BEYOND THE *shadows*

by E. Abraham

Dedication

For Emily:
This is me being nice to you with words. Suck it, bitch.

Trigger Warnings

Trigger Warnings:

Attempted Murder/Murder
Blood
Death
Criminal Activity
Violence (guns/knives/pipe)
Mentions of kidnapping
Physical Abuse (not by MC)
Mentions of torture techniques
Fire
Hospitalization/Needles
Misogyny/Sexism (not by MC)

Content Warnings:

Adult Language
Adult Sexual Scenes
Light BDSM-Spanking, Hurt/No comfort
Lack of safeword

One

Roman

This is bullshit.

I've been running Synd for all of two days and I'm already over it. I never wanted to be in charge, at least not of *this* city. I'm basically cleaning up the messes I made, which was never in the plan. Although, none of what my life has become was in the plan in the first place.

When I came to Synd five months ago, I thought I was waltzing toward my own destruction with vengeance in my heart, convinced I was avenging my father's and sister's deaths.

Now, my entire life has flipped. My sister might still be dead, but none of the men who run Synd were at fault. My father, who is, in fact, alive and well, was the one who snuffed out her life. He spoke in riddles when he rose from the grave, as he's wont to do, but I lived under his rule for so long, I could easily read between the lines.

I'm not even surprised he took up with the Guild. Anders Drake is an opportunist first and foremost. I have no idea how he fell in with them. Anger ruled him after we left Synd, probably before as well. Rage was always destined to be his downfall. I can only hope he pisses someone off enough that they kill him. It'll take away the satisfaction I'd have of watching the light leave his eyes as I gut him, but at least he'd be dead. For real this time.

Still, I imagined taking over for the Kings and Byrns would be the toughest challenge I went up against. I was so fucking wrong. A huge hiccup in my quest to right my wrongs is standing in the middle of Mason Byrns's driveway in the pouring rain.

At first I thought she was a mirage, a specter come to haunt me because I'm in over my head. Now, I'm convinced she's here to kill me for some imagined crime. It's probably Samantha Byrns, dressed as the Wraith, fully ready to take me out. She wasn't exactly happy when the rest decided to leave me in charge of Synd.

When the figure lifts her head, though, a chill runs down my spine. This isn't Sam, darling of Synd and secret assassin. The curve of her cheekbone catching the light, the curl of her plump lips, the wisp of scarlet curls, all point to the one person from my past I thought I'd long dispelled from my mind.

Even now, I'm lying to myself. At fourteen, she captivated me. At seventeen, I was well over my obsession. I went from silently wanting her to wanting nothing more than for her to disappear. I remember every single moment with her, despite my best attempts to erase them.

Closing my eyes, I remember her smugness as she informed me of my younger sister's midnight escapade to Synd to chase after a boy. Little Miss Know-it-all thought she had all the answers, not understanding the consequences of her own hubris. She even provided the car that ushered Aelia to her death. She wasn't so smug when my sister didn't come back.

Dark eyes pierce me from the shadows of her hood. The downpour obscures their glittering green depths. At least, that's how they used to be in another place and time.

"What do you want, Ember?" I call, and she tilts her head.

She'll make me wait if she's anything like she was when we were younger. I haven't seen her in almost ten years, right after Aelia was killed. Ember Hayes—the chaos to Aelia's calmness. They were inseparable, closer than Aelia and I ever were. I couldn't compete with Ember's fierceness. At least she was loyal to my sister until the bitter end.

The figure turns, taking off for the trees lining the driveway. As she goes, she lifts her middle finger in the air over her shoulder, and I glare at her back. As the rain swallows her form, I return to the warm interior of my temporary home. The final words she said to me echo in my ears.

The stars will fall from the sky, the earth will shatter beneath us, the rivers will drown all of humanity before you see the day I yield.

Two

Ember

I hate it here. Synd itself isn't all that bad compared to other cities I've been to. It's actually kind of nice if I ignore the barren strips of land skirting the river running smack dab in the middle. And overlook the various buildings that seem like they've seen the wrong end of a fuse. And that my nemesis currently resides here.

All in all, Synd would be a good place to raise a family if I ever planned on having one. Except I don't.

The very lifeblood of this city runs through the veins of the mafia families who have seemingly abandoned it. The word from the media is they're on business, extending ties to Rima. Four hours is a bit of a stretch for helping a neighboring metropolis, but to each their own, I guess.

The hotel I found is better than any I've stayed at in a long while. Hot water, soft sheets, and room service are all well and good until the bill comes. I'll only be here one more night before I'll move on to another place, probably whatever abandoned house I find along the way.

I sigh, letting the hot water run down my body and ease the tension in my muscles. I'm pretty sure the exhaustion is permanently etched into my bones. No shower or massage will erase the stress I've carried for years. At twenty-six, I should be able to relax. Hell, I should be settling into a job, or going to the club, or fuck, anything other than chasing a ten-year-old obsession. I told myself the last city was the last one.

Moving on with my life was no longer an option when I got wind of Anders fucking Drake coming back to Synd. Just thinking about him makes my blood boil, and I slam my hand on the handles, cutting the water off. Goosebumps scatter across my skin, and I grab a towel, almost dropping it I'm so distracted. Chalking it up to my low-burning rage toward Anders, I dry myself before loosely wrapping my hair.

I'm not fooling myself. Being pissed at a former mafia man would be a normal reaction, especially when he's responsible for my best friend's supposed death. But those feelings are a constant burning in my gut. The feelings coursing through my body now have nothing to do with him and everything to do with his son.

I shouldn't have spied on Roman Drake. Is it really spying if I made sure he knew I was there? Hell, I flipped him off as I flounced away as if I was in some fucked-up musical. I know he saw. I could feel his eyes boring a hole in the back of my head until I vanished from his view. What he didn't realize was I tracked his progress through the house when he ran back inside.

Huffing, I wrap the robe around me, not bothering to deal with my hair. I'll hate myself in the morning, but that's nothing new. I've grown used to the self-loathing that's dogged me ever since I left Westmont the day I turned eighteen.

My parents didn't care. In fact, I'd be surprised they even noticed. They ran in the same circle as the Drakes. Self-centered didn't even begin to describe their type of people. I was too much to fit into their perfect little world, which was perfectly fine with me. Part of me wanted to pop their little bubble and tell them what Anders actually did to acquire all his money, but I could never bring myself to do it.

I pivot a second before there's a knock on my door. Room service isn't always this reliable, but with this fancy of a place, I would be pissed if they were late. I stop, raising an eyebrow as I try to remember the last time I ate. Shaking my head, I check the peephole, scanning as far as I can with the limited view. The cart sits outside, unattended, exactly as I requested.

Still, I grab my dagger from the table, tucking it behind my forearm. I'd rather not stab an unsuspecting server and deal with the clean-up. I should probably be concerned with the fact they're innocent, but I've been doing this long enough, I've found there's not that many people out there who don't deserve a little light stabbing every once in a while. I bet it would deter a lot of people if they knew that was the consequence of their actions.

Standing behind the door, I ease it open and count to thirty before peeking around the wood. Light winks off the silver cover keeping my food warm. Ducking my whole head out, I glance up and down the hall and then tug the cart inside.

The scent of waffles envelops me and my mouth waters. Plates rattling, I push it further inside before kicking at the door. I roll my eyes as it slowly clicks shut. One downside of such a high-end place means soft closing doors, which is great for the other patrons, but terrible for people who are paranoid about being attacked.

When I whip around, the towel slides, covering half my face. I bend over, flipping the fabric from my hair. Straightening, I push the mess back, contemplating whether I should deal with it now or after I've eaten. It'll frizz if I leave it, but I don't want my food to get cold.

"What the hell are you doing here, Ember?"

I squeal, spinning around. I flip my knife toward the source. I drop into a crouch, grabbing the only other weapon I can find. A spoon won't help me much, but I'll make due.

My gut twists when my mind finally catches up seconds before my eyes settle on Roman Drake. His hand slowly reaches for his ear. When he pulls his fingers away, blood stains his skin, painting it a bright red. I fight a grin when I realize I nicked him. Bastard deserved it for sneaking up on me.

I match his scowl, setting the silverware down and readjusting my robe. His eyes flick down before he glances away, a tick in his jaw marking his frustration.

"I could ask you the same thing, *Drake*."

"Don't call me that," he growls, crossing his arms.

I smirk, raising an eyebrow at him. When we were younger, he insisted we call him Drake instead of Roman. Aelia and I made fun of him every chance we got. A bolt of pain slices through me when I think of my best friend. She was light and carefree, even if she was a bit spoiled. The same could be said for me, probably. Pushing thoughts of her from my mind, I glare at him.

"There a reason you decided to break into my hotel room through the"—I search the room, trying to figure out where he slipped in—"balcony door?"

The lock hangs in pieces. He must have come in when I was in the shower, and I scold myself for not thinking about it. Usually, I don't stay in places that have another exit to secure. Now that he's rammed his way through, I'll have to move tonight instead of tomorrow, like I planned. Bastard.

"There a reason you decided to play the part of a killer in a horror movie in my driveway?"

I shrug even as anxiety shoots through me. I didn't have a plan when I snuck through the trees in the middle of a storm to catch a glimpse of my past in the flesh. Honestly, the fact he was there and came outside at that exact moment was serendipitous. Giving him the finger was just icing on the cake.

"You didn't like my welcome basket?"

He gives me a sharp look, a flash of panic in his ice-blue eyes. "What welcome basket?"

I could fuck with him, let him search for a non-existent box, but that seems cruel.

I wave away his concern. "Settle down. Not like I dropped off a bunch of cooked grenades. I was talking about flipping you the bird."

"I can see your attitude hasn't improved."

"I can see you still haven't acquired a sense of humor."

As angry as I am at him, I can admit I missed this. The banter between us was always top-notch. Rarely would anyone engage with me, but Roman always gave as good as I did. He said it was because he was trying to teach me manners, but secretly I think he loved it.

He sighs, tucking his hands behind his neck and tipping his head back. The move sends a bolt of lightning through me, and I force my gaze away. I obsessed over Roman Drake for much of my teen years. Aelia teased me incessantly about my crush, but I was convinced I was in love.

Scoffing, I tip my chin up and skip to the cart. He can stand there being frustrated all he wants. I'm fucking starving, and I'm not going to let it go to waste.

"Tell me what the fuck you're doing here, Ember," he demands.

"My, my, someone's not getting laid."

He makes a choking noise, but I'm already stuffing a strawberry in my mouth. The chef even cut them into cute little flowers. I smile at one before I pop it in my mouth, the sweet tangy juice exploding over my tongue. I barely hold back a moan, the sound sliding down my throat along with the fruit.

"Would you knock it off?"

I freeze, fork halfway to my mouth as I stare at him. "What?"

"Why is it so fucking hard for you to just answer a question?"

"Uh, first of all, you came busting in here, interrupting *my* meal. So don't get pissy because I'd rather eat than talk to you. Second of all, your question isn't just *a* question. It's one that will lead to another and another and another and I find that annoying. Third of all—"

"For fuck's sake," he grumbles.

"Third of all"—I raise my voice to drown him out—"you should realize I'm doing the same damn thing I've been doing for the past ten years."

Shock flits across his face, followed closely by the mask he was taught so well. Every emotion shutters, cutting off any hope I'd have of reading him.

"What do you know?"

"What's the male equivalent to resting bitch face?"

He drops his chin to his chest, pulling in a deep breath. He's probably summoning some bullshit inner strength to deal with me. Seems like not much has changed since we were teenagers.

"There isn't one."

"Guess I'll just have to call you a bitch then, huh?" I throw him a simpering smile.

"I can see you haven't changed in the slightest. I expect you to be gone by morning," he growls, marching for the balcony.

"How 'bout no," I mumble around a mouthful of perfectly cooked waffle.

He spins back, planting his hands on his hips. "This isn't a discussion."

"It hardly ever is." I roll my eyes. "However, I will refrain from getting in your way."

His nostrils flare as he scans me up and down, a curl forming on his lips. "Leave it be, Ember. You're not qualified to deal with the shit you're chasing."

When fire burns in his eyes, the rage I've buried deep comes bubbling up, engulfing my senses. He's so set in his ways, so convinced he's right, I'll never be able to change his mind, not that I wanted to.

"How are you still such a fucking asshole? You'd think after all these years—"

"I'd what? Get over the fact my sister is dead? Get over your involvement in her death? Get over my entire fucking world burning around me? Is that what I should just 'get over'?" He's panting by the end of his speech, hands flexing over and over.

"You'd think after all these years you wouldn't try to push me around," I whisper, fighting back tears.

His throat bobs, and he marches past me and to the hallway instead. He halts next to the cart, grabbing the glass of champagne and downing it.

"Next time try not to throw a knife at my face," he growls.

Slamming the glass down, he stalks to the door and rips it open. I swallow the giggle when he tries to slam it behind him, but then I remember how we ended this latest altercation.

Who knew after ten years we'd still get under each other's skin? I'm not surprised. Even with all the training I sought, all the places I've traveled, all the cities

I've searched, I'm still the sarcastic girl I was when I was sixteen. Growing for me didn't include losing my attitude.

My stomach turns and I stare at the feast in front of me. Picking up a purple grape, I roll it in my hand as I turn, dropping onto the white love seat. The exhaustion from earlier swamps me, and my eyes droop.

For the first time in a long while, I felt something other than numbness. For a moment in time, I was staring not at a looming void of nothingness, but a mosaic of colors swirling through the air, all stemming from the one man I can't afford to feel anything for.

Slipping into our old roles was as easy as breathing, but I can't fall under his spell again. Hatred rumbles in my chest, remembering how he dismissed me all those years ago. I came to him, the one person I thought would understand—that would help. He dashed any hope I had at finding Aelia alive, forgetting her in the blink of an eye. The pain in his eyes tonight was real, but he's still convinced she's dead. And I can't believe that.

I refuse to believe that. She's out there, somewhere, waiting for someone to save her. If her own brother won't help me, then so be it. I'll go alone, like I have all these years, following a trail long since gone cold.

It's not until the juices trickle down my wrist, I notice I've crushed the grape in my fist. A single drop hits the fabric, bleeding into the whiteness, and then disappears. Staring at the spot, I wonder if my hope will vanish just as easily. Like my name, it's merely an ember struggling to keep burning.

A heavy sigh leaves me as I push up, dropping the mess on the tray as I pass. The big bed that was begging me to dive into its fluffiness mere hours ago seems desolate now, exactly like my future. I turn off the lamps before crawling between the covers, settling in a for a long night of reliving my encounter with Roman. The dawn breaks before I finally fall asleep.

Three

Roman

"Mr. Edwards—" I sigh, pinching the bridge of my nose.

"Please, call me Pierce." The man shoots me a bright smile, showing way too many teeth.

"Mr. Mayor, this is mostly a figurehead position. You'll report to me or my men. You've seen what happens when someone tries to go off on their own."

I level him with a look, but his face doesn't change. Honestly, I wonder if he's had so many injections, he can't move the muscles. Tilting my head, I'm mesmerized by the orange sheen covering his face. Add in his perfectly coiffed hair and he looks like he stepped out of a daytime soap opera. He wasn't *my* first choice, but the others voted. There was a lot of yelling at that meeting. I don't know how they dealt with the political sphere, so I'll have to do it my way. At least I'm well versed in dealing with the elite who only think of themselves and their money.

"Mayor Edwards, let me be clear. Do not make major decisions without consulting with us first. I don't tolerate mistakes."

He nods, his hair flapping with the movement, but settles exactly where it was before. It defies the laws of physics, and I find it hard to pull my eyes away. Mentally shaking myself, I take a sip of the black coffee, holding back a grimace at the taste. I'd rather have a tea, but their selection here is shit. For a fancy breakfast place, they have subpar drink options.

"You may go." I wave him away.

He trips out of the booth, and I press my lips together. They couldn't have picked a more incompetent person for the job, but I suppose that's the point. Leaning back in the booth, I close my eyes.

Immediately, Ember's face floats behind my lids. Images of her have been plaguing me since I confronted her two days ago. I've been putting off checking if she's left Synd or not. Another altercation will only suck me further into her orbit. I can't afford the distraction, and that's all Ember Hayes is.

An ache twists in my chest as I remember her disheveled appearance the other night. I would never admit it out loud, but I couldn't pull my gaze away from her body when the belt of the robe she wore slipped, exposing a sliver of pale skin. With her red hair a riot around her head, she looked like she'd just been ravished.

I snort, shaking my head. Who the hell says the word "ravished" anymore? Trying to erase any sexual thoughts of her from my mind proves difficult, which is not what I need right now. Not ever. She's a poison running through my veins. She'd kill me slowly, bleeding the strength within my body, and I'd merely cry out for more—more of her, of her body, of her venom—until the bitter end. She'd laugh as she waltzed away, leaving my heart shattered in her wake.

"You realize anyone could come up and slit your throat, right?" As if I've manifested her, Ember's lilting tone floats over me. Maybe if I ignore her, she'll scamper back to whatever city she's been holed up in. Preferably not this one.

"I'm not going to go away just because you ignore me," she sneers. "Oh, how lovely, but I don't prefer coffee. Do you perhaps have tea?"

Peeking at her from slitted eyes, I find a starstruck woman trembling in front of Ember. Her bright red hair and twinkling green eyes are enough to pull most people in, but she's now adopted a formal British accent. To my knowledge, she's never even been overseas, much less knows how they speak.

"Unfortunately, the selection is quite small," the young woman says, a slight lilt to her tone, as if she's imitating Ember.

"Ah, well, that is disappointing. However, I shall have a small orange juice please and a chocolate muffin. He'll be paying." She flashes me a brilliant smile, eyes begging me to disagree.

"Of course, madam." The server scurries away as I roll my eyes.

"The accent is a bit much," I mumble, crossing my arms.

"You're a bit much," she mutters, dropping the charade. "Why don't we get this over with. Then we can go our separate ways for another ten years."

"Five."

Her eyebrow ticks up, a smirk forming on her plump red lips. "If you'd like to rendezvous in five years, just say the word, Drake."

Huffing, I straighten in my seat before leaning closer to her. "It's been five years since we've crossed paths, not ten."

I can't tell if she's fucking with me or actually forgot that I called her half a decade ago. It was only a ten-minute conversation, but it's been etched in my mind ever since. Apparently, it was more impactful to me than it was to her.

"Nu uh. The last time I saw you was when you were unceremoniously tossing my ass out into the pouring rain, leaving me to walk home," she hisses, curling her body over the tabletop. "And when I got there—"

Ember jerks back, a blank mask sliding over her features. I shouldn't care what happened after I threw her out. She deserved it for not giving up when all I wanted was to mourn in peace. No matter what I said, she just wouldn't stop talking. She pushed me too far when she insinuated I didn't love my sister. If her parents finally took notice of her, though, I can't imagine what they did to her that would be so terrible she's held onto it all these years.

"I didn't throw you." It's the only response I can muster.

She lets out a sharp laugh, glancing around at the other patrons. We're tucked in the corner, surrounded by unoccupied tables. I'm pretty sure it's standard practice for mafia leaders, though I doubt they'd classify me as such.

"So, tossing me over your shoulder and hauling me out the door before throwing me in the mud doesn't count as throwing me out?"

"What the fuck. I set you down gently on the front step. You're the one who tumbled off and fell into the puddle. Are you going to blame me for everything that's gone wrong in your life?"

I swear her chin quivers before she ducks her head. The server hovers just out of earshot. At least I hope she didn't overhear us. The last thing I need is gossip swirling through the masses about us. I'd rather no one speculate on who she is or why she's here.

"Are you going to tell me where Anders is? I'm assuming you weren't colluding with him if Synd's mafia leaders left you in charge."

When she lifts her head, she's completely erased all emotion from her face. Her monotone voice is so at odds with who she is, I almost don't recognize her. She's literally biting her tongue, though. Only once have I watched her break, when she was begging for my help. I thought it was an isolated incident.

As much as Ember gets under my skin, she's one of the strongest people I know. Not that I know her that well anymore. Ten years is enough time for someone to change. Except, every interaction I've had with her so far points to her being precisely the same as when we were teenagers.

"Well? Are you going to answer or stare at me like I've grown a second head?" she demands, and I start, so lost in my thoughts I forgot she asked me anything.

Revealing that my father went to Rima would be disastrous. I'm sure he's cocooned within the inner circle of the Guild, helping them destroy humanity one kidnapping at a time. Ember and I may have issues piled between us higher than Mount Everest, but that doesn't mean I want her in their sphere. They'd snatch her up and throw her straight into the Auction. I've heard they reserve the feisty ones for the VIPs to bid on before the winner tears them apart, breaking them so completely, they're better off dead. It's one small facet of the Guild's operation, but I still don't want Ember anywhere near that shit.

"Not sure. I just know he's not here any longer. Why don't you go home? Stop chasing after this mirage."

She huffs, pushing out of the booth. She stops as she pulls on pure white gloves, complete with pearl buttons at the wrists.

"If you change your mind about sharing information, here's my number." She slips a black business card from her pocket, sliding it across the table with one finger.

"I won't be needing that," I say, nostrils flaring.

She shrugs before pivoting on her heels, her dark green dress swirling around her hips as she glides past the other tables. She wiggles her fingers at a man whose jaw is practically in his eggs. The man blushes, scrambling, and almost upends his champagne flute.

When the bell chimes, announcing her exit, I pull my eyes away. The server tiptoes forward, her timidness a sharp contrast to Ember's confidence. She can't be much older than eighteen. I hardly have time to coddle an almost child's feelings.

"I won't be needing that," I grunt, waving her away. She squeaks before rushing back to the kitchen, leaving a trail of orange juice in her wake.

Pulling out my phone, I check my email. In the forty minutes since I last looked, I've received a dozen new inquiries, ranging from minuscule issues someone else could deal with to borderline catastrophes I need to address.

I grew up hearing the stories of Synd. I spent half my childhood here, but we left when I was so young, I barely remember most of it. My father didn't start telling me anything until I proved I was loyal. I shudder at the memory of the tests he put me through at the tender age of eleven.

Now I realize why the city was split into three territories—four if one counted when my family oversaw the south side of Synd. It's large enough there's no way someone could run all of it as successfully as the others have done for so many years. The fact I'm trying to do it now is ludicrous. At least I don't have to deal with Reapers territory. The MC has their own laws and ways. No one would follow my leadership up north, anyway. Thankfully, Hawk, the Reapers' VP, stayed behind with his woman to keep things running.

Staring at the phone, I try to muster up enough energy to keep going. When Ember glided out the door, it was as if she took all color with her, painting my world in a myriad of grays and blacks. Everything is muted and cold without her presence.

I shake my head, pushing out of the booth. Throwing a wad of cash down, I stalk out the door, an older man dashing out of my way. In the month since the decision was made for the Kings, Byrns, and Helms to fuck off to Rima to help bring down the Guild once and for all, I was paraded before the public by each of them. I attended so many galas and charity events, I'll be glad if I never see the inside of a ballroom again. The argument was always that I needed to play the part, establish the story of a long-lost founder of Synd, and be seen as a force to be reckoned with. Apparently it worked, if the man profusely apologizing to me is any indication.

Slipping into the car, I breathe a sigh of relief. When it takes off for Byrns's mansion, I push away all the thoughts of Ember twisting together in my mind. They settle next to the ache in my chest, curiously close to my heart. No good can come from thinking about her. There are more important things to focus on. She's a needless complication in an already volatile situation. Ignoring her is my only course of action unless I want to force her out of Synd.

Four

Ember

I scowl at the sky, wishing there were clouds to cover the moonlight filtering between the buildings. It's like a spotlight, content on making me the star of the show, lighting my path in the most inconvenient way possible. I've been in Synd for less than a week and yet it's rained every day until the one night it could help. Just my luck, I guess.

Finding information here is ten times worse than any other city I've been to. Usually, I have a contact already established, which leads to another and another until I uncover enough intel to guide me to the next place.

Synd, on the other hand, is locked up tighter than a nun's asshole. Roman is the only person I know here, and he's made it quite clear he's not talking. In fact, he's ignored me every time we've crossed paths since the incident at the restaurant, which is perfectly fine with me. I thought I could stay out of his way, but apparently fate is a cruel hag, dangling him in front of me whenever I go for coffee or to eat.

If I was back at the hotel, I could avoid him, but after he broke in, I figured it was best to move on. I'm at some motel on the north side that seems like a set to a horror movie or a porno, but it's far enough away from the Byrns mansion, Roman shouldn't accidentally spot me.

"Just 'cause the girly's gone don't mean we take kindly to someone else trying to take over," a gruff voice says from behind me.

Whipping around, I swing my knife, ready to defend myself. Mountain man is the only way I can describe the burly person standing in front of me. With beefy hands planted on his hips, and a scowl buried behind a bushy orange beard, his hair looks like mine after I wake in the morning. I bite my lip, barely keeping back the tirade I desperately want to throw at him for sneaking up on me. I need to get my shit together so this stops happening.

"Don't know who the girly is, but I'm not trying to take anything over. Just out for a midnight stroll."

He snorts, glancing off down the alley before swinging his eyes back to me. "No one strolls in the Barrens."

Scrambling, I try to place what he's talking about. I've never heard of the Barrens, but I'm assuming it's the area we're currently standing in. Darkness permeates the air down here, suffocating the light from the few streetlamps that work. Most of the buildings are abandoned, complete with a plethora of broken windows and more than a few that have been burned to the ground. I'd rather not admit to this man, who could probably rip my limbs from my body with no effort, that I don't know what the Barrens are. I might not have a choice, though.

Tucking the knife against my arm, I straighten and plaster on a bright smile. "I'm sorry, not from around here. Could you explain?"

Folding his arms over his chest, he mutters under his breath as he scans me from head to toe. "You know the girly?"

"Uh, maybe?" I mean for my tone to be confident, but it comes out like a question instead.

He stares at me for another minute, not moving a muscle, and I shift back a step.

"Well, as much fun as this has been, I'm going to skedaddle. Lots of shit to do."

"Who you lookin' for?" he calls as I turn, and I end up pirouetting to face him again.

"Who said I was searching for someone?"

"Been around long enough, lass."

I quirk my eyebrow at the nickname, but let it slide. Normally I would scold whoever thought they could assign me a pet name, but with the gentle lilt to this man's voice, along with his coloring, I'm pretty sure he's Irish.

"Anders Drake." Narrowing my eyes, I track every twitch of his face, though with the beard it proves more difficult than usual.

"Why?"

"I have questions only he can answer." A deadly smirk graces my face.

He nods, lumbering toward me, and I tense, gripping my knife tightly. As he marches past, though, I cock my head.

"You comin', lass?" he calls over his shoulder, and I scramble after him.

Could he be leading me to my death? Possibly. Can I fight him off? Maybe. Am I willing to risk it for any type of lead I can get on where Anders went? Absolutely. We wind through the desolate streets, past pockmarked buildings, coming closer to the river with every step. I expect it to smell like a dumpster fire, but the gusts of air have a hint of winter in them.

Living most of my life hundreds of miles to the south of Synd, snow wasn't in our vocabulary. A couple winters ago, I was following a lead up north. When the fluffy flakes fell from the sky, I giggled, something I hadn't done in years. Ironically, the first person I thought of was Roman Drake.

On the rare occasions we weren't sniping at each other, we would talk about hopping in a car and driving until we found the ground blanketed in white. It was a dream that died a fiery death. He probably doesn't even remember. He's probably purged every memory except the ones that support his perception of me.

I scold myself for letting my mind wander in the middle of this place while I follow a man I just met. The various trainers I've had over the years would kick my ass for it. I brush my hand over my back, the press of my gun comforting me. Knives may be my specialty, but I'm not about to go out without another weapon.

A low hum of voices pops up, as if from nowhere, and I glance up. Light filters between two squat apartment buildings, and I lean around the man's frame.

"An Irish bridge," I murmur, mesmerized by the sight before me.

"What's that?" he asks, glancing over his shoulder.

"It's an Irish bridge, although usually cars drive over it instead of people setting up a fucked-up farmer's market. They're low-water crossings, but they flood when there's a lot of rain."

The man grunts, tilting his head as he scans the area. Metal gates protect the openings on each side, complete with armed guards, but they're more ragtag than militia men. Stalls line each side, a couple even setting up shop right in the middle of the road.

"Won't let ya in, but I'll go get her." He lumbers off before I can ask who the hell he's talking about.

Tucking myself further into the shadows, I lean against the building. When he reaches the gates, one of the guard's eyes bug out, and he rushes to clear a path for my temporary tour guide.

He disappears between the bodies of dozens of people mingling together. Kicking my foot against the wall, I start counting. If I hit a certain number, I'll take off and find someone else to help me. I don't know what the threshold is, though, which probably will send me into a spiral. I never know when I've waited long enough, always thinking as soon as I leave, they'll show up. It's fucking terrible, living in the gray space of never understanding other people.

I'm in the middle of arguing with myself on whether to wait or just go when the man appears at the gate, an attractive woman probably ten years older than me trailing him. Pushing off from the wall, I scan the area, but it's silent. The last thing I need is them ambushing me with a horde of accomplices.

"*This* is her, Mack?" the woman asks, eyeing me.

"Reminds me of the girly way back," Mack says gruffly.

He still hasn't explained who the girly is, but apparently this woman doesn't have the same issues I do. Jealousy writhes inside me like a serpent threatening to swallow me whole. I beat it back, but it'll return, waiting for the moment to devour me completely.

Never staying in one place long enough along with the mission that's consumed my every waking minute and most of my dreams means I never form relationships. The last meaningful one I made was violently ripped from me. I refuse to deem what Roman and I had as a relationship. If anything, it was an auxiliary kinship, connected only by the thread of Aelia. Without her, we unraveled, leaving a mess we both walked away from.

"I see what you mean. Thanks, Mack."

He grunts, shuffling off into the dark. Turning back to the woman, I eye her just as she did me. How she's not freezing in a short-sleeve shirt and jeans is beyond me. I have three layers on and I'm shivering. Spring hasn't sprung this far north yet. She brushes her bleach blonde hair over her shoulder as she purses her lips. If she's waiting for me to start, she'll be sitting here awhile. I've done this enough to understand the unspoken protocols.

"What's your name?" she asks, planting a hand on her hip.

"Depends what you're going to do with it," I say, mirroring her stance.

She chuckles. "Cautious. I like that. Listen, honey, I don't have a lot of time, but Mack said you were looking for Asshole Anders."

"Any info on him, really. I'm not picky."

She nods, sucking her lip in her mouth. "Not much to tell. He moved on about a month ago."

"I heard. Any idea where he went?" I ask, but she's shaking her head before I've even finished.

"Can't say. Another relation might be your best bet."

I recoil, forgetting to mask my reaction. Schooling my face, I raise an eyebrow at the woman, and she laughs outright.

"Oh, honey. I'm guessing you know Roman Drake, then?"

My face drops and I mutter, "Something like that."

"May be time to get reacquainted with that fine specimen. When you see him, you tell him Nicki said he's no longer banned, but if he steps foot in the Egg, I'll cut his balls off and feed them to Rocky." She smirks, knowing I have no clue what the hell she's talking about.

"Rocky your dog?"

She laughs, spinning around and sauntering off. Glancing over her shoulder, she calls, "He's one of the guards."

Slipping into the shadows, I go back the way I came. I should take another route, but I'm afraid I'll get lost. These streets have no rhyme or reason to them, not like the rest of the city. The more I explore Synd, the more I'm convinced the two sides of the river mirror each other.

Roman probably has the answers to all my questions, down to the most mundane. How to pry them from him is another mystery I'm not sure I want to solve. He's pretty set on my leaving, giving up my quest to find Aelia. As if I'd go back to Westmont. My parents would try to marry me off to some dull man twice my age who only wants me for a brood mare. Maybe they'd choose one with good status but no money, who will live off my inheritance.

I stutter to a stop, checking the next street before dashing across the empty space. I thought my parents would cut me off as soon as they noticed I was gone. For some reason, they're still funneling cash into the fund they started when they got annoyed with me asking for more money. I rarely touched it once I figured out it was to make up for their neglect. They might still think I'm off on holiday or something. It's the only reasonable explanation why it's still fully funded.

A sigh of relief huffs out of me when I reach the edge of the Barrens. Music pounds from a few blocks down, bright lights flashing through the night. There must be hundreds of people hustling through the biting wind to the various clubs with their doors thrown wide open, spilling bass notes into the streets. In another life, I'd probably be mashed in with them, sweating my tits off while leering men watched from a VIP balcony overhead.

Rolling my eyes, I swing away from the noise. I never wanted to be a part of that crowd, anyway. Shaking my ass at a nightclub seems like a good way to get groped. Even in another life, I doubt I'd enjoy that scene. I crave silence too much to be inundated with a cacophony of sounds I can't escape. I'm built for staying in and reading or stalking the streets with my knives.

As I flag down a taxi, I rack my brain for a solution that doesn't include Roman Drake. I can't think of one and I'm running out of options. The trail for finding Aelia went cold over two years ago, yet I'm still chasing her ghost. Leaving her to the fate her father handed her isn't something I can live with. Finding Anders is my only lead, and I won't let my nemesis stand in my way.

Five

Roman

"Something I can get you?" the server asks, a slight curl to her lip.

"Earl Grey tea and the breakfast skillet," I grind out.

I've been sitting here for at least ten minutes, waiting for her to come over. She was too busy chitchatting with the cook to bother with me. She rolls her eyes, not bothering to write anything down, and I realize I'm fucked. Only being here once before apparently doesn't afford me good service. Huffing, she pivots, marching away as if I've asked her to deliver me the moon.

The bell above the door chimes, and I glance up, tracking Hawk as he scans the diner. When he spots me, he stalks over, sliding into the opposite side of the booth. He waves at the server, and she nods. The biker must come here a lot if she's not giving him the same treatment I received.

"Ready to throw in the towel yet?" he asks with a smirk.

"Everything is fine," I grunt.

"You sound like Byrns. And we saw how that worked out."

"With him in love?" I quip and my chest tightens.

A soft smile blooms on his face, and I duck my chin, scowling. All these men have found who they want to spend the rest of their lives with. The man sitting across from me has Willow, Helms has MacKenzie, and the Kings have Samantha. Mason and Lacey might not have been together very long, but they're very much in love.

For a month I was surrounded by couples with stars in their eyes staring at their partners as if they hung the moon. It was annoying and exhausting and that hasn't changed in the two weeks since the others left. Willow is usually attached to Hawk's hip, completely in love.

Gritting my teeth, I shove what I'm sure is jealousy deep within my chest until it suffocates. I have no time or inclination to entertain the bitterness that refuses to die. At one time in my life, the path to a happily ever after was bright and promising. Harboring naivety isn't something I struggle with. Finding someone who could fit into my life was never going to be easy, but I was hopeful in my youth. Hell, at one point I thought Ember Hayes was made for me, that destiny was on my side for once, and we'd ride off into the sunset, leaving our shitty lives behind. Until my world was flipped upside down, with the help of the very person I thought I'd marry one day. I took up the mantle of vengeance, scrubbed her from my life, and never looked back.

"Being in love isn't a death sentence. You know that, right?" Hawk says, derailing my train of thought.

"Why the hell are we talking about love?" I grumble, crossing my arms.

Hawk chuckles. "Might be good for you to get out there and meet someone. Then you'd be too busy falling to turn on us."

"If I was going to turn on you, I wouldn't put this much work into rebuilding shit. I'd just burn it all to the ground as soon as the others left."

He nods, probably searching the space for the server. "We need to get the shipments back on track. If we can bypass Rima, that might help. You have connections in Westmont we could tap into?"

I run my hand through my hair as my stomach jumps. Westmont was a vile cesspool of snobby elites, bent on using their privilege to lord over the general masses within the town. The Drakes may have come from money, but I was taught not to flaunt it, lest someone look too closely at where it was coming from. I was dubbed inferior before I reached high school.

They held tight to that belief until I proved myself to be more than just a pretty face with some extra cash. The underground fighting ring was the only reason I was allowed to hoist myself up from my subordinate status. Aelia hated when I went, but at least it stopped the others from picking on her. Just imagining reaching out to any of those people gives me hives.

Ember's face pops into my mind, the voice in the back of my head whispering that I could ask her, but I dismiss it. Requesting anything from her is liable to get me killed. She probably hasn't been back to Westmont in years. I can't imagine she goes home for holidays.

Plus, I've been ignoring her. She assumes she's being sneaky, holing up in a shitty motel near Reaper territory. There's no telling what the hell she's still doing in Synd. I refuse to give her any information about my father. If she's anything like she was five years ago, she'll blast off to Rima and get herself killed.

I don't know exactly how she morphed into a badass, but from what I was told, she's skilled at making people talk. None of it matters, though. Her entire adult life has been focused on finding Aelia. What is she going to do when she finally accepts that my sister is dead? Maybe she never will. Maybe she'll spend her whole existence chasing a ghost.

I do a double take when the front door pops open. As if she stepped straight from my mind, Ember breezes in. Gone is the elegant sun dress she wore a week ago, replaced with ripped jeans and a black leather jacket thrown over a blue sweater. Her high ponytail swings over her shoulder as she shoots a dazzling smile at the server. I duck my head, hoping they put her on the other side of the diner. There's no way I'll get out of here without her seeing me.

"Who are you staring at?" Hawk asks, swinging around.

Curling my fingers into a fist, I tuck my hand under the table. "No one. Turn the fuck around."

"She's hot. Looks like she could break you in half too," he says, craning his neck.

"She's all of five foot three. What makes you think she could do that?"

"Got that air about her. Like Sam. Seems like she's got a beast simmering under the surface."

He finally faces me, but not before Ember's eyes catch mine and she smirks. Pulling my gaze away, I level a look at Hawk, urging him to keep his mouth shut if she comes over here. He's too busy texting to notice. Glancing over his shoulder, I track Ember's movements as she chats with our server. Our food languishes in the window, baking under the heat lamps, and I grind my teeth together.

"Want me to play wingman?" Hawk's voice pulls my eyes back to him.

"Excuse me?"

He snorts, throwing his phone down before scrubbing his hands over his face. "When was the last time you got laid?"

"Is there something else we needed to discuss, Hawk? Or would you prefer I put you through the window?"

He holds up his hands in surrender, a twinkle in his green eyes. When he turns, my palms itch to follow through on the threat, but he waves at the server, and she hurries to grab our food. Dropping my plate first, she sets Hawk's down gently, and I suck in a breath. Shoveling a forkful in my mouth, I swallow the potatoes along with the vitriol I want to spew at her. I doubt I'll be coming back, no matter how much the others rave about the Flaming Skillet.

I expect her to leave, but she turns her back to me, leaning on the table to chat with Hawk. I swear they're talking about the fucking weather. A ringing in my ears prevents me from taking in any of their conversation. Concentrating on my meal, I reach for my mug, but it's nowhere to be found.

Clearing my throat, I knock my knuckles on the table. I gain Hawk's attention, but the server ignores me.

"Tea," I grunt, boring holes in her back.

"We're out. You get coffee or nothing," she says, not bothering to turn around.

"Will I even get that?" I mutter, and Hawk smirks, as if this is actually funny. Newsflash: it's not.

Glancing over her shoulder, she glares at me. I don't know what the hell I did to her, but she clearly hates me. I don't fucking care. There's plenty of people who despise me, but they're not the ones I'm trying to get a goddamn cup of tea from.

"Time to go, Mia," Hawk says, smothering his grin.

She rolls her eyes before retreating, which is probably for the best since I'm liable to blow up at her. Mia stomps off, her old-fashioned dress swishing as she does. Posting up at the counter in front of the window to the kitchen, she glares at us.

"What the hell is her problem?" I grumble, dropping my fork on my plate.

"She's the kind you have to earn her loyalty, but once you have it..."

"Doesn't excuse her from doing her job," I mumble.

Peering around, I try to see where Ember went, but she's nowhere to be found. I search out the window, but only Hawk's bike and the car I took are in the gravel lot. My stomach twists, thinking about her flitting around Synd by herself.

Over the years, I've heard of her training. She's probably more skilled than I am, which means nothing really. I'll still worry, even though I shouldn't. She's a grown-ass woman who can clearly take care of herself if she's survived this long.

"You must be Hawk." Ember's voice filters over me, seeping into my pores and filling me up in a way I haven't been in a long time. Closing my eyes, I rein in the urge to grab and shake her.

"Go home, Ember," I growl, still trying to school my features into some sense of neutrality as I face her.

She's holding her hand out to the biker as his eyes jump back and forth. Of course, she ignores me, waiting for his response. Hawk smirks and I internally groan, reading his intentions plastered on his face.

"Ember, it's a pleasure to meet you. Why don't you join us?" Hawk says, gesturing next to me.

"She can't. Go away, Ember. Your presence isn't wanted here."

Shock flits across Hawk's face, and he drops the dopey grin. Adjusting my tie, I clear my throat. I won't take back my words, even if they were harsh. She won't respond to anything else. And I can't afford Hawk divulging my father's whereabouts to her. The sooner she moves on, the safer she'll be. I could lie, say he went west, or hell, even back to Westmont, but she'd never believe me. I've never given her a reason to trust me.

From the corner of my eye, I catch her waving away my words, or maybe Hawk's reaction to my harshness. Whichever it is, I don't care. If I repeat it enough, maybe I can convince myself that I feel nothing but resentment toward her. I doubt I'll accomplish such a feat. Her presence does nothing but torment me, both from her role in my sister's death and her inability to accept the truth. I refuse to acknowledge the pain of her betrayal. It doesn't matter in the grand scheme of things. It'll reside within me, blackening my already hardened heart.

"I'd love to join you, however, I'm on my way to a meeting. I just wanted to introduce myself, since Drake here is an asshole and won't," she says sweetly.

I snort, glancing out the window again. Like hell she's going to a meeting. If anything, she's off to terrorize someone. She could be running down what she thinks is a lead, but she'll be disappointed, just like every time before.

He chuckles. "Well, okay then. Come visit Reaper territory some time. I can show you around."

"You're too sweet. It was such a pleasure meeting you, Hawk." She passes him the same black business card currently residing in my wallet. She turns to me, pursing her lips. "Drake."

Gliding away, she wiggles her fingers at Mia on her way out the door, disappearing around the corner instead of going across the lot like I expect. I push my plate away, then grab my cash and drop it on the table. Waiting around for the bill would be a lesson in futility.

"Don't run off, *Drake*. You're not getting away without explaining whatever the fuck that was." His tone holds a hint of laughter, as if he's still lost in the fantasy of setting me up.

"Whatever it is, text me. I'm not about to discuss my relationship with that woman. Leave it alone, Hawk," I say, sliding from the booth.

"Relationship, hmm?" Tapping his finger against his lips, he raises an eyebrow, and I scowl. "Willow could use a friend while Mac and Sam are in Rima."

"Absolutely not. Believe me, Hawk. You don't want her in Reaper territory. And you certainly don't want her influencing Willow. Her tactics for extracting information are second to none, and you won't even realize what she's doing. Be very careful when dealing with Ember Hayes." I've probably given too much away, but I can't afford to be subtle with this.

He leans back against the booth, tilting his head. "What exactly *is* your history with her?"

"I knew her in Westmont and that's all you need to know. I'll reach out to some contacts, see if I can set up some new routes. Text me if anything comes up."

I'm halfway to the door when Hawk calls my name and I turn.

"Don't fuck it up, but when you do, grovel."

I have no idea what he's talking about, but he's clearly not referencing the distributions of products.

"I don't fucking grovel."

Six

Ember

Lying to Roman never works. The minute the words of a meeting were out of my mouth, I knew he didn't buy it. The only time I ever got away with anything with him kicked off the worst period of my life. I never want to experience anything like that again. Which is exactly why I didn't care that he knew I was spewing falsehoods at the diner.

Hours later though, I actually do have a meeting of sorts. I've been waiting for thirty minutes for the man to arrive. The dark corridor isn't the best place, but this is more of a rendezvous than anything else. Back-alley meetups don't usually scream trustworthy and reliable. If it was a few weeks from now, my reputation would proceed me. I haven't had the time to build up credibility, so people think they can fuck me over.

I fucking hate it.

Sighing, I twirl my knife around, eyeing the blade as it glints off a sliver of moonlight. It reminds me of Roman's hair, glowing—ethereal and otherworldly—as he makes his way through the shadows. Smacking my head against the brick wall, I try to dislodge him from my mind. The memories of him have haunted me for years, chasing me from city to city, never giving me peace. I thought if I ran far enough, I'd forget the pain. I should have known better.

"You Cinder?" a gruff voice calls from the end of the alley.

"Depends on who's asking." My response echoes off the buildings, just as I planned.

It took a bit to find the perfect spot. The alley needed to be dark enough to hide in the shadows, but light enough to still catch someone sneaking up on me. And the acoustics had to be perfect with enough reverb to disorient whoever I trapped down here.

"I'm not about to play games, girl."

A dark shadow shifts from a covered doorway, closing in on where I'm hidden in plain sight. He crouches and I swallow the giggle threatening to escape. I almost lose it when he spins around, prowling away from me. Putting him out of his misery would be the kind thing to do. Too bad I've never claimed to be particularly charitable.

When he reaches the mouth of the alley, he twists, glancing over his shoulder. I have no idea what the hell he's doing at this point. I'm clearly not hanging around in full view of the road, complete with a streetlamp for a spotlight. What a tool.

"Wrong way, dumbass," I call in a singsong voice.

Growling, he swings around and charges toward me. I can't keep the giggle down this time as he charges past me. He stutters to a stop, then pivots, and I twirl the knife again. The streetlamp behind him flares to life, keeping his face in shadows. His dark hair hangs in clumps, as if he gelled it to within an inch of its life, but in his dashing back and forth, it's become disheveled.

"Whoa there," I murmur as he tugs a gun from his back. "No need for that."

"You have information and you're going to give it to me."

He shuffles until I'm facing him straight on, and I scan him from boots to face. Patches cover his ripped leather jacket as if someone took a weedwhacker to it. One stands out, a viper curling around a gun with VP scrawled in pretty script under it. The only motorcycle club I've heard of in Synd is the Reapers, so I'm not entirely sure where this guy is from.

"Name?" I ask, using the tip of my knife to clean one of my nails. Rage shimmers around him, engulfing the alley in waves of fury.

"You're the one who contacted me," he snarls.

I finally raise my eyes to his face and my mask almost cracks. Someone used him as a punching bag, that's for fucking sure. One of his eyes is almost completely swelled shut, which makes me a little nervous. An unhinged man with a gun is dangerous. An unhinged man with a gun who also can't see? Volatile.

"Mad can't actually be your name. Nickname, perhaps?"

"Like I'd tell you."

He gestures me away from the door frame, which is silly. Mad clearly doesn't know how to corner someone. Maybe he hasn't had to threaten many people. I don't know if that makes me feel better or worse about the situation, honestly. I almost wish he'd try to fight me, if only for something to do.

The people I've met so far range from those who I'd feel bad taking out to Roman, because he's at the other end of the spectrum. I wonder how much he's learned since I saw him last. His father trained him, like the good little mafia father he is, but how much did Roman keep up with? Only time will tell.

I jump off the step, keeping my back to the wall as I tuck the knife behind my arm. He seems the type who wouldn't notice a blade unless I was waving it in front of his face. He might be one of those pretty boys whose bark is worse than their bite.

"Information. Now," he snaps, shoving the barrel practically up my nose.

Pushing it away with one finger, I raise my eyebrow. "You'd do well not to point that thing at my face, lest I carve up yours just a little bit more, hmm?"

He tips his head back, letting out a maniacal laugh. Sighing, I roll my eyes, waiting for him to finish. I don't have time for this. Actually, I do have time for this since I have absolutely nothing else to do right now, but it's the principle of the thing.

"MacKenzie Raines. Where is she?" he snarls, his face awash with vitriol.

He steps back, though. The name taps on the back of my mind, but it takes a minute to place who he's asking about. As far as I know, she's embedded with the Reapers.

"No idea where she is. I can probably find out if you're willing to give up anything."

He shoots me a lascivious grin and lowers the gun slightly. Gross.

I swallow the sneer begging to escape and paste on a simpering smile. "You're in luck, lover boy. Your night might end better than it began if you play your cards right."

He licks his lips wantonly, and it takes everything in me to stop the disgust from showing.

"Unfortunately, I have a prior engagement. But if you'd like to meet up later, I'm sure we can arrange something," I say, infusing my voice with regret.

His face contorts and I tense, letting my knife fall into my hand. After a good twenty seconds, though, his features smooth out and I slowly exhale.

"I don't fuck sluts. Find my sister and maybe I'll let you keep breathing."

Tilting my head, I track his subtle movements—the shifting of his weight, the flexing of his fingers, the whoosh of air. I duck when it all aligns, slashing toward his stomach. A bullet ricochets into the wall behind me, chunks of brick pelting my back. The first sign I've hit my mark is the give of his flesh under my blade. His cry of shock and pain is the second.

I purposefully kept the cut shallow, so he really has no room to complain. I could have spilled his guts across the alley until the rain washed away his blood. He should be thanking me. Instead, he's cursing me to high heaven, stringing together expletives in one of the most creative ways I've ever heard.

"My, my," I murmur, wiping my knife on my black pants. "Such language. You'd think you'd refrain from calling me a dirty cunt after I sliced you open, but not everyone is as smart as they are pretty."

Hands pressed against his stomach, he slumps against the wall across the alley. Personally, I think he's being quite dramatic. There isn't even any blood seeping from between his fingers. I've cut myself deeper with a razor. What a pansy.

"You bitch," he spits out, staggering to his feet. "This isn't over."

"Unless you want to start losing fingers, I think it is," I say sweetly.

I flip my knife around, advancing on him, and he scrambles toward the mouth of the alley. Grinning, I slip the blade into the sheath under my sleeve. As he stumbles off into the night, I wonder if I should tell someone about Mad, brother of MacKenzie Raines. I'm sure he's important in some scheme, though whether he's worried about her or ready to kill her, I couldn't quite tell. I'm living proof that people go to extremes when their loved ones are threatened. Hopefully, MacKenzie knows what kind of guy her brother is. I'd hate to be the one to tell her he's a fucking creep.

Not only did he piss me off by wasting my time and giving me absolutely no information, he also took off in the same direction I needed to go. Studying the streets and actually walking them are very different, especially when a barren wasteland spanning several blocks on either side of the river splits the entire fucking city. Navigating around isn't as easy as I thought it would be.

I don't think I'm that close to the river, but I do know I'm on the Byrns side. Bright lights flash across the low-hanging clouds, pulsing as if to a beat only the gods can hear. It's over a mile away, and long past midnight, yet the clubs are still going strong.

Plodding steadily along, I wonder if I'll be able to flag down a taxi before I reach the clubs. If I walked the whole way to my room, I'd probably get there at dawn. I could crash at the Byrns house—estate—whatever the hell they call it. It's a ridiculously large mansion with more rooms than they probably know what to do with. I never understood why rich people need a bazillion spaces they barely fill. The house I grew up in is almost the same size. Great for hide and seek and sneaking out, terrible for invoking the feelings of home. Snorting, I glance down another street.

As I walk, I imagine every way I could slip into the mansion. Roman might never find me—the ultimate test to how great their security system is. I could fuck with Roman, pulling pranks on him, maybe convince him a ghost is haunting him. It would be the most fun I've had in years.

The grin that popped up on my face dissolves. Aelia and I used to pull that shit on him. Every slumber party game we could find, from a face full of whipped cream to putting his hand in a warm bowl of water, we tried. Even back then, he was a spoilsport about it. But after he scolded us, as Aelia would turn away, I'd catch his expression softening, a smirk playing at the corner of his mouth. No matter how much he hated me—hates me—he always had a soft spot for her. It was hard not to.

I'm lost in my thoughts as I duck down another alley. I'll blame Roman for the fact that I'm now surrounded by three men, all bigger and, some would say, scarier than I am. Pressing my arm against my side, I dislodge my knife, but don't draw it. No use letting them see I'm armed before they state their intentions. This could just be a simple mugging. If robberies can ever be described as "simple," that is.

"Nice night for a stroll, isn't it?" I ask, turning slowly to keep them all in sight.

One snorts, but they don't say anything as they slowly circle me. Silently, I curse my luck and fortune, adding Roman's name to the list, too. It's his fault I was distracted. Now I'll have to deal with bullshit I didn't want to fuck with. I wanted to lie low, but with each pass of these men's eyes, that opportunity slips away.

"You don't want to do this, guys. I mean, you *really* don't want to do this."

From the corner of my eye, I spot the man to my right tensing. I skip to the side as he lunges, a knife tight in his grasp. He dances back, grinning. The one to my left shuffles forward as if he can sneak up on me and slit my throat. I swing my gaze to him, and he stutters to a stop.

"Stop toying with her," the man in front of me growls.

I duck as his accomplices rush me, letting my knife drop into my palm. We're not far from a main street, which could either be incredibly good or incredibly bad. More people doesn't always mean help. Sometimes it spells disaster.

Kicking at the right man's kneecap, I lash out with my knife toward the other one. The first guy crumples, clutching his leg. I don't know why they're not pulling a gun out to shoot me. Unless they're after something other than murder.

Shuddering, I skip back. My knife missed its mark, and one of my trainer's voices screams obscenities in the back of my head. I can't remember his name, but I think it started with a J. I *do* remember every time he cussed me out, though.

"Seriously, this is a bad idea. You could just walk away, and we can pretend this never happened."

Can I take these three down? Yes. Can I drag them all to the river instead of leaving them to bleed out on the concrete? Probably not. I'd *really* rather not have to call Roman and beg him to clean up my mess. The humiliation alone would be too much.

"Not a chance. Everyone has a price," the leader says, and I groan.

"Fine. But don't say I didn't warn you."

Slipping my other knife from my back, I flip them around and wait for the men to attack. Kneecap stands up finally, waving his weapon back and forth in intimidation. It doesn't work. The leader stays in the shadows as the other man lunges. I dodge his thrust, twisting my blade around and slicing his forearm. His cry echoes through the alley, but I'm already dealing with Kneecap's assault.

He's more skilled than his friend, blocking several of my blows. I skip back, breathing heavily. If all three of them attack at once, I'll be lucky to get out of this without an injury. The leader seems content to let his minions deal with me for now, though.

A burning sensation sears across my shoulder and I let out a curse. Crouching, I charge toward him, catching his stomach with my uninjured shoulder. We tumble to the ground. I roll off him as he brings his knife down, and he stabs himself in the process. How he accomplished such a pathetic feat is beyond me.

"Should have brought better men if you wanted to kill me," I say, giggling.

Kneecap charges me, and I brace myself. Right before he hits me, I duck, letting his momentum send him sailing over my body. He lands with a sickening crack and an "oof."

He gasps for breath as blood seeps from the knife wound in his stomach. I wince as he grips the handle. Pulling it out will only make him die faster. Then I won't be able to question him.

I let out a whoosh of air when his hand falls to his side, leaving the dagger in place. Neither is dead, but they're incapacitated enough I can catch my breath before finishing them off.

The scuffle of a boot behind me is the only warning I have. I try to run, but the leader throws a thin rope over my head, yanking me toward his body. My knife clatters to the ground, skittering off into the dark. Tears fill my eyes, both from the lack of air and the knowledge that I fucked up. I forgot about him, gloating too much over what I thought was my inevitable victory.

Nausea bubbles in my gut, and I try to swallow. The burning of the rope rivals that of the cut on my arm. My feet shuffle on the concrete as he pulls up. My mind blanks—all my training disappearing into the black spots dancing across my vision. As my fingers slip against the roughness against my throat, a sense of calm overtakes me, and I remember.

Pulling my knee up, I slam my heel down on his foot. He grunts. It's not enough for him to release me, but the rope loosens a little and I gasp. Renewing his efforts, he cuts off my air again. I've already fucked up. There's no great escape plan and all my training has gone down the drain. I have nothing left to lose at this point.

I slam my fist into his crotch, and he groans. I do it again and again until the pressure at my throat eases, and he stumbles away. Coughing, I trip, falling onto my hands and knees. He roars and his footsteps thud against the stone as he rushes me. Seconds before he's on my back, I grip the handle of the knife still deep in the other man's stomach. I roll, taking the dagger with me, and brace myself for impact.

The leader doesn't have time to do anything other than widen his eyes as he falls on the blade. As his body lands on mine, the end of the handle digs deep into my ribs, and I swear I hear one of them crack. If I survive this, it'll be annoying. If I don't, well, I won't care.

The man on top of me groans as he tips to the side. I release my grip. My aim wasn't perfect, but from the way he's gasping, I nicked his lung.

Scrambling up, I glance at Kneecap. He's gaping at the two dying men as he struggles to his feet. Turning wide eyes to me, he wobbles and leans against the wall. Clearly, they all thought I was a helpless female they could easily take advantage of.

"Don't move," I warn him as I approach the leader. "What's your name?"

He snarls even as his hands flutter around the knife, as if he wants to pull it out but knows he shouldn't. I smirk, wrapping my bloody fingers around the handle and tug it from him. The slurping sound it makes as I do sends my stomach into a riot. His cry echoes off the buildings.

I glance around, hoping to avoid anyone else sneaking up on me and taking advantage of my vulnerable state. I fucked this up entirely and would rather no one else witness my mistakes.

Gripping the man's hair, I force him upright. Kneecap's cry of outrage is lost in his partner's moans. I grin, setting the blade against Leader's throat. Only one of them needs to be alive at the end of this, and Kneecap will do just fine.

"Going to start talking, or should I slit his throat?"

I'm taking a risk, using them against each other. I have no idea if either of them would care if the other dies. Kneecap stares at my hostage.

"Do it," the leader snaps and Kneecap nods shakily.

As Kneecap reaches behind him, I drag the knife deep across the other's throat and cock my arm back. The blade sinks into Kneecap's Adam's apple and his body crumples, dead before he hits the ground. Panting, I drop the leader and turn my attention to the survivor, but he's disappeared, a trail of blood leading away from the alley.

"Well, fuck."

Seven

Roman

I sigh, leaning against the wall of the warehouse. It's an open space, much like the room I almost died in a few months ago. That was a turning point in my life—one of only a few. I wonder how many more I'll have before I finally settle wherever I'm destined to be.

"Pinch wants to meet with you after this," TJ, one of Byrns's top men, murmurs.

I nod, scanning the men unloading the latest shipment. We don't have that many coming in these days, which is exactly what I'm supposed to be rectifying, according to Hawk. I haven't had much luck. Westmont is a dead end and reaching out for new leads isn't that easy in this lifestyle. It's not like calling up a manufacturer.

"Willow called as well, said she's got some questions for you."

"Remind me to call her tomorrow. Who's that guy?" I point my chin at a young man.

He's thin, sweat dripping from his shaved head. I almost crack a smile when he staggers under the box of guns dropped in his arms.

"Dig was an initiate. This is his first assignment as a member. He's a good kid even if he is a bit on the scrawny side." TJ chuckles, leaning next to me.

This isn't usually what we'd do. Well, it's not what *I* would do. Being involved in every part of the operation is crucial, but overseeing shipments isn't at the top of my list. I have no idea how Byrns or Shane King normally does things.

"Do Byrns or King come down here?" I ask.

"To the warehouses? Sure. I think Shane sends Alex and Ren more often than not. They were talking about setting up another operation like the Depot on their side of the river," TJ says, nodding to a man I don't know.

"With Byrns's help? Or are they branching out on their own?"

TJ gives me a curious look, and I wave my question away. I don't need the answer at the expense of making him suspicious. I'm no longer set on bringing down the mafia families who run Synd. I'm here to pay penance, not only for my mistakes, but for my father's as well.

"When's the next one scheduled?" I ask as they unload the last box.

"Not until next week." He sighs, shaking his head. "Drake, we can't keep going like this. The guys don't have enough to do. They're getting squirrelly and I don't know if that means anything to you—"

"It does. I'm working on it, but if you have any suggestions, I'm all ears."

The truck pulls away, and Dig pressed the button for the overhead door to close. I stride through the dimly lit hallways until I exit to the alley. This warehouse is on the edge of the Barrens. Lights from club row dance into the sky, painting a myriad of colors across the low-hanging clouds.

Glancing to the right, I see a man stumble past. At first, I dismiss him as a drunk, staggering home on a Friday night. The longer I watch, the more I realize he's injured. Clutching at his stomach, he falls to his knees, then tips to the side. I grit my teeth, waiting for him to stumble to his feet again, but he remains unmoving.

Leaning back through the door, I call to TJ, who takes entirely too long to respond. He scowls as he makes his way toward me, as if I interrupted something important. I hate the in-between space I'm occupying—not enough power to command full respect and too much to be a mere member. Working within the guidelines of someone else's territory grates at my nerves.

"What is it, Drake? We still need to move this shit tonight," he growls.

I step from the doorway, sweeping my hand toward the body at the mouth of the alley. He shoots me a quizzical look and my jaw twitches.

"Who's our clean-up for this area?" I ask.

TJ squints, probably trying to identify who the man is. "Did you kill him?"

"When would I have had the time to do that? We still need to remove him."

"Why?" If his question didn't seem genuine, I'd be ramming my fist into his face.

"I'd rather not have random bodies collapsing about, leading to more questions about what is going on around here."

He chuckles, shaking his head. "Won't be necessary, but if it'll make you feel better."

He disappears back inside, and I glare at the door as the heavy metal clicks shut. Closing my eyes, I pull in a calming breath, willing away the rage bubbling within my gut. I'm not pissed at TJ, but this job is too much for one man. Even with the Reapers' help, I'm drowning under the weight of responsibility. Rebuilding is a thousand times harder than dismantling Synd piece by piece, and I barely scratched the surface of destruction. My father did more in the few months he was here, with little to no planning than I did with ten years of preparation. My heart was never in it, though.

I took up my father's cause when I had nothing else to live for. It wasn't a loss when I thought my father had died. But losing Aelia was soul-crushing. Ember's betrayal only added salt to an open wound that's never fully healed. My father's vendetta was my only way to move forward. As intertwined as it was with my sister's death, I doubt I would have been able to break free.

Looking back, though, I realize I was stagnant—stuck in the past with no hope of moving on. Now I can barely bring myself to care whether or not I avenge her. I tried to kill my father and failed. I'm no longer worthy of seeking retribution on her behalf.

I stroll toward the other end of the alley, away from the body. Even though TJ gave me shit for it, I trust him to take care of the man languishing in the street. They may not like me being in charge, but they're quickly learning I follow through on my promises. Being down here when shipments arrive, setting up new contacts, and keeping them informed goes a long way toward gaining their respect. I'm not used to it by any means.

When we moved to Westmont, my father swooped in quickly and quietly, ousting the gang who ruled the underbelly. He led through fear, telling me they'd never respect him if he didn't control them with an iron fist.

It was the same way he parented. I tried to shield Aelia from him as best I could, but that meant I took the brunt of his extreme techniques. When I took over after he supposedly died, I tried to implement subtle changes, but the damage had already been done. Leaving them all behind was more of a relief than anything.

Synd is different in ways I'm not entirely sure I understand. It seems to work for them even if adapting to their methods is a shock. I'm no longer here to upset their process. When they return from Rima, I'll have to decide where to go. Every time it crosses my mind, I skip past it, refusing to delve deeper. Changing the structure within Westmont would be a lesson in futility. I don't have the energy.

As I round a corner, I shake my head. This is not the time, nor the place, to be distracted by things I can't change right now. Focusing on my job here is the only thing I need. I stutter to a stop when I spot one distraction that could derail all my short-term goals.

Ember leans against the brick wall, red hair obscuring her face. A body lies not far from her, mostly in the shadows, but I'm pretty sure he's dead. Sliding into the darkness cast by the building, I wait for her to move. She's so still, I wonder if she's locked in a flashback or paralyzed from killing someone. The only reason I kept track of her over the years was so I'd know if she was headed back to Westmont. At least that's the lie I've told myself. It no longer holds weight.

"Ember?" I call softly after a few minutes.

I expect her to whip her head around or straighten, but she doesn't move. Tilting my head, I study her lithe body, and a shiver runs down my spine.

"Ember," I say forcefully.

Finally, she turns toward me, peering through her hair. "Can I help you, Drake?"

"I'm guessing you're responsible for the body three blocks over?"

I edge closer to the body. I'm assuming he's dead, but I'm not going to take any risks.

"One of them got away," she says bitterly, hanging her head again.

"Can't catch 'em all," I mutter as I dig my toe into the man's shoulder. I can practically feel her eye roll.

The man at my feet is most certainly departed from this world, and when I glance at Ember again, I realize there's another one mere feet from her. I have no idea what happened, and I doubt she'll tell me. Though I knew she was trained, I didn't realize what that entailed.

I kept tabs on her for years, mostly to feed the one kernel of hope she'd find something about Aelia. As much as I spout that my sister is dead, I always wished Ember would find something. The last sliver within my heart never fully accepted that Aelia was gone. I blame Ember for keeping the hope alive.

Clearing my throat, I skirt closer to her. "Luckily, I'm pretty sure your runaway stumbled past one of the warehouses. I called a clean-up. I'll get these out of here too."

"I don't need your help," she spits out.

"Are you hurt?" I ask, tilting my head to see her face more clearly.

"No. Go away."

"Now isn't the time to be a hero, Ember. If you're hurt…" I don't know how to finish the sentence.

I tuck my hands in my pockets. No reason for her to notice how they're trembling just from the thought of her being injured. She's still standing, obviously well enough to spit fire at me, but she's probably been trained to hold the pain at bay. If she went through the same teachings I did, she is probably adept at holding it inside until she's alone. I can't walk away knowing she's hurt.

She snorts, shaking her head, and her breath stutters. I'm at her side, gripping her arm before I fully comprehend I've moved.

"I just killed three men. I am *not* the hero of any story, Drake. Let me go and take your happy ass back to your temporary mansion and leave me be. I don't need your help. I don't want your help. I will fight you every step of the way if you try to force your help on me." She's panting by the time she's done with her little speech.

"Fine. Suit yourself," I mutter, dropping my hand to my side.

I make it to the end of the alley before I glance back. She pushes upright, tipping her head against the brick. I swear there's a thin, red line across her throat, but with the shadows, I can't be sure. When she presses a hand against her ribs, my body leans of its own accord, my mind screaming to go back.

Shaking my head, I walk away, pulling out my phone. After I send a quick text to TJ to add two more bodies to the list of shit to deal with, I walk the three blocks to my car. The cool leather seat sends a shiver through me. Or maybe it's the fact I left Ember standing in an alley, obviously injured and needing help, no matter what she claims. I learned a long time ago I can't save someone who doesn't want to be saved.

I grip the steering wheel, fighting the urge to drive to her and force her into the car. No good will come from that decision, and I can't add another thing to fix on my list. Ember is a grown-ass woman who can clearly take care of herself.

As I drive back to the Byrns estate, the feeling I fucked up persists. Even two hours later, I'm still thinking about her. TJ said she was gone by the time he got there, but I don't know if she made it back to the hotel. Sliding into bed, I fall asleep, doubt plaguing me.

Eight

Ember

"You've got to be fucking kidding me," I mutter as the skies open up, dumping what seems like an entire swimming pool on my black hood I've pulled up to cover my unruly hair.

Should I be skulking around in the forest outside of the Byrns estate? No, I shouldn't. I should be working my way into Hawk's good graces, but for some reason, my feet took me here instead. Now I'm wishing I would have fought the urge. I'm sure Roman hasn't noticed I've been following him. Yet all he's done is attend one boring meeting after another.

I thought I was on to something when he went to a huge warehouse closer to the river, but it was locked down with keypads at every entrance. All the men coming and going looked to be made men, and I doubt they'd talk to me. The risk isn't worth the reward in this instance. I'd rather not get shot—again.

Swiping my sleeve against my face does nothing and I sigh. After almost two weeks, I should have found something, but I'm starting to think Nicki was right and the only person I'll be able to pry anything from is currently pacing the halls of this mansion.

I resign myself to tromping through the mud and going back to the shitty motel. Hot water is apparently nonexistent for them, and electricity is intermittent, leaving me in a shitastic mood. I wish I was back at the fancy hotel, or even sequestered with Roman. He's got plenty of room in that huge house. I'm still thinking about sneaking in. He would never know. Except staying away from him is already proving to be a problem for me. One I need to nip in the bud sooner rather than later.

I thought I could be in the same city as him without feeling anything, yet emotions I haven't felt in years have risen to the surface, suffocating me. The reality is, I never actually hated him. Blaming him for protecting his heart isn't fair. If I'm honest, I'm more hurt than anything. He dismissed me so thoroughly, never giving me a chance to explain why I clung to Aelia being alive, chalking it up to a gut feeling.

Explaining the evidence I gathered would have been shouting into the void of his grief. I was too young, too rash, too much for him to believe me, anyway. Shaking my head, I stumble over fallen branches, brushing against wet bark. The trees are thick here, trunks growing so close together in some places I have to squeeze through. It's strange, as if I've stepped into another world in the middle of the city.

A crack of thunder overhead startles me, and I crouch, searching the dark for ghosts that don't exist. I really shouldn't have come out tonight. There was no indication it was going to storm, but I'm starting to realize this happens a lot here. As lightning flashes across the sky, I breathe out a sigh and double my efforts to get away from here before I freak myself out even more.

When I finally tumble from the darkness, I fall into a hedge, cursing as the branches scratch my face. I'm not usually this clumsy, but between the weather and the mud coating my boots, I'm struggling to keep my feet underneath me.

Frustration courses through me, piling on top of the embarrassment already staked within my chest. Chasing after Roman Drake is the worst idea I've ever had. I'd argue with myself, but I know how that would end, and I'm not a masochist.

Across the street, a car door slams, and I peek through the bush, trying to make out who it is. The last thing I need is someone sneaking up on me while I'm wallowing in the shrubbery, complete with a little path running down the middle. Another car pulls up almost directly in front of me, and I turtle, pulling my bandanna from my neck to cover my face.

This can't be normal, at least not for this part of town. I half expect them to pull out a brick of drugs, but the first man just leans on the open driver's window. Over the rain, I won't be able to hear what they're saying. I can only hope they move on soon because I'm getting more soaked by the minute.

"I can't just shoot 'em in the fuckin' head," the first man yells, throwing his hands up.

I can't make out any of the features of the driver, not even to distinguish if they're a man or woman. They obviously answer though, since the man leans in again. They spend the next several minutes talking before the man starts for his car, turning back halfway across the street.

"If I get killed because you want 'em taken out, I'll fuckin' haunt your ass."

The car takes off as the man gets into his, and he speeds off in the opposite direction. I'm frozen in the hedge, analyzing what little I heard. They could have been talking about anyone. This town is probably filled with people who have a hit out on them. There's no reason to suspect they're after Roman. Even in my head, the lie doesn't stick. I may be pissed at him, but I'm not about to let him get assassinated.

Sighing, I untangle myself from the hedge, opting for the long way around instead of going back through the trees. I'm banking on the two cars not sticking around, which might not be the smartest decision, but there's no way I'm going to get stuck in the mud again.

The guard shack comes into view, a light burning inside. Shivering, I rehearse what I'm going to say, but at this point I'm just hoping they don't shoot first and ask questions later. A man with arms the size of tree trunks eyes me as I approach, and I realize this is not my finest moment.

Opening the door, he crosses his arms, scanning me with a scowl on his face, and I wave.

"Hello there. I was wondering I could talk to Mr. Drake." I wince as I say his name, wondering if I should have said Roman, since it feels more personal.

"He's not taking visitors. Best you move along," he says, a gruffness to his voice.

"Ah, well, see, I have some information for him," I stutter out and then bite my lip. My stomach twists, as if a can of worms burst inside me. The mental image that evokes makes me crinkle my nose in disgust.

"You can give me the information and I'll pass it on to him."

Swallowing, I lean around the small building to eye the house. Most of the windows are dark now, which isn't surprising, since it's almost two in the morning. Getting past the burly security guard isn't looking good. He won't pass on the information I have, no matter if it was as vague as it actually is or not.

An engine revving down the block catches my attention and I glance over, my blood running colder than the rain slashing at my face. A lot of people drive a four-door sedan, but this one bears a remarkable resemblance to the one I saw not ten minutes ago, carrying a man who screamed about killing someone.

Time warps as I whip around, shouting at the guard to get down. Instead, he lurches toward me, pulling a gun from fuck knows where. Before I can run, he grabs my arm, jerking me behind him, and I crash to the ground, my upper body protected by the rain now. Gunshots ring out and I curl into a ball, attempting to make myself as small as possible. With his body blocking my view, I won't be able to return fire, but the guard seems to hold his own as he unloads round after round at the passing car.

Tires screech and he turns, eyes swimming with fury as he points the barrel at me. All of my training flees as I stare down the chamber, bracing myself for the burning pain of a bullet between my eyes. Maybe I won't even feel it before I slip into unconsciousness. Knowing my luck, he'll be three centimeters off, and I'll experience every aching second of it until I'm swallowed in death's hold and dragged down to the fiery pits of hell. Although, that might be nice after the freezing cold still pumping through my body.

"Who the fuck are you?" he growls, pulling the hammer back slowly, as if it's any scarier than doing it quickly.

I press my lips together instead of answering. Little men made of pure nerves are doing a tap dance in my stomach right now, and I'm sure they'll try to escape out of my mouth if I try.

"Moss, what the hell is going on?" Roman's voice winds through the deluge still falling from the sky and a wave of dizziness rolls through my head.

"Get back in the house, Drake, and let me do my job," the man bellows back, eyes still fixed on me.

"Like fucking hell I will."

Roman stomps around the corner, taking in the scene in front of him, and his eyes widen when they reach mine.

"What the fuck are you doing, Ember?" he demands, and an unbidden whimper escapes me. "Put it away, Moss. She's not here to kill anyone."

"Sir, she was used as a distraction for an attempted hit. You need to get back in the house and let me handle it."

Roman's eyes find mine again and he runs his hands through his hair, though it's plastered to his head.

"What happened?"

I don't know if he's talking to me or Moss, but I shake my head, refusing to get involved. The guard can tell him, then he can't say I'm lying.

"This woman came up saying she had some information for you. Then a man in a vehicle tried to take me out, I'm assuming so you'd be left unprotected. I'll take care of her, sir." Moss still hasn't taken his eyes from me, and my skin starts to itch under his scrutiny.

"Ember, were you a distraction so someone could kill Moss?"

I shake my head as my muscles begin to cramp from my position. Skipping my workouts while I've been here was a bad idea if I can't even hold myself on my elbows for five minutes. If I get out of this, I swear I'll never miss a day until my body can no longer keep up.

"See? She wasn't a distraction. Moss, I'm taking her inside. If she comes back, just let her in. It saves me from having to replace the windows."

"As if I'd break a window to get in. I'd clearly find some secret entrance or just walk through the damn door," I say, not able to keep the words in any longer.

Roman rolls his eyes before stepping between me and the guard, who finally tucks his gun away.

"If you think I'm carrying your ass like some damsel in distress, you'll be sorely mistaken. Get up and get in the damn house. It's fucking late and I'd like to get to bed. Alone."

"As if I'd share a fucking bed with you," I mutter, pushing up.

My wrist gives out, pain shooting up my right arm and I collapse, narrowly avoiding bashing my head against the tile floor. Stars dance in front of my eyes as black licks at the corner of my vision. The tap dancers are back in full force, begging to be freed, and I groan as I roll to my side.

"Shit," Roman murmurs.

He hauls me to his chest, straightening way too fast, and I swallow back the bile building in the back of my throat. Opening my eyes, I slam them shut again when the world fractures around me, sending a bolt of pain through my temples.

"Why are you running?" I moan, curling closer to his warm body as the rain pelts my face.

"I'm not," he says, but concern laces his tone and the jostling ceases.

Blessed warmth brushes my face as he crosses the threshold, but with my clothes soaked, I still shake uncontrollably. I didn't notice until I was out of the deluge, and now I'm convinced I'll never be warm again.

"What were you thinking, being out in the fucking rain like that? And at two in the morning?"

"It wasn't raining when I got here," I mutter, tucking my face into his chest and breathing in the scent of sandalwood emanating from him.

It's like a long-lost memory rising to the surface—familiar and comforting with an underlying tinge of regret. The smell lulls me and I relax in his arms, letting the shadows sweep me away.

Nine

The urge to drop Ember on the bed overwhelms me, but I set her down gently. I don't think she passed out, rather her adrenaline seeped from her body. That, coupled with the warmth, lulled her into some semblance of twilight sleep. Her eyes open and she stares at me lazily.

"What was so important you came by in the middle of the night only to get shot at?" I grumble, stomping to the closet.

I took over a random room not that far from Mason's. I don't have much, yet I can spare an extra shirt and some sweatpants. They'll probably fall right off her if she stands, but at least they'll warm her up. Coming back to the room, I find her cocooned in my comforter, as if she grabbed the edge and rolled.

"Get up. I don't know where the extra comforters are and I'm not about to go searching for one because you got mine all wet."

She groans, unwrapping herself before lying spread-eagle on my bed. Despite closing my eyes, the image is seared into my mind, and my cock hardens. There must be at least thirty bedrooms in this place, and another several empty rooms I could have dumped her in, yet I brought her here—to mine. Reining in the thoughts of everything I want to do to her body, I glare at her.

"Knock it the fuck off and get changed," I growl, tossing the clothes on the end of the bed before marching from the room.

Slamming the door behind me, I can't make out the snarky response she's yelling. TJ is leaning against the wall and he raises an eyebrow. Explaining would take more time than it's worth, especially when something thuds against the wood behind me.

"Something I should be worried about?" TJ asks, smirking.

"No. I'm dealing with her."

TJ's smirk turns into a full-blown grin, and I inwardly groan.

"I've heard that line before, not too long ago, actually. Unless this is a situation like she won't leave you alone and thinks she's destined to be with you. In that case, you should let someone else deal with her."

I wave away his concern as I make my way down the hall. There are supplies in my bathroom, but I needed the excuse to walk away from her. Ember tests my patience right along with my resolve.

"She's from my past. Hopefully, she won't be staying long."

He nods, following me into Sam's old bedroom. "What happened outside? Moss is grumbling about mistakes being made and no one listening to him."

"Ember came up to the guardhouse and wanted to see me. Car came by and started shooting at her. Moss assumes she was the distraction. He'll get over it. I'm more concerned with why someone is targeting her," I mumble, digging around the cabinet in the bathroom for a first aid kit.

"You sure they're really after her?" He leans against the door frame, crossing his arms.

"She wasn't a distraction. She works alone, and as much as we despise each other, she wouldn't try to have me killed."

He holds up his hands. "Wasn't saying that, but they could be targeting you. Wouldn't be anything new in our line of work."

"At two in the morning? Right when she walked up to the house? And with a drive-by? It doesn't make sense."

Finally, I find a small black case stuffed with bandages and ointment. I push past him, intent on my room. The sooner I can treat her, the sooner she'll move on. If someone is after her, I'll need to convince her to get out of Synd. I'm not entirely sure what she's mixed up with.

"Not a lot makes sense until we get to the end, I've found. Seems like you've got some shit to deal with, but we need to meet tomorrow. There are some issues with the rebuild popping up I need you to sign off on."

Leaving him in the hall, I kick the door shut behind me. Ember jolts upright from her spot on the floor, wincing as she cradles her wrist. The clothes I gave her are lying on the bed and a bolt of frustration hits me square in the chest. I have bigger issues than dealing with her stubbornness at wearing them.

"What the hell are you doing on the floor?" I say, tossing the bag next to her.

"Well, you bitched about your sheets, so I figured the best place was on the floor, where I apparently belong."

She snatches up the bag with her good hand. I let her struggle to unzip it for a minute before I grab it. Dumping the contents on the floor, I rifle around until I find a bandage to wrap her wrist.

"Give me your arm," I say, holding out my hand. "You never answered my question."

She sighs dramatically, thumping her head against the mattress. Gritting my teeth, I prod at the bones, noting when she jerks away. It's not broken, but she clearly landed on it wrong.

"I *may* have seen that particular car before it came barreling down the road, intent on peppering my hide with bullets."

Whipping my head up, I narrow my eyes at her. "You think they were after you?"

"No, I think they were after *you*. Or maybe Byrns, but that doesn't make sense. I was a couple blocks down and two cars stopped to have a little chitchat in the rain. Seemed a little suspicious, so of course I listened in as best I could. Sounds like one was telling the man in the sedan to take someone out."

"What exactly did you hear?" I ask, securing the end of the bandage and sitting back to lean against the wall.

"Something about shooting someone in the head. Thinks he's going to get killed, apparently. Listen, it could have nothing to do with you, but now that they came around like twenty minutes later? Yeah, not lookin' good for you, Drake." She gives me a look, and a pang shoots through me.

I didn't realize how much we've shared over the years. The sassy expression on her face is the same one I saw countless times, usually when I'd made an ass of myself. As much as I saw her as my little sister's friend, she was mine as well. The connection buzzed beneath the surface, never being fully acknowledged. I wonder how much deeper the betrayal would have run had we been anything other than friends.

"Why are you still chasing her ghost?" I murmur. "Ten fucking years, Em."

Her breath hitches and she ducks her head. "Are you actually going to listen?"

"You're obsessed, Ember. There's no way this ends well. Aelia is—" I clamp my lips together, closing my eyes. "She's dead."

We sit in silence, refusing to look at each other. We'll never see eye to eye. She's too stubborn and set along this path, no matter what I say. I should give up trying to convince her—to get her to go home. Under all the rage, I still want to save her like I couldn't save Aelia. It won't rid me of the guilt, but I can't stop.

"Ember, he told me. He said she served her purpose. Even if she didn't go to Synd, he would have killed her eventually." The words are ripped from me, with little regard to the emotions they evoke.

"If he lied about being alive, why wouldn't he lie about this?" she whispers.

"You didn't know he was alive until, what? A month ago? Maybe two?"

She snorts, giving me a mocking look. "I've known he's been alive for ten years, Drake. You can't honestly think I put this much effort—my entire fucking life—into something without proof."

My stomach twists, and I dig my fingers into my neck. I never told her I searched for them. At seventeen I came to Synd, prying into their world here to find if there was any chance my father and sister had made it out alive. Exploring the rubble left behind from what everyone said was an attempted coup but was really a systematic take down of the leaders, yielded nothing. The men who took over, the sons of those who drove my family out of our rightful place, were barely older than I was. I didn't care about them at that point, I was so lost in my grief. It didn't matter, anyway. There was nothing to find. Someone would have floated their bodies, or buried them in an unmarked grave, as if they had no one who cared.

"What proof?" Maybe if she tells me, she'll finally put this to rest and move on with her life.

"As if I'd tell you," she says, but there's no bite behind her words.

"Want to explain that?"

"Maybe I just like holding shit over your head. Are you going to tell me where Anders went?"

"No. You can't follow him. You'll get yourself killed and then I'll..."

"You'll what? Avenge me?" She snorts, shaking her head.

Pushing off her good hand, she struggles to her feet before cringing as she pulls at her wet shirt.

"I gave you clothes. You could have worn them," I grumble, gazing up at her.

"At what cost? I'm fine. I told you what you needed to know, and now I'm going back to the hotel. Unless you're willing to give me a ride."

Staring at her, I bite my cheek. She's right. There's no reason for her to stay here. And from her perspective, I'm sure it seemed as if the gunman was after me, or maybe Moss. I can't let her walk away without asking her about the possibility of her being the target.

"Ever run into any trouble?" I ask, watching her face closely.

"You're going to have to be a lot more specific."

"Anyone after you? You piss someone off or something?"

Realization dawns on her face, and she chuckles, though it holds no humor. "They weren't shooting at me, Drake."

"I beg to differ. They were definitely shooting at you, Ember. So, what kind of trouble have you landed in and why are you too stubborn to ask for help?" I push to my feet, towering over her. Of course, she doesn't back down. That was never her way.

"I *may* have pissed some people off in the last city, but there's no way they'd follow me all the way here to kill me. It wasn't that serious." She waves away my concerns, but I'm not convinced.

"Then it won't be that big of a deal if you move your things here instead of staying in that shithole on the outskirts of Reaper territory, will it?" I cross my arms as her mouth drops open. "You didn't seriously think I wouldn't keep tabs on you, did you?"

She marches for the door, spinning around to jab her finger at me. I can't help the smirk overtaking my face. One of my favorite things these days is riling her up—watching her explode in a kaleidoscope of colors. It's a glorious sight and never fails to ease the ache that permanently resides in my chest.

"You asshole. I get that you have some god complex or something, thinking you rule the entirety of Synd, but that doesn't mean you get to order me around. I'm not some damsel in distress and you sure as hell aren't Prince Charming. Cut the bullshit and tell me the real reason you suddenly want me around."

Crowding her against the door, I lean my arm against the wood above her head. Her breath hitches before her face shutters, but not before I catch the desire flashing in her green eyes. My gaze dips when she pulls her lip between her teeth. Brushing my thumb against her jaw, I tug it out, all the while knowing I should step back. No good can come from this, but I can't force my feet to move. Ember draws me in like a moth to a flame. I'll get burned every time, but resisting her is proving to be harder than I imagined.

"As much as you piss me off, I'd rather not see you dead when I could have protected you," I murmur, skimming my fingers across her cheek before settling on her throat.

"I don't need your protection. I'm perfectly capable of taking care of myself."

"Is that so?"

Pushing my knee between her legs, I lean in, and she sucks in a sharp breath. I tilt her head to the side with my thumb, brushing my lips against the shell of her ear.

"Then why haven't you pushed me away yet?" I whisper.

She shudders before my words filter through the lust I've stirred in her body. Then a strangled cry leaves her and her hands smack against my chest. I chuckle, refusing to move. Pulling back slightly, I nip at her jaw.

"Let me go, Drake," she growls, wiggling against my thigh.

"Your words aren't matching your actions, Em."

Sliding my hand from her throat and down her side, I latch onto her hip, and she stills.

"Go to hell," she breathes, all while her head tips back, a pretty blush crawling up her freckled skin.

I chuckle, nuzzling her neck. "Already there, sweetheart."

Ten

Ember

Roman's scruff brushes against my skin, scattering goosebumps in its wake. My mind screams at me to stop him, but my body refuses to listen. Instead, I tilt my head, granting him better access to my flesh, and realize I've lost. Any upper hand I ever held with him is dashed with that minute move. Everything else could be explained away. Not this, especially coupled with my fingers tangling with the fabric of his shirt, nails digging in his chest.

I could get away if I wanted—if I was in control of my limbs. A wanton woman has eclipsed my usual pragmatic self, burying her beneath lust I've long denied. Even when I was skipping away in the rain, flipping him off the entire way, a bolt of awareness shot through me, settling right between my legs. Every encounter, I've studiously ignored each lick of desire.

The fog clears from my mind for a second, and his face comes into focus. Searching his eyes, I expect to see the lie. He must be fucking with me, using me to further his own agenda. There's no reason he thinks the man was shooting at me. I'm not the one in danger here.

"You going to push me away?" He grins as if this is some big joke.

I narrow my eyes, imagining all the ways I could gut him right here, and his smile drops. When he tilts his head, a wicked grin overtakes my lips. Realization blooms on his face a second before I slam my fist into his stomach. Grunting, he doubles over, the top of his head almost pressing into my chest.

I lean in, brushing his ear with my lips. "Think very carefully how you proceed, Drake."

His shoulders shake and his hand squeezes my hip, sending another bolt of desire through me. Placing my hand on his shoulder, I dig in my nails and he tenses.

"You think just because you're oozing sexual pheromones, I'm going to fall at your feet? You think a few pretty words and a brush of your lips across my skin will wrap me around your finger? I suggest you take a step back and mind your fucking manners before I mind them for you," I hiss, shoving him.

It's like pushing a fucking brick wall. Slowly, he straightens and his eyes meet mine. There's no laughter in them now, just frustration. Planting both hands on either side of my head, he boxes me in.

"I suggest you think about whose house you're in. I've allowed you a ridiculous amount of freedom within Synd. Perhaps you should remember you're only here because of my good graces."

"You pompous ass, thinking you control all of Synd. This isn't even your house. As if you could control me and what I do."

A seductive glint enters his eyes as he smirks. "I think you like the idea of giving up control to me, don't you, Ember?"

"In what fucking fantasy world do you live in? For fuck's sake. No wonder you're all alone. No one can stand to be around you for more than ten minutes without wanting to pull out their goddamn hair. I swear—"

He growls low in his chest, cutting off my tirade. I didn't even know what I was going to say next, anyway. Roman bounces from one emotion to the next, settling on whatever suits his fancy in that moment before flitting to the next. It's the ultimate manipulation—playing with my feelings as if they're not easily damaged. I suck in a breath at the thought, realizing he's the only one who could possibly break my heart.

"I'd think very carefully how you want to finish that sentence, Ember, or else you'll say something you'll regret later."

Tipping my chin up, I glare right back at him. I can't let him see my vulnerability. He'll use it against me, breaking me down until nothing but my scattered bits blow away in a gust of wind. To think I ever believed we could find peace between us.

Since coming to Synd, the possibility of finding our way back to each other has been sitting in the back of my mind, demanding attention. The more time we spend together, the more that hope dies. I refuse to acknowledge it was ever an option. It's easier than accepting the truth.

"Can I go now?" I huff, glancing away from his probing eyes.

"Run away, little bunny," he whispers, stepping back.

Staring at him, I bite my tongue as the many retorts I want to throw at him gather in the back of my throat. When he turns to walk away, I can't hold back any longer.

"I'm not running away."

His gaze starts at my feet, crawls up my body, and settles on my face. "Seems like running to me."

Throwing my hands up, I let out a strangled groan. "You are so fucking infuriating. How the hell did we even get to this from where we were? I came to tell you someone is trying to kill you. End of discussion. But *no,* you had to bring up other shit and then start to...what? Seduce me? As if that would make me forget everything else?"

"As if it would have taken that much effort," he scoffs, crossing his arms. "Admit it, Ember. You're only focused on finding Aelia because you have nothing else. And when someone points out the uselessness of your life, you run. You did it when we were younger and you're still doing it now."

Ten fucking years and he still knows exactly which buttons to push. Rage swirls in my gut, clouding my better judgment. This is the perfect opportunity to walk away, but I can't stand him thinking he's the reason I'm running. Because I'm not. I merely don't see the benefit of continuing this conversation. At least that's what I'm going to tell myself.

"You're one to talk. You've spent the last decade chasing someone else's revenge plot. As if your father would have given two shits whether you avenged him or not. You chased after a legacy that didn't amount to anything other than a burned shell of a mansion and an empty dynasty that wasn't worth saving in the first place."

He stalks closer, hands flexing at his sides, and I tense. Roman won't hurt me, but the move throws me so forcefully into the past I slam my eyes shut, crawling out of the hole trying to suck me in further. I brushed off Roman's concerns before when he asked about the last city I fled. No one would follow me here, even if they did track me, but fighting off the ghosts still chasing me from my time there is proving harder than I imagined.

"I don't have to explain myself to you. You're nothing but a stubborn, spoiled rich girl, begging for someone to give you a purpose. Newsflash—you don't have one," he snarls.

"Fuck you, Roman Drake. Up on your high horse, thinking you're any better than me. Spoiled? You're the fucking definition of the word. Lashing out at me isn't going to make your own life worthwhile."

He slams his hands next to my head, and I flinch. His face transforms, easing into concern. Shame swirls in my gut as a flush burns my cheeks, and I grit my teeth. Even as my rage toward him courses through me, he's setting my body on fire. Maybe it's just been so long since I've played bedroom bop-it, anything will send me over the edge. Even as I think it, I know I'm lying to myself. It's him. It's always been him.

"Em..." he breathes, eyebrows pulling low.

"Don't." My nostrils flare as I fight for control. "Don't you fucking dare. I don't care if you think I'm wasting my time. Just because you gave up doesn't mean I have to. Go be a pompous ass to someone else."

As he tips his head back, his throat bobs. and I have the urge to sink my teeth into his exposed flesh, but I dig my nails into my palms, using the pain to resist the impulse.

"Why are you so fucking infuriating? Just once it would be nice to have a goddamn normal conversation. But no. You just can't fucking help yourself, can you?"

"I can't help *myself*? Look in the fucking mirror. You're so enamored with yourself—"

His lips slam into mine, cutting off my tirade. For a split second, I stiffen, then my eyes fall closed and I melt. Stars explode behind my lids as he devours me, his tongue tangling with mine. Pressing closer, the heat from his body seeps into me, matching the inferno consuming me from the inside out. All rational thought flees, leaving me with only the sensations he's conjuring within.

Roman's hand snakes into my hair, gripping the strands as he tilts my head. My mind screams for me to do something—anything—to gain control, and I sink my teeth into his bottom lip. Growling into my mouth, his other hand grips my hip. His leg slips between mine, and I moan.

Ripping his mouth away, he skims his lips along my jaw, tipping my head back. My jacket doesn't leave much skin for him to explore, and he growls again. The sound reverberates through my chest, electrifying the air between us. I don't recognize the needy noises falling from me as he bites into my neck, most likely leaving a mark. I'm so far gone, I don't even care.

Frantic thudding on the door behind me has him leaping away, leaving me bereft in a sea of desire. Another knock sends me scrambling away, running my hands over my hair before tugging my hood up to cover the mess. There's nothing I can do about my swollen lips or flushed cheeks, but hopefully whoever is on the other side has more important things to worry about.

Roman scowls at me as he stalks to the door, but I pretend not to notice. Dropping to my knees, I gather up the first aid supplies he dumped on the ground, shoving them back in the bag as he opens the door.

"Drake, we have a problem," an older man says gruffly.

"What is it, TJ?"

To anyone else, Roman probably seems his normal asshole self, but I hear the strain in his voice. I duck my head to hide my smirk. He can pretend all he wants he wasn't affected by whatever is between us. I'll let him live in his fantasy world as long as he likes. It's not like I'll be taking things further, no matter how much my body begs me.

While sleeping together would be explosive, the aftermath would leave a smoldering wreckage in its wake. Our past renders our future a stark wasteland, destined to be barren of anything other than biting remarks and unresolved issues.

"Safe house on the Kings' side is going up in flames. Fire marshal called to tell us he wasn't going to send anyone down there. Something about teaching us a lesson." TJ's face twists and a string of curses leaves Roman.

I slowly stand, trying to not draw attention to myself as Roman stomps to the closet, slamming the door behind him. Pursing my lips, I glance at TJ, finding him already staring at me.

"I understand you were outside when the gunman came through?" he asks as he tugs at his salt and pepper beard.

Clearing my throat, my eyes jump to the closet door before settling back on him. As much as Roman pisses me off, I'd rather he was here for this conversation. I don't particularly want to be interrogated by one of Mason's men about something I'm not involved in. Often, men don't believe me when I say I had nothing to do with things. At least in my recent experience.

"Uh, yes." I resist the urge to add "sir" to the end of my sentence, instead clamping my lips together.

"Any reason you decided the middle of the night was the best time to deliver whatever news you had for Drake?" He crosses his arms and raises an eyebrow. I'm sure he thinks he looks nonchalant, just someone making conversation while we wait, but the tick in his jaw says otherwise.

"Don't bother, TJ. She won't reveal anything." Roman steps from the closet as he finishes straightening his tie.

My mouth waters as I take him in. When he catches my eye, he smirks, and I grip the bag I'm still holding tighter. Best not to throw it at his head when a person who is probably paid to protect him is in the room. I'd be lying in a pool of my own blood before it even touched him. Dropping the supplies on the desk, I sidle closer to freedom.

"Drake, I think it best we—"

"Is it on the north side? We'll need to stop and grab her some clothes," Roman says.

"I don't think that's wise." TJ eyes me, but I'm already glaring at Roman.

"Don't worry, TJ. I won't be coming."

"Not yet," Roman mutters as he pulls on his coat. I bite my cheek to stop myself from commenting on the fact he's wearing a peacoat with more buttons than the last dress I wore.

"In that case, we should get going. I'm sure"—TJ gestures in my direction, clearly searching for my name—"she can find her own way home."

Roman opens his mouth to continue to argue, but I slip past TJ into the hall. Turning the corner, I stop, closing my eyes and listening for any indication they're behind me. I'm not about to team up with Roman to help solve whatever mysteries are going down in Synd, but if something is happening that can point me to Anders, I won't let it pass me by.

"Moss will make sure she leaves the premises," TJ says.

"I'm not concerned with Ember being here. She's not a threat to us, and your skepticism isn't appreciated. If Ms. Hayes wants to frolic on the lawn, naked in the moonlight, you'll do nothing but avert your eyes. Understood?"

I smother a chuckle behind my hand at the image. As if I'd ever frolic, naked or otherwise. TJ murmurs something and I lean closer.

"Regardless, you'll tell the others and let me handle Ember. Now, where exactly are we going?"

A door shuts and I shuffle deeper into the shadows, praying they don't come this way.

"Just south of the Flaming Skillet."

Their voices fade away and I smile. Time to find out how observant Roman Drake actually is.

Eleven

Roman

"I suggest you get your men down here immediately, Brewer, or we're going to have problems."

I pace the sidewalk across the street from the blazing inferno. I'm already pissed it took the fire chief ten minutes to return my call. The fact that he's beating around the bush on whether he's going to send trucks infuriates me. Fighting against their pushback to my authority feels too much like when I was younger, grappling for my place within the hierarchy. I should be at the top of this food chain, and yet I still have to assert my control.

"Mr. Drake, you're new, so I'll clue you in on something—"

The phone is ripped from my hand, and I spin, my fist already swinging. Hawk blocks me as he holds the device to his ear, the fire chief still spouting excuses.

"Brewer, get your shit together and get down here or we'll float your ass by morning."

The biker hangs up, tossing me the phone as he stalks back to Willow. She shoots me a concerned look before gazing back at the smoke billowing into the night. Thankfully, no one was in the safe house, but the residents on either side are huddled half a block down from us, a woman sobbing into a man's chest. If the firetrucks don't get here soon, their houses will catch fire, too. If it spreads, we're fucked. Between the damage I caused and my father continued, there's enough to repair in Synd. I can't afford more.

"Anyone see anything?" Willow murmurs as she steps next to me. Hawk is on his phone, probably talking to Helms or the Kings.

"No, but that's not surprising. How did you two hear about this?"

She smiles, giving me a look, and I shake my head. The Reapers have enough contacts that someone probably informed them before me. Most of their concentration has been on finishing the repairs left over when a rival MC swept through. Not to mention the shit my father pulled in their territory. I planned on leaving them alone when I was stuck on bringing down the leaders of Synd. It wasn't worth the effort, and I figured I could strike a deal with them after everything was said and done. My plans fell apart, making them my unlikely allies.

"I know it must be hard taking over for them, especially when no one seems to fully trust you, but I think you're doing fine," she says, patting my arm.

"There a reason you're being so friendly toward me?" Crossing my arms, I peer at her from the corner of my eye.

She sighs, eyes fixed on the fire. "I think you see yourself as a terrible person whom no one will ever see as anything other than the man who messed up. But when you took me, you weren't a monster. You didn't shove me in the trunk or tie me up. You never threatened me. In fact, you went out of your way to assure me that your quarrel wasn't with me and I was free to go after."

"I still kidnapped you against your will," I say gruffly.

Her musical laugh rings into the night, but she smothers it when she catches the couples down the block watching us.

"All kidnappings are against someone's will, Roman. I should know. It's happened to me more than expected, even in my position." She turns toward Hawk, waving as he smiles at her. "Loving someone who lives in the shadows isn't easy. If I could do it all over again, skipping all the pain, I'd still choose him. Every single time. I'd take all the suffering I endured just to spend one more minute in his arms."

The image of Ember, head tipped back, completely submitting to her desire, flashes across my mind. I dig my nails into my coat to quell the itch on my palms, remembering my hands gliding across her soft skin. Even the taste of her dances on the tip of my tongue. Shaking my head, I try to push her from my mind, but it's no use.

"I'm glad you found someone." I clear my throat, ducking my chin to my chest. "Things should have gone differently."

"Is that your version of an apology?" A sly smile graces her lips as she turns to me.

"Perhaps it is," I murmur as sirens finally blare in the distance. About fucking time.

"It's a piss-poor one, then. You should work on that."

When I fully face her, she tips her head up, an expectant look on her face. Hawk stutters to a stop just out of earshot, eyes bouncing between us. I realize this is something I need to do if I ever have a hope of fully gaining their trust. Admitting I was wrong, regardless of the fact I was operating on false information, is proving harder than I thought.

"I apologize for the undue stress I caused by using you as bait." My words come out gruff but steady.

Willow tilts her head, narrowing her eyes before the corner of her lips tip up. "I accept your apology. Please refrain from doing it again. I have a lot more training now, and I'd rather not have to stab you if I can help it."

I snort, turning back to the flames as the fence surrounding the property catches on fire. A firetruck whips around the corner, the sirens cutting off abruptly when they pull in front of the house, blocking most of my view.

"Willow, we need to go." Hawk grabs her hand. "Drake, we still need new routes. I'm thinking Harris unless you've got anyone in Westmont."

I shake my head, eyes fixed on the firemen hooking up hoses and yelling into their radios. A lone truck pulls onto the street, stopping just down the block. I can barely make out a man behind the wheel, but I'm pretty sure it's Brewer. I take one step before a hand on my arm stops me.

"Not worth it. We'll just have to find someone else to replace him. Then we'll need to break them in. If you're still pissed tomorrow, we can slash his tires and egg his truck," Hawk says with a laugh.

"I'll deal with the residents. They won't be allowed in their houses tonight, at the very least," I say, still eyeing Brewer.

He claps me on the shoulder. "Don't stay out here alone. Too many people want to take a shot at you, see if they can overrun Synd in the others' absence."

"I'll be fine."

"Even with shit going down earlier?"

"I wasn't the one being shot at," I mutter.

"Shooting at the house is just as telling as if you were standing in front of them. Everyone in the city knows it's a surefire way to earn a one-way ticket down the river. Don't let complacency get you killed, Drake."

With that final warning ringing through the air, he tugs Willow toward his bike. I track them until their taillight disappears into the night before I watch the firefighters battle the blaze. I expected this production to be louder, but it's a fairly quiet affair other than the water gushing from the hose. No one shouts or runs around frantically. Shaking my head, I make my way over to the people still huddled on the sidewalk.

A man not much younger than me steps in front of the woman and what I'm assuming is his child. The other two men step up next to him, blocking my view.

"Gentlemen." I nod to each of them, keeping my distance. "Unfortunately, you won't be able to return to your homes tonight. I'm sure they'll be able to stop the fire before it spreads, but if you have any damages, please send the invoices to me. I've arranged for a car to come and take you to a hotel for as long as needed. Supplies will be provided, and you can request anything else from the driver." They exchange wary looks, but I'm already turning away.

"Mr. Drake?" The woman's voice calls, pushing past the men. One grabs at her arm, keeping her next to him. "Was anyone hurt?"

"No. The house was empty. We'll rebuild it and sell it. The house will no longer be an issue for you."

"Oh, there was a young woman who stayed a few nights. She was kind—bright red hair. I thought maybe she was still inside. Are you sure?"

My stomach drops and my heart races as I whip my head toward the fire. No one could survive if they were stuck inside. The entire thing is a loss. Stepping off the sidewalk, a rumbling followed by a crash reverberates through the night, and I stutter back. The woman's cry echoes in the lull and her partner dashes past me. I seize his arm, hauling him back.

"Stop," I bellow as he fights my grip.

"Oh, thank god," the woman sobs and we both turn.

She's fallen to her knees, hands pressed to her cheeks and eyes fixed behind us. Whipping around, relief flows through me at the sight of Ember. She's not the only person with red hair living in Synd, but my mind was convinced she was the squatter trapped inside the house, earmarked to die.

Ember rushes to the woman, landing on her knees next to the woman. She glances up at me as the woman collapses in her arms. I'm not surprised she's here, whether to check up on me or hoping for more clues to find Anders. How a fire at a safe house could help her, I don't know. I've kept track of what she's been doing over the years, but looking too closely sends a rush of rage through me, so I never examine her dealings deeply.

"Ma'am, the car is here," I say, gesturing to the two vehicles down the street.

Ember helps the woman stand, then lets her go as the group shuffles away. Gritting my teeth, I wait until they're safely on their way before latching onto Ember's elbow and tugging her between the dark houses.

"What are you doing squatting in one of my safe houses," I growl, pushing her against the side of the house.

"*Your* safe house? I was under the impression it was the Kings'." She smirks, crossing her arms.

"Does it fucking matter? Why were you there? And how did you know it was one of ours?"

I plant my hands on either side of her head, pulling back when it reminds me of our time earlier. The last thing I need is to kiss her again. I don't know if I would be able to stop myself the next time. Shaking my head, I vow there won't *be* a next time. She'll be on a train home soon if I have any say.

"You're not the only one with contacts in Synd, you know. Besides, I only stayed for two days and then moved to the hotel."

"You mean the shithole motel that looks like it'll collapse on itself without warning? Great upgrade," I scoff.

"Seeing as how *that* house is currently in flames? I'd say it's better. Can I go now? I'd rather not have to listen to you bitch about shit that has nothing to do with you any more than I have to."

I spin away, planting my hands on my hips, as I pull in a deep breath. Her unique ability to get under my skin with a few choice words is just one reason I should stay as far away from her as possible. From the corner of my eye, I track her movements as she slips toward the street. The irrational urge to stop her—to yank her back to me—overwhelms my senses.

As she steps onto the sidewalk, a ticking fills the air, and she cocks her head as if she hears it too. Horror sweeps through me, and I lurch forward, grabbing her arm as a shock wave hits us.

Ember ducks into me and I spin us as a concussion of air and fire envelops us. Curling my body over hers, I force us to the ground as orange flashes across my closed eyes. The heat hits me then, bubbling along my back, and I tuck closer to her.

Twenty seconds and the world falls silent. At least I think it does. I shake my head, trying to rid myself of the ringing in my ears. Ember pushes against me and I roll, still holding her tightly against my body.

Glancing over my shoulder, the fiery remnants of a vehicle sit along the curb across the street. If Ember would have kept going—if I had let her walk away—she would have been caught in the blast.

I shudder, tucking my face into her neck and breathing her in. There's no way this was a coincidence. The safe house was set on fire as bait, the car bomb the trap that I walked right into.

Ember pushes at my arm, and I unlock my muscles one by one. I'm not ready to let her go, but I have no reason to make her stay. I expect her to scramble away. Instead, she turns, tucking her face into my chest as she trembles. I wrap my arms around her again, content to lie here for another minute before I have to get up and deal with all the shit suddenly happening around us.

"Are you okay?" she whispers, fingers digging into my chest.

"Fine. We need to go."

Reluctantly, I tug her to her feet, keeping my arm around her waist. The last thing I need is her running off again. She'll get herself killed. The firefighters have already converged on the car, spraying it down with some type of foam substance. Brewer loiters next to the firetruck, peering around as if he's searching for something—or someone.

Pulling Ember deeper into the shadows, we disappear into the night. Once we're far enough away, I'll call a car, but I'd rather not deal with Brewer any more than need be. Peeking down at her as she brushes her hair away from her face, I sigh. There's no doubt in my mind that this was an attempted hit. The only question that remains is who was the target—myself or the woman next to me?

Twelve

Ember

"Why are we here again?" I grumble from the backseat next to Roman.

He's acting like the car exploding a dozen feet from me was a calculated attack. While I might agree that it was suspicious, assuming it wasn't just a freak accident caused by the house going up in flames is ludicrous. Glancing at Roman as he runs his fingers through his hair for the sixth time since we got in the car, I wonder what's got him so riled up. Sure, it sucked, but this isn't as big of a deal as he's making it.

"I'm not going through this again, Ember."

He runs his fingers through his hair again, mussing it up. When we were teenagers, he only did it when I was around. He never touched his hair otherwise. Teenage Roman was too sophisticated to show his frustration. Personally, I think he was too vain.

"One more time. Be explicit, please." I mirror his expression as he raises an eyebrow. "What?"

"I'm just not used to you using your manners," he murmurs.

Closing my eyes, I pull in a deep breath, trying to suppress the urge to strangle him. "Answers. Now."

"We're here to gather your things. Clearly, someone is after *you*, not me. Therefore, staying in this"—he wrinkles his nose as he gazes at the motel—"establishment is unacceptable. There are plenty of rooms at the Byrns mansion. You can take your pick."

"And what if I want your room?" I raise my eyebrow, but when he smirks, my eyes widen. "I didn't mean it like that."

"Oh, Ember. You're more than welcome to share my room whenever you want. However, as you probably noticed, there's only one bed."

He pushes from the car, holding out his hand to help me exit. I hesitate before placing my own in his, swallowing hard as it envelops mine. He tugs me from the car, keeping hold of me as we walk to my door. I scoff when I realize he knows which room is mine.

"You couldn't have at least picked a hotel so the doors would be on the inside? Seriously, you're just asking to get shot in a place like this."

"It was cheap, and I didn't have to register a name, so yeah, this is where I picked. Plus, it's on the edge of the bikers' territory, so I assumed they were, like, in charge around here or something."

"And now?" he asks, leaning into my body as I unlock the door, jiggling the handle as I do.

"Now apparently doesn't matter, since you're forcing me to move in with you," I grumble as the door pops open.

Stumbling over the threshold, I suck in a breath as his hand slides around my waist, preventing me from tumbling to the floor.

"Force is such a strong—"

We freeze, then he yanks me back into his chest. The room is in tatters, mattress cut open, exposing the springs. The pillows are strewn about, along with all my things. Dresses are ripped apart, and toiletries are scattered, bleeding out on the floor.

"I know you weren't tidy when you were younger, but this seems a bit excessive," he murmurs in my ear.

I can't form a response. I'm still paralyzed by the thought of someone in here, searching for fuck knows what. They clearly didn't find it, since I'm not hiding anything. All the information I have is stored on the cloud and accessed through a computer that is currently in two pieces by the sink. No one else would care about my search to find Aelia, unless her father is behind this.

"Drake, you need to tell me where Anders went."

He stiffens, dropping his arm and stepping away from me. "You think this was him?"

Spinning, I plant my hands on my hips. "I can't think of anyone else who would do this. I haven't exactly been quiet about wanting to find information on him."

"What happened in Harris, Ember?" he asks, and it's my turn to stiffen as my stomach rolls.

"Nothing. I pissed some people off and then I left," I mumble, turning away to take in the destruction again.

He sighs and I can feel his eyes burning a hole in the back of my head. Hopping over a spilled bottle of lotion, I peek into the bathroom, finding the rest of my things in the shower, soaking wet and covered in what smells like bleach. I'll have to buy an entire new wardrobe, along with all the other things. I can afford it, but it's the principle of the thing. Dealing with the aftermath is always shitty, which is usually why I skip town before shit hits the fan.

"Why are you avoiding this, Ember? You realize it only makes me dig harder."

Walking back into the room, I pick up both pieces of my laptop and then toss the screen back into the sink. I may not be able to salvage anything from it, but there's always a possibility. They should have taken it, honestly, seen what the hard drive had on it. Unless they had someone with them that could tell they wouldn't be able to lift anything from it. I cringe as my cheeks burn, followed closely by my ears. Tucking my hair back, I bite the inside of my cheek, trying to will the blush away.

"Get it over with and tell me what the hell happened," he growls. "Why won't you just fucking say it?"

"Maybe because it's none of your damn business," I yell as my heart races and my chin trembles. I clamp my mouth shut to stop it, but I just keep shaking, unable to control myself any longer.

"What is so bad that you can't tell me?"

"I'm fucking embarrassed, okay?" I scream, tears filling my eyes. "Is that what you want to hear? Do you want me to flay myself open for you to inspect and judge? Perhaps you can tell me all the ways I fucked up, instructing me on how you would have handled it so much better. Then you can lord your superiority over me, and we can once again establish the hierarchy. How about that?"

Tears stream down my hot cheeks and I toss the broken computer down, swiping angrily at the wetness. I catch his reflection in the mirror over the sink as his mouth hangs open, disbelief etched on his face. My head swims, dark spots dancing in front of my eyes and I close them.

I hate this. I hate everything about what's happening. I'm never vulnerable, protecting myself with a solid brick wall that no one should be able to break down. But of course, he did. He always could, which is why I've stayed as far away from him as possible. I thought I could handle it now. I thought enough time had passed where he would no longer affect me. I was so fucking wrong and I fucking hate it.

He takes a step toward me. "Em..."

Pivoting to face him, I hold up my hand. "Don't. I don't want your fucking pity. Just...just leave me the hell alone."

His face falls, twisting the knife that's been stuck in my heart for too fucking long. "I can't do that."

Sighing, I yank my hair back, shoving it into a ponytail. It's unruly and strands hang down by my face, but I don't care. It matches the emotions rolling around inside of me, never knowing where to settle. I could handle this if I didn't feel so much.

"Let's just go home," he murmurs, turning for the door.

As he disappears into the night, I can't help but whisper, "This isn't home."

I fell asleep in the car. My usual default of snark failed me today and the flood of emotions drowned my system, I suppose. I wake up in Roman's arms, halfway up the stairs at the Byrns place. A guy with the blackest hair I've ever seen opens the door as we approach, and I almost say something. Instead, I snuggle closer to Roman's body, breathing in his scent. I'll hold on to this moment, reliving it in the future whenever I become a morose bitch again.

"I know you're awake," he mumbles as he turns down a hallway.

"Well, put me down then," I say, but he keeps walking.

I expected him to bring me up the stairs, sticking me in a bedroom close to his to keep an eye on me. Should I care about where he's taking me? Probably. Do I? Nope. Not even a little bit.

I'm tapped out for the night. I haven't cried in front of someone in ten years. It hits me that the last person I broke down in front of was Roman, and I snort.

"What's so funny?" He stops in front of a nondescript wall with birds plastered all over it.

"Nothing. Are we waiting for a portal to appear to Faeven?"

"Where the hell is Faeven?"

"I read it in a book," I say innocently.

He gives me a look before pressing his foot into the baseboard. It clicks and then a panel pops out, revealing a landing with stairs going up and down. He eyes the darkness and then purses his lips, and my gaze dips down. I can't help it. Even if shit is weird between us, I still can't stop my body from reacting to him. He sighs before setting me on my feet and pulling out his phone.

"Shut the panel," he says.

A shiver runs through me as I do, plunging us into total darkness. I yelp as he grabs my hand, tugging me up the stairs, probably going slower than he normally would. After living here for a month, I'm sure he knows all the ins and outs of this place. He stops on a landing, and I almost plow into him. Maybe he doesn't actually know where he's going.

"Are we lost?" I whisper, leaning around him and squinting into the shadows.

"No. Why are you whispering?"

"Seemed appropriate for the current circumstances. Plus, you're whispering too." I stick out my tongue, even though he's not facing me.

"I saw that," he says before tugging me to the left as I roll my eyes.

He pushes open another panel, revealing his bedroom. Stepping through, he drops my hand, spinning around and holding his hands out as if he's presenting a glorious prize.

"Great, you got us to your room. Fantastic," I deadpan.

He rolls his eyes, stalking to his closet. The clothes he tried to give me earlier are still lying on his bed, mocking me. I should have put them on, but my stubbornness got in the way. I told myself if I didn't accept anything from him, I could go about my life as if we weren't tangled together in a mess of the past and present. A bunch of fucking lies. That's all I was telling myself. I seem to be doing that a lot.

Snatching up the clothes, I march to the attached bathroom, scoffing at the ornateness of the room. For a place you pee and shower, it's pretty fucking fancy. It reminds me of my childhood home, which makes where I lived seem quaint when it was anything but. At least Mason's house feels a little lived in. My own was a museum filled with neglect, judgment, and disappointment.

I kick the door closed and peel off my damp clothes. If it would have kept raining, the house fire would have been easier to control. In fact, I'm surprised it went up as quickly as it did. Some sort of accelerant must have been used to help it along, but without getting closer, I'll never know what it was.

Tossing the only clothes I own over the edge of the tub, I tug on the sweatpants, rolling the hem several times so I don't trip. Sandalwood infiltrates my nose as I pull the shirt over my head. I gather the fabric in my fingers, breathing deeply.

A soft knock on the door has me dropping my hands, as if he caught me doing something wrong. I wasn't, but it would be embarrassing.

"What?" I call, spinning around as I try to figure out what the hell I'm supposed to do now.

"Are you taking a shower?"

Pulling my ponytail over my shoulder, I examine the strands. Just thinking about the hot water rushing over my skin has my muscles easing, but it's almost five in the morning. It's a problem I can solve tomorrow, along with the plethora of others bouncing around in my head.

I yank open the door, revealing a dressed down Roman leaning his arm against the doorframe, and I squeeze my thighs together. Roman in a suit is hot. Roman in gray sweatpants and a soft black t-shirt is devastating.

Biting my lip, I glance past him to get my shit together. Hooking up with him would be amazing and reckless and unhinged. Doesn't mean my mind will stop conjuring up all the things he could do to my body.

"No. Just show me where I can crash for a couple hours, and then I'll be out of your hair." There goes the knife in my chest digging in again. I really need to get the hell away from him.

He scowls as he straightens. "We'll talk about that tomorrow, or rather, later today. You're sleeping here."

"With you. In this bed." I meant for it to be a question, but it comes out closer to a statement. "That's not going to happen."

"I'd rather you not slip out without a word. Plus, after the night we've had, I hardly think you need to worry about me ravishing you." He pushes off the doorframe and settles on the bed.

Marching after him, I plant my hands on my hips. "Who the hell says ravishing anymore? Second of all—"

My sentence is lost in a shriek as he launches upright, wraps an arm around my waist, and yanks me onto the bed. Rolling us, he tucks my back to his chest. Somehow, he kicks the comforter over us, tugging it the rest of the way until I'm bundled up, warmth seeping into me.

Opening my mouth, I intend to rip him a new one, but he grunts, cutting me off.

"Don't fucking start. Just go to sleep," he mumbles.

"The lights are still on."

He sighs, reaching up to hit the wall, and the lights cut out. Asking what the hell just happened is too much work. Arguing about sleeping next to him is too much work, too. Even waiting until he's asleep and slipping out is too much work. Instead, I'll just settle in and soak up the feeling of safety that settles over me. I'll deal with everything else tomorrow.

Thirteen

Roman

"Going somewhere?" I whisper as Ember shimmies across the bed.

She huffs, settling next to me again. "I already went somewhere. Namely, to the bathroom. But I'm still tired, so I figured I'd come back. Now stop talking so I can get some more sleep."

I grin, peeking at her from under my lashes. She's practically hanging off the other side of the bed, staring at the ceiling. All the reasons we should stay far away from each other and not be involved have fled, leaving a contentedness behind I shouldn't trust.

For one morning, though, I'd like to pretend. I want one moment in my life that's not dictated by what I *should* do. The anger and betrayal I felt just days ago are simmering now instead of boiling over.

Having her waltz back into my life so abruptly had all the old emotions bubbling up, threatening to pull me under. The more time we spend together as adults without the other bullshit surrounding us, the less I feel that tug to bury her. If anything, I'd like to bury my cock in her, leaving us both satisfied. The thought sends a rush of blood south. I try to adjust myself under the covers, but she narrows her eyes at me.

"What are you doing?"

"I'm reminiscing about how you melted under my touch, love." I smirk as I skim my hands along her side, dipping my finger under the hem of her shirt.

"Ack. Abso-fucking-lutely not. You will not, under any circumstances, call me 'love' again. Walking fucking cliché." She makes another gagging noise but doesn't move away from my questing hand.

"No pet names. Got it."

I walk my fingers across her stomach, smirking as she trembles and goosebumps scatter across her skin. Her face flushes as she purses her lips.

"Thought you said no ravishing?" Her breath hitches as I skim my hand higher.

"That was last night. Today is a brand-new day," I murmur, and her eyes finally find mine.

Her mouth parts and her heart thunders under my palm. I'm sure she thinks she should cuss me out, scramble from the bed, but her body wants this. At least while we're here, we can pretend we're two people who merely want each other. We can find solace in each other's bodies with nothing else getting in the way.

Clinging to the edge of the comforter, she mumbles something under her breath, going back to stare at the ceiling.

"You can't deny you want this. So why not just let it happen?"

I don't even know what I'm saying. Ember is the last person I should ask to have a fling. We have too much baggage. Even if we didn't, I would want more—more of her, more of us, just more. Lying to myself won't get us any closer to some mystical world where we're not destined to be enemies.

"You have got to be kidding me," she mumbles, rolling her eyes. "This is bullshit, and you know it. I'm not fucking you just because your dick is begging to disappear into my cave of wonders."

Rolling off the bed, she takes half the covers with her, leaving the sheet low on my hips. She scowls at me before stomping to the closet, slamming the door behind her. Tucking my hands behind my head, I close my eyes.

I'm loath to admit that she's right. Getting involved isn't the wisest decision, but getting my cock on board with that line of thinking is proving to be harder than I imagined. Every time she opens her mouth, my blood boils, sending my thoughts spiraling. All I want to do is sink into her and make her body sing. Kissing her last night opened a floodgate.

Reaching down, I grip myself through my underwear, attempting to ease the pressure. The sweatpants I had on got kicked off in the night. Squeezing my cock doesn't help, though. All I can picture is Ember's body pressed against mine, the scent of her filling my pores, the feel of her soft skin under my hands, her needy sounds filling my ears. She's starred in most of my fantasies for so long, to finally have her in my arms was overwhelming.

Slipping my hand underneath the waistline of my boxer briefs, I grab my cock. My breath catches in my throat as I peek under my lashes, fixing my gaze on the closet door. I shouldn't jack off with only a door separating us. The idea of getting caught has my balls tightening and I stroke myself once, twisting as I get to the tip.

My eyes fall closed again, and I repeat the move slowly. I'll stop in a minute, when the tension eases a bit. I'll stop when she opens the door, so I don't get caught. I'll stop…probably never. I'll never picture anyone but her in these moments. I've been with other women, but their faces blur together, never fully registering. They were flings and my stomach turns when it hits me I tried to put Ember in their ranks.

Groaning, I tighten my grip, moving my hand faster. Having her only feet from me, with no clue to what I'm doing, is intoxicating. Part of me hopes she catches me. Maybe it'll convince her she should be sitting on my face instead of denying what we both want.

A sharp intake of breath has my eyes flying open. My heart races when our gazes meet, and I find hers dripping with desire. I slow my movements, stroking myself as I imagine it's her wet pussy stroking me instead of my fist.

The corner of my mouth tips up and her fingers grip the hem of her shirt. No, not her shirt—mine. The sight of my clothes draping her body is almost too much, and a sense of possessiveness overtakes me. She has no idea what she's doing to me. As her eyes dip lower, though, I'm sure she can see exactly how she affects me.

I tip my chin up, my gaze traveling down the length of her body. "Take them off."

My voice is gruff, laced with the burning urge to see her splayed under me, in front of me, hell, I'd take her any way and every way she'll let me. She shakes her head, even as her hand sneaks under the waistband of the sweatpants. Even from here, I notice how her body shudders. I can tell the exact moment her fingers reach her pussy, as her eyes fall half-closed and her lips part.

"That's it. Imagine it's me stroking that wet pussy."

She gasps as her head thumps against the wood and her pants slip down her hips, exposing more of her flesh. My black shirt blanketing her body bunches as she slides her other hand under the fabric. I tug the band of my underwear down and grip my hardened cock again.

"Look at me while you touch yourself," I breathe.

I swear my heart skips a beat when she does as she's told. A flush crawls up her neck, splashing across her cheeks and making her freckles stand out. Her hand moves faster, pants falling down and exposing just a hint of curls, and I quicken my pace at the sight. She's going to be my undoing, and I don't even care.

Suddenly she stops and I follow suit, groaning at the need building within me. She pulls her hand from her pussy, fingers glistening, and I shudder. Pushing upright, I lean against the headboard, waiting for her next move. Panting, her eyes meet mine, and I run my tongue along my bottom lip.

"Come here," I command, bracing my hands on the bed to keep from touching myself.

She stumbles forward, tripping over the hem of her pants. When she reaches me, I latch onto her wrist, bringing her fingers to my mouth. She shudders as I suck them clean, the taste of her exploding across my tongue. I moan as my eyes fall closed. Her hand wraps around my cock, forcing a grunt from me. She strokes me once, twice, and my resolve breaks.

Lurching forward, I hook my thumbs in her waistband and shove them down before gripping her hips and hauling her on top of me. A squeal falls from her, morphing into a moan as my cock rubs against her clit. Her nails digging into my shoulders are the only thing centering me enough to not thrust inside her and explode.

Sliding my hand into her hair, I grip the strands, yanking her head back to expose the column of her throat. I pull her closer, licking at her skin before sinking my teeth into her flesh as she quivers. A low moan leaves her as she grinds on my cock, coating it with her wetness.

Nibbling on her lobe, I whisper in her ear, "Be a good girl and ride me, Em."

Her body curls, nails scraping down my chest, leaving red streaks in their wake. I lift her up, then sink into her warmth, tipping my head back as I groan. When I'm fully seated within her, we stop, panting as she spasms around my cock. I've been dreaming of this moment for years, imagining how her pussy would feel around me. My fantasies didn't even come close to reality.

She tips her head up, bright green eyes meeting mine, and a frenzied edge comes over us. Slamming my mouth to hers, I sweep my tongue inside as she rocks back and forth. She's driving me mad with her slow, sensual moves. I rip my mouth from her and my head smacks against the headboard. As much as I love having her in my shirt, it covers too much.

"Take this off," I growl, twisting my fingers into the fabric.

She whips it over her head and I groan, leaning forward to capture her nipple in my mouth. Fingers dig into my hair, urging me to the other one. Flicking it with my tongue, I scrape my thumbnail over the one I abandoned, and her pussy clenches around me.

Nipping at her nipple one last time, I grip her hips, plunging into her hard and fast as her head falls back, red hair cascading across her flushed skin. I want to live in this moment with her riding me, her body on full display and pleasure coursing through her. Giving up control, she falls onto her hands, arching as I thrust into her.

She whimpers, my name falling from her lips as her pussy spasms, and she sails over the edge. I slow, easing her through her orgasm. When she sighs, I slide my arm around her back and tug her to me. Pressing our damp bodies together, I kiss her long and slow as she purrs.

I grasp her hips and pull her off my cock, my eyes rolling to the back of my head as I do. She gasps, body trembling as she flops onto her stomach. Digging my fingers into her waist, I yank her ass in the air, and she yelps. This exact image was one I imagined many times over and I almost don't believe it's real. I skim my hand along her spine before tangling my fingers into her hair and tugging her head back.

Slipping the tip of my cock into her pussy, I lean over her. "I'm not done with you yet."

"Because you didn't come? Is that what this is?" she sneers, even as she pushes back, trying to take me deeper.

"Because you deserve everything."

Rearing upright, I plunge into her, gripping her sides. Her fingers curl into the sheets as she cries out, her voice muffled with her face buried in the mattress. I'm close, but I won't let go until she's come once more for me. I wrap my hand around her waist, tugging her up so her back is fused to my chest. My hand goes to her throat, squeezing gently and she shudders, body trying to curl into itself. My arms are the only thing keeping her from collapsing.

Thrusting into her, I bite the soft skin on her neck and she hisses, tilting her head. I lap at the mark I've made, soothing the flesh.

"Play with your clit," I grunt as her hand flies to her pussy.

Demanding pleas fall from her lips as her fingers rub the small bud and she thrashes in my grasp. I roll her nipple between my fingers, drinking in the noises coming from her.

Her pussy clamps around me as she comes again and her fingers slow. She goes pliant in my arms, and I pull out of her before flipping her on her back. Gripping my cock, I pump it in my fist three times, and I sail over the edge into oblivion. A deep satisfaction rolls over me at the sight of her body painted in my cum.

She glances down, wrinkling her nose. "What the fuck."

Fourteen

Ember

"I can't believe you blew your load all over my stomach," I grumble for the fifth time.

It's been hours since he did it, but I'm still miffed. I had to take at least three showers before I felt clean. He smirks, glancing out the car window at the traffic we're stuck in.

For some reason, he had the brilliant plan to come down to club row. The dress he bought me rides up my thighs as I squirm, remembering our morning activities. I grab the hem, pulling it down for the third time. I shouldn't even be with him still, yet here I am letting him dictate my day. And my night apparently.

His finger taps out a vaguely familiar rhythm on his leg. "I can't believe you said 'cave of wonders' as if it was completely normal."

"Well, I certainly showed you a whole new world."

He snorts, rubbing his hands along his pants. The trunk is filled with bags from our shopping excursion and a brand-new laptop rests between us. I told him not to buy me all this shit, but he wouldn't take no for an answer, and I was too tired to argue. I'll pay him back, but I'll have to dip into my offshore account. At least I had the foresight to move money years ago from an account my parents controlled to one of my own, especially since I'm estranged from them now. They may have been richer than gods, but that doesn't mean they wouldn't cut me off at some point. I've spent the last several years living off that money. If I don't have a breakthrough soon, I'm going to end up in a very bad way.

Glancing at Roman, I wonder how he's been able to keep going. Anders drained at least one of the family accounts shortly after he supposedly died. It's the proof I've been keeping from Roman, the same information I had when I went to him all those years ago. He never gave me a chance to tell him until now.

With the way things have been between us since coming to Synd, I didn't want to reveal anything. I let my petty shit get in the way, withholding all the information because I didn't want him to interfere. Because if he wasn't going to tell me about Anders, then I wouldn't tell him about the money. He could be in the dark as much as I was.

Petty bullshit.

"Where are we going again?" I cross my arms and slide down in the seat, causing my dress to ride up yet again.

Roman's hand lands on my thigh, squeezing, and I shudder. "We're going to check out a lead."

"A lead for what?" I ask, then shake my head.

Peeling his fingers from my flesh, I toss his hand away. Just because we slept together doesn't mean I'll allow him to get all possessive. Our little rendezvous will be a onetime thing. It was a line we never should have crossed in the first place. We've blurred the boundaries, a haze settling upon our relationship. Our *nonexistent* relationship. All we really have is a past filled with longing and pain and friction, which is enough to have me falling on his dick, but not much else.

An ache blooms in my chest and I press my fist to it, willing it away. Random bouts of anguish I can't explain have plagued me since I came to Synd. I chalked it up to the aftermath of the incidents in Harris or my waning hope at finding Aelia, even with the proof that Anders is alive. Now, I'm wondering if it always centered on the man sitting next to me, fingers digging into the leather seats.

Roman leans forward, knocking on the glass between us and the driver, and it slowly lowers.

"Let us out here," he says, and the car eases to the curb.

He pushes from the vehicle, the thudding bass filling the space between us as he does. I sigh as he slams the door shut and then find the handle, but it's ripped away from me as he opens it.

Presenting his hand, he stares at me, a smirk gracing his face. I wrinkle my nose before accepting it, the warmth from his skin seeping into my palm.

A young man whistles as I emerge, and Roman scowls at him before tucking my hand in the crook of his arm. I smack him against the chest, huffing. No reason to bring more attention to ourselves than necessary.

"You going to tell me why we're here?" I mutter, but I doubt he can hear me over the people mingling in line and the music flooding from the open doors of the nightclub.

He nods to the bouncer, and I shoot the man a bright smile, causing him to blush. The crowd parts as we make our way to the bar, and I glance up at the balcony area overlooking the crowded dance floor. I didn't realize people would recognize him, but they're scrambling out of our way as others point and talk behind their hands.

I want to ask him what the hell is going on, but I'll have to wait. The bar is even more crowded than the dance floor. A spot magically appears, and I roll my eyes as Roman tips his chin at the bartender. She saunters over, a sultry smile on her face. She braces her elbows on the bar and I look away. I doubt I'll be drinking regardless of what he orders. I use the time to peruse the faces in the flashing lights.

"What can I get you?" she asks, her voice piercing through the others.

"Ember, pay attention," Roman growls in my ear, sending a shiver through my body.

Spinning back, I find her blue eyes fixed on me, and she bites her lip. Releasing the flesh slowly, she licks her lips. "I asked what you needed, sweetie."

Blinking rapidly, I glance at Roman, who isn't even paying attention. "Um, rum and Coke, please."

"Coming right up." She winks at me before spinning away.

Roman ducks his head, murmuring, "Promise me you won't try to run off with the bartender." He presses a kiss behind my ear and then nips at the lobe.

"What the hell is happening right now?"

He tips his head back, laughing. "I believe you're being hit on. I'm merely staking my claim."

He tugs me closer, sliding his arm around my waist and digging his fingers into my hip. A flash of heat runs through me that has nothing to do with the press of bodies around us. Laying my hands on his chest, I give into the feelings swirling through me. I'll probably regret surrendering, but I can't help myself. Being in his arms makes me feel something I haven't in a long time, if ever. Whether it's safety or peace or something else, I don't know. I refuse to examine it too closely. I'm afraid as soon as I do, it'll evaporate in a puff of smoke.

The bartender sets our drinks on the bar, smirking as she bounces to the next person. Roman's arm drops from my hip, and he hands me the glass, seizing my fingers to tug me toward the stairs.

The bouncer doesn't even bat an eye as we pass him, and I wonder again about the type of pull Roman has in such a short amount of time. Once we're settled on a private couch, I turn to him.

"Why are we here?" I set my glass on the low table in front of us.

He glances around before leaning back and widening his stance, taking up most of the space. Gritting my teeth, I scoot closer to the armrest, but his hand snakes around my waist and tugs me to his body. His fingers dig into my thigh as he slides my leg over his, and I yelp. We're in a curtained-off section, yet still exposed to the people on the dance floor below us. It's dark, but I don't know if it's enough to hide my thong.

"What the hell are you doing?" I demand, squirming in his grasp.

"I could tell you I'm playing a part," he says as he runs his nose along my jaw. "Or perhaps that I can't stop thinking about how sexy you look when you come. Maybe I just want to feel that wet little cunt greedily clinging to my cock again."

My pussy clenches at his words, heat flooding my body, and my cheeks burn. A strangled noise leaves me as he pulls his arm from my back. As he trails his fingers from my knee up to my inner thigh, I melt under the caresses. If I don't stop this, I'll be a puddle on this couch before long. When his head dips and he sinks his teeth into my neck, though, my mind blanks, giving in to the sensations.

He toys with the elastic on my thong, featherlight touches along the lace. I suck in a deep breath, easing my legs further apart. His low chuckle skates over my skin and goosebumps scatter across my body. His finger dips under my underwear, stroking my pussy, and I shudder.

"Look at you, so wet for me already."

"You going to do something about it, or are you just toying with me?" I squirm against his hand.

He runs his lips along my jaw as he sinks his finger into me, and I clench around him. It's not enough, and a whimper escapes. His thumb finds my clit, rolling it over the sensitive nub. I moan as my eyes fall closed, my hips moving in time with his stroking.

He shushes me, adding another finger. "You wouldn't want someone to die, would you?"

I gasp, eyes flying open. "What the hell does that mean?"

His free hand cups my face, turning my head until I'm staring into his blue eyes ablaze with lust.

"No one is allowed to hear those delicious sounds but me. No one is allowed to see you come but me. They both belong to me."

He claims my mouth before I can respond, as if he knows I'd object. I wouldn't though. Not with the tidal wave of pleasure he's flooding me with. He licks along my lips, tongue sweeping in to duel with mine as his fingers thrust into my pussy. It's still not enough. Nothing but sinking onto his cock will fill me like I need.

Jerking back, I pant, trying to catch my breath. His fingers slow before pulling out completely and I whimper again.

"I can't fuck you properly on this couch. Not with someone right on the other side of that curtain," he growls, pushing my leg off his and standing.

He grabs my hand, tugging me behind him into a dark hallway, away from the prying eyes of those dancing below. A black door looms ahead, and he pulls me inside. This isn't the shitty bathrooms I've seen at so many other nightclubs. It's VIP, complete with a sitting area tucked off to one side. He drags me to the counter with a mirror behind it.

"Are you going to lock the door?" I breathe.

He smirks, pointing to my dress. "Take them off."

"Uhhh, I'm not getting naked in a nightclub bathroom, especially when you haven't locked the door."

He rolls his eyes, crowding me back into the counter. He brushes his lips over mine. "Your panties, Em. Take them off."

Stepping back, he crosses his arms, narrowing his eyes when I hesitate. My underwear is already soaked, so I might as well remove them. Hitching up my dress, I hook my thumbs into the waistband and tug them down. It isn't easy to get them off over my heels, but I manage, and he snatches them from my fingers.

"Hey," I cry as he shoves them in his pocket. "Those are brand new."

One corner of his lips tips up. "I'm aware. I'm the one who purchased them, remember?"

Running his palms along my legs, he pushes my dress up farther, latching onto my waist, and picking me up.

"No, fuck. Absolutely not," I hiss as he goes to set me on the counter.

He jerks me to his chest, holding me close to him. Alarm flashes across his face as I scramble to keep my ass away from the tile.

"What the hell is wrong with you?"

"I'm not putting my bare ass on a counter when fuck knows what else has been on there. Absolutely not."

He laughs, ducking his head into my neck as his shoulders shake. Setting my feet on the floor, I tug from his grasp. Spinning, he grabs a towel from a basket on the counter facing us and our eyes meet in the mirror. He grins and it hits me,

I'll be staring at myself while he fucks me. My stomach tightens and I press my thighs together. He spins, flourishing the towel, and leans around me to spread the fabric over the cold tiles.

"Now can I get back to fucking you?" He grips my waist and picks me up.

My retort is lost when he covers my mouth with his. Stepping between my legs, he presses his hard cock against my bare pussy, and I wrap my legs around his waist. Kissing his way down the deep vee of my dress, he pushes the fabric to the side, exposing my breast. His lips wrap around my nipple. I fall back on my hands, tipping my head back, and I hit the mirror. I barely feel it through the sensations rolling through me.

Releasing the nub with a pop, he peers up at me. "Take my cock out. Now."

I scramble to obey him, undoing his belt and button before shoving his pants and underwear down his hips until his cock springs free. Now would be a great time to protest him bossing me around, but my desire overrides every argument as soon as it pops into my head. I lick my lips, just imagining sinking to my knees and making him come undone for me.

I reach for his cock, but he bats my hand away. When I glare at him, he tips my chin up with his finger while he lines himself up, slipping the tip into my pussy.

"We don't have time for that, but I'll let you suck my cock soon. I'll even let you swallow every fucking drop of me," he murmurs.

My reply is lost in a moan as he thrusts into me, his own groan mingling with the sound. Falling back on my hands, I give myself over to the sensations building within me. With every thrust, my ass slides a little further back. He grips my hips, digging his fingers in to keep me right where he wants me. His gaze is fixed on where we're connected as he pounds into me.

"Play with your clit, Em. I need you to come before someone walks in," he grunts, never slowing.

If he keeps up this pace, I won't even need the extra stimulation, but I slide my hand between my legs.

"If you would have locked the door," I gasp, rubbing my clit as bolts of lightning flash through my body.

Tipping my head back, I wrap my legs around his waist and lock my ankles. A whimper echoes through the space, and he grunts as I clench around him.

"Come for me. Now."

His words send me spiraling into ecstasy. He groans as I spasm around his cock. One last surge and he buries himself deep within my pussy, leaning over my body as he shudders. His usually slicked back hair falls over his forehead, brushing my bare chest and I shiver. I wish I could live in this bubble, both of us content without the biting words or destructive past looming between us.

A thud outside the door has him jerking upright, sliding from me without a word. Tossing a towel at me, he grabs his own, cleaning himself off before tucking his still hard cock away. I wipe away the evidence of what we did and then scoot to the edge of the counter.

Roman throws the towels into a bin tucked under the counter and then wraps an arm around my waist. I expect him to let go when my feet are on solid ground, but he buries his head into my neck.

"Next time, I'll be the one cleaning you up. And I'll do it with my mouth."

Fifteen

I'm two seconds away from ripping someone's hand from their body as I watch the older man reach for Ember, clearly flirting with her. She's sidestepped his wandering grasp about five times so far, but she's still engaging with him. I have no idea if she's purposefully trying to piss me off or getting the information we need. It's the only reason I haven't stopped it yet.

Ember throws her head back, her light laugh floating over the music and conversations swirling through the nightclub. I scowl, glancing away to scan the crowd as I lift my drink to my lips, but it's empty. Gritting my teeth, I slam it down on the table, and the glass top rattles. From the corner of my eye, I spot Ember turning to me and I push from the couch.

Not even an hour ago I had her body on display for me, begging me to fuck her on this very piece of furniture and now she's talking up some random man. I'm not jealous. I'm pissed. We have more important things to deal with than her next conquest. Thankfully, the curtains are pushed back now, giving me a clear view of her, or I just might lose it completely.

The VIP bar tucked in the back of the space is empty save for the bartender. I'm surprised the main level is so busy on a Wednesday, but this exclusive area is deserted other than a group at the other end of the balcony. They're grating on my nerves as they take shot after shot, progressively becoming louder as the night goes on.

"Whiskey on the rocks," I say, and the bartender nods.

I can't help but turn to watch Ember as I lean against the bar. She's still chatting away, ducking her head, a smile playing on her lips as the man waves his hands around. The ache in my chest is back, never fully giving me peace.

As pissed as I am, I'm still fucking hard, staring at her in the short black dress I bought her. She didn't want to model it for me at the shop, but I insisted she change into it before we left the boutique. I almost took her back into the dressing room and fucked her right there.

"Trouble in paradise?" a lilting voice says next to me.

Glancing over, a woman with a tight dress and a whole lot of cleavage leans on the bar. She smiles at the bartender, setting her wineglass on the counter. Her blonde hair slips over her shoulder as her eyes meet mine. I try not to glare. I'm sure she's exceptionally wonderful or some such nonsense, but I don't have time for her. Nor do I want to make time.

"Was there something you needed?" I ask, glancing back at Ember.

"Oh, no. I was just making small talk," she murmurs.

A man yells something from the other side of the space, anger lacing his tone, and she jumps, leaning away from me, although we're not even touching. He's glaring at her, arms crossed over his crisp white button-down. I wonder if his face is flushed from the amount of alcohol he's consumed or the fact that his woman is speaking to me.

"Are you in danger?" I ask, reaching for the glass the bartender finally sets down.

"What? Oh, no. Andrew just—" She swallows, hand fluttering in front of her. "Had a bit to drink. It's fine."

I meet the bartender's eye, and he nods. I pull my phone from my pocket to send a text to TJ. Walking away, I scowl again as I find another man has joined Ember next to the railing. They box her in, pressing her against the glass. She's still smiling, but there's a tightness in her face that wasn't there before.

Neither of the men notice as I approach. Ember's green eyes flash to mine, widening the slightest bit. I contemplate detouring to the couch again, letting her handle them herself, but my feet carry me to her. They always take me straight back to her. Which is not what I need, especially now. Her hold over me only increases the more time we spend together. I should cut ties, vow to stay away from her, and for fuck's sake, stop salivating over her body.

"Time to go," I say, gaze fixed on her.

She steps toward me as the man on the right swings toward me, his lip curling. He slides between us before I can reach for her.

"I believe the lady would like to stay here with us. Why don't you go back to ignoring her as you have been all night?" Lip Curl says, turning his body to further block her.

"Oh Richard, I think the word you're looking for is 'ogling,' not 'ignoring.' And Brent, I don't know what you thought, but I was nowhere near following you and your father to the bathroom for a quick fuck," she says, her voice laced with mirth.

"I suggest you listen to her before she makes a scene," I say, straightening my cuffs.

Brent scoffs, running his hand through his already thinning, light brown hair. He peers at his father, as if the older man will make me walk away with a few words.

Richard snorts. "There are two of us and one of you. I don't think the scene will go the way you think it will, buddy."

Ducking my head, I smirk before lifting my gaze over his shoulder at Ember. "I think you misunderstand. I won't be the one making a scene."

Brent stiffens, eyes going wide. Based on the smile Ember has, she's pressed a knife to some part of his body, letting him feel the prick of her blade. Richard's confusion morphs into panic, and he takes off for the stairs, leaving his son behind.

Ember leans closer to Brent's ear, whispering something I don't catch. Whatever it was sends him scurrying after Richard, who's already lost in the sea of people dancing below. Ember slips the small knife back into her cleavage and then bounces forward, landing in my arms.

All the promises I made to myself about staying away from her dissolve as her laughing eyes meet mine. My arms wrap around her of their own accord, holding her tight against my body. My heartbeat settles and my muscles ease. I didn't even realize how worked up I was when she was tucked behind them. The feelings rolling through me are foreign, and I tense again.

My lips brush her ear, and she shivers as I say, "I hope that whole spectacle was worth it, and you actually have information to share."

She stiffens, nails digging into my chest. "Did you learn anything from the woman you were flirting with at the bar?"

Ember leans back, but I keep my arms tight around her. She raises an eyebrow, lips pursed and the overwhelming need to kiss her floods me. Mentally, I shake the feeling away, smirking instead.

"Of course. She's coming home with us."

Her nostrils flare, a flush blooming on her pale cheeks and her knee pops up, attempting to hit me in the balls. I block her, digging my fingers into her side.

"That wasn't very nice," I murmur. "Your jealousy is showing, my dear."

A choking noise falls from her lips. Sliding my hand up her body, I grip her neck, bringing her closer to me. I scrape my teeth across her skin, teasing her flesh with my tongue. She doesn't protest, whatever vitriol she was about to spill lost to the pleasures I'm visiting upon her body. Convincing myself I'm doing this to fuck with her is harder than I thought it would be.

I step back suddenly, releasing my hold on her, and she stumbles, blinking away the desire in her eyes.

"Asshole," she snaps, smoothing her dress down in an attempt to pull herself together.

I grab her hand, pulling her toward the stairs. The man I was supposed to meet here tonight didn't show. There's no reason to continue loitering around a nightclub, especially when all I want to do is take her back to the bathroom and fuck the frustration out of us both.

As we pass the group, the man, Andrew I believe, bellows at me over the noise. I don't bother to turn, advancing on the woman from the bar.

Tugging Ember to my side, I mutter from the side of my mouth, "Do not bitch about this."

Stalking toward the woman, I snag her upper arm and pull her along with us. She doesn't resist, so the bartender must have done his job. The woman stumbles on the stairs, and I steady her. Ember glances back as Andrew rushes after us. When we reach the bottom, I drop my hands, and Ember latches onto the woman's arm, tugging her away from me as I pivot next to the bouncer.

"This man is to be removed from the club and banned from all establishments along club row. See that it's done."

The bouncer, Spencer, nods, blocking the stairs, and Andrew barrels into him. His words are lost in the surrounding noise. Andrew attempts to leap over Spencer, pointing his finger at me as if I'll be intimidated. I could put him on the ground, beat him so badly he would think twice the next time he put his hands on a woman. Especially with how much he's had to drink, I could pulverize him within minutes.

Stepping closer, I reach over Spencer's shoulder, grab Andrew's throat, and squeeze until a strangled cry leaves him. The bouncer slides from between us and I pull Andrew closer as he struggles to pry my fingers away from his neck. His already flushed face reddens and satisfaction flows through me at the fear in his eyes.

"Continue to beat women and I will find you. I will rip your throat out with my bare hands and feed it to the ducks. I hear they're quite hungry this time of year," I growl. "Blink if you understand."

He blinks rapidly as a blood vessel pops in one eye, red overtaking the white. I toss him back, striding away without a backward glance. The crowd parts as I prowl through the club, intent on the rear exit. When I reach the hallway, I find the woman, tears streaming down her face as Ember rubs her back, whispering something in her ear. Our eyes meet, approval shining in hers.

"Let's go before he gets the bright idea to try to retaliate." I usher them to the back door.

Two cars wait for us. I open the door to the first one, and Ember guides her inside. The woman stutters back when she spots TJ, almost falling into Ember's arms.

"Ma'am, this is TJ. He works for me. He'll get you to a safe place. Andrew will no longer be allowed within Synd. If he attempts to return, we'll take care of him. Please let TJ know if there's anything else you require," I say.

Ember rolls her eyes, crouching down to address the woman. How she's able to stay on her feet in those heels is beyond me, but she has been attending society events for most of her life. I'm sure she's had plenty of practice.

"Paisley, I promise they're not going to hurt you. You'll be safer away from him."

Paisley stares at Ember until finally she nods, scooting closer to TJ. I help Ember to her feet before closing the door. Their taillights flash and then they're gone, on their way to a safe house on the Kings' side of the river. This feels like the most productive thing I've done since the mafia leaders left.

"How'd you know?" Ember whispers, eyes still fixed on where the car disappeared.

"She had bruises on her arms and throat, along with a burn mark on her wrist. That, coupled with the way she reacted when he yelled, told me all I needed to know. However, the bartender also slipped me a note when I picked up my drink."

I pull the napkin from my pocket, a message scrawled across it—*get her out*. It's why he took so long to make my drink. There aren't many opportunities I have to save someone, but it's always bittersweet. I'm capable now, when before I wasn't. I was too young, too naïve, too weak to save my sister.

Stepping away from Ember, I stalk back to the car, wondering what the hell I'm doing with her. I've held onto my rage toward her for so long, I thought I'd never be rid of it. And at the first chance, I fucked her, letting her through the defenses I never thought she could breach. I need to get my head on straight when it comes to Ember Hayes. I can't claim to hate her one minute and then sink my cock into her the next.

Shaking my head, I vow to stay away from her, or at minimum, her body. It's the least I owe to Aelia. I'll keep Ember safe, since that's what my sister would want if she were here. Doesn't mean I have to treat her as anything other than the enemy she is.

Sixteen

Ember

"What the hell is your problem?" I bellow as Roman stalks up the stairs.

He hasn't said three words to me since we left the club. I don't want to chase after him, but this house is huge and I'm pretty sure I'd get lost if I lose sight of him. Mason Byrns will find my body years from now and wonder who the hell snuck into his house and died.

When Roman doesn't slow, much less answer me, I tromp after him. I can't exactly stomp my feet in these heels, but I want to. He's being a dick again, probably pretending we didn't cross that invisible line. I'm just grateful he didn't leave my ass at the club at this point. I'd leave, but I actually have information for him, not that he deserves it.

"Hey, asshole. Want to give me two fucking seconds of your time so I can take this damn dress off?" I shout when I reach the top. He's already halfway down the hallway, like he ran as soon as he was out of my sight line.

"If you wanted me to bed you, Ember, all you had to do was ask," Roman says, his voice barely carrying back to me, and I scowl.

Someone clears their throat to my right, and I flush when my eyes meet TJ's brown ones. He glances at Roman's still retreating back before swinging to me again. He's fighting a grin and my stomach rolls. I shouldn't care what these people think. Convincing my mind of that, though, isn't as easy as it should be.

"Sorry, Ms. Hayes, but there was a package left. We believe it's for you," TJ says.

"Um, that can't be right. No one knows I'm here and even if someone did, they wouldn't be sending me packages. Kind of a loner here. You should tell Drake about it. I'm sure he'll throw a conniption fit if you tell me something and not him." I huff as I crane my neck around TJ only to see Roman disappear around the corner.

"It's addressed to 'the lady of the manor,' and while that could be Lacey, Mason's woman, I doubt it. We put it in the conference room." He gestures back the way he came.

Glancing once more at the end of the hall, I sigh. "Lead the way."

TJ's footsteps are silent on the hardwood floor, but my heels click with every fall of my feet. Could I be silent? Of course. Am I secretly hoping that Roman will come looking for me, using the clack of my shoes as a guide? Also, yes. He won't though. The further we travel into the twisting landscape of wainscoting and wallpaper, the more the silence swamps my senses. Even if he was jealous over my actions with Dick and his equally misogynistic son Brent, he never gave me a chance to explain. Besides, he's a smart guy. He should have figured it out.

Unless he's had enough. A few romps and he's had his fill. I bury the hurt deep underneath the rage. I should have shucked off his advances, since I knew this would happen. Roman Drake has never been and probably never will be long-term material. Even without our past getting in the way, he's a playboy at heart.

Actually, he's not even a playboy. That requires some pizazz and charm. Roman merely looks at a woman and her panties catch on fire. That's the charisma I was drawn to when I was younger—exactly like every other girl in our school. He didn't even have to try, and they'd chase after him, salivating. I'm sure his sharp cheekbones and intense eyes helped, but it was just an aura he exuded, and he hasn't lost that all these years later. In my case at least, it has intensified.

I knew all this and yet I practically dashed for his dick like it was the last piece of cheesecake at the party. Sure, it was delicious, and I'd totally have another slice, but now my stomach hurts from stuffing...my face.

"Who the fuck does he think he is?" I mutter under my breath. TJ glances over his shoulder, giving me a questioning look, and I wave him onward.

I can't tell if I'm more pissed at Roman or myself, so I'll just have to settle for him being the villain of my story. I'll ignore the fact that he gave me no promises or declarations of love and devotion. Actually, I won't even think of him at all. I'll tell him what I found out and then I'll bounce.

My plans don't involve Roman unless he's going to reveal to me where his father slithered off to. Since he won't tell me, I'll just go back to figuring shit out on my own. I've done it long enough, even if having him by my side would make things infinitely easier. It's not worth it. If I say it enough, maybe I'll believe it.

TJ pushes open the door and I shake my head as I cross the threshold, vowing to leave my erratic thoughts in the hallway. Whoever sent this package probably isn't wanting to give me a gift. I don't have many enemies, if any, but I certainly didn't leave Harris on the best terms. They wouldn't be able to find me, though. I've covered my tracks enough, wiped enough of my identity, that no one should be able to locate my whereabouts. It eats at me that Roman freely threw my last name around here. Ember may not be a popular name, forcing me to stand out, but giving someone my full name isn't something I've done in years.

"Why did you bring the package up here?" I ask.

I eye the nondescript brown box. There's no label, just "lady of the manor" scrawled across the top, just like TJ said. It's not even that big, barely the size of a hatbox. I snort, realizing how bougie that statement sounds even in my own head. TJ leans against the table, crossing his arms.

"Moss didn't want it in the guard shack."

"You mean Moss didn't want *me* in the guard shack." I mimic his stance, rolling my eyes. "So, you brought it here, but did you check it?"

"What do you mean? We don't have an x-ray machine to send it through," he says, chuckling.

"Uh, because it could be a severed head? Or a bomb?"

I back away from the box, hoping it doesn't blow with us in here. That'd be just my luck. Roman would be in an even shittier mood then. I snort, shuffling toward the door. If this package really is a bomb and it really does explode, Roman's attitude will be the least of my problems.

TJ unravels his limbs, grunting as he pushes off the table. He's not exactly old, but I'm sure in this business your body breaks down faster than others. Except for Moss and TJ, the others are young guys, a couple women, but none of them are much older than me.

"Maybe you shouldn't," I say, hesitantly as he rounds the table.

He reaches for the box, flipping a knife out. "Would you rather me not tell you if it's a severed head? Are fingers okay?"

I reach toward him, panic lacing my words. "TJ, no!"

His smiling face is the last thing I see before the room fills with a deafening crack. A small fireball quickly engulfs the box and white smoke infiltrates the room. I drop to a crouch, covering my head as the explosion rolls over me. Screaming fills the room, and I clamp my lips together to stop it. Tears stream down my face, but whether from the smoke or fear, I don't know. Now isn't the time to figure it out.

My stomach cramps and I tip forward onto my hands, gagging, but nothing comes up. Flames lick at the edge of my blurry vision, and I realize the curtains are on fire.

I crawl toward TJ's prone body lying between the table and the fire threatening to consume him. A choked sob leaves me when I reach him. His face is a mess of blood and soot, barely recognizable as the smiling man from just a minute before.

I can't carry him, but I'm not about to leave him here to die, if he's not already dead. Sliding my hands under his shoulders, I grip him tightly before pulling him back. I drop his limp form, coughing into my arm as the smoke chokes me. Another sob leaves me as I grab him again, trying to yank him toward the exit.

If someone doesn't come soon, the house will go up in flames. The fire is faster than I am as I drag him toward freedom. I'm only halfway when the door behind me bangs open, Roman's roar filling the space. His arm circles my waist, taking me clean off my feet.

"No," I cry, kicking my feet out, but his arm is a vise around me. "Save him."

He dumps me in the hall, charging back into the room before I even find my feet. Guards pour into the hallway when he appears again, carrying an unconscious TJ. One guard bumps into me and I shuffle back, pressing my body into the wall as I cough. Another man charges forward, holding a fire extinguisher, and they race into the burning inferno. Roman stalks past me and I scramble to follow him.

One hallway after another, I chase after them, my lungs screaming at me to slow down. There's a rattling in my chest that isn't normal, but I'm more concerned with TJ. He must still be alive if Roman isn't giving him CPR. Unless he doesn't know how. Roman struggles down the stairs, his pace slowing the further he's forced to carry TJ's body.

I stumble, falling into the wall. Doubling over, I wheeze, attempting to pull enough air into my lungs. My vision blurs again, black dots flashing in front of me, and I slam my eyes shut before I puke. Footsteps pound up the stairs, but I can't stop coughing.

A large, calloused hand seizes my arm, jerking me back the way I came. My ankle gives out and I yelp as pain shoots up my leg. Opening my eyes, Moss's face swims above me, set in a thunderous scowl. He doesn't give me time to get my feet under me before he's dragging me into a small room that's probably supposed to be an office, but it's devoid of furniture. He throws me against the wall, and I crumple to the floor.

"Start talking," he snarls, producing a gun from his side and pointing it at me.

Swallowing hard, déjà vu floods me, but at least it's not raining this time. I only have my knife on me and Roman's probably halfway to the hospital by now. He's where he needs to be, but he won't be saving me this time. Opening my mouth, my throat closes, and I press my hand to my chest, willing the air inside. It doesn't work.

"The package. It was a bomb. I don't know who it's from," I croak.

"Then why is TJ the one hurt and you don't even have a scratch on you?" He pulls back the hammer, narrowing his eyes.

"Put the gun down, Moss." Roman's voice, as if crafted from shadows, sweeps over me, easing the tension riding me.

"Drake, you don't think clearly around this woman."

"I'm well aware."

Roman steps into view from the wall and my mind short circuits. There's no way he just appeared. This isn't some paranormal show where people can walk through walls.

"Where the hell did you come from?" I squawk before remembering I still have a gun pointed at my head.

Roman pulls in a deep breath, clearly biting the inside of his cheek. It's his "shut the fuck up before you get yourself killed" face. Fortunately, I know it well and press my lips together.

"Moss, I understand the implications of this situation, but we clearly have enemies outside these walls. Let's not make the people within them our adversaries as well. Go do your job and I'll do mine."

Roman's eyes find mine, a promise floating within the striking blue, and I shiver. I shrink a little, pulling my limbs in to make myself smaller. Roman and I have had plenty of run-ins, especially recently, but the look he's giving me right now is nothing like the others. This time, I might not survive his wrath.

Seventeen

Roman

"Moss, you can either get the fuck out or I'll shoot you myself, consequences be damned." I say it calmly, but he jerks back as if I've hit him.

"Remember your place, Drake," he sneers, swinging to face me, but he drops his gun to his side.

I cross my arms, tilting my head as I stare at him impassively. Moss may be an asset to Byrns, but he's been nothing but a thorn in my side since I took over. Every decision I've made he's challenged, whether openly or behind my back. I'm sure he doesn't realize I'm aware of who he's speaking to. I've let it slide, if only because I've been preoccupied with other things. Who knows if the others will even follow me if I deal with Moss in my usual way?

"You've overstepped one too many times, Moss. This is your only warning. You can either put your gun away and walk out of here with the full knowledge that you will be following my orders until Byrns gets back or—"

"Or what?" he sneers.

I grind my teeth together, digging my nails into my arms. "Or I can float your ass."

"Byrns would—"

"Mason isn't here right now. And they put me in charge. You can either get your shit together and help keep this city intact until they return, or you can leave this world with a bullet in your head."

He scoffs, but whatever he was going to say is cut off by a knock at the door. I nod toward it, waiting for him to decide. Explaining to Byrns I shot his head of security and threw his ass in the river isn't something I want to do. It's not like I can call Byrns up, either. We've had minimal contact since they fucked off to Rima. Plus, I don't need him to fight my battles for me. I'm capable of taking care of shit myself, no matter how out of my depth I might feel.

He glares at me for another ten seconds before stomping over to the door and ripping it open. Rigger, a mid-level Byrns guy, stands in the doorway, brown eyes wide as his gaze skips from Moss, Ember, and then to me.

"TJ is in critical condition. He'll go into surgery if they can stabilize him, but it's not looking good."

Moss curses, swinging away to glare at Ember as if this is her fault. I may be conflicted having her around, but she's not the type to kill off people indiscriminately. From what I've seen, she avoids it at all costs. Her fight-or-flight response leans heavily toward flight. I fully expect that at some point she'll take off in the dead of night, and I won't talk to her for another five years. Although, since our relationship has shifted, maybe I'll never see her again.

"You can go, Rigger." Even I can hear the exhaustion in my voice.

Rigger closes the door slowly, grimacing when the hinges squeak. Moss shakes out his limbs, putting his gun away before turning back to me. Tucking my hands in my pockets, I wait for him to speak. He opens his mouth, snapping it shut and scowling. He marches for the exit, but hesitates when he reaches the door, not bothering to face us.

"If he dies, there will be hell to pay. And it won't come from me, Drake. Keep that in mind while you interrogate your little girlfriend."

With his warning floating in the air, he leaves, slamming the door behind him. Sighing, I glance at Ember, still cowering on the floor. Add a little mud and take the edge out of her green eyes and we'd be transported back to the night she came to me, begging for help.

"Come on," I grunt, making my way to the exit. I may not want to have this conversation, but avoiding it will only breed more resentment.

She follows me upstairs, keeping at least five paces between us. It's a strange feeling, knowing she's right behind me when not even two hours ago she was at my side. Putting distance between us is the only way I'll get out of this unscathed. If that means physical as well as emotional, so be it.

"Where are we going?" she whispers as we turn down yet another hallway.

I don't bother to respond. If I open my mouth right now, I'll end up yelling at her, and fuck knows what will come out. My nerves are shot, every sense on high alert, and I swear if I have to deal with one more issue, I'm going to lose it. I could call Hawk, tell him this is bullshit, and I didn't sign up for any of it, but we'd both know I was lying.

This isn't anything new to me, running a territory. Synd is vastly larger than Westmont, though. Add in winning over men who have no loyalty to me and filling half the political positions within the city, and I'm in over my head. Hawk can only help so much, and besides, he's dealing with his own problems. The Reapers may not have been hit as hard as the Kings or Mason, but they're still recovering from when a rival MC blasted through with a vendetta. Hawk made it clear if I can't hack it, then I might as well admit defeat before the rest even leave, letting them divide and conquer. My pride wouldn't let me. Not to mention I'm at fault for some of the destruction.

I push open the door to my temporary office, flipping on the lights as I go.

"Shut the door," I say, then point at a chair opposite me as I settle behind the massive desk.

Shuffling up the papers strewn across the surface, I scowl at the latest report of supplies coming through. Most of the contacts Byrns had before are slowly coming back, but we're still short on stock and some of our vendors in other cities are refusing to answer. With nowhere to funnel the guns and other things coming through, we won't have a steady cash flow. I'd like to have done something other than just survive by the time the others come back. Reestablishing our supply routes and buyers is top of my priority list, along with a shit ton of other things.

I sigh, realizing I'll never be able to deal with all this on my own. There aren't enough hours in the day and I don't have enough pull. Dealing with Ember will go a long way toward dealing with my personal shit so I have more time to dedicate to the real problems.

"What happened?"

"How'd you walk out of the wall?" she murmurs, finally meeting my eyes.

I close my eyes, gritting my teeth. "Focus, Ember. What the fuck happened in the conference room?"

"If I tell you, are you going to tell me what changed between fucking me in the bathroom at a nightclub and when we walked out?"

Slamming my hands on the desk, she flinches. She tries to hide the action with a defiant look, but her knuckles whiten as she grips the arms of the chair.

"This is not a negotiation. I've got a man in the hospital who might fucking die. Another one thinks you're the one who put him there, and the longer you deflect, the more I'm inclined to agree with him." The lie turns to ash in my mouth as her face falls and then shutters.

"When you took off, TJ said I had a package in the conference room. I told him he must be mistaken, but it was addressed to the lady of the manor. He thought it must be me instead of Lacey, whoever that is," she says, her lip curling the slightest bit.

"It's Mason's woman. What next." It's a demand, not a question.

She stares over my shoulder, and I resist the urge to glance behind me. Her eyes flash with pain as she relives the events.

"Moss didn't want it in the guard shack, so TJ brought it up. There was no return address. I told him it could be a severed head or—" She clears her throat, her mask cracking a little before she composes herself. "A bomb. I said it could be a bomb, and he laughed. I tried to stop him, but he opened it."

Her version of events doesn't seem like TJ, which only supports Moss's thinking. I can't believe I'm considering that Ember is behind this. If we didn't have history, though, I'd assume she was at the heart of everything that's happened—the shooting, the house fire, the car bomb, even this.

Swinging toward the computer, I wake it up, pulling up the cameras. Lacey ran me through the basics, though most of the more technical jargon was over my head. I know enough to navigate things, but nowhere near what she's capable of as a hacker.

Hell, five years ago I had to ask Ember for help to uncover who Nemesis was. I shudder, remembering how I had to hype myself up to even reach out to her, rage overshadowing my decisions. I'm surprised she even helped me, considering how I spoke to her.

"Any other questions, or am I free to leave?" she asks, sarcasm tinging her words.

"Don't fucking move," I growl.

I'm sure the footage will be cut off, but hopefully I can salvage something from before the bomb exploded. It couldn't have been particularly large, since the house didn't blow and immediately kill both of them. Clicking on the file, the video starts playing from the last hour and I speed it up until Ember comes into frame, playing out the scenario she just told me. TJ's laughing face appears as he flips his knife out. A bright flash shatters the image before the screen goes black.

Leaning back in my chair, I chew the inside of my cheek. Unless Ember delivered the package to herself or had an accomplice, there's no way she's involved in this. Deep down I knew she wasn't, but with all the other shit going on, I'm letting outside forces skew my thoughts.

"What did those men tell you at the club?"

She crosses her arms, glancing out the window. "They had some business dealings with Anders that fell through when he disappeared. Oh, and apparently someone reached out to them recently to ask about you. They didn't realize it was actually you, but yeah."

"What the hell does that mean?"

She rolls her eyes, finally bringing them back to me. "They knew who you were, but not that you were sitting twenty feet from them. Can I go now?"

"So eager to run? Not that I'm surprised. You may go."

Hurt flashes in her eyes, then she blinks, and it's gone. Pushing from the chair, she dips into a low curtsy, lip curling before stalking from the room. I fully expect her to slam the door behind her, but it clicks shut softly. Cursing, I drop my head in my hands, my elbows thudding onto the desk. I dismissed her as if she was nothing more than an underling. Keeping my distance is one thing, but disregarding her completely sends a bolt of pain through me.

Shoving to my feet, I stalk after her, intent on finishing the many conversations we've danced around for the last week. Fuck, we've never had an honest one since I threw her out of my house all those years ago. Once we finally set the record straight, I'll be able to wash my hands of her, and the guilt that's been riding me for ten years will finally dissolve. I'll be able to let her go without it breaking me.

Eighteen

Ember

Whoever brought up the shopping bags just dumped them on Roman's bed. I'd assume it was Moss, but I'm pretty sure he's waiting outside the door, ready to shoot me. I doubt he'd be hauling around boxes and bags full of clothes and toiletries.

Sighing, I glance around the room. I don't know what I'm looking for. There's no way I'll be able to carry all of this. I didn't want to get this much stuff anyway, but Roman insisted.

"Bunch of bullshit," I whisper, upending the contents onto the bed.

I'll go through it all and pick the pieces I need and then bag the rest of it up. He can deal with the hassle of returning them. Grabbing one of the empty paper bags, I throw the underwear and bras, along with a few shirts and pants inside, leaving all the dresses and pretty shoes. It pains me to abandon them, but I don't have much use for that type of shit anymore.

I left behind most of the extravagant parties and galas when I abandoned that life at eighteen. Actually, my parents stopped forcing me to go when I was much younger, but I kept attending for Aelia. I wasn't about to leave her to the wolves. Usually, we'd find a quiet corner and make fun of the stuffy old people who spent their time trying to subtly one-up each other. All they ever talked about was how much money they had, attempting to make everyone jealous of what they own.

Aelia was much kinder than I was. She spent a lot of the time reminding me we were in the same boat, growing up with a shit ton of money. I always justified it by saying we were nothing like them. Looking back, I was a fucking snob.

I wish she could see me now, how much I've grown since then. Although, thinking back on the last ten years, I don't have much to show her. She'd probably tell me I've been a dumbass, wasting my time.

I bite down on my tongue, holding in the tears. I've been promising myself I wouldn't shed a tear for her until I find her. Until I came here and reconnected with Roman, I hadn't cried in years. One encounter with him was all it took to break down the walls I had built around my heart. I don't know what that says about me.

Sighing, I grab the box containing a brand-new laptop and start for the door. There's no reason to stay, especially when my presence is getting people hurt. Finding who sent that package isn't something I want to do. Hopefully once I leave, they'll disappear into the ether, dissolving into the shadows to bother the residents here no more.

As soon as I set my hand on the knob, it turns and I stutter back, almost tripping over a shoebox I didn't see before. I'm impressed I keep my feet in these heels. The laptop slips, and I scramble to grab it before it hits the floor.

"What the fuck, Ember," Roman growls, reaching for me.

"Get away from me," I snarl, gripping the computer and finally finding solid ground.

"We need to talk."

He glances behind him before shutting the door. As he leans against it, I realize he won't let me leave until he gets to yell at me some more. While I'd rather not have this conversation, it's been a long time coming. I don't have to participate, though. He can just talk himself into silence and then I'll run, because that's what I do best.

"Going somewhere?" he asks, crossing his arms as he scans the items in my arms.

"Not yet. Might as well get this over with," I say, tipping my chin at him.

When he glances at the mess I've left behind, he scowls. Pulling in a calming breath, I set the things in my arms down and march over to the bed. As I shove clothes back in the bags, I realize my hands are trembling and I speed up. The sooner I get this done, the sooner I can escape his judgment.

"Would you knock it the fuck off?" he snarls, marching over and ripping the bag out of my hands.

Stepping back, I run my hands down my dress, smoothing down the fabric. My damp palms tingle and I repeat the move. I wish I had pockets, but this dress is so fucking tight I doubt I'd be able to even add some. I snort softly when I remember I also don't know how to sew.

"What are you even doing?"

"Clearly, I was dealing with the mess. I hope you saved the receipts," I mutter, glancing away from his prying eyes.

"I bought this so you would actually use it. Not paw through it and pick whatever you could carry before you ran."

He throws the bag on the bed with the rest, then runs his hand through his hair. Whatever is going through his head, it doesn't seem like it's going to be good for me. Which is precisely why I wanted to be long gone before he came back.

I would have left it all behind, but I really do need something other than this slinky dress to wear. The computer is my lifeline at this point. With all the shops closed, I need something to get me through the night, at the very least.

I cross my arms, popping my hip out. "I wasn't running. You told me to go. Don't get all pissy because you can't control when I leave."

"This shit is hard enough without having to deal with your temper tantrum," he grumbles, pacing between the end of the bed and the closet door.

"This is the furthest thing from a temper tantrum, Drake. And if I make your life *so* hard, then why stop me from leaving?" I hold up my hand when he opens his mouth. "I don't need an answer. I know *exactly* why you want to keep me around."

His face darkens, eyes narrowing, and I fear I've gone too far. Thinking back on my words, I realize the implications of what I said.

"I didn't lock you in the house, Ember. I'm not about to justify myself to you. Fucking you wasn't something I planned, but if you're so eager to point to that as the reason you're here, so be it." He spins away and rips open the door before slamming it in his wake.

"What the fuck," I whisper, smoothing my hair back from my face.

The red strands flop right back, tickling my cheek, and I shiver. Whatever just happened, it certainly wasn't a conversation. Half of the things I said, I didn't understand myself. Every time Roman turns those icy blue eyes on me, I lose my head. And then he storms, leaving me with whatever bullshit is left over, and wondering what the hell just happened.

"I can't keep doing this," I sigh.

A lone pair of leggings languishes on the floor, half-shoved under the bed. Dropping on the comforter, I slip off my heels and toss them into the mess. I snatch up the pants and shimmy them up. Thankfully, the zipper for the dress is on the side, or I'd never be able to reach it. It's not until the fabric is bunched at my waist that I realize I'll never get the thing over my hips, and I start pulling it up. I'm wriggling, arms straight over my head, when the click of the door echoes through the room.

"I fucking swear if you say a goddamn word I will stab you in the kidney," I snap through the fabric over my face.

"Oh, for fuck's sake," Roman mutters.

He yanks on the dress, but the zipper catches in my hair and I let out a yowl.

"Stop! Fucking shit. Stop." I try to pull away from him.

"If you'd stop fucking moving, I could get it off," he snarls.

"It's stuck in my hair." A sob makes my voice break.

He breathes out a curse and the tugging stops. I duck my head so I can breathe, and a tear drips off my nose. Roman's hands slide along my head until he reaches where it's tangled. A knock on the door has us both freezing.

"What do you want?" he calls.

Then he shoves me, I'm assuming behind his body. I trip over my shoes and tumble onto the bed, crumpling paper bags beneath me as I squeal.

"Uh, am I interrupting something?" Hawk's laughing voice seeps through the fabric and my cheeks burn.

"Why don't I help her and you two can go talk," Willow says, and I groan.

I wiggle, the bags crinkling under me, and then a shoe box pokes me in the jaw. Whimpering, I realize I'm doing more harm than good at this point.

"I can handle this. What the hell do you two want anyway?" Roman growls, his hands wrapping around my waist and setting me upright.

"Can we not have an entire fucking conversation while my dress is halfway over my head?" I snap.

I swing my arms around, still stuck above my head, attempting to smack Roman, but I meet nothing but air. Willow's giggle is cut off and all the fight leaves me deflated. Crumpling to the ground, I slump against the bed, resigning myself to living like this for the foreseeable future. They're too busy bickering to notice.

Willow's small hands brush against my side, and I jolt. "Sorry, I'm just going to get this unstuck, okay? I've been imprisoned by many a dress in my day."

"Can you get them out of the room first? I don't have a bra on," I mumble.

Her hands stop pulling at my hair. "Why don't you two head to the conference room and we'll be right along?"

Silence meets her suggestion, but there are no doors shutting or shuffling of feet, so I'm sure they're still there, staring at me. At least I got pants on before I found myself in this mess. I can't imagine how they would have reacted if my whole ass was hanging out. My thong is still hidden in Roman's pocket.

"Go now," Willow commands, steel lacing her tone.

"Don't let her out of your sight. She comes with you, or I'll have to hunt her ass down and I'm fucking tired," Roman grumbles.

"I will make sure she's exactly where she needs to be. Now get the hell out."

Finally, the door clicks shut, and Willow's hands leave me. Seconds later, the lock snaps. Then her hands are back, gently tugging the strands from the zipper. She works in silence for a few minutes and I'm about ready to tell her to rip them out instead of dealing with the mess.

"Was there a reason you two dropped by?" I ask, if only to break the suffocating silence.

"Hawk will explain, I'm sure. Unless you're actually leaving?"

One last tug, and she yanks the fabric over my head with a cry. I meet her triumphant gaze and her face falls. I'm sure I look a mess, eyes puffy, nose running, and hair a riot around my head.

"Oh dear, I'm so sorry. Here"—she grabs a shirt tossed on the back of a chair and holds it out to me—"put this on. You'll feel better when you're not free balling it for everyone to see."

I snort, not noticing my mistake until the fabric slides over my face, Roman's scent flooding my nose. My muscles relax and my breathing slows as I take a deep breath. Sandalwood should not have this effect on me. Shaking my head, I yank it the rest of the way down, scowling by the time I can see Willow again.

"Something wrong?" she asks, tilting her head as she twists her fingers in front of her.

"Nothing. I'd rather not make an enemy of you, Willow, but there's no way you're forcing me to go to the conference room. I may be persuaded if you give me an incentive, though."

The last thing I want to do is sit in a room with them as they hash out what they're going to do about the fire chief or when the next shipment is coming in. I still haven't fully grasped what's *in* those shipments, but I assume it's the same type of things the Drakes dealt with in Westmont. It took years for Aelia to admit to me they ran guns, drugs, and information, keeping the criminal underworld afloat. The way she described it didn't seem much different from what my parents did, actually.

"Like a snack? I don't have any with me, but I'm sure I could find something in the kitchen."

"A what? No, I meant if you could just tell me what it's about. Roman's the one who can be bribed with snacks." I wave my hand toward the door.

She tips her head back, a full-bodied laugh overtaking her. I have no idea what's so funny. Roman doesn't make a big deal of it usually, but I wonder what he's been up to that Willow seems to know him so well. I'm not jealous because that would be ridiculous.

Roman has had ten years to become someone else, living his life completely separate from mine. In fact, I've lived my whole adult existence striving for a dream that might never be achieved. Expecting him to do the same would be...

I shake my head, pushing the thoughts from my mind. He made the decision for me to walk this path alone, conveying in no uncertain terms I was chasing after something that would ultimately break my heart. Which is exactly why I need to leave as soon as possible.

Maybe I'll go to Rima, explore the possibilities there. If everyone else fucked off to Rima, there's a good chance that's exactly where Anders is. I've heard rumors of the Guild setting up shop there, and while I'd rather not tussle with them, I'm confident enough that I can flit through the shadows. They'll never know I'm there.

"Sorry, I just have had personal experience with Roman and his snacks," Willow says, chuckling again.

"Mmhmm."

Jealousy curls in my gut. No, not jealousy, nervousness. That's what this is. I'm merely worried about getting out of this house without Roman waylaying me again, insisting on another asinine conversation that will go absolutely nowhere. That's all this is.

Standing in the middle of the carnage of shopping bags, I resign myself to lying, even if it's only in my own head. I'm getting quite adept at it and I don't plan on stopping now.

Nineteen

Roman

Hawk prattles on about contractors like he has been for the last twenty minutes, but my eyes are glued to the door. I never should have left Ember alone with Willow. Standing outside the bedroom waiting for them felt creepy, though. Willow will never be able to physically keep Ember from leaving, though she's quite persuasive when she sets her mind to something.

"Hawk, is this really what you came to talk about at"—I glance at my phone—"two in the morning? Because frankly, I could give a shit whether your contractors are fucking you over. In the morning, perhaps I'd have more patience for it, but not this late at night."

He clears his throat, glancing at the door. "I was actually waiting for the girls to come in. Figured it would be easier to only have to tell this shit once."

"I highly doubt Ember will be—"

The door swings open, revealing both Willow and Ember. My breath stalls in my lungs as my eyes catch on what she's wearing. The dark blue shirt hangs halfway down her thighs, hiding most of her curves. It's merely a T-shirt, nothing extravagant, but it's mine. I wore it three days ago, tossing it onto the chair with every intention of throwing it in the laundry, but I never got around to it. Now it's gracing her body and the possessive beast within my chest wakes from its slumber, demanding I claim her as my own.

"Highly doubt I'll be what?" she asks, dull green eyes finding mine. Willow nudges Ember on her way to the chair next to Hawk, but Ember doesn't move.

"Let's get this over with, Hawk. We've had a shit night," I say instead of answering her question.

She blushes, crossing her arms and leaning against the wall. When our eyes meet, I raise a brow, looking pointedly at the chair next to me, but she tips her chin, focusing on Hawk.

"Got a message from Helms. Says shit is going sideways in Rima and things are a lot more complicated than they thought. Doesn't think they'll be home for a while. Apparently, they're having trouble infiltrating, even with Lacey doing her hacker thing. Also, there's a gala we need to attend," Hawk says, laying his arm over the back of Willow's chair.

"Fucking hell. Why the fuck do we have to go?" I swipe through my calendar on my phone.

It's riddled with meetups involving contacts and appointments with political big shots. I don't have time to go to a fancy party, glad-handing with rich people who have nothing better to do than subtly one-up each other. Most of my teenage years were spent being dragged to one party or another. Ember and Aelia always slipped away, tucking themselves into an alcove and giggling.

"Listen, I'm not all that happy about going either, but people need to see that we're still around, so they don't start running amok."

Ember snorts, smothering her grin behind her hand, and I roll my eyes. Willow swings her chair around, tilting her head. Ember's chest jumps as she tries to hold in her laugh. I sigh, tipping my head back and resigning myself to what's about to happen.

"Amok, amok, amok," she mumbles, then doubles over as her entire body shakes.

"Are we supposed to know what that means?" Hawk asks in a staged whisper.

"It's from a movie. Ignore her," I mutter as Willow giggles, adding to the slow breakdown of this conversation.

"Nothing we can do to help them other than not letting Synd go to shit. Send me the details on the gala. We'll be there."

At my statement, Ember straightens, face sobering as she stares at me. I'm sure she'll have something to say about this later, but hopefully she'll keep it to herself until they leave. From the storm clouds gathering in her eyes, I gather I have about three minutes before she explodes and tells me off.

"Anything else?" I ask when the silence stretches.

"Yeah, I think someone is trying to kill you. Not sure who, but there was a guy in Trigger's tonight asking about who lived in the big mansion in the forest. Wasn't very subtle about it or very good at subterfuge, so I doubt he'll be successful. With all the other shit happening, I figured I should mention it."

Willow clears her throat. "Personally, I don't think he's after you, Roman."

"Willow," Hawk hisses, a warning tinging his voice.

"I believe he's after Ember."

He leans down to whisper to her, but his voice carries, regardless. "*Mo dóchais*, you don't have any evidence to suggest that."

"Well, you don't have much to go on either, Hawk. By the look on Roman's face, I think in this instance I may be right. So, if you could stop dismissing me and my observations, that would be wonderful." She pushes from her chair. "We can bicker about this at home. Ember is about to fall asleep while standing up, so we should go."

She's right. Ember slumps against the wall, lids drooping as she struggles to stay awake. I'm surprised she's lasted this long, considering everything that's happened tonight. I push from my chair, opening the door for Hawk and Willow.

"We'll talk about this later. Send me the details on the gala."

Hawk claps me on the back, smirking when he glances at Ember. "Don't fight it too long."

I have no idea what he's talking about, but it doesn't really matter. When I wrap an arm around Ember's waist, she jolts upright, blinking rapidly. The anger coursing through me just an hour ago has faded into a dull ache in my chest. I wonder if that's what it's always been—rage masking the hurt underneath.

All these years I've wondered what would have happened had I listened to her instead of throwing her out. I was drowning in too much grief and anxiety. Days away from turning eighteen, I lost everything. Sure, I gained a criminal empire with more money than I knew what to do with. But along with it came a vendetta I never wanted to pursue. The revenge burning deep inside me was just the icing on the cake.

Ember twists away, forcing me back to the present, and I grip her tighter, yanking her toward me.

"Let me go, Drake," she huffs, turning her face away.

I sigh, resting my chin on her head, and her hair tickles my face. "We need to talk, Ember, but not tonight."

"I have nothing to say to you," she whispers harshly, hurt lacing her tone.

"Perhaps not right now, but maybe tomorrow. Let's go to bed." I tug her along, leading her out the door.

"I'm not sleeping with you."

"Again," I say, smirking. "I'm well aware of that. However, I don't trust that you'll stay where I put you, and we need to have this conversation. It's been a long time coming, and we can't keep putting it off."

"Why are you such an insufferable asshole? So goddamn pretentious, thinking you can boss everyone around. *You're* ready for talking, so *everyone else* better get on board or there'll be hell to pay."

I can't help smiling at the slight drop in her vowels. She must be exhausted if she isn't masking it behind the proper vocal technique her mother drilled into her. Well, probably not her mother. That woman was the furthest thing from a parent. Veronica Hayes most likely passed off Ember's dialect training to someone else, as she did most things dealing with her daughter.

"You and I both know we need to hash things out before this shit gets out of control."

She stiffens, but whether it's from my words or the fact that I've led her straight to my bedroom door, I'm not sure. Regardless of what she thinks, I can't leave her by herself. She'll slip out, just like she was attempting to do before Hawk and Willow came. The irony isn't lost on me. The fact that I'm still vacillating between whether to toss her ass out again and keeping her as close as possible is ridiculous. Every time I think I have things figured out, my mind flips, feeding me shit I can't fully commit to. This needs to end.

Reaching around her, I open the door, ushering her inside. It clicks softly behind me, and I lean against the wood, crossing my arms. She scoops up bags and the computer she discarded before and then spins around. She narrows her eyes, clutching the items closer to her chest.

"Are you going to move?" she asks, and I shake my head. "God-fuck-ing-dammit, Drake."

"We can have this conversation now or tomorrow. Personally, I'd like to wait since tonight has been shit and I don't see how it'll get any better."

The momentary burst of adrenaline leaves her, and her shoulders drop. She blinks slowly, glancing around the room.

"You're really going to make me crawl out the window, huh? Thought you'd just toss my ass out the door. Wouldn't be the first time," she mutters.

Sighing, I shake my head. "It's been ten fucking years, Em. When are you going to let it go?"

As soon as the words are out of my mouth, I know I fucked up. Her face flushes, but then the mask falls over her features and her dull eyes meet mine. I open my mouth to say something, anything, to take back the implications of my words, but she slowly shakes her head.

"Don't bother. I know what you meant," she says dejectedly. "Can I at least get my own room?"

Pushing off the door, I go to the bed and start tossing the boxes and bags into a pile on the other side. I can feel her eyes on me, but I refuse to answer her. My response will only piss her off, and she knows what I'll say.

Glancing from under my lashes, I realize the look on her face isn't the mask I've seen over the last few weeks. She's blank, staring into space while her body sways. I toss the last box into the pile and the top pops off, spilling a pair of bright red heels.

"Ember," I murmur, straightening. "We both know you'd be gone before I even shut the door. We can't keep running from this. Clearly, someone is after you and ignoring that will only get you killed."

"What exactly are we running from?" she asks, rolling her head toward me.

"Don't do that," I whisper harshly. "Don't act like you don't know what the fuck I'm talking about."

"No one is after me. Unless your illustrious father has discovered that I'm searching for him and sent someone to take me out. Although, I wonder why he would be more worried about me than you," she murmurs, readjusting the shit she's still holding.

"I doubt you're even on his radar." I take a deep breath. "But he's run back to the Guild."

The blood drains from her face before she ducks her head. I'm not surprised she knows who the Guild is. Ember isn't the type to go about her life without knowing what the hell is going on.

"Ember, you can't go after him," I warn, stalking closer to her.

She tenses, glancing at me from the corner of her eye. "You think I'm stupid enough to go after the Guild? Even if…"

Her eyes take on a far-off look and she tilts her head. I can practically see the gears turning in her head, rejecting ideas and slotting others into place. If she's anything like she was ten years ago, as soon as she decides, she'll close her eyes, sigh, and make her next move. I watched her do this exact same thing from the dark window after she stumbled from my house in Westmont. The rain soaked her almost immediately, flattening her hair and hiding her tears.

When her eyes fall closed, I clear my throat. "What did you just figure out, Ember?"

"He took all that money. He took it and ran to them. Maybe a couple years? Probably took him a while."

She's muttering more to herself than anything. Slowly, I tug the paper bag filled with clothes and toiletries from her hands and then ease the computer from her arm. She barely moves, her hands merely falling to her sides. I cup her cheeks to remind her I'm here, and her eyes flutter open.

"What did you figure out?" I whisper.

"Oh," she breathes.

Her bright green eyes finally focus on mine, then she pulls away from my grasp. Tucking my hands into my pockets, I sigh. I don't have time to deal with another fight, but as I gaze at her, I realize I don't have a choice. Shit is going to hit the fan whether I like it or not.

Twenty

Ember

"Are you actually going to listen to me this time?" I spit out, tucking my arms around my waist.

He sighs, running his hand through his hair before slipping it back into his pocket. I'm not in the right head space to have this conversation, but he won't let me go unless I do. Over the last week, he's pulled my emotions in a million different directions. It would have been too much even if we hadn't slept together. The situation is messy, mirroring the emotions swirling inside of me.

He rolls his neck before settling his gaze on me. "I'd rather go to fucking bed than deal with this now, but you've figured something out and I'd like to know what it is."

"It's the same thing as always. Aelia is alive and I think she's with Anders," I say, tipping my chin up.

His face drains of emotion, a stony expression taking over. It's the same song and dance we had ten years ago. And five years after that. And again, just recently. We're so far into whatever this is, I don't even know where we go from here. Part of me wants to slip out the window and run, just like he said I would. The other part, though, wants to curl up next to him and forget every issue between us.

"Don't," he warns harshly, and my gaze snaps to his. "Don't you fucking dare."

Swallowing around the lump in my throat, I shake my head, all the fight draining from my body. Between the bomb that might have taken out TJ and the threats from Moss, I don't have it in me anymore. It may not be a great decision, but all I want to do is pretend we're normal. I want to feel like I belong somewhere, even if it's a lie.

"I don't want to do this right now," I mutter.

Exhaustion settles in my bones, and I shuffle to the bed, collapsing onto the comforter. My eyes close before Roman even moves, but I peek at him as he stalks to the closet, leaving the door open behind him. I'm sure he thinks I'll sneak out while he's changing if he closes it, but I can't even bring myself to slide under the covers, much less make a break for it.

He doesn't even bother stepping to the side, instead stripping down to his underwear in full view of me. I should look away, but seriously with that specimen undressing in plain view, who could blame me? His back muscles ripple as he bends over, grabbing his pants and tossing them into a hamper.

My mouth goes dry, and I turn away. Even with everything we've been through, I still want him. It's a desperate craving that's lived deep within me for years.

I float in that space between awake and asleep, still trying to track where Roman is. I don't come back to reality until he's sliding his hands under my knees and back.

"What are you doing?" I mumble, curling into the heat of his body.

"Can't sleep on top of the covers, love."

The cool sheets slide against my skin, and I sigh. Tonight was a drain on more than just my body. I've dealt with plenty of men who shove a gun in my face, threatening to kill me, but never someone I have to interact with. There's always the option of leaving—packing up shop and moving to the next lead. I know the reason I'm hesitant to leave Synd, and it lies solely with the man sliding into bed next to me.

I give myself up to the darkness, hoping when I wake, I'll finally be able to walk away.

"Sir, you can't believe she has nothing to do with this. We should at the very least put her downstairs." Moss's voice infiltrates my dreams, and I peek at them from under my lashes.

Roman leans a hand against the door frame, dropping his head. "Our focus needs to be on securing the property, Moss. Not chasing after false leads."

"Just because you're fucking her—"

Roman lunges forward, wrapping his hand around Moss's throat and shoving him backwards. I shoot up, peering through the open doorway as Roman slams the man against the wall.

"One more word and I'll tear you apart with my bare hands. And I won't feel an ounce of regret at losing you," Roman growls, his voice laced with barely suppressed violence.

Moss's eyes meet mine over Roman's shoulder, and I tip my chin up. I don't blame him for his reservations. From his perspective, I'm a random woman who flounced into their world, bringing bullets and destruction with her. If I were in his position, I'd assume I was at fault, too.

Moss makes a choking noise, his hand finally reaching up to wrap around Roman's wrist. He tries to speak, but Roman's fingers squeeze tighter. Moss's face turns red and his head thumps against the wall. After what feels like an eternity, Roman drops his hand and steps back.

"Get out," Roman sneers as Moss coughs.

The guard's eyes meet mine again, bloodshot and full of loathing. He stumbles away and I sink onto my back, pulling the covers up to my chin. Roman's defense of me is jarring after he practically accused me of the same thing hours ago.

Swallowing hard, I track Roman as he prowls into the room, searching for an outlet for the pent-up rage that's still obviously riding him hard. His eyes skip over me, as if he doesn't even notice I'm awake. When he doesn't find whatever he's looking for, he stalks to the bathroom. The door rattles on its hinges when he slams it shut.

"Oookay," I mutter, slipping from under the covers.

I tiptoe to the window and peek between the curtains, bright sunlight greeting me. Dropping the edge, I glance toward the bathroom as the shower starts up. I would give almost anything to join him. I can almost imagine the hot spray easing all the tension coursing through me.

Getting relaxed and clean isn't on the agenda for today. I skirt the pile of boxes and bags left in the middle of the room, intent on finding the essentials I packed last night. Skipping into the closet, I find the computer on top of the built-in dresser, but the rest of my stuff is nowhere to be found. Roman probably hid it to deter me from leaving. He forgot that I have my own money and can just buy more shit. The expensive shops he took me to yesterday probably won't let me in without him, but I don't need to buy a designer hoodie or ridiculously expensive underwear.

The only problem now is finding shoes. I don't want to dig through all the boxes and I'm on a time crunch here. Sneaking back into the room, I drop to my knees to check under the bed for footwear. If Roman gets out of the shower anytime soon, I won't be far enough away to escape him. The thought pulls me up short. Do I honestly think he'd keep me here if I really wanted to leave?

It takes me longer than I like to come to the conclusion that he wouldn't stop me. He might make me beg and plead. He'd definitely try to talk me out of it. But in the end, he'd let me go, if only so he wouldn't have to deal with me anymore.

"What the hell are you doing on the floor?" Roman asks, framing the doorway in just a towel.

Water droplets slide down his tattooed skin and I track one as it reaches his stomach before disappearing into the fabric. Licking my lips, I drop my chin to my chest. No reason he needs to see how much he affects me.

"I'm looking for shoes," I mutter, peering under the nightstand.

"Going somewhere?"

I sigh, glancing up at him again. "I can't stay here forever, Drake. And clearly, you've got some shit going on."

He scowls and crosses his arms, reminding me how very naked he is. Not that I forgot. All I would need to do is lean forward the tiniest bit and I'd be able to spy under his towel, seeing all his delicious parts. Shaking my head, I bite the inside of my cheek, copper exploding across my tongue.

"I took care of it. Besides, we have a gala on Friday," he says as if I'll give in if he doesn't give me a choice.

"Why would I go to a gala with you? I hate those things." I push to my feet to check the closet while mumbling, "Bunch of rich snobs bidding on shit they don't need and subtly judging everyone around them."

He follows me, grabbing clothes from the dresser. "Neither of us like them, Ember, but I have to show my face."

"And how does that have anything to do with me?" I ask, raising a brow at him.

"That package was addressed to you. Or at least who they think you are. Someone is trying to kill you. If you'd rather leave Synd and let them follow you to the next place you land, then by all means." He sweeps his hand out, presenting the way.

My gut turns, and I glance toward the bedroom. He's not wrong, but I'm still not fully convinced. There's a voice in the back of my head whispering that Roman is in danger. Losing Aelia was hard, but it would be infinitely harder when I find her to say I didn't protect her brother when I had the chance. No matter where our relationship stands, I can't let her down like that. I ignore the whispering that it would break my heart, too.

"You're so fucking stubborn," I mutter.

"You're one to talk," he snaps, dropping his towel.

"What the fuck. You think if you drop trou in front of me I'll ride your dick till sunset and things will be peachy keen?"

He grins as he pulls on his underwear. "If you want to ride my dick, love, all you have to do is beg."

"The saying is 'all you have to do is ask.'"

He steps forward, crowding me against the wall and bracing his hands on either side of my head. I barely suppress the shiver rolling down my spine. I can't stop my nipples from hardening though, or my pussy from tingling with anticipation. He skims his nose along my jaw and my eyes close.

His lips brush my ear, and I swallow hard. "Asking wouldn't fulfill my fantasy of seeing you on your knees, begging me to fuck your mouth."

"I will never beg." False bravado rings through my tone.

But the image of me sinking to my knees as I gaze up at him is now planted in my brain. He'd twist his fingers into my hair, holding me still as he pushed the tip past my lips. The wanton part of me that can't help but crave him would open wide, giving him full access. I'd moan, swirling my tongue along his length. And when the time came, I would swallow every single fucking drop.

I open my eyes as he leans back, trying to school my face into one of boredom. He smirks, probably spotting the desire in my eyes and the blush on my cheeks. When his nostrils flare, I know I'm fucked.

"Tell me you don't want me. Lie to me. Say you're not fucking soaked fantasizing about choking on my cock."

Pressing my lips together, I tip my chin up, refusing to answer even as I dig my nails into my thighs to distract myself from the images running rampant through my mind. All the times we've fucked before replay in my head, and wetness gathers between my legs. Pretending he doesn't affect me isn't working. Lying won't accomplish anything either. He'll know, mostly because my body will betray me—horny bitch.

"You think you're such a fucking rock star in bed that I can't control myself around you?" I snort, turning my face away. "Your ego knows no bounds."

I gasp when he swoops down, biting into the soft skin of my shoulder. My hands fly to his chest, ready to push him away, but I dig my nails into him as he works his way up my neck, nibbling and sucking. His hand falls to my waist, sliding around to my ass and kneading the flesh.

"You were saying?" he whispers in my ear before latching onto the lobe, and I shudder, eyes shutting again.

"Fuck you." The vitriol is lost in another gasp as he works my body into a frenzy.

He cups my chin, fingers digging in until I meet his bright blue eyes. His thumb brushes over my lower lip.

"Your mouth will look so pretty with my cum painting your lips."

Twenty-One

Roman

"Mr. Drake, hello. I'll take you right up to Mr. Smith's room," the elderly nurse says.

"Thank you," I murmur, glaring at the young nurse who kept asking me who I was.

She leads me through halls that all look the same. I'm not entirely comfortable in hospitals, but the time I've spent inside one has been limited. The nurse glances back a few times, a small smile playing on her lips.

"I'm sorry about Jacklyn. She's newer, but also very protective of her patients. Not a bad thing until she meets someone like you," she murmurs.

"Someone like me?" I ask, even though I know exactly what she means.

Byrns must have done a lot more preparation than he told me if nurses at the hospital know who I am and the role I'm fulfilling. She stops suddenly and I almost run into her. When she spins, I lift an eyebrow, tucking my hands in my pockets.

"I took care of Mason Byrns when he was in a coma, sir. I've also personally seen to Samantha and Alex King when they were here. So, as much as I appreciate your need for secrecy, let's assume that I know a lot more than you."

She pats my arms, shooting me another smile before continuing. I follow her, ducking my head to hide the smirk gracing my lips. TJ couldn't be in better hands, apparently.

"Is he out of the woods?" I ask as we reach TJ's door.

"For the most part—"

Whatever else she was going to say is lost when my phone rings. She shoots me a disapproving look before marching back the way we came. Mason's name flashes across the screen and I sigh.

"Byrns, what can I do for you?"

"Drake, we have a problem. I need you to call Sam. I can't get ahold of her." Mason's frantic voice rings down the line, crackling for a second, and I worry I've lost him.

"Why don't you just call one of the Kings? I'm sure they're glued to her side."

"You think I didn't fucking do that?" he shouts, then lets out a string of curses. "Something's wrong, Drake."

"Fine, I'll call them."

I hang up before he can yell at me some more. Calling Sam ends up a dead end. Alex's phone goes straight to voicemail, which doesn't bode well. He's usually the only one consistent enough to pick up. My hand trembles by the time I pull up Shane's contact. It connects, static filling the line.

"King?" I wait for thirty seconds before the line goes dead.

Ren didn't even want to give me his number, but Alex slipped it to me with a grin before they left for Rima. I'm sure Alex expected me to prank him or something, but I haven't used it until now.

"Hello?" Ren's dejected voice fills the line.

"Ren, what the hell is going on over there? Byrns called me in a panic, saying he couldn't get ahold of Sam. Called the rest and no one's picking up," I hiss, glaring at a doctor who hurries past.

"She's gone. No one's left."

Twenty-Two

Ember

I've held fast for the last three days without giving in to Roman's suggestions. That's what I'm calling all the dirty words he's been whispering to me. We've pretended the other shit didn't happen.

TJ may be in the hospital. Someone might be gunning for one of us. Moss definitely has it out for me, whispering into Roman's ear every chance he gets. Roman also hasn't brought up my theory of Aelia being with Anders. He's ignored it all, opting to walk away every time I bring any of it up.

Watching him straighten his tie in the bathroom, I wonder how he'll answer questions about me at the gala. I haven't asked and I don't plan on it. He can do all the talking. I attended plenty of these occasions throughout my childhood, but I was never very good at it. I was too outspoken—couldn't keep my mouth shut enough for my parents' liking.

"Put your shoes on, Ember. The car will be here soon," Roman calls, breaking through my thoughts.

"Is someone going to sweep the car before we get into it?" I ask.

"We don't have to worry about the car. Put your damn shoes on."

Rolling my eyes, I slip my feet into the heels, wincing when they pinch my toes. I tug them off again, tossing them against the wall.

"Seriously, Ember? It's not that big of a deal. Fancy fucking food, conversations with self-absorbed people, and bidding on shit no one needs. We've played this song and dance a million times over. Not putting your shoes on isn't going to stop me from throwing you over my shoulder and dumping your ass in the car. You can go barefoot for all I care," he grumbles, then tucks a gun into the holster under his jacket.

"Slow your roll, asshole. I just need a new pair."

I wade through the bags until I reach the boxes stacked in the corner. We're in a stand-off with what to do with them. Two days ago, Roman tried to put them away in his closet. I waited until he was on the phone and tossed them all back into the bedroom. Yesterday, he hung all the dresses in the other closet I hadn't noticed before. I threw them on the floor, then kicked them into a neat pile in the corner, and there it all stays.

Finding a pair of flats in this mess isn't easy, but I finally cry out in triumph, brandishing them in the air. He scowls, and I'd put cash money down that he's biting his tongue right now. Hopping on one foot, I slip one on, grinning. Apparently, his resolve isn't as good as mine since he clears his throat.

"You can't wear flats to a gala," he mutters.

"The fact you know that these are flats is kind of amazing." I slide the other one on.

I tense when there's a knock at the door. Roman shoots me a look I can't decipher as I slip into the smaller closet and peek around the frame. A young guy, a guard probably, whispers to Roman, his eyes bouncing around the room. I can't tell if he's nervous to be standing in front of someone as powerful as Roman or if he's searching for me.

"It's fine, Rigger. Don't worry about Moss. He'll come around."

"But, sir, he's saying he called Byrns." Rigger's eyes finally settle on Roman, widening.

"I'm well aware. I'm also aware of what was said. The question is, do you trust Byrns enough to follow my orders?"

It's not an actual question. It's a warning, delivered with a brutal promise laced within the words. If Rigger sides with the head of security, it'll be seen as a betrayal against the Byrns family. Roman could put a bullet in Rigger's head for his actions. I desperately want to know if Roman did talk to Mason Byrns or if he's merely bluffing. Like hell I'll ask him.

Rigger is smarter than his weaselly face suggests and nods, backing away from the door. His brows pull low as he stares at his feet before nodding again and shuffling down the hall. Roman glances back at me, raising an eyebrow, daring me to ask the questions burning on my tongue.

Instead of giving him the satisfaction, I grab my clutch, checking that the small dagger is still safely tucked inside. It's not the only weapon I have, but the others are strapped to my body. They won't be as easily accessible as this one, even though the weapon is smaller.

Tiny objects can do a lot of damage if wielded properly. I guess the same could be said for women as well. Most people would look at me and assume I'm not a deadly force to be reckoned with. Plenty have made that mistake before and regrettably didn't live to tell the tale.

"Well, are we going or not?" I tap my toes against the hardwood floor.

"Change your shoes first," he commands, leaning against the door.

"Why the hell should I do that?"

"You're wasting time. Change into heels. Now."

I bite my tongue. Tonight is going to be a disaster if he keeps pushing me. I didn't want to go to the gala in the first place. The only reason I'm entertaining it is because Roman's been dangling the promise of information in front of me. He's been handing out tidbits about who's going to be there, as if I have any clue who any of them are. They all have fancy-sounding names, though. I don't know if that matters or not.

"You realize if I wear flats I'll be able to run, if need be, right?"

He glares, scanning me up and down. Just when I think he's going to give in, he marches past me to the pile behind me. He digs around for at least an entire minute before pushing to his feet. He shoves a pair of red heels into my hands as he passes. They're half the height of the ones I originally had on.

"Put them on, Ember, or I'll put them on for you," he growls, resuming his guarding of the door.

Biting my lip, I kick off my flats and pull them on. It's not worth the argument.

"Are you going to be a controlling asshole the entire time we're there? Do you want to choose what I eat as well? Is this dress okay, or do I need to change?"

"Don't push me, Ember. Now let's fucking go." He opens the door and sweeps his hand out for me to exit.

I think about refusing just to piss him off, but it's not worth it. When we're done with this, maybe he'll stop blocking my attempts to leave. To be fair, I haven't tried all that hard. I'd be lying if I said it wasn't easier being here.

There's food whenever I want, and enough space I don't have to be looking over my shoulder all the time. Not to mention his bed is amazing, and not because he's occupying it. It's big, fluffy, and the best damn thing that has come into my life in the past ten years.

Huffing, I slide past him, and his hand brushes my hip. The move sends a shudder through me, and I skip away from his fingers. He's been playing this game for three days now. Little touches, dirty comments, and sly looks abound.

We'll have to put on a show at the gala, but that doesn't mean he needs to start it early.

His hand lands on my lower back, and I'm suddenly cursing the dress I chose. The exposed back is the last thing I need. Heat spreads through my body, and I trip over my own feet. His hand slides around my waist, gripping my hip to steady me. When I try to pull away, he doesn't let go. As he ushers me into the backseat of a town car, it hits me I'm totally in too deep.

Twenty-Three

Roman

Shaking yet another old, rich man's hand is slowly draining my soul. I'm ten seconds away from suggesting Ember pretend she's twisted her ankle or something. Then we'd have an excuse to bail. I've made the necessary contacts, let the media take their pictures, so we should be able to make a quick getaway.

"Let's get out of here," I murmur in her ear.

If the saying "if looks could kill" was literal, I'd be dead.

"You told me there were people here with information for me," she hisses through gritted teeth.

Her mask falls into place, a bright smile plastered across her face. I sigh, resigning myself to another pointless conversation.

"Besides, free food," she mutters.

I lead her into the main ballroom, filled with round tables, and a stage set at the front. They put us at a table near the podium someone will stand behind and drone on for longer than anyone wants to listen. We won't even be able to slip out the back when we get bored.

"What other information do you need, exactly?" I murmur in her ear as I push her chair in.

She tilts her head, and I brush my lips across her temple. Trailing my fingers across her bare shoulders, I suppress a smile as she shudders.

I take my seat, nodding at the couple across from us. Pierce Edwards, the new mayor, starts to make his way to us, but a chime overhead sends him scurrying for his seat two tables over, and I breathe a sigh of relief.

"I need to know everything about Anders. Maybe I can trace where he's been all these years and I'll be able to see where Aelia went," she says quietly as she fidgets with her clutch.

"That's what you're after? For fuck's sake, Ember. You're wasting your..."

I shake my head, settling into my seat. Now isn't the time to get into all of this. It never feels like the right time. Eventually, we'll have to address everything. We started the other night, but we never seem to finish. Like most of our interactions.

"Wasting my time? Yeah, well, some would say *you're* a waste of time, but I've never said it. Out loud, that is," she murmurs, picking up the knife and twirling it between her fingers.

Wrapping my hand around hers, I slip the handle from her grasp and set the knife next to her fork. No reason to make the other guests nervous because she can't keep her hands still. A man sits next to me, then tips his head back, his laugh echoing over the crowd.

"Mr. Drake, what brings you here tonight? I didn't think we'd be seeing you after the whole debacle." Henry Pritchard, the new police commissioner, is practically shouting.

Most would call him boisterous. I think he's merely annoying. I'd rather not spend my night making small talk with someone who doesn't understand volume control. He also has no clue how to keep shit to himself, which is a terrible trait for the position he's in. Byrns said it wasn't easy to find someone to take the job after the last few fucked up. Not that I had a say in any of the appointments they made after my father disappeared.

"What debacle would that be, Mr. Pritchard?"

I know exactly what he's talking about, but I'm going to make him say it. He thinks he can pass judgment on matters that have nothing to do with him. Personally, I think he just likes to gossip. Then he takes that information and spreads it around to raise his own status. If he starts spouting about the Barrens and the renovation of the Egg in the middle of this gala, though, I might have to put a bullet in his head. We don't fuck with the people down there.

Pritchard leans in, a smirk playing on his lips. "Your little issue with Brewer. Not exactly good to have the fire chief against you in a town like this."

His mock whispering carries around the table. I see red when he claps me on the shoulder, laughing. He's about to lose his hand if he touches me again. The woman seated across from me giggles, and I stare at her until she drops her gaze.

"Mr. Pritchard, I'm surprised," Ember says as her hand lands on my leg.

"And you are?" he asks, a slight sneer in his tone.

"No one of consequence." She waves her other hand, and I catch the flash of silver before she tucks it under the table.

"Then I'd advise you, little missy, to continue being the arm candy I'm sure Drake intended for you to be," he snarls, then grins at me, as if he's done me a favor.

I could slit his throat. Or I could shoot him, like I've been imagining since he sat down. Hell, I could just smother him in the soup the server places in front of me. Ember's nails dig into my leg, pulling me from my fantasies of all the ways I could kill him.

"No need to get testy merely because you're unable to find a way into the Barrens. I'm sure you're not too happy with being bested by a woman, but that's no reason to be nasty to us all," Ember says, smiling sweetly.

Pritchard's face reddens, the flush spreading down his thick neck. Rage flows from him in waves, cascading over the others at the table. Ember appears unfazed as she picks up her spoon and starts in on the squash soup, as if his wrath parts around her. Just as he opens his mouth, probably to spew more vitriol upon her, Willow slides into the seat next to Pritchard's wife.

"Hello, I apologize for our tardiness. The soup looks delicious, doesn't it, Hawk?" Willow's voice has a calming effect on everyone, and they scramble for their silverware.

"Sure. Whatever you say," Hawk mutters, eyeing the soup as if it's going to reach up and slap him.

"Mr. Pritchard, I saw your interview the other day. I think it's an excellent idea to clean up the river in the south of the city. How do you plan on dealing with the potential flooding?" Willow asks.

He swings to face her, glancing back at Ember once before giving his full attention to Willow. They strike up a conversation, and I realize Pritchard only attacked Ember because of me. He's pissed because I keep blocking his attempts to continue the pet projects Jason Grayson, the original police chief, started. The only reason he's saying anything about Brewer is to start shit. The last thing I want to do is have to call Byrns and tell him we have to pick a new police commissioner.

The thought pulls me up short. I haven't seen myself as a part of their group. I'm an outsider who fucked with their shit and now I'm paying reparations. Lumping myself into those types of decisions is completely different. I've held firm to the belief that as soon as the Kings, Byrns, and Helms return from Rima, I'll be gone—vanished from the history of Synd once again.

"Drake," Ember hisses, and I tilt my head toward her. "Stop daydreaming ways of killing Pritchard and pay the fuck attention."

"Contrary to what you believe, I am."

"Then stop staring at that poor woman. I'm pretty sure she's about to have a panic attack."

I whip my head to Ember, pulling my brows low. When I peek at the woman, though, terror radiates from her. Muttering a curse under my breath, I pick up my spoon. One bite is all it takes to realize I still hate squash, especially when it's in soup form. I'm about to choke down more when a buttered roll appears on a plate by my elbow. Ember goes back to her goop in a bowl, and I grab the bread.

The rest of the meal is an intricate dance of words, woven through with subtle moves and very few missteps. As soon as the dinner is done, a woman approaches the lectern to start round after round of speeches. Ember excuses herself, smiling gracefully at the others, then walking away.

Hawk gestures for me to follow him and we make our escape to an alcove tucked away toward the back of the room. Hawk peers back at the table. Willow raises her eyebrow at Pritchard, her lips twisting into some semblance of a smirk.

"Oh, she's about to eviscerate him," Hawk says, eyes fixed on his woman.

"What are you doing here, Hawk? Thought you couldn't attend tonight."

A server shuffles to us, bearing two glasses of amber liquid. I hesitate, unsure where they came from. Some poisons only take one sip to put a full-grown man six feet under and I'm not about to take the chance. Hawk doesn't have the same reservations, though, or he may just not have thought someone would try to kill him.

"It's from your lady, sir," the server murmurs, gesturing to Ember.

She lifts her glass to us before returning to her conversation with the woman I apparently frightened. I take the glass, swirling the whiskey around before letting the alcohol burn its way down my throat. It's not my first choice to deal with the anxiety building in my gut, but since it probably would be uncouth to fuck Ember in the middle of the dining room, this is the best option.

"You going to tell me how you know Ember finally? Or am I going to have to call Lacey to figure that shit out?"

"As if Nemesis has the energy for that shit. She's busy trying to infiltrate the Guild. She won't waste her time," I scoff.

He chuckles, then sips his own drink. "Drake, that woman could find a needle in a stack of needles if it's on the internet."

"Well aware. Why do you care?"

"Just wondering when I'm going to have to tell you you're fucked. Again. Listen, there's some issues we're dealing with up north. We're still cleaning up from when the Night Slayers came through. The bridge we blew up is almost done, but some of the businesses are still struggling," Hawk says.

Another person starts their speech, droning on about all the money raised for various organizations. What he's actually bragging about is what he's personally given to causes he doesn't care about. It's a status grab since he's been trying to break into the upper echelons of Synd. Disgusting, but not surprising given the company present at the gala.

"I'll give you whatever support I can, but we're dealing with a fair bit at the moment," I murmur as the mayor struts past, nodding his head to us.

"TJ still in a coma?"

"Yeah, but they think he might pull through. You heard from Helms? I've tried to call Byrns, but there wasn't an answer."

After the last call I had with Mason, I didn't even have time to tell him about TJ. When I tried to get ahold of him after I spoke with Ren, his phone was off. In fact, everyone's phones are off now.

"Helms told me they were going dark, so I expected this. Are you sure Ren said what he did? Maybe he meant something else?" Hawk asks, rubbing a hand over his forehead.

"Maybe..." I sigh.

"Don't fucking patronize me, Drake," he growls. "I'm going to enjoy my night, spend a little of Helms's money, take Willow for a spin. Maybe I can get another statue to drop at the Kings for when they get back."

I shake my head as he walks away. I'm not sure whether he's going to take Willow for a ride on his bike or something else, and I'd rather not know. Ember's hips sway as she makes her way to me. I lean against the wall to track her progress, wondering what game she's playing now. She flashes me a mischievous smile and my cock hardens. Her eyes flick down, probably noticing the effect she has on me. When she passes a vacant table, her fingers trail across it.

One second she's sauntering toward me and the next she's making a hard left, ending up at the bar. Tipping my head back, I let out a chuckle. Fucking woman, provoking me. The last few days I've been riling her up, waiting until tonight to strike. I can wait a little longer, but I'm ending the night deep inside her pussy.

Twenty-Four

Ember

The bartender is flirting with me. I've been trying to pay attention to her quips, but I can feel Roman's eyes on me. It's making it difficult to concentrate on anything other than him and the desire he's stirring within me. I thought I could play his game—beat him at it—instead, I'm left clenching my thighs together and hoping the wetness between them doesn't run down my legs. I'm finding it probably wasn't the best idea to go commando. It was another ploy I intended to wield tonight. All my carefully laid plans are disappearing faster than the drink I'm downing.

"Whiskey on the rocks." Roman's voice flows over me, easing the tension I didn't realize was locked in my muscles.

He sets his glass down, leans on the bar, and smiles at the woman. I don't have the heart to tell him she won't be interested in his flirtations. I duck to hide my grin, but not before I catch her eye, and she shakes her head as she focuses on his drink.

She finishes, placing the glass in front of him, and gives him a sultry smile, pressing her arms together to accentuate her cleavage. He runs his tongue over his teeth, then pulls his lip between them. I bite my cheek to keep the giggle at bay. Whoever this woman is, she's my new favorite person.

Just as he opens his mouth, probably to say something utterly ridiculous, thinking he's getting under my skin, she rolls her head toward me. Her tongue darts out, wetting her bottom lip.

"Isn't it amazing how docile they become when they think they're going to get their dick wet?" she murmurs.

I tip my head back, finally releasing the laugh from the prison of my throat. Tilting my head toward Roman, I find him scowling.

"Actually, I'm surprised this one fell for it. He's usually better at this type of thing," I say, challenging him.

I count down from ten, waiting for the moment he puts his foot in his mouth.

"I'm excellent at 'this type of thing,' as you know, Ms. Hayes, among other endeavors. Should we give her an example?"

He finally turns to me, then picks up his glass and downs the contents. How he's able to do it without wincing is lost on me. His throat bobs, and a flush spreads up his skin. I don't know if he's embarrassed or if the alcohol is taking its toll on him. I snort, hiding my smirk behind my hand. No way Roman Drake is embarrassed. He's never been flustered in his entire life, as far as I know.

"There's a club downtown that can accommodate those types of kinks," the bartender says, and confusion clouds his face. "If you need an audience to get it up."

He scowls, then grabs my hand. I grin at her as he pulls me away and she winks. We pass by the double doors to the silent auction, and I tug to get him to stop. Hawk and Willow hover over a statue of some kind. I swear it's a duck with a squirrel riding its back. Before I can get a good look, Roman drags me past and through another door.

Cool spring air brushes my flushed skin, and my eyes fall closed. He drops my hand, leaning against the railing to gaze out at the distant lights of Synd. Stepping next to him, I run my palms along the cold metal, scanning the forest surrounding the property. It's as if the building was dropped into an oasis, the trees standing guard against the encroaching city. One last bastion of nature holding on by a tendril as the industrial world creeps its way ever closer.

The door behind us snaps closed, and I whip my head around. Couples wander past, none the wiser of our presence. Faint music filters through the glass—a waltz I can't quite place. Dancing couples move in time to the rhythm, matching my heartbeats. Turning away, I press my lips together, and my eyes flutter closed again.

Roman's warmth presses into my back, wrapping around me like a safety net. It's a dangerous feeling, a dangerous path, a dangerous existence to live in. His hands land on either side of me, his body pinning me against the railing. He dips his head, nuzzling my neck, and I tilt my head, revealing more skin to him.

The strap on my dress slips down my arm, and his teeth graze my exposed shoulder. I should stop this before it goes too far. I've held myself in check for the past three days, telling myself it was better this way.

My body doesn't agree as fire erupts in my stomach and wetness gathers between my legs. Every time I promise myself I'll stop, I find myself right back in his arms. It feels too right to be wrong.

When his hand glides along my thigh, gathering the fabric, I shudder. His questing fingers brush along my skin, and I bite my lip, keeping the moan inside. I'll deny him the satisfaction of knowing how much he affects me until I either muster up the courage to walk away or I'm too far gone to care.

"No cutting words?" he murmurs before nibbling on my lobe.

"Fuck you," I breathe as his fingers skate to my inner thigh.

Soon he'll find out I'm not wearing any panties, bare to him and whoever happens to walk across the lawn below us. At the thought, my eyes fly open, and I tense. He grips my thigh, fingers digging into my flesh.

"Don't run away now. We're just getting started."

"We're a little exposed out here," I say, leaning forward to check for security guards making rounds.

"That's part of the fun. Anyone could walk by. Someone could need some fresh air and suddenly they have dinner and a show."

Turning my face toward him, the scolding I intended is lost as his lips crash into mine. In the same moment, his finger dips between my legs and he groans into my mouth. My legs turn to jelly as he flicks his thumb across my clit, then slides lower. I lose the battle raging inside and give myself over to the desire, letting the flames consume me.

My knees buckle when he pushes two fingers deep into my pussy. His other arm snaps around my waist, holding me upright. Tipping my head back, his lips trail down my neck as he works me into a frenzy. My hips move in time with his thrusts, and I swear he's going to make me come in record time. A cry escapes me when he pulls them out, leaving me cold and breathless, my orgasm dancing just out of reach.

"Turn around," he commands, stepping away from me, and my dress flutters back into place.

When I spin, I'm ready to rip him a new one, but he's already fisting his cock, pants around his hips. I want to ask how he got undressed so quickly. Instead, I cough, my mouth suddenly dry. His hooded gaze meets mine, the corner of his mouth tipping up. His eyes travel the length of my body, leaving licks of fire in his wake. I grip the fabric of my dress, squeezing my hands into fists.

"Higher," he grunts, and I glance down.

The silky material swishes as I inch it up, revealing my ankles, then my calves. His nostrils flare, and he glares at me. Teasing him before didn't work well in my favor. Now, he's practically chomping at the bit, and all it took was a flash of skin. I bite my lip to hold the grin back, but he growls, and I realize I wasn't trying very hard.

He steps closer to me, and the railing digs into my lower back. Yanking my dress up, he exposes me to his hungry eyes.

"Tell me, Ember. Did you not wear any panties to drive me mad? Or were you planning on fucking me tonight?" He trails his hand along my inner thigh, making me quiver.

"Bold of you to assume it had anything to do with you," I whisper, the tremble in my voice still coming through. If his smirk is any indication, he hears it, too.

"Hold your dress. And for fuck's sake, do not fucking scream," he growls.

His hands wrap around my waist, and my feet leave solid ground. A cry leaves me, but I clamp my lips together to cut it off. My ass balances precariously on the railing and a wave of vertigo washes over me. Latching my arms around his neck, I bury my face into his shoulder, a chuckle rumbling through him.

"You think I'm going to let you fall, love?"

"This is not sexy, Drake. Put me down," I gasp.

Whatever other demands I want to make flee as he grips his cock, rubbing it against my clit. His other arm holds me around my lower back, but that doesn't seem like enough to catch me if I tip backward. My mind is torn between pleasure every time his cock circles my clit and remembering the three-story drop right behind me. This is either going to be incredibly thrilling or ridiculously unsafe.

"I'm going to fuck you just like this. Dress wrapped around your waist, pussy clinging to my cock, fear of the fall feeding your pleasure."

"Roman," I groan, half desire and half exasperation lacing my tone.

He thrusts into me, and I whimper. My ass shifts back, and I cling to him, eyes flying open. He doesn't give me any time to adjust, slamming into me while I hold on for the ride. After all his teasing, I'm already cascading over the edge. His lips brush my ear, whispering encouragement while I shudder around him.

"Roman," I gasp. "Please."

I don't even know what I'm asking for. I don't want him to stop, but my breath has stalled in my lungs. A break, that's all I need. He slows, but I make the mistake of lifting my head. The glass doors do nothing to hide what we're doing. I was so concerned with the possibility of tumbling to my death I forgot we might be putting on a show for a bunch of rich dicks.

"The doors," I mumble.

"Let them watch you tumble into oblivion again. Let them see how much you crave my cock."

His words send another shimmer of pleasure through me, and I pant as I watch couples laughing and drinking, mere feet from where we are. Roman's fingers slide down, digging into my ass as he pounds into me harder. Raking my nails along his back, he grunts with each thrust. Another orgasm floats through my body, and I spasm around him once, twice.

"Legs around me, love."

I obey almost immediately, locking my ankles as I wonder when I started taking orders from him. He dips his head, latching onto my nipple, and I shudder. I didn't even notice my dress slipped so low, not that I'm complaining. His teeth graze the sensitive bud.

"Be a good little whore and come again for me," he growls against my skin.

He slams his mouth on mine, devouring the scream that leaves me and I shatter around him. He groans, long and low, ripping his mouth from mine as he tips his head back. Stars dance in my vision, my body going limp. A weightlessness overtakes me as he holds me while I quiver in his grasp.

It doesn't escape me that no matter how much I fight it, I run straight back to him. Resisting him is a lesson in futility, at least according to my pussy. She's a greedy bitch, constantly at war with my mind.

He slides out of me, and the remnants of our actions coat my thighs. This is why I usually wear underwear. I snort as he sets me back on my feet. I never do shit like this—fucking someone on a balcony. The idea that I use my panties to clean myself up after is ridiculous.

"Something funny?" he asks as he tucks his cock back into his pants.

"No," I whisper, still holding my dress around my hips.

He produces a handkerchief from fuck knows where, flourishing it out to me.

"I'd clean you up myself, but I think we're pushing it in the privacy department," he mutters, gaze fixed over his shoulder.

"How exactly would you doing this be any different than me?" I swipe at the wetness, sighing. There's no way this tiny bit of cloth will take care of the mess.

"Oh, Ember." He chuckles, ducking his head until his lips brush my ear. "Remember, I'd be cleaning you with my mouth."

I jolt as his phone blares through the silence and his hand wraps around my arm, steadying me. When he's sure I won't tumble to my death, he steps away. Keeping one eye on him while he retreats to the corner of the balcony, I finish wiping away the evidence. I really don't want to stuff a cloth wet with his cum into my clutch, but I might not have a choice. Roman's angry whispers float to me, and I narrow my eyes. He curses, then hangs up before stalking back to me.

"Are you done?" Steel laces his tone.

"Sure. Anything else we needed to do here?"

He doesn't bother to answer, opting to text someone instead. Lifting onto my toes, I try to peek at his screen, but he angles it away from me.

"What's going on?" I ask, tilting my head.

He still doesn't answer, and he paces away. Regret and rage and shame war within me, each clamoring for dominance. I don't know why I expected anything different from him. His pretty words aren't enough to cover his actions. I'm a quick fuck on a balcony, an annoyance who might be useful, so better keep her around. I'm convenient and familiar, an almost from the past he finally has the opportunity to conquer.

It hits me then that he's never promised me anything. I read between the lines, hoping he'd want the same things I do, all the while knowing he doesn't. I knew going in that he would never falter, never give me more. He made himself clear and I fucked up. The walls around my heart crumbled just enough for the possibility of an us to slip through and now I'm paying the price. Being pissed at him for my own mistakes won't mend the brokenness within me.

As I drop my dress, the cold finally seeps into my body, the last remains of desire shattering from me, pieces drifting away with the rustle of the wind. I spin around to gaze at the forest, the lights, anything to keep my eyes from Roman. I'm not scanning the lawn for threats this time, and I sigh.

"Ready?" he asks.

"Why am I here, Roman?" I wrap my hands around the railing.

"Several high-powered people here. Thought you'd be able to gather some intel."

"Liar," I breathe. "Why are you keeping me so close?"

He sighs, dropping his head. "I'd rather you not take the kill that's meant for me."

"If you were worried about that, you'd have gone to Rima with the others."

He sighs again, as if he can't pull enough air into his lungs. As if the lies are tiny cotton balls, slowly stuffing themselves into his throat. Eventually they'll dissolve like cotton candy, and he'll snap. It's just a matter of time, but I've never had a lot of patience. Waiting for him to admit I'm here because he loves the control isn't easy. All these years later, he hasn't changed in that regard. With his life spiraling out of control, he's merely seizing whatever is left—namely me.

"Let it go, Ember," he mutters, leaning his forearms on the railing.

The handle is cold in my grasp, numbness spreading up my arm and seeping into my veins.

"I'm leaving tonight," I say.

He snorts, feet shuffling against the concrete. "I'd like to see you try."

"Synd isn't working out. I'm leaving, Drake."

"Don't," he whispers, stepping close to me.

"Then give me a reason."

No matter what he says, I have to go. Coming here was a mistake. I don't regret it, but I've been here long enough. Too long maybe. If I don't get out now, I never will. Roman will suck me in and I'll end up following him around like the last guest at a party no one wants to kick out.

"Because I can't watch you walk away again."

I spin, crossing my arms to keep myself from reaching for him. His stony expression shows me nothing, but anguish drips from his eyes.

"I didn't walk away before. You did. You were the one who refused to listen. You were the one who said I was obsessed, overcome with grief. You were the one who didn't care. Even if I had walked away, you wouldn't have noticed."

"I did. When you disappeared, I noticed. Every moment, every city, every move you've made over the past ten years, I've tracked."

I scoff, waving his words away. "You told me you barely kept tabs on me when we spoke a couple years ago."

"I lied," he growls, crowding into me. "No matter where you've been, I've known. You crawled into my veins, wrapping your essence around me. The farther you've run, the tighter those tendrils have become, squeezing out everything except you."

He rests his forehead against mine and I breathe him in, basking in the peace I find within this sliver of time.

"It doesn't matter." I swallow hard, digging my fingers into my arms. "It doesn't change anything."

He pulls in a deep breath, then spins, prowling back to the railing. My heart cracks, but I have to stay strong. Roman and I don't have a future. We never did. Maybe before Aelia vanished we had a chance, but we're too at odds. Our goals don't match. Plus, we'd be at each other's throats every other day. It would never work.

Still, a small voice in me cries out for him. I smother her underneath the pain and heartache.

"I'm sorry," I whisper, then slip through the doors.

He doesn't turn around.

Twenty-Five

Roman

All the things I should do run on a loop through my head. I should go after Ember. I should stop her from leaving. I should give up chasing after her. Because that's what I've been doing—chasing after her. Whether or not I've been lying to myself doesn't matter in the end. Either way, she's leaving, and I desperately want her to stay.

As soon as I admit it, even if it's only in my mind, it's as if a weight is lifted from my shoulders, easing the tension, and I can finally take a full breath. I didn't realize how much I was avoiding my own thoughts. Our relationship goes beyond fucking each other to relieve the stress of our lives.

Sighing, I scan the city beyond the dark trees. Gripping the cold railing, I drop my head, staring at my feet. Minutes ago, I had her balanced right here. The only time I've felt centered is when my cock is deep insider her. Giving that up—giving her up—will be the hardest thing I've done since Aelia was killed.

All my missteps pile up, stacked upon one another until they've formed a wall between me and the outside world. I have enough to occupy my mind, to distract myself from having my heart torn from my chest. When the others come back and I leave Synd, though, I'll flounder. A clean cut is the only way I'll survive.

"Roman Drake?" The man's low voice is almost lost in the gust of wind, and I pivot.

He hides in the shadows, next to a decorative tree. His silhouette shifts, separating from the darkness.

"Can I help you?" I straighten my cuffs, then casually tuck my hands in my pockets.

Usually I'd be more wary of someone cornering me on a balcony at night with only the stars as witness. At a function like this, only a fool would try to do something like shoot me. He could try to stab me, I suppose. Again, I'm not worried. I may not be as skilled as Ember, but I have been trained. My father made sure I knew what the hell I was doing. I wonder why if he always intended on killing me in the end. I suppose I couldn't have dismantled Synd and done his dirty work if I was dead.

"Confirmation was all I needed," he sneers.

The moonlight catches his face, hidden within a hood I didn't notice until he steps toward me. The edge of a grin peeks out, and I tense. Perhaps I should be more concerned. A flash of light scatters between us from the barrel of a gun he flourishes from under his jacket. Rocking back on my heels, I wait for him to make his move.

"You realize this is a suicide mission, right? We're in the middle of a gala and your gun doesn't have a silencer. You won't get past the dining room before someone accosts you. Sure, you might hit me, but killing me? That will take skill—skill I don't believe you possess."

"That won't be your concern."

I let out a sharp laugh, shaking my head. "Sir, you are severely mistaken if you believe I won't be coming after you once I've picked myself up off the floor. Then I will retaliate."

He chuckles, gun wavering. "They said you were scary. Said it'd be hard to kill you. Turns out this won't be so bad after all. Then I'll go after that little woman of yours. Maybe we'll have some fun before I kill her."

I smirk, knowing he won't get anywhere near Ember. She'll eviscerate him long before he lays a finger on her. I won't allow him to go after her, though.

"If you choose to go after her, I will hunt down your associates, your friends, your family, and I will end every single one of them until I get to you. Then I'll repay the favor. Slowly."

He scoffs, shaking his head. I probably don't need to threaten him. In fact, I rarely do in these situations, and I've been in them more than a couple of times. This feels different, though. If I can get him to tell me who he works for, I might actually get to the bottom of all our problems. Ember will be safe to leave. And I won't have to be constantly looking over my shoulder.

"You going to tell me who 'they' are? Or should I guess?" I ask, tilting my head.

"Any last words?" He shuffles in front of the doors.

A couple walks past, mere feet from the man with the gun. I failed to mention to Ember that it is one-way glass. No one would have been able to see her when she orgasmed unless they came out here. With the temperature falling at night, I took the risk.

"Might as well get on with it," I murmur.

The gun wavers in his hand before he drops it to his side, and I arch an eyebrow. He smirks a split second before he rushes me. My back slams against the railing as his shoulder rams into my gut, expelling the air from my lungs.

I wrap one hand around the railing and the other squeezes the back of his neck. For a skinny guy, he has a strength I didn't anticipate. He digs in, then heaves upward, trying to throw me over the side.

I grunt, my center of gravity tipping me farther toward open space. It was one thing to set Ember on the railing and fuck her, using the thrill to override her other senses. This is nothing like that.

I wish Ember was here.

The thought flashes through my mind without warning. Shaking my head, I renew my efforts to dislodge the would-be assassin. My feet leave the ground, toes scuffling against the concrete. Soon, it'll be too late.

Suddenly, his weight leaves me, and I suck in a breath. He hits me again, and I flip over the railing. Latching onto metal, I hang over the side, resisting the urge to kick my feet. I reach with my other hand, but my fingers keep slipping.

Seconds later, a body sails over my head, and I track it as he lands on the lawn two stories below. Ember appears over the side, a sardonic smile plastered on her face. Her eyebrow pops up just as my fingers begin to slip.

"Little help?" I wheeze.

"Didn't I do enough?" She cocks her head, tongue darting out.

Red strands frame her face, clearly coming undone from the elaborate updo. My breath catches at the sight, until I realize how much I'm trembling. Swinging my other hand up again, my fingers slip off the metal. I grunt, piercing her with a glare.

"Ember," I growl in warning.

"I should make you beg, but I'm pretty sure we'd be here all night before you got it right."

She wraps her fingers around my wrist, then reaches with her other hand for mine. There's not much I can do other than try not to be completely dead weight while she struggles to pull me up. After several tense moments, I collapse on the balcony as Ember pants next to me.

Staring at the stars marching across the sky, I wonder how much longer I'll last. This world doesn't lend much time to those of us who live the lives we do. Eventually, our luck runs out.

When the warehouse blew up, I thought it was over. When I was stuck in the Byrns's dungeon, I resigned myself to my fate. When my father shot me, I just wanted it to end. I thought I was tired then. It's nothing compared to now.

Ember's fingers brush mine, and I grip them tight, as if they're my only lifeline back from whatever hellhole this is. She's not dragging me back into the light, since we don't operate there. No, only the shadows hold any salvation for people like us. If anyone can pull me into them once more, it's her. She's the only one I'd even let try.

"Who do you think is trying to kill you?" I whisper, unwilling to break the connection between us.

It's more than just our linked fingers. It's being in this space, a solid moment of peace. Maybe it's the shared experience of killing someone. Whatever it is, I don't want to lose it. In this bubble of safety, I don't want to leave Synd. I can admit leaving would break me.

But Aelia is still out there, probably waiting for someone to remember her—to save her. Giving up isn't an option. Roman may hold his sister in his heart, letting her death drive whatever fucked-up motives he's had for years. Since I'm the only one who thinks she's alive, then it's safe to assume I'm it—the last miracle she has.

"Still not convinced they're after me," he murmurs.

"A man tried to shove you off a balcony. If that's not all the evidence you need, then we have bigger problems."

He snorts, squeezing my hand. "Thought you were leaving."

"You're my ride," I remind him.

Could I have called a car? Yes. I totally could have. Walking anywhere to find a taxi wasn't an option, and they don't exactly hang around these fancy events. Everyone has a driver anyway. Willow slipped me her number, but there's no way I'm getting on the back of a bike. Plus, all my things are still at the Byrns estate.

"Admit it, Em."

I turn my head toward him, and our eyes clash as a breeze gusts over me, making me shiver. Or maybe it's the light circles he's drawing on my wrist. Either way, I'm going to ignore it.

"What exactly am I admitting to?"

"You don't want to leave. Especially since you're not completely convinced I'm the only one with someone after me."

I scoff, gazing back at the stars. At least he's conceding that he's in danger. My mind drifts back to the men who cornered me in the alley. I brushed them off as annoyances, an attempted mugging gone wrong. If I'm completely honest with myself, though, I knew someone sent them. Most likely, the men from Harris followed me. How, I don't know, but I intend to find out. If they're searching for me, trying to kill me, then no matter where I run, they'll find me. It's not sustainable. I'll have to deal with them and here is as good a place as any.

"Harris was...not the best experience," I murmur.

"So I gathered. You finally going to tell me the specifics? Or are you going to force me to dig?"

"Bold of you to assume I left a trail."

He lets out a chuckle. "Told you, Em. I've kept tabs on you."

I roll my eyes, tugging my hand from his grasp, but he grips me tighter. He won't just let me go. He's always pulling me back into his orbit, refusing to let me go about my business. Roman may think he's been sneaky, enlisting a mishmash of people to follow me around, but I knew. Of course I fucking knew. He's not half as cunning as he thinks he is.

"Nemesis might be the most experienced hacker I've ever met, but that doesn't mean she's the only one," I murmur.

"I never used Nemesis."

"Which means you weren't using the best." I glance at him as he rolls his eyes. "You really walked into that one."

"We should go. I need to call a cleanup before someone starts screaming about a dead body at a fancy party." He releases me from his hold as he pushes himself up, groaning.

I wince as I sit upright, pressing against my side. When I pull my hand away, blood coats my palm. I glance at Roman, hoping he didn't see, but he's leaning over the railing. A giggle bursts out of me when I imagine pushing him over. I wouldn't, yet I can't get the image of him flailing as he falls, shock splashed across his face.

Pushing to my feet, I use my arm to put pressure on the wound. The last thing I'm going to do is admit to Roman I fucked up. He'll bluster about, making a big deal out of a small cut. Then I'll have to deal with his hovering. Except I have no idea if that's what he'll do. The last time I was injured, he walked away. He left me in an alley, knowing I was hurt. I was nothing more than a hindrance to whatever he had planned that night. I can't blame him, but it still stings. Going back to the

Byrns house is out too. With Moss there, he'll take advantage of my vulnerability and finish the job.

"How about you deal with that, and I'll call the Reapers? I'm sure Hawk will want to weigh in on whatever this is." I wave my hand to encompass all the shit we're dealing with.

He nods absentmindedly, already engrossed in his phone. Stepping through the balcony doors, I stumble, but right myself before I face-plant. I smirk at the woman dripping in diamonds feet from me. She lifts her chin and sniffs. As she flounces away, I flip her the bird. I didn't think people actually snubbed others like that anymore. It's been so long since I've had to suffer through one of these things, I forgot how stuck-up people could be. It's part of the reason I refused to attend them if Aelia wasn't going to be there.

I find an alcove, thankfully devoid of others, and pull out my phone. It rings out, Hawk's voice filling the line to tell me to leave a message. Huffing, I call Willow, half hoping she doesn't pick up either. The longer I stand here, the more likely it is I'll pass out. At least my dress is dark enough to hide most of the blood seeping from my side.

"Ember? Are you okay?" Willow's frazzled voice crackles as she cuts in and out.

"Fine. Drake's seen better days. Someone tried to push him off the balcony. Thought you guys would like to know." I grit my teeth as a wave of pain floods me.

Closing my eyes, I pull in a slow, deep breath, urging the nausea away.

"You don't sound fine. We're heading back."

"Don't bother. I won't be here, anyway. Drake's calling a cleanup, but maybe try to get him to move to the Kings' house. Probably won't do much, but it might confuse some of the people after him." I peek around the corner, tracking Roman's figure as he paces toward the dining room, obviously searching for me.

"Too late. We're already out front. Do I need to come in and drag you out, or are you capable of walking on your own?" An edge laces her tone now.

If I knew the building better, I could probably slip out the back way, but someone would catch up to me sooner or later. Especially with my time being lucid steadily counting down. I'd rather pass out when I'm with them than in some random alley.

"Fine, but don't tell Drake. He's got enough to deal with."

I peek around the corner, but Roman is nowhere in sight. There aren't many places he could go other than the dining room. I'd have noticed if he walked past me, since the crowd has diminished now. Most of them are milling in the next room, perusing the items for the silent auction. I wish I could be in there, my only mission being to find the most ludicrous piece and bid on it. I'd gift wrap it, then drop it on Roman's doorstep.

"I'll be there in a couple minutes," I whisper before hanging up.

Stumbling from the alcove, I straighten my spine and walk toward the front. The massive doors appear, several workers milling around them and two of them pull the heavy wood open.

I breathe a sigh of relief when I step outside, glancing back once more. Still, there's no sight of Roman. I don't know why I expected him to chase after me. He probably hasn't even noticed I'm gone.

The wind has picked up, whipping through the air. Thankfully, I spot Willow waving frantically from the shadows. Gripping the metal, I ease down the stairs, forcing myself to stand upright. A wave of dizziness floods my head as I reach the bottom and I pull in another deep breath. Apparently, the stab wound is more than a scratch.

"Ember?" Willow's concerned voice floats along the wind, seeping into my thoughts gradually.

I totter to her, my feet lead as I drag them along. Willow's blonde hair wavers when she glances over her shoulder. Hawk appears from out of thin air and a giggle escapes. He bounds toward me, barely catching me before I crumple on the ground.

"Shit. Willow, call Drake," he barks, his voice piercing the fog swirling in my mind.

"Don't. Body." I cough, and wetness coats my chin.

Swiping the back of my hand over my mouth, it comes away red. The crimson shimmers in the moonlight. Or maybe that's the streetlamp. My head muddles, my body floating with the breeze. I'll lose consciousness soon. I can feel the dark beast of nothingness seeping along the edges of my mind, beckoning me into its embrace. Letting go would be blissful, easy, comforting. I fight its allure, struggling to speak.

"No hospital," I wheeze.

"Ember, just stay awake," Willow says, then mumbles something to Hawk I don't understand.

Heat envelops me, seeping into my body. I didn't realize how cold I was until I'm put in the backseat of the car. My eyes fly open, and I gasp, pain engulfing me. Whatever the bastard did, it's more than just a scratch. I might have fucked up by not telling Roman. He's going to be pissed when he finds out.

"Ember, stay with me. Hawk, hurry the fuck up," Willow says, her words blending together.

"Call Drake. We're taking her to Ink, but he's going to be pissed," Hawk replies, tires screeching, and my body tips to the side.

Willow hauls my body back onto the seat, and I groan. The wound burns when she leans on it, muttering something about pressure. I arch my back, trying to get away from the pain, but it's everywhere, stealing through my body and erasing every other thought. Willow curses, but I can't help it.

"Sorry," I gasp when the surge of strength drains away.

"Don't be sorry, just stay awake. I don't fancy dragging your unconscious body around. I've done that once and it wasn't pleasant. Who stabbed you?"

"Don't know. He's dead."

"Small miracles," Hawk chimes in.

"Don't call Drake," I moan, clutching my side.

Willow has a phone pressed to her ear. I have the irrational urge to knock it from her grasp and toss it out the window. My lungs seize, just imagining what he's saying, as her nose scrunches up.

Willow huffs, her annoyance stamped across her face. "Well, I hate to tell you this, but no."

"What the fuck to you mean no?" a man yells on the other end.

"Calm your tits or I'm hanging up. We're almost there, Ink." Pause. "She said no hospitals." Pause. "Stop yelling at me. I'm not the one who stabbed her."

"He's yelling at you?" Hawk barks out, his hand grappling toward us. "Give me the phone, Willow."

"Keep your eyes on the road," she growls, and I let out another groan.

The last thing I need is for everyone to be bickering because of me. I should have left when I told Roman I was. He'd be dead then, but at least I wouldn't have to listen to their bullshit.

A choked sob leaps unbidden from my lips, and I slap my hand over my mouth to keep the rest in. Willow's wide eyes dart to mine. I shake my head, hoping she doesn't think I'm about to lose it. I am, but I'd rather not do it in front of a bunch of people I barely know.

"Just get shit ready. We're two minutes out," Willow snarls, then cuts off his yelling by hanging up on him.

"He's pissed," I wheeze.

"He'll get over it. Ink isn't a bad guy, just hates we keep getting hurt. Another minute and we'll get you stitched up. Just stay with me."

Her reassuring words echo through my mind as the darkness crashes over me, pulling me into its depths.

Twenty-Seven

Roman

"I'm well aware of how much I've called you. Not much I can do about it unless you'd rather be cleaning up my body instead," I snarl at Jax, Byrns's cleanup guy.

I don't understand why he's so pissed, since he's making hand over fist lately with how many bodies he's had to get rid of. I'd call someone else, but we're still on the east side of the river. He's all I have.

"If you'd like me to call someone else, by all means, text me their number," I growl, hanging up before he can keep bitching.

The last bit of energy I have drains from my limbs and I drop my hand to my side, pressing to where the bullet grazed me. Ember didn't seem to notice I was hurt, and no one started screaming when he shot me, so I could get away with no one knowing. Hell, I didn't even realize the gun went off until I was lying next to Ember.

Blood smears across my skin as I hold it up to the moonlight and I wince. Maybe it's more than a graze, but I'm still standing. I just need to rest and then I can go home.

I slide down the glass separating me from the other guests. I fix my eyes on the dark smear on the railing where I almost died. If Ember wouldn't have shown up when she did, I'd be the body lying in the grass three stories below. I never thought I'd owe Ember Hayes anything, yet here I am. She may not understand a life debt, but in my world, it's serious. Not that it means much more when it comes to her. I'd protect her with my life either way.

Shaking my head at the thought, I plant my hand on the stone to push myself up. My palm comes away wet, and I grit my teeth. I hate having sticky hands and there's no telling what the hell I just got all over me. Stumbling to my feet, I wipe it off on my pants, pressing my other hand more firmly to my wound.

When I glance down at the spot, horror floods my senses. It's the exact spot Ember was lying after she pulled me back from the edge of death. Which means the entire time we were talking, when she stumbled out the door, when she disappeared to fuck knows where, she was bleeding. She was hurt and didn't say a goddamn word. Of course she didn't. Why would she? She's always been stubborn, refusing any help, especially from me.

I grab my phone to call her, but my heart drops. I don't have her number anymore and the card she slipped me is sitting on my nightstand. Refusing to put it in my wallet was a small act of defiance—a ridiculous one—to prove she meant nothing to me. I pull up Hawk's name instead. Ember gave him one too, so hopefully he has a way to contact her.

"Drake?" Hawk asks, exhaustion lining his tone.

"I need to get ahold of Ember. Do you still have the card she gave you?" I say, not bothering with pleasantries.

Pain pulses through my side, and I wince. Swallowing hard, I concentrate on his breathing.

"Uh, yeah, I have her number."

"Send it to me," I growl, doubling over when a wave of nausea comes over me.

"Drake, are you okay? Why the hell don't you have her number?" Hawk's voice is a million miles away, ringing quietly through the night.

When I open my eyes again, I realize I'm squeezing my phone to within an inch of its life. Hawk is becoming more frazzled by the minute, demanding answers to questions I no longer remember.

"Hawk," I wheeze, crashing to my knees when my wound pulses again. "Find her. She's hurt."

"Are you still at the gala?" he asks, the pounding of his feet accentuating his words.

"I'm fine. Find Ember."

"We have her. She's here. Tell me where the fuck you are, Drake."

I drag in slow, steady breaths, willing away the pain. She's safe. She'll be fine. My mind swims, warping the world around me, and I close my eyes. The gunshot wasn't that bad. I barely felt it and I haven't bled all over the place—not like Ember. Getting my shit under control should be easy.

"I'm coming to the gala. Don't bleed all over the place. It's harder to explain that shit away."

Hawk hangs up, and I tumble back with a heavy sigh, leaning against the cool glass once more. I don't know how long I sit there, staring at the stars as they blink in and out of existence. That may be the blood loss, though.

The doors next to me burst open and I roll my head toward Hawk. He towers over me now, hands planted on his hips.

"What the fuck are you doing?" he spits out.

"Is she okay?" I ask, then clear my throat.

"She's fine. Well, not fine, but Ink seemed optimistic when I left. Get up. I'll take you to her."

I can't remember how my limbs work. Numbness freezes me in place, but I'm not sure if it's shock or the wind that's picked up in the last half hour. Hawk drops his chin to his chest, sighing heavily. He mumbles something I don't catch before he crouches in front of me.

"What the fuck are you doing, Drake." It's a statement more than a question.

I tilt my head, studying him as his words slowly seep through the fog that's taken up residence in my brain. Opening my mouth, I snap it shut again when I realize I have no idea how to answer him.

Ever since Ember waltzed back into my life, I've been unmoored—floundering around, unsure of who I am or where I'm going. It started before she came, though. Pinpointing the exact moment I no longer had a purpose is harder than I imagined. It could have been when my father was found alive and well. Or when the warehouse blew up around me, sending my plans up in smoke. Or when I came to Synd.

In reality, it was long ago, when I lost Aelia. All the dreams I had of stealing my sister away from this life died with her, along with my hope. I've been existing ever since. Until Ember sauntered back in, snarky attitude and sexy smirk in tow.

She's more of a distraction than anything, but it's one I needed. I'd never tell her, but I admire her tenacity—her single-minded drive to find the truth, no matter how many people tell her to give up.

It hits me that I'm jealous of her. We may not agree about Aelia's fate, but at least she doesn't give up. I gave up, accepting the words of others to convince me of my sister's death. If it turns out Ember is right, I'll never hear the end of it. And I'll drown in the newfound guilt that I gave up on Aelia. She'll want nothing to do with me, and rightfully so.

"Come on. I'll take you to Ember. Get you stitched up." Hawk slides his arm around my shoulders, then braces himself to force me to stand.

"I don't need stitches," I mumble, but my words are slurring.

"With the amount of blood you're losing, I'd say you do. But I'm no doctor, so how about we let Ink decide that?"

I finally get my feet under me, swaying as I blink rapidly to clear the black spots swimming in my vision. Hawk's grip on my arm is the only thing keeping me upright at this point. There's no way I'll be able to make it through the gala space without someone noting my condition. Hawk glances through the glass, probably coming to the same conclusion.

He ducks his head through the doorway, flagging down the bartender from earlier. Leaning against the glass, I force my body to relax, ignoring the pain pulsing through me with each heartbeat.

"Any way you could get us out without using the front door?" Hawk asks, giving her a grin.

She raises her eyebrow, then spots me, hopefully looking like I'm lounging instead of about to crumple to the ground. She scans me, eyes narrowing, then she lets out a soft "Oh," and scurries away.

Hawk fiddles with his phone, slipping it back in his pocket when she returns not even a minute later with a man in tow. His uniform is a bit wrinkled, but he pulls a suit coat on over the mess.

"It's Krysten, by the way. Not that you ever bothered to learn my name," the bartender whispers, wrapping her arm around my waist. "Hawk, you go ahead with Mark. We'll be right behind. Mark, play the part."

Mark flushes, then tentatively places his hand on Hawk's arm. Hawk has a gun resting under his chin before Mark can react.

"What the fuck, Mark. Pretend like you're making a deal, not feeling up the fucking VP of a motorcycle club. His woman will carve you up if she thinks you're trying to seduce him," Raven hisses, shaking her head.

Hawk tucks away his weapon, opening the glass doors and gesturing Mark through. Raven and I follow, and she mostly holds me up.

"Smile, asshole," she says through her teeth, her own grin in place.

She throws her head back, laughing as if I'm the funniest man in the world. Logically, I understand she's playing the part, but it doesn't make it any easier.

"I don't smile," I grunt, laying my arm over her shoulders as I stagger forward.

She steers us after Hawk and Mark toward a door off to the side. She mutters a curse, then ducks her head to my chest.

"What the fuck are you doing?" I mutter.

"Just get your ass to the door and we'll be good. Fast as you can, sailor."

"Did you just call me sailor?"

"Totally did. Let's not get caught up in the details. Mind the stairs."

I trip down the first one, groaning when pain radiates up my side. At the bottom is another set of doors, already open, a car waiting for us. Mark jumps forward, waving Hawk away before he can help me into the seat.

"I'm not sitting in the back. It's not that bad," I growl, dropping my arm from Krysten's shoulders.

Mark slams one shut before opening the passenger door, sweeping his hand out, and I give him a look. Krysten smacks him, glaring, and he flushes again.

"Thanks, Krysten," I mutter as I slide inside the warm interior.

Hawk passes me a wad of cash from the driver's seat. When I try to hand it to her, though, she scowls.

"I'm not taking your fucking money. I like the idea of you two owing me one instead," she says, smirking.

Mark slams the door shut before I can respond. Hawk is halfway around the building before I remember I'm still holding his money. I stuff it in the center console, my mind muddled.

"Put pressure on that. Blue is going to be pissed two people bled all over his car."

"She was bleeding?"

Hawk nods, and my head thumps back against the seat. Closing my eyes, I wonder what the hell I'm doing. I should tell Hawk to bring me back to Byrns's house. My phone buzzes and I jolt upright, fishing it from my pocket.

"Who is it?" Hawk asks.

"Moss, what do you want?" I snarl.

He's been toeing the line since I put his ass against the wall and threatened him. If I was truly in charge, he'd be long gone. I probably wouldn't have floated him, but I'd have him as far away from Ember as he could get.

With TJ in a coma, and very few people I can truly trust left, I can't afford to lose him. I've texted Mason, but he hasn't responded, which sets me more on edge. And also tells me that Moss has been spreading lies to the others. Sowing dissent within the ranks isn't much better than lying straight to my face.

"Sensors and alarms are going off all over the property. Haven't seen anyone yet, but we don't have enough men here to deal with it. You need to get back here."

I hang up, not willing to give in to his demands. I planned on moving shit to the King's house later, but I'm going to have to move up the timeline if Moss keeps this up. Especially if Ember stays with me like I hope. Having her in the same house as him—keeping her in my back pocket-—will only piss off both of us.

"Hawk, if I pass out, make sure Ember doesn't leave."

"Based on how she was when I came to get you, she's not going anywhere anytime soon."

"She won't care. She'll run, just like she always does," I mutter, closing my eyes again.

"Maybe this time she'll run toward you, instead of away," Hawk says as we pull into Reaper territory.

"Here's hoping."

Twenty-Eight

Ember

Ink might be their version of a doctor, but his bedside manner leaves something to be desired. Typical, but doesn't make it any easier to listen to his mutterings. I bite my tongue to keep my opinions to myself and grit my teeth against the pain. Maybe I should have gone to the hospital instead. At least they'd have pain meds that could knock me out.

"How much longer?" I ask, then yelp when the needle pierces me again.

"Whine a bit more. Maybe that'll make me go faster," Ink growls.

"You're a dick."

His dark eyes meet mine, brows pulled low. "You really want to call me names when I'm literally sewing you up? Thought Willow said you were smart."

"I'm incredibly smart. Sorry I don't have rainbows shooting out of my ass. I did get fucking stabbed."

"Well aware." He shoves the needle back into my flesh, and I wince.

"Are you sure you don't have morphine?"

I struggle to stay conscious. Willow disappeared as soon as Ink stomped in, phone pressed to her ear. Hawk barely made it out of the car before he was crawling back in and taking off into the night. They left me with a bunch of bikers milling about while I lie on a hard table in the middle of the Reaper's headquarters as Ink jabs me.

"We *have* morphine. You just aren't allowed any." He states it so matter-of-fact-ly, it takes a bit for my mind to process his words.

"What the fuck!" I struggle to sit up.

"You might have nicked something important. So, either you do this without morphine or I take you to the hospital for imaging."

He bares his teeth and I drop back, pursing my lips. This entire night has been a shitshow. I don't know what I expected, but it certainly wasn't to be put on display in a biker's club with an extra hole in my body.

The worst I imagined was falling asleep, extremely satiated, in Roman's bed. To be fair, that would have been the best outcome too. It doesn't matter either way, since Roman is probably still at the gala. Taking on everything he has to keep Synd running is enough. If he's right and someone *is* after me, then I'm putting more shit on him.

"Can I go now?" I watch as he ties off what I'm hoping is the last knot.

"If you move, your lungs will fill up. So, if you'd like to drown in your own blood, then by all means, I'll stop wasting my time."

"I thought you said he didn't hit any major organs."

"It might have nicked your lung. Unlikely, but again, hospital is still on the table. If you get worse or start hacking up blood, don't come back here. Hopefully, it'll work itself out, but don't go jumping off a bridge or something."

I raise an eyebrow. "Does that happen a lot?"

"Once or twice. Depends on how much the prospects piss Tank off," he says, grinning. "Alright, sit up."

"Thought I wasn't supposed to move," I grumble.

Ink wraps an arm around my shoulders, helping me, and the stitches pull, sending a different kind of pain radiating from my side. Soon my torso is swathed in crisp, white bandages. I tug down the shirt Willow gave me over them, wondering what the hell I'm going to do now.

The double doors behind us burst open and I twist around, yelping when it pulls at my wound. Ink growls at me as he passes. Hawk stumbles under the weight of keeping Roman on his feet. Roman sways, almost as if he's drunk. Unless he was hurt when he almost fell, I can't imagine what is wrong with him.

"What the hell happened now?" Ink grumbles, grabbing Roman's other arm.

Hawk strips off Roman's suit coat before they place him on the table next to me. Roman groans, the vein in his jaw pulsing with each heartbeat. Flecks of crimson bleed into the crisp white shirtsleeve. When Ink cuts the fabric from his body, the biker reveals a small hole with blood seeping from it. A wave of nausea washes over me, and I turn away.

"Shot was clean through. I don't think anything was hit, since he was bitching the whole way here," Hawk says as he presses a towel to the wound.

Taking advantage of their distraction, I slide from the table. I'm immediately lightheaded and use the chair to keep myself upright. Closing my eyes, I wait until the dizziness leaves before opening them again. No one notices when I start for the door.

An ache settles in my chest, pulsing with each step. I don't blame them. None of them really know who I am other than Roman, and he's currently being drugged. I doubt he even realizes I'm here, and with the amount of painkillers they're probably going to give him, he won't remember I was here in the first place.

"Ember," Roman groans, voice stuttering, and my heart skips a beat.

When I glance back, though, his eyes are closed, a grimace on his face. Ink wields a needle, probably full of the morphine he denied me. Hawk murmurs in Roman's ear and he relaxes. I stumble away, not wanting to witness Ink piercing his skin with anything.

Maybe I was mistaken and he wasn't even saying my name—calling for me in his time of distress. There are a million other words that sound like Ember. I can't think of any right now, but I'm sure they're out there.

Cool spring air slaps me in the face when I stumble over the threshold, clearing my muddled head. Pressing my hand to my wound, I wince and swallow hard. I shuffle into the shadows and lean against the wall to rest for a minute. Just a minute, then I'll disappear into the night. I already told Roman I was leaving Synd, so he shouldn't be surprised. Leaving a note when I gather my stuff from his house should be enough. He'll be pissed but eventually see it's best this way.

His accusation that people are after me has been rolling around my brain for two weeks. Admitting he might be right is physically painful, but if he is, then I'm only bringing more trouble to his life. Clearly, someone is attempting to kill him as well. He doesn't need me to pile on.

"I'm guessing you're not out here to catch your breath," Willow murmurs from the shadows, then leans next to me.

"Drake was shot." Saying the words out loud sends a bolt of terror through me, though I know he'll be fine.

"Hawk told me. He's going to be fine. You know that, right?"

I nod, gazing out at the sleeping neighborhood. From this view, here in the dark, no one would know it was biker territory. With everyone tucked away in their beds, matching houses marching down the street, it's a peaceful scene. Yet not even a dozen feet away, Ink is tending to a gunshot wound after dealing with my stabbing. From his demeanor, I'd say this type of thing happens more often than not.

Willow sighs, tipping her head against the wall. "You want to talk about what's going on?"

"Seems like someone is trying to kill me. And Drake. It's not entirely surprising." I'm trying to be blasé, but even I can hear the strain in my voice.

"Actually, I meant with you and Roman, but sure, we can talk about that too. I'm surprised you're willing to leave while danger is afoot," she murmurs.

"Danger is afoot? Have you been reading Sherlock Holmes or something?"

She giggles, a light tinkling sound that seems strangely out of place in a biker gang. She doesn't answer my question, opting for silence. I scramble for something to say, but I'm not used to this. Small talk isn't my strong suit anymore. I haven't had cause to use it in years. Add in the fact that I haven't talked to someone casually in almost a decade without some ulterior motive, and I'm floundering.

"So, you're just going to leave, then?" Willow turns toward me and crosses her arms over her chest.

"What's that supposed to mean?"

"Nothing. I'm just wondering when you're going to stop running and actually face whatever demons that are following you."

"You say that as if I have no purpose," I grumble, and she gives me a look. "I'm looking for my best friend."

Her face morphs, taking on a semblance of sympathy. I hate it—the forlorn looks, the sad half-smiles, and eventually, the sighs. I don't tell many people who Aelia is to me. Usually they assume she owes me money or I'm trying to kill her. I let them think whatever they want. They're not the type of people to put themselves in the line of fire to hide someone.

"How long have you been searching for her?"

"Does it matter?"

"No, it really doesn't. I imagine if it were me, I'd never stop. If Mac was missing, I'd move heaven and earth to find her. Not everyone understands that way of thinking," she says, leaning against the building.

"No, they don't," I whisper, ducking my head.

This is the most real conversation I've had in a while, other than with Roman. And since he's constantly at odds with me over the subject, it feels like I'm beating my head against the wall most of the time.

Maybe Willow does understand but asking her for help won't do anything. Not really. She'll sympathize and bolster my arguments and then...nothing. There's nothing she can do. I'll move on and she'll be here, living this life that seems peaceful on the outside, yet is volatile in nature. And I'll be alone once more. Her support might help in the present, but opening up any more won't amount to much when I'm in the next city.

"You shouldn't go to Rima," she says after a while.

"I don't really know what I plan to do yet."

"You sound surprised. I'm sure Roman told you not to go there." She levels me with a look.

"I was just expecting you to say something else."

She grins, and I can't help but smile back at her.

"You thought I was going to harp on you about staying here and how you're safer and all that nonsense, weren't you?"

"Something like that."

She shakes her head, gazing up at the stars. "Six months ago, I probably would have. Keeping to the status quo was how I stayed alive for a lot of years. And when I came here, I didn't want to be a burden, but I thought I needed someone to save me."

"What changed?"

I don't know Willow well, but she doesn't seem the type to let someone else step in and fight her battles for her. Looking back, I've caught glimpses of the person she's describing, though. How she transformed herself into the woman next to me in only a few months is beyond me.

I've lived so long with a single-minded focus, I don't even know who I would be if I gave it up. Maybe she's merely reverting to who she's meant to be. The thought sends a bolt of regret through me. I don't know who I am—who I'm meant to be. This is all I know, searching for someone who might be long gone from this world.

"I know a lot of people will tell you it was love and all that nonsense. I mean, Hawk gave me the space to figure out who I was, but it was more than that. Honestly, it wasn't until I met Sam that I figured out I could."

"Could what?"

"Do whatever the fuck I wanted," she says, laughing, then she sobers. "I killed my stepfather. I knew I had to be the one to do it, but I'm not exactly built for something like that. Or at the very least, I wasn't trained. Sam tried to help, giving me lessons, but I was...scared."

"And then?"

"And then when I asked Sam for a weapon, she didn't talk me out of it. She didn't tell me I should ask Hawk for help or try to go with me. I found out later she followed me, had someone she knows watching to make sure I didn't actually die, but she trusted I could kill him. No one ever told me I was capable of taking care of myself."

I huff, trying to figure out why I'm suddenly pissed, and then it hits me. I never had that. I never had anyone telling me I was capable of taking care of myself, of learning all the shit I have. Aelia would have supported me, but I wouldn't have had to learn how to kill someone seventeen ways to Sunday. I wouldn't have learned how to hack into someone's personal life and eviscerate them. I would have had a normal life, whatever that means.

Maybe Roman and I would have been something more than two people constantly at odds. Although, with his lifestyle, I probably still would have learned how to stab someone.

"Ember, I don't know what's really going on with you and Roman, but at some point, you need to face the truth."

I let out a short laugh, more of a snort than anything. "And what, oh wise one, is the truth?"

"Well, when it comes to Roman, you're completely fucked—figuratively and literally, I'm pretty sure. But maybe that isn't such a bad thing."

She gives me a small smile, her small hand landing on my arm and squeezing before she ducks inside. Roman's curses filter through the open door, then are abruptly cut off when it snaps shut. Glancing around the quiet street again, I wonder what the hell I'm going to do now.

Twenty-Nine

Roman

"Where is she?" I ask through gritted teeth.

Ink ignores my question as he stabs the needle into me again and again. When he mentioned he had plenty of morphine since Ember couldn't have any, I refused it as well. I'm starting to regret that now. He said she was bitching the entire time, no worse for wear, but now no one can tell me where she slipped off to.

"She's hanging around just outside the front doors, deciding whether she's going to take off or not," Willow says despite Hawk's attempts to shush her.

"And you decided to just let her?" I growl, attempting to roll off the table.

Hawk shoves his arm against my throat, and I choke, head slamming back onto the hard surface. I've been around long enough to see most of Hawk's moods, but this isn't one I've encountered before. He bares his teeth, pressing harder, and then slowly releases me.

"I've got enough problems without you running after her with a needle trailing behind you. Get your shit together first. Then you can decide whether you're worth it."

"What the fuck is that supposed to mean," I wheeze.

"You're fucked for that woman, but you're clearly not ready to admit it. So, get your shit together and then figure out if you're worth her time."

I bite my tongue, refusing to confirm or deny anything he's saying. Hawk may be living his perfect little life with his other half, but he knows nothing of what's going on between Ember and me.

Everyone around here seems to think they can stick their nose in everyone else's business. I've watched the consequences of that shit. I informed them all that loving their women made them weak. I stand by that statement. What I failed to tell them was it's also their greatest strength. They have something more to fight for than just their territories. Byrns learned the hard way what it's like to feel the wrath of complacency.

"Are you almost done?" I snap, not bothering to continue this conversation. It's none of his business, anyway.

"I'm quitting after this. You all fucking suck," Ink grumbles, throwing down a pair of tweezers.

He slaps on a bandage, taping both the front and back before gathering up his tools.

"I'll get a prospect to clean up the blood, Ink." Hawk turns hard eyes to me. "Say thank you, Drake."

I mumble my thanks, holding up my tattered shirt and scowling. I slide on my suit coat, then storm out the door, intent on confronting Ember. Halfway across the gravel parking lot, her laugh calls to me from behind.

Slowly I pivot, finding Ember shaking her head, eyes fixed on the stars. When they meet mine, though, the ache in my chest practically takes me to my knees. I stagger toward her, not entirely sure what I plan on doing, but if I don't touch her right now, make sure she's real, whole, I'm going to lose something vital.

She lifts an eyebrow, mouth twitching, but the mask drops when her eyes meet mine. Her brows pull low as her shoulders droop. My hands slap against the wall next to her head and I breathe her in. She doesn't look any worse for wear except for a tightness around her eyes.

She opens her mouth, then snaps it shut again as if she's not entirely sure what to say. The door next to us opens, but I don't pull my gaze from her. I don't know what I'm waiting for. I'm banking on recognizing it when it happens. Maybe it's a flash within her emerald-green eyes, or the tilt of her head. Anything to guide me on the right path.

Except we're not strolling on a nice, well-kept road. Ours is fraught with brambles and hidden passageways, designed to deceive us at every turn. I keep waiting for the shadows to clear or the moon to light our way, but it never comes. Maybe we're meant to weather the storm together. Or maybe we're supposed to be on different journeys, and we're fucking ourselves over by crossing paths.

"Drake, we've got a problem," Hawk says, and Ember blinks, breaking the connection between us.

"Unless something's on fire—"

"Funny that's your threshold, because the Depot is on fire."

"Where the fuck is Brewer? He'd better get his ass down here now if he wants to keep his head attached to his body," I growl into the phone.

Hawk yells something I can't hear, and I curse. The blaze may be confined to the warehouse, but that doesn't give the chief the right to withhold a firetruck—again. I don't know what Shane was thinking, allowing this excuse of a human being to run shit.

Apparently, they've been having issues with Brewer for months now. With everything else they've been dealing with, replacing him has been at the bottom of their list. I tried to get Hawk to choose someone, but he keeps telling me it isn't his place. It's probably not my place either. Shit is getting out of control now, though. It's only a matter of time before Brewer fucks up and fails to save some poor, innocent family's house, thinking it's one of ours.

"Hawk, I don't have time for this. It's going to get out of control if we don't have some help."

"Sorry, Drake, but you might have to deal with this one on your own."

The line cuts out and I pull my phone away and glance at the screen. It's completely black, won't even turn on, and I let out another curse.

"Problem?" Ember asks from her spot on a bench.

She posted up there after hemming and hawing about coming along. Now she's lounging on her back, pretending she's not about to pass out. I'm pretty sure I ripped my stitches already and I really wish I still had a shirt instead of just my suit coat. Ember keeps smirking every time it falls open, showing off my chest.

"You could get up and help, you know," I mutter, even though there's nothing she can do. In fact, she'd probably only muddle the situation more.

"No idea what you expect me to do. Find a fire extinguisher? Battle the flames myself? Perhaps you'd like me to organize a bucket brigade?"

"Yes. I would love for you to form a bucket brigade and put out the fire," I snap.

She pushes up, groaning as she does, and marches off to Moss, who showed up ten minutes ago. They have a heated conversation I should probably interrupt, but I'm too exhausted. Clearly, the head of security doesn't want to have anything to do with her. He waves her off several times before she produces a knife, snarling, and I'm forced to act. Before I can make it over there to diffuse the situation, though, he's nodding, then shaking his head. Ember smirks, then trots back over to her bench and plops down again.

"You know you should fire the fire marshal. Chief? Whatever the hell he is. He's quite bad at his job," she mumbles, closing her eyes.

"I'm well aware. I'm not exactly in the position to find a new one, though, am I?"

"Because of your temporary status in Synd?" She peeks at me from beneath her lashes. "Say, what do you plan to do after they all get back from their sojourn to Rima?"

"Do you even know what sojourn means?" I growl, mostly to steer the conversation to something other than my nonexistent future plans.

"Used it correctly, didn't I? Is that your way of deflecting because you have no fucking clue what you're going to do?"

"Perhaps I would rather not tell you. For all I know, you'd probably pop back up in the next city and harass me some more," I say, but there's no bite to my words.

We both know we're at a crossroads. With both paths shadowed and murky, it's not clear which will lead me to salvation. Aelia would tell me to follow my heart. She wouldn't understand my ability to love died with her. Even if I had anything left to give Ember, she'd never accept it, anyway.

"You really are the most insufferable asshat I know," she mutters.

"Glad I'm at the top of two of your lists."

"Which other list are you supposedly at the top of?"

"Best at making you come, love. Thought that was obvious."

She scoffs but can't hide the slight pull at the corner of her mouth. Sirens ring in the distance, finally, and I let out a sigh of relief. I scan the dozens of men milling about, some of them stealing glances at Ember. Moss has disappeared, and I run my fingers through my hair.

The stitches in my side scream and my shoulder feels like flames are licking along the muscles instead of inside the building. I need a shower and a nap, neither of which I'm getting any time soon.

Stomping toward the corner of the building, I spin back to Ember.

"Stay," I growl.

"Woof," she says sarcastically, eyes remaining closed.

It's darker on this side of the Depot, many of the lights absent so we don't have to worry about spies. Most people around here know the Byrns and Kings are mafia, but there's no reason to display it out in the open for all to see. I doubt

Moss wandered off on his own, but there's less chance he went into a burning building, especially since we evacuated it.

Skirting around the bushes, a flash of white catches my eye. I rush over, crashing to my knees when I recognize Moss's shirt. Quickly, I check his pulse, the tension leaving me when I find one. It's thready but there, and that's what counts. A scuffle of a shoe against concrete has me scanning the darkness, away from the clamor at the back of the Depot.

A rustling in the bushes beyond Moss has my head on a swivel, trying to spot who knocked him out. I grab his legs and pull him further onto the sidewalk, and spot crimson seeping into his shirt, staining the white fabric by his shoulder. His head lolls to the side, revealing a gash, and blood mats his hair. I probably just infected whatever wound he has, but it's better than leaving him to die.

A branch snaps at the same time as a bullet whizzes by my ear. Instinctively, I duck, covering Moss's body.

Another bullet lodges itself into the building, and I struggle to keep my head down while pulling my weapon from the holster on my back. The third bullet is what does me in, slamming into my shoulder and paralyzing my arm instantly. Ten seconds is all I have before the burning sensation sets in, sending heat rushing down my side.

My head becomes muddled as I sit up, swaying and struggling to stay conscious. I must be hallucinating, because there's no way Ember is crashing out of the trees and diving for Moss's body. She's hissing something, but my ears have stopped working. I blink rapidly as red overtakes my vision.

The fierceness on Ember's face is a sight to behold. I knew she'd been training, learning all she could in her quest to find Aelia. I've never seen her in action. Sure, I caught the aftermath of her tussle with the men in the alley, but to see her grabbing Moss's gun from his side, rolling onto her knees, and taking aim over his body.

One eye closes as she fires, the gun kicking back slightly, and I smile as I tilt to the side. Turning to me, her mouth forms a perfect O, one of her sleeves hanging off her shoulder. She reaches for me, but I land on top of Moss.

My hearing switches back on as she takes another shot, and the stars wink out of existence. Or maybe that's my vision turning off. Either way, unless Ember can get help, I think this might be it for me. I expected rage or vengeance to flood my system—keep me going—but peace steals over me instead.

Ember's face fills my vision, head floating within the blackness, and a rush of fear engulfs me.

"Drake, stop flailing. I have to move you," Ember snaps.

Her hands slide under my shoulders, hooking around my arms, and I'm floating. I have no idea if we're actually getting anywhere, but I kick my feet and she growls.

"Would you knock it the fuck off? You're not helping." She's breathless, words strained as she pulls me along.

I close my eyes when nausea threatens to upend the fancy meal we had earlier. It's hard to imagine it was only a few hours ago, yet we've been through hell and back.

Light flashes behind my lids, and I swallow hard. The last thing I want to do is puke. A cacophony of voices swirl through the air as her lips brush my forehead, then she's gone.

Thirty

Ember

Men swarm around Roman, who's passed out on the sidewalk. I don't know if I did any more damage by dragging him, but I couldn't leave him there. I didn't even stop to think about getting more men to help. It would only put more of them in danger. It would put Roman in more danger.

I grab one man's arm, I think his name is Rigger, to get his attention, but he shrugs me off. He's focused on Roman, as he should be.

Glancing around, all I see is chaos. The fire still rages on, now licking around the large warehouse doors. Others are shouting into phones, though who they could possibly be talking to is beyond me.

I suck in a deep breath and tear back into the shadows—toward Moss, toward the shooter. I'm pretty sure I hit them, but where there is one...

Moss is right where I left him, chest shuddering with each small breath he manages. He might be the same height as Roman, but his bulk will make it harder to drag him to safety. My stature isn't going to help, even if I am stronger than I appear. Hefting Moss's dead weight around may be a feat I'm not capable of.

Grabbing his ankles, I shuffle him around, trying to listen for the telltale click of someone cocking a gun. The last thing we need is for me to be shot as well. When I finally have him positioned, I scramble to his head, then gather him up under his arms. I don't want to drop him on his head, but I swear this man gained another fifty pounds in the few minutes I was away.

"Fuck this shit. You don't even fucking like me. You tried to get Roman to kick me out. You probably would have killed me, given the chance. And here I am, saving your sorry ass so you don't fucking die. If I don't get a thank you for this, I'm going to shoot you myself," I grunt as I tug him along. "If I rip my stitches for you and have to have that maniac attack me with a needle again, you and I are going to have a private acupuncture session."

Inch by inch, I shuffle backward, tipping my head up to scan the darkness every few feet. A shot pings through the air, and I duck, covering Moss's body with my own. I dropped his gun when I was saving Roman. It's lost among the bushes, I'm sure. Plus, there's no fucking way I'm dodging back into the fray in hopes of finding it.

Another barrage of bullets whips through the night, cracking the stone as they hit the building, each one closer than the last.

I grin, sliding the small knife I tucked into a holster at my thigh. My dress split when I was tussling with Roman's assassin, making it easy to reach now. Whoever is shooting at us is clearly not a sniper, basically taking potshots at us blindly. I imagine they didn't even realize they were shooting at Moss instead of Roman.

All their wild attempts at hitting us have helped me pinpoint roughly where they're hiding. It's farther than I've ever hit a target before, especially when all I can make out is a darkened shadow among the trees. Worst that can happen is I'll miss and be in the exact same boat. One last bullet slams into the concrete between Moss's legs, and I wonder how he'd feel if he lost one of his balls.

Pushing upright, I flip the knife so I clutch the blade, the edge digging into my palm. It's not ideal, but I'm hoping the weight of the handle will carry it far enough to reach them.

I swing my arm back, then forward, letting the knife go, and praying to whatever gods have abandoned me I've calculated shit correctly. I soft thunk tells me I've either hit a small tree, or a body. Another louder thud follows, and I breathe a sigh of relief.

Blood drips from my hand onto Moss's blindingly white shirt. Grabbing him again, I resume our arduous journey toward safety. I doubt there's more than two of them, but I'm not taking any chances. Moss groans but doesn't open his eyes.

I don't know if I want him to wake up or not. Roman kept trying to help me, making my job all the more difficult. I can't expect Moss would be much better. I'm panting by the time I round the corner.

"Don't fucking die, you bastard," I wheeze as I contemplate dropping him. Instead, I set him gently on the ground.

My ruined dress tangles around my feet, and I collapse onto my ass. I wave at a younger guy, probably an initiate, whose eyes widen before he hurries off, hopefully to get help. As the adrenaline leaves me, I tip to the side, gaze fixed on Moss's pale face. His lids flutter, body twitches, and I hold my breath.

Roman's wound was most likely superficial. I'm pretty sure the only reason he passed out was from the shit earlier. Moss, on the other hand, was hit in the side. I'm not a doctor, but I wouldn't be surprised if his kidney was damaged. We need to get him to a hospital sooner rather than later. Maybe Moss and TJ can share a room. I snort at the thought.

"Is he breathing, Rigger?" Roman's strained voice calls from behind me.

"Barely. I'm calling it in," Rigger says, leaning over Moss and pressing a cloth to his side.

"Call one of ours. No fucking way is he riding in an ambulance," Roman growls.

"You need to go too, Drake."

My eyes are glued to Moss's chest, watching it rise and fall irregularly. If he doesn't get help soon, it won't matter that I saved him. He'll probably blame me for that too, opting to haunt me from the other side or some shit.

Groaning, I roll onto my back, and my dress pulls against my skin. My side is wet, but I don't know if that's from the blood I lost before or if I truly did rip my stitches. Ink isn't going to be very happy with me.

Willow's voice echoes over the din, demanding answers that no one gives her. I raise my hand, closing my eyes and hoping she spots me in the mass of people. A sharp report of a gun rings out, silencing the crowd, and I jolt upright.

"Now then. You are going to go meet the firetruck and direct them back here. No, don't go around that way. Two people were just shot going that way." She shakes her head, obviously done with the lot of them. "You, help Drake into the car. No, that blue one there. We're not waiting for some random car service and hoping they're going to let him bleed all over the backseat. You and you, take Moss to the other car and get him to the hospital. If he dies on the way, I'm holding both of you personally responsible."

I let out a chuckle, easing onto my back once again.

"Something funny?" Willow asks, and I peek up at her.

"You're kind of a ball buster. I like it," I wheeze.

"Oh, for fuck's sake. You ripped them, didn't you? Ink is not going to be happy. Prepare yourself for a lot of bitching. Roman is fine, by the way. Not that you asked."

"I'm the one who pulled his sorry ass from the line of fire. I know he's fine. Moss, on the other hand..." I wave my hand toward where Moss was just a second ago, but he's not there anymore. They must have already loaded him up.

"You think this was a setup?" Willow asks, plopping down next to me.

"No. I think it was an initiate who made a mistake and started a fire. Then someone was at the right place at the right time. They didn't seem to know the difference between Moss and Roman. You'd think they'd realize their mistake since Roman's hair is like a fucking spotlight in the dark, but apparently they're not very bright."

"Well, this is going to be a shitshow to clean up. I hope you know that."

I snort, laying my arm across my eyes. "This whole city is a shitshow. I doubt one more incident is going to put us over the edge."

"Us, huh?"

I peek at Willow, scowling. "I didn't mean it like that."

"Sure you didn't. Are you going to ride with Roman back to Ink? I think you should, since you're bleeding. Again."

"We need to check on the shooters. I think I hit at least one of them. Maybe," I mumble.

I push up, groaning as a stab of pain hits my side, doubling me over. I breathe through the sensations rolling through me.

Staggering forward, I pretend I'm not about to pass out. We've already had enough of that tonight. Willow's hand wraps around my upper arm, and I lean into her.

"We'll pretend this didn't happen if it makes you feel any better," Willow says.

"Not necessary. I don't mind accepting help. Unless it's Drake, then he can suck my—"

"Alright, I got it. This probably isn't a great idea in your state."

I shove away from her, intent on making it on my own. I don't have a problem accepting help, but there's no way I'll let anyone think I'm not capable. Keeping my shit together is the only way I've survived this long.

"You know, this might all be because of me," I whisper, not entirely sure if I can say it outright.

If I admit it out loud, fully and with my whole fucking chest, I'll be responsible. Willow will tell Hawk, who will tell Roman, and then...then nothing. He'll tell me to get out of Synd or try to protect me. Either way is unsustainable. I keep waffling between staying or going. Every time I make up my mind, something tugs me back in. Fuck Roman and his magnetism. That's what I'm blaming. Not my own ridiculously wishy-washy personality.

"It's not. We both know who's behind all this. Roman knows too, though he's loath to admit it, even to himself," Willow says, glancing behind at the sound of Hawk's bellows.

The darkness swallows us up as we make our way down the path. Hopefully, it hides the blush staining my cheeks. I'm not entirely sure where the shooter was, but I have a rough estimate. Leading Willow along, I push through the bushes, searching the ground for any sign of a weapon or blood.

"You hit him alright," Willow murmurs from a few feet away.

I crash closer to her, parting the brambles until a pair of feet appear. A middle-aged man, his pudgy stomach straining against a black sweatshirt, stares at the foliage, a bullet hole piercing his forehead. Even I'm impressed at what was clearly a lucky shot. Sure, I knew his general location, but the chances that I'd stick him right in between the eyes is nothing short of a miracle.

"Well, you're a lot more skilled than I thought," Willow says, glancing around.

"Lucky shot. I think there was another one, too."

I grumble as I tug my dress from the brambles. The other shooter was farther away, and I stumble toward where I assume he was. A knife is a lot less deadly from a distance than a gun, but maybe I hit them and they'll bleed out. Or get sepsis. We should talk to the hospital in the hopes they need to be sewn up. I let out a whoosh of air when I spot a dark pool of blood.

"Uh, Willow?"

"Did you find them?" she asks, coming up behind me.

As I round the trunk of a tree, my eyebrows raise. "I'd say so."

"Well shit. Was this a lucky shot, too?" She laughs, planting her hands on her hips.

We stare at the body of the man with a knife sticking out of his throat. I have no fucking clue how I did it, but Willow looks suitably impressed. I let out a snort, covering my mouth with my hand as my shoulders shake. Willow's eyes track me, but I can't seem to stop the laughter from bubbling out of me.

"Uh, not a normal reaction to a dead body, but to each their own, I suppose," she mutters.

"I just...how the fuck..." I wheeze, doubling over again and holding my side.

I groan, still not able to get my shit together. An ache settles in my chest, and Willow rubs my back. My emotions are all over the place.

"Alright, why don't we go back and I'll call a clean-up crew. I think you're a little bit in shock."

I straighten, breathing deeply. "I'm fine. I totally have my shit together."

"Course you do, honey. Let's go find a ride back to Reaper territory."

She guides me back down the path and despair crashes through the tenuous control I had over my emotions. I crumple to the sidewalk, ducking my head as tears spill from my eyes. They streak down my face, soaking into my ripped dress and splashing on the concrete, small pools the only evidence of my breakdown. I can't keep going like this, adrift in a strange city filled with nothing but heartache. Yet I can't let go. I've spent the last ten years with a tether around my heart, twisting and squeezing the life from me.

If I run now, I won't survive. But if I stay, I might not either.

Thirty-One

Roman

"Get your fucking ass in the car, Drake. I'm already catching hell from Ink. I'm not pushing my luck with him," Hawk says.

He's been trying to get my sorry ass in the car for the last ten minutes, but we keep getting waylaid by Byrns's men, wanting some sort of direction. I'm ready to tell them Willow is in charge since they all seemed to get their shit together when she showed up.

Staring at the open car door, I sway, trying to place why I can't leave. Something holds me back, but I can't remember why I need to stay here. My thoughts are covered in molasses, slowly rolling around my mind. It's like I'm missing a limb. Glancing behind, I almost fall over, catching myself on the car.

Someone giggles, the musical sound floating above the chaos still rumbling through the air. I close my eyes, pulling in a deep breath, letting Ember's laugh fill my lungs, my body, my heart. It's not the same chords I've caught when we're alone, when we were younger. There's a manic edge to it, as if the weight of the world rests within the notes.

That's what I forgot—what I was missing. Her.

"Drake?" Hawk's voice cuts across the peace, and I strain to hear her again. "Roman."

He sighs, knocking his fist on the hood. "I'll get her. Just...just get in the car. You're no good to her if you're dead."

His footsteps fade away, eaten up by the sirens and men shouting. It's a miracle I even heard her laugh over the noise, as if fate intervened, graciously throwing me a much-needed win, slight as it may seem.

I'm tired, exhausted to my bones. I'm sick of fighting against the world, both as a temporary leader within a city I was intent on destroying mere months ago and as a man with no direction. Though I may not agree with Ember's mission, I refuse to punish her for it anymore.

"Roman?" Her voice is soft, softer than I've heard in a long time.

Slowly, I open my eyes, my vision blurring until all I see is her. Curly red hair a riot around her head, blowing across her face in the breeze, but it doesn't seem to bother her.

Reaching for her, I tuck the strands behind her ear and her throat bobs. She shivers, goosebumps erupting along her arms. I snatch up my coat from the seat behind me and slip it around her shoulders. Thankfully, Hawk gave me another shirt or I'd be out here half-dressed.

"You're about to pass out," she whispers.

I glance at Hawk, who grabs Willow's arm and drags her toward Rigger. Firemen rush in and out of the building, but the truck sits abandoned except for Brewer. He leans against the side, arms crossed as he glares at the fire. His eyes skip to mine and he smirks as if he's won something.

"Sorry about your dress," I murmur.

Her head snaps up, shock flooding her face. She narrows her eyes and her tongue darts out, pulling my gaze down to her mouth. I swallow hard, resisting the urge to haul her into me and devour her.

"Did you just..." She clears her throat. "Did you just apologize?"

I roll my eyes, a soft chuckle leaving me. "We've had a shit night and you're focused on the fact I said I was sorry about your dress?"

"I don't think you've apologized a day in your life, Roman Drake."

She tenses, spine straightening. She's slipping away, or rather, pulling on the mask she wears in front of everyone, including me. I've never hated it more than right now, when our bodies are riddled with wounds and a fire rages just out of sight.

I can't let her go. I need her with me. She's the only reason I'm still functioning—the only reason I'm here. Even when I was following my plan of destroying Synd and men who ran it, I wasn't invested. Having Ember with me, pushing me, challenging me has made all the difference in the world.

"I'm about to pass out, so why don't we get in the car, and you can yell at me," I say, a slight slur to my words even I can hear.

She tilts her head. "And what exactly am I going to be yelling at you about?"

"Whatever the hell you want."

She glides into the car, graceful even with a shredded dress and a wound in her side. I wish I could say I slide inside with dignity, but my body collapses, and my vision darkens. Hawk better get here quick or they're going to be hauling my body into headquarters. Slightly humiliating, but I might not have a choice.

"Is Moss going to make it?" she asks, tracking the chaos outside.

In here, there's a bubble of safety—a space removed from everyone else. Soon someone will come along and burst it. I'm exhausted and don't have the energy to deal with everything. I only have enough for her.

"He wants you dead," I say, resting my head against the seat.

My hand finds hers and I lace our fingers together. I need something to ground me to the present right now, and I'll choose her every time.

"Maybe I'm insecure enough to want him to like me."

I snort, squeezing her hand. "You saved both of us, Em. If he doesn't appreciate that, then fuck him."

"You can't afford to lose him."

"I'd rather not talk about Moss right now. He's on his way to the hospital and he'll either make it or not. Nothing we do now will change the outcome."

"Would you like me to yell at you?" she asks, and I peer at her from under my lashes.

Her head turns toward me, exhaustion hanging heavy in her eyes. If Hawk doesn't get here soon, I won't make it to Ink before succumbing to the darkness licking at the edges of my vision. At least her face will be the last thing I see.

When I turned into a fucking sap isn't important. Maybe if I wait long enough, the feeling will go away. Even if I do admit there may be something more between us other than animosity and torment, I won't be spouting poetry any time soon. I can barely keep my eyes open as it is, much less tell her how things have changed.

"It was stupid of you to go down a dark path when someone is trying to kill you," she says, her words bursting through my thoughts.

"It was stupid of you to follow."

"Except I'll be lauded as a hero for saving the clueless mafia leader. The history books will not look kindly upon you."

I snort, then groan, holding my hand to my side. "Bold of you to assume anyone will write about either of us."

A sound of indignation erupts from her, and she presses her hand to her chest as her mouth drops open.

"Men will write sonnets on my beauty. Women will expound on my amazing feats. Everyone will remember the name Ember Hayes. We'll see who's laughing then," she says haughtily, tipping her chin up.

"The only person who will wax poetic about you will be me," I murmur, and her gaze snaps to mine. "They'll be tragedies, but I'll still write them."

She rolls her eyes, trying to pull her hand from my grasp, but I cling to her. If she retreats now, I'll lose my grip and slip away. Her face softens, concern swimming in her green eyes. They're muted now, laced with a hint of pain.

"What happened?" I gasp, then wince as a throbbing pain rolls through my head. She scoots closer to me, and I close my eyes again.

"You were shot—again."

"I mean on the balcony?"

"Maybe we should talk about this later."

"No. Your voice is the only thing keeping me here. Just keep talking. Tell me anything," I wheeze.

Wind whips through the car as she rolls down the window, shouting something. The chill recedes as she closes it again, cuddling closer to my side.

"About six months ago, I got a tip on Anders. So, I chased it down to a town, probably fifty thousand people? I was worried about blending in. After a week, I realized I'd been bamboozled and fed bad intel. Problem was, I had nowhere else to go. Been there before, so it wasn't that big of a deal. If I waited long enough, something would come along, and I'd chase down something new."

"Did you stay in a shitty hotel there, too?"

She laughs, laying her head on my shoulder, and the ache in my chest eases the slightest bit.

"No, I was actually at a bed-and-breakfast. Little old lady there thought I needed a husband to keep me in line. So, I told her I was married."

"You lied to an old lady so she wouldn't set you up with the baker's boy?" I can just imagine Ember dressed in a frilly sundress trying to not scare some innocent man who has no idea why his grandmother insists on setting him up.

"He was an accountant, but yes." She sucks in a deep breath. "When she asked what my husband's name was…I gave her yours."

Hawk rips open the door, yelling at Rigger to get his shit together before sliding into the driver's seat. Ember clears her throat, shuffling back to her side of the car. When she tries to pull her hand away, though, I growl, gripping her tightly. She huffs, but keeps her fingers entangled with mine.

"Still alive or should I drive straight to the morgue?" Hawk says, laying on the horn until Byrns's men scatter.

"Depends on whether your so-called doctor is actually going to give us pain killers this time or not," Ember mutters.

"Wait, I thought you didn't need any?" I snap, glaring at Hawk in the rearview mirror.

She waves away my concern, but her eyes are still tight, barely holding in the pain.

"Something about a possible nicked something-or-other and drowning in my own blood. Drugs will stop me from breathing or whatever. I don't know since I'm not a doctor. It's fine, but I'm going to need more stitches. Maybe I'll ask Willow to do it instead so I don't get yelled at again," she mutters.

I open my mouth to demand answers, but Hawk clears his throat.

"Willow is probably the last person you want to sew you up. Great at baking a cake. Terrible at darning a sock."

"Darning a sock and sewing up someone's flesh are two different skill sets," Ember says, gazing out the window.

"Obviously, but she can't sew up a hole whether it's fabric or flesh."

"Might choose her anyway, but darning a sock is different than sewing, no matter what medium you're working with."

Why the fuck they're arguing about this shit is beyond me, but it's giving me a headache. That could be the multiple wounds I've suffered tonight, as well as all the stress, though. I'm blaming them either way.

"Would you two shut the fuck up?" I lean my head against the window.

"Your girl here needs to get her priorities straight, Drake."

I sigh, letting the coolness seep into my heated skin. "My *woman* merely focuses on random shit so she doesn't have to deal with her emotions."

Hawk crows in triumph. I'm too tired to ask what the hell he's on about now. I'll ask him tomorrow. Or next week. Or not at all. Fucker doesn't deserve my curiosity.

"Roman, you need to stay awake." Ember's words weave in and out of my thoughts.

Bright lights burst behind my lids, dancing along with the melody her voice creates within my head. The notes tether us together, creating a song all our own that will never fade.

"Hawk, is Willow going to be okay?" Ember asks even as she squeezes my hand.

"She'll be fine. She can hold her own, especially with them," Hawk says, then mutters a curse.

I snap upright, my side and shoulder screaming in pain. "What's wrong?"

"Someone is following us. Duck down, just in case. Blue will fillet me alive if I fuck up his car. He's already bitching about the blood."

Ember slides down, wincing. I don't have anywhere to go, though. My legs are too long, already bunched up against the passenger seat. Ember's wide eyes meet mine and she pats the seat next to her.

"Lie down. I'll crawl in the front."

"No. You'll be more exposed. Just stay where you are."

"Drake," she whispers, a warning in her tone.

"Do not fucking move," I growl. "I'd rather get shot in the fucking head than have you get hurt again."

Her mouth falls open slightly as she stares at me. I won't take back what I said. Her life is worth more than mine. It always has been. And that will never change.

Thirty-Two

Ember

I always thought it was creepy when people watched others sleep. Every time I read it in a book or saw it in a show, it gave me the ick. What can I possibly accomplish by counting breaths and measuring the spaces in between? Yet still I'm propped against Roman's headboard, eyes fixed on his chest. It rolls with each intake, like the waves splashing against the shore, over and over again.

My stitches pull as I readjust, reminding me I should be sleeping too. Ink's scathing lecture rings in my ears, my promises to rest not forgotten, but definitely ignored. I tried to, but every time I closed my eyes, the fear Roman would die while I was lost in the darkness would take my breath. My chest would tighten and my stomach would roll.

After an hour, I gave up. He hasn't stirred in several hours. The moon has disappeared, and the world outside holds its breath for the sun to make its appearance.

Roman mumbles, still fast asleep, and I lean down to hear him. My side protests and I sit upright again, huffing until the pain subsides. I jolt when Roman's hand brushes my leg, then latches onto my inner thigh. When he tugs, I yelp, eyes flying to his face. He smirks, digging his fingers into my flesh. Even in sleep, he's a dominating asshole.

I shimmy down, his hand gliding along my skin, pushing my shirt up. He pulls me close, curling his body around mine. I tense, waiting for him to continue his seduction, but his hand settles over my stomach as he sighs.

We're both too wrung out for anything other than sleep. Resisting him would be a feat, though. The pull between us is too strong for me to deny him. That's what I figured out while I watched him sleep. I'm not strong enough to fight my own feelings.

"Add another wall," I whisper, tucking my chin to my chest.

"What are we building?" he murmurs, his breath ghosting across my ear.

"Go back to sleep."

"Why more walls?" He nuzzles into my neck, then presses a kiss against my skin, and I shudder.

"No more walls. They don't keep you out, anyways. Now, go back to sleep."

He groans, rolling onto his back, and I mourn the loss of his warmth surrounding me. When I scoot away, he grips my wrist, holding me in place.

"Come here," he says gruffly.

"I'm right here."

"Closer. I sleep better when you're here."

I roll my eyes even as my stomach flutters. The change within him in the last twenty-four hours is stark, and I can't tell if it's the drugs Ink pumped in his system or something else. Maybe the pain engulfed him, loosening his tongue. Except I never imagined he'd be spouting the things he has been.

Flipping toward him, I forget about my wound and wince. He tugs my leg until it's between his own and I rest my head on his shoulder, my hand on his heart. His arm loops around me, pulling me flush against him, and my body melts into his.

Obviously, this isn't the first time we've slept in the same bed, but cuddling on purpose wasn't on the agenda. Mostly it was sex or exhaustion, our bodies migrating toward each other of their own accord.

"Don't leave," he murmurs, brushing my hair from my forehead and kissing me softly.

"I don't have anywhere to go."

It's a cop-out. We both know it, but he lets me live in my delusion. Something shifted last night when he was shot and I saved him—twice. I thought the change would be subtle, only felt by us, or rather me. Instead, it was a poorly kept secret, known to everyone.

Hawk laughed when he dropped us off, telling Roman he was fucked. Willow's knowing smirk was almost too much. It was Ink that put me over the edge though. He kept reassuring me that Roman would be fine with some rest, as if I wouldn't be able to live if Roman died.

Roman's hand skims up my back, tracing circles as he goes. I shiver, trying to move my pussy so he can't feel me clenching. He chuckles, his fingers lacing with mine to keep me still.

"Ink said you should sleep."

"He also said you should as well, but I get the feeling you've been watching me the whole night."

"We didn't even get home until four hours ago," I snap, more annoyed at myself than him.

His breath hitches and he freezes. I try to sit up, but his arms are a vise around me.

"Roman? What's wrong? Did you rip your stitches? Let go so I can call someone."

I wiggle, not wanting to hurt him, though I could get away if I really wanted to.

"I'm not—" He clears his throat. "I'm not hurt. You said...never mind."

He shakes his head, resuming his perusal of my body. Each pass sends heat pooling between my legs. He's trying to distract me from questioning him. Unfortunately for him, I can do two things at once. Rubbing my foot against his leg, I press my knee into his cock, and he grunts.

"What exactly did I say that's got you in a tizzy?" I ask, untangling our fingers and running my palm down his bare chest.

"Are you trying to seduce answers out of me?" He's trying to sound unaffected, but the gruffness in his voice gives him away.

Tipping my head back, I raise an eyebrow. "Depends. Is it working?"

A primal noise rumbles in his chest, and I squeal as he rolls me on my back, covering my body with his own. His hips rock into mine, his hard cock hitting my clit. I wrap my leg around his waist, gasping when a stabbing pain lashes through my side. He props himself on his forearms, lifting his body. Concern flashes through his eyes as he scans me.

"What's wrong?" He grabs the hem of the shirt I'm wearing—his shirt—and lifts it, checking my bandages.

I bare my teeth as a blush rushes to my cheeks. "Nothing. I just forgot I was hurt. Stop fussing. It's weird."

He glares at me, brows pulled low. "It's weird that I'm worried about you?"

"Yes," I cry, trying to pull the fabric from his fist. "You're not sweet and gentle, concerned for my safety."

He ducks his head, and his hair brushes my skin, making me shiver. When his eyes meet mine, there's a softness within them I haven't seen in years. I lick my lips and his gaze follows the movement, so I do it again. I brush the blond strands off his forehead, but a lock falls back into place, disheveled from sleep.

"Maybe I just never showed you before," he murmurs.

"I don't like it." My voice lacks the steel I wanted to infuse into it.

He smirks, then swoops down to capture my lips with his. I gasp and he takes full advantage, sweeping his tongue in to tangle with mine. As I squirm beneath him, the desire hits me full force, as if it never fled, and I'm left panting into his mouth. Suddenly, his weight is gone as he rolls to the side. Before I can start cussing him out, he hauls me into him, my back pressed to his chest.

"What the hell, Drake," I snarl.

His teeth latch onto my earlobe, and I grip his thigh, digging my nails in to center myself.

"I can't fuck you properly right now, but that doesn't mean I can't make you come," he whispers.

"Who says I'm going to let you..." My retort is lost in a moan when he cups my pussy through my thong, the heel of his palm grinding into my clit.

"I say. This pussy belongs to me. Your pleasure belongs to me," he growls.

"Fuck that," I gasp, my eyes rolling back in my head as he strokes me through the thin strip of fabric.

"You're going to be a good girl and come all over my fingers. Then you're going to sit on my face. Once you're all wrung out, I'll put you on your knees. You're going to let me come down your throat."

"Why the fuck would I do that?"

"You may be a fucking brat, but you love my cock."

I jerk my hips, fleeing from the slow torture he's putting me through.

"So, you think my pussy belongs to you, but you'll request to fuck my mouth?" I snap, scrambling to find my dignity within the swirling pool of desire he's drowning me in.

"Oh, Em. Your pussy is my property. Your mouth is a gift."

My mouth drops open, not that he can see. He's back to nuzzling my neck, fitting me against him again. His finger slips under the fabric of my thong and swipes along my slit.

"Look at how wet you are for me," he murmurs, his voice laced with approval.

He holds his glistening fingertip up for my inspection. I lean forward, sucking it into my mouth, and he groans. He yanks his hand away, wrapping it around my throat.

"Such a dirty little whore, aren't you?"

"Bold words for someone who keeps corrupting me every time I'm in your bed."

He laughs, his chest rumbling, sending warmth through me. It's rare to hear Roman truly laugh, but over the last few weeks I've heard it more and more. I don't know if it's the responsibility of running Synd or something else. I'm hesitant to think it's me—or us being together.

I'm lost in my thoughts when he snaps the elastic on my thong, bringing me back to the present. He growls when they don't slide down my hips. He pulls his arm from under me, then grabs the edges and yanks them down my legs. The look on his face has me tensing. The corner of his mouth tips up and his eyes dart to mine.

"What are you thinking?" I ask cautiously.

"Just wondering if I need to stuff these in your mouth."

My mouth drops open, and I snap it shut before he acts on his unhinged suggestion. He smirks, raising an eyebrow before tossing them over his bandaged shoulder. He crawls up my body, nipping at my inner thigh, my hip, my nipple before tipping to his side.

I expect him to start yanking me around, but his touch is gentle as he guides my leg over his, opening me up to him. His fingers dance along my skin, never reaching where I need him most. I didn't expect Roman to be a tease, to work me into a frenzy before giving in. To be fair, I didn't imagine him being gentle, ever.

When I was young, I had a fairytale vision in my head of what our lives would be like. I thought he'd be my Prince Charming. Instead, I got the morally gray villain with the dirty fucking mouth. I can't say I'm disappointed. The things I wanted when I was a teenager were envisioned through rose-colored glasses.

I've changed, morphed, and figured out what I want. It wasn't easy since I move so often. Jumping cities doesn't exactly encourage relationships. Not that I cared about that shit. I wasn't looking for one, probably because I was too busy secretly pining after the man currently rolling my nipple between his fingers.

"Stop thinking." His teeth sink into my neck, and I shudder.

"Stop talking. Stop thinking. What the hell exactly am I supposed to do then?" My hips jerk toward his hand as it skims across my stomach.

"You're going to stay still, or I'll tie you to the bed," he growls.

I try to hold back the shiver rolling through me, but his chuckle says I didn't succeed. He's still playing with my body, stoking the flames within me until there's a roaring in my ears.

"Maybe I'll tie you to the bed instead." The bite in my words is lost in a gasp as he strokes my pussy, then circles around my clit.

"That'll have to wait until my wounds are healed. You wouldn't want to hurt me, would you?"

A moan leaves me as he pushes a finger inside, slowly pulling it out. He repeats the move over and over, curling when his palm cups me. He stops and I writhe under him. At this rate, I'm never going to come, but if he doesn't move at all, I'm going to lose my mind.

"Answer the question, Ember," he demands.

"What question?" I whine, and he grinds the heel of his hand onto my clit.

"You don't want me to get hurt, do you?"

"What the fuck kind of question is that?"

I cry in protest as he pulls out of me. He slaps my pussy and I jolt, surprised at the move and the lick of pleasure shooting through me. His fingers return, plunging into me again. His chest rumbles in approval as I move with him, my stomach tightening.

When he stops again, leaving me bereft, an involuntary sob bursts from me. His lips brush the shell of my ear, shushing me as he brushes my hair from my flushed forehead.

"I can do this all day, love. You might as well give in and tell me how much you want to stay. How much you want me safe."

He circles my clit leisurely as if we have all the time in the world. We don't. Everything is falling apart around us, someone is trying to kill one or both of us, and more than a few people are in the hospital now. He has responsibilities to attend to other than giving me an orgasm.

"You want me to spill all my innermost thoughts?" I pant, digging my nails into his side, urging him to go faster.

He freezes, then props himself up on his elbow and gazes down at me. His blue eyes blaze with desire and an edge of something else I can't name. His lips pull into a smirk and my eyes widen as I realize what I've inadvertently revealed to him.

"What other desires are you hiding deep inside?"

The words stick in my throat, though they're begging to be set free. Roman leans into me, scraping his teeth along my shoulder before biting down, most likely leaving a mark. I tilt my head, giving him more access as my eyes fall closed. His hand caresses my hip, then glides to my inner thigh.

"Give me a secret, Ember," he murmurs, burying his fingers into me once more.

My breath stalls in my lungs as he thrusts hard and fast, but it's not enough. I move with him, chasing the high dancing just out of reach. He slows, I whine, then he picks up the pace again. He repeats the cycle, and I realize he won't let me come until I give him what he wants.

"You bastard," I wheeze, clamping down on him when he lingers, pressing on my clit with his thumb.

"One little secret."

"Fine, I want to fucking stay!"

He turns my face to him, covering my mouth with his as he fucks me with his hand, thumb rubbing my clit. I sail over the edge, moaning his name as his tongue dances with mine, as if he can drink my pleasure up one lick at a time.

When he finally pulls back, I don't know if my flushed skin is from my climax or embarrassment. I hold my breath, waiting for him to say something—anything. But as he nuzzles my neck, I worry he won't say anything at all.

Thirty-Three

Roman

Ember's body is pliant in my arms, her pussy no longer spasming around my fingers. I should reassure her that her secret is safe with me, but the words won't come. She fought me, and while I wanted to watch her come, I couldn't help but punish her. The beast within me, usually slumbering peacefully, demanded her submission, and I couldn't deny him. It's rare I let him out of his cage. I can't say I regret doing it, though.

"Such a good girl. But you still owe me more." I lick my fingers clean, the taste and smell of her overwhelming me, and I groan.

"And what exactly do you think I owe you?" she spits out, her skin still flushed from her orgasm.

"I'll give you a choice." I untangle my limbs from her, kneeling next to her hip. "Tell me more of your secrets, and I'll make you come for each one you reveal. Or you get on your knees and I fuck your mouth."

Her eyes narrow even as they dart down to my cock straining against my underwear. I'm hard most of the time when she's around, but this morning it's bordering on excruciating. I grip myself, squeezing to relieve some of the tension, and she bites her lip.

"What will it be, Ember?"

I pull out my cock, and my blood heats as she tracks me stroking myself from tip to base. Her tongue darts out, swiping across her bottom lip. With her legs splayed open, pussy glistening, it's like she's a feast laid out just for me. I roll my neck, resisting the urge to make her come on my face like I promised. I'll wait until she's forgotten before I strike.

"Both," she says breathlessly.

I refuse to show how satisfied I am with her answer. She'll gloat, and I'll have to make her pay for it. While that might be enjoyable for both of us, my energy is lagging. I haven't had enough sleep and the heaviness around her eyes tells me she hasn't either.

"Did you sleep?" I ask, running my hand up her leg.

She blinks at me, red curls creating a halo around her head. Even exhausted, she's a vision.

"Wouldn't be smart if I didn't."

I raise an eyebrow, digging my fingers into her flesh, and she sucks in a sharp breath. A scowl overtakes her face as she attempts to snap her legs closed. I growl, sliding from the bed and latching onto her ankles. She squeals as I tug her until her ass hangs precariously on the edge of the bed, and I drop her feet.

"Knees. Now," I command, glaring when she doesn't move.

She smirks, a gleam in her green eyes. She props herself up on an elbow, tilting her head and I brace myself.

"Make me."

"Oh, Em. You might regret that."

I drop to my knees, biting back the groan threatening to escape me. Between the wound in my shoulder and the one in my side, I probably shouldn't be doing this. Her pussy is too intoxicating, though. She squeezes her knees together and I run my hand up her thigh. Her resistance won't last long. It never does. She wants my head buried in her pussy as much as I do.

Her legs tremble and her arousal surrounds me as I lean down, sinking my teeth into her flesh. She yelps as I lick the mark, then move higher. I repeat the move several times, satisfaction rolling through me. I grin against her skin when her muscles relax, knees falling open.

"I thought you wanted my secrets." Her voice holds a hint of accusation as if I've tricked her.

"You'll be singing them when I refuse to let you come."

I lick from her core to clit, moaning as the taste of her overwhelms my senses. She jolts as I flick my tongue against the small bud. A whimper echoes through the room, and I press a kiss to her thigh. I could spend all day right here, teasing her into a frenzy, and be perfectly content. When I glance up, she's fallen to her back, fingers digging into the sheets and twisting them.

I nip her thigh, then slide her leg over my good shoulder. Burying my head between her legs again, I resume bringing her closer to the edge. Her nails dig into my scalp, tugging on my hair as her hips jerk forward. Pushing two fingers into her pussy, I suck her clit into my mouth, waiting until she's clenching around me before I stop.

Her huff of frustration is warranted. As I slowly stroke her pussy, her fingers slide from my hair. Then there's a stinging sensation in my forehead.

"Did you just fucking flick me?" I glare at her.

"Fucking edge me again," she snarls.

I curl my fingers inside her and her face goes slack, giving into the desire I'm building in her body. She pants, squirming as I flick my tongue on her clit. When her legs start to tremble, I glance up at her from between her legs. I suck on the bud, then let it go.

"Secret, Ember," I remind her, lapping at her again.

"I blew up a building in the last city," she gasps, glaring at me.

I reward her by burying my face in her pussy, thrusting my fingers into her. She shatters, crying out her release. Her hands grab at the sheets, and then she groans, curling toward her injured side.

Instantly, I'm up, gathering her in my arms. She shudders, but I don't think it's from the pleasure coursing through her veins.

"What's wrong?" I snap, laying her on her back.

Running my hands along her skin, I avoid the bandage on her side. It might not have been deep, but I'm sure it's still sore. She bats my hands away, shaking her head.

"Stop it. I'm fine."

"Clearly, you're not," I growl, standing by the bed.

Glancing around for my phone, I run a hand through my hair. As much as I'd rather not call Ink, I can't afford to put Ember in danger. The thought pulls me up short, and I shake my head. The more time I spend with her, the more important she becomes. Before long, I'll be putting her above everything else.

You already are, the voice in my head whispers, and I swallow hard.

I don't have it in me to give more than I have already to her. I should have known this would happen when she showed up in Synd. She's wormed her way under my skin, and I can't even regret it.

I'm jolted from my thoughts when her lips wrap around my tip, hand circling the base of my cock, and I groan. My mind empties as her cheeks hollow out. Her nails burrow into my thighs as I grip her hair. I've imagined fucking her face, making her take all of me until she gags. I want to see tears streaming down her face as she swallows every last drop of me.

I doubt today is that day, though. We're both weak from blood loss and using sex to distract us from all the other problems plaguing us. Will that stop me from coming? Fuck no.

"Take it all, love."

Her gaze lifts to mine as I thrust into her mouth deep, hitting the back of her throat. The sight almost sends me over the edge, and I cup her cheek, wiping away a tear from her eye. Maybe I will get my wish after all.

"You look so beautiful with my cock in your mouth," I murmur, pumping into her harder.

Her eyes roll back, then fall closed as she hums. When her free hand drops between her legs, I quicken my pace. The needy noises fall from her lips, muffled by my cock as I fuck her. She shudders as she rubs her clit, letting me take over completely. The base of my spine tingles and my balls tighten. She sucks hard and I explode, groaning as I come.

Her body jerks, throat bobbing as she swallows repeatedly. Pulling from her mouth, I wipe my thumb over her bottom lip as she pants, then grins at me. Her fingers are still buried between her legs. I slide my hands under her arms, picking her up. I sit on the bed, then pull her toward me.

Grabbing her hips, I lift her onto my lap and plunge into her dripping pussy. She gasps, ducking her head to my chest as her fingers scratch against my shoulders, scrambling for purchase.

"I thought you couldn't fuck me properly," she whines even as rides my cock.

"Changed my mind. Play with your clit, Ember. Use me."

My fingers dig into her skin, probably leaving bruises behind. Her head tips back as I bury my cock in her over and over. Her fingers find her clit, circling fast and hard and I can't pull my eyes away from the sight. Every time I disappear inside her pussy another spasm shoots through me.

"Come for me, Em."

She shudders, grinding down as she climaxes, ripples of pleasure rolling through her body. I lean forward, sucking her nipple into my mouth, and she hisses as her pussy pulses around me. Her eyes fall closed as she comes down, a delicious flush spreading across her skin. I'll never tire of watching her fall apart for me.

I stand up, still deep inside her heat, and she wraps her limbs around me. I stutter toward the bathroom, almost collapsing, but I grit my teeth. Getting shot wasn't my first choice of things to do and now it's interfering with fucking Ember. If I could bring the men back and kill them again, I'd do it slower. Although technically, I didn't take out any of them. How someone so bratty can be so deadly is beyond me. As much as Ember and I bicker, I hope I never get on her bad side. She'd probably fuck me, then stab me. She'd walk away laughing the whole time, too.

I bite the soft juncture between her neck and shoulder, and she yelps.

"What the hell was that for?" she cries as I slip from her pussy and drop her to her feet.

"You owe me more secrets," I grumble, pointing to the toilet. "Do your business, then we're going back to bed."

I lean against the counter, dizziness invading my head. She huffs as I wash my hands and splash my face with cold water. After a minute, the toilet flushes, and she bumps me out of the way.

"So, we're at that point now? Peeing in front of each other? And if you think you're going to start dictating my hygiene habits..." she scoffs.

I stalk to the toilet, and she practically runs from the room, my laughter chasing her. Until she said something, it didn't even occur to me. I wash my hands again, then prowl back through the door. Planting my hands on my hips, I glare at her already under the covers.

"If your pussy gets sick because you didn't piss after I fucked you six ways to Sunday, then I don't get to fuck you for a while. I told you she was mine, so it's in my purview to keep her healthy."

"I have so many questions, but I'm tired. I spent the last twelve hours saving your ass. Think you can stay out of trouble while I nap?"

Rolling my eyes, I crawl in next to her. As much as I'd like to continue to bicker with her, I'm exhausted. I tug her close, melding our bodies together as we drift off. Hopefully, people can keep their shit together long enough for us to rest. I'm not betting on it, though.

Thirty-Four

Ember

"Would you just let me put a fucking bandage on you? For fuck's sake, Drake." I plant my fists on my hips, glaring at him while he studiously ignores me.

I throw my hands in the air, scoffing as I stomp from the closet. He's been getting ready for the last ten minutes, pretending I haven't been harassing him. He thinks four days is plenty of time to heal from getting shot twice. In one night. He didn't like when I told him how ridiculous he's being.

"Don't go gallivanting off when I'm gone," he calls, the low timbre vibrating through me.

"You're not my keeper, Drake. You'd do best to remember that," I yell from the bathroom.

I splash water over my face, attempting to erase the flush on my cheeks. It's from frustration, not flashes of memories of his face buried between my legs. Squeezing my thighs together, I slap my hands over my eyes.

"Being your keeper and worrying about you being killed are two different things," he growls from directly behind me, and I jolt upright.

Glaring at him in the mirror doesn't deter the smirk on his lips. I contemplate stomping away, but there are only so many places to retreat to in this room. He'd catch me long before I made it to the door. Then he'd never get to the hospital. I could still try, though.

As if he can read my thoughts, he presses against my back, trapping me between his body and the counter. I track his movements in the reflection as he trails his fingertips up my arm, leaving goosebumps in their wake. I shiver when he brushes my hair from my shoulder, then dips to press a kiss to my neck.

"If you're good, I'll reward you when I get back," he murmurs before nibbling on my earlobe.

My eyes fall closed as his other hand slips under my tank top, skimming along my stomach before cupping my tit. When my knees go weak, he wraps an arm around my waist, all while rolling my nipple between his thumb and finger. His lips keep up their assault on my skin and the flush returns. His hand moves from my chest to my throat and he tips my chin up.

"Look at you," he whispers, and my eyes flutter open.

I pull in a shaky breath, wondering when things changed. Sure, we've been fucking for the past several weeks, but this image isn't just lustful. It's a snapshot of desire meshed with something more. The possessiveness in which he holds me overrides the doubts plaguing me.

His eyes darken when our gazes meet. In this moment, I believe him when he says I'm his—wholly and completely. I'm at the mercy of his hands, his lips, his words. That thought used to frighten me, worried I'd lose myself in his magnetism. I was wrong. So fucking wrong.

"Exquisite," he murmurs before kissing my neck again.

He steps away, hands dropping from my body, and I grip the counter to steady myself. I don't know what the fuck just happened. It's as if everything else falls away when he touches me. Every thought, worry, inhibition evaporates, leaving only him. I don't know if that's healthy, but with the way our lives are, I doubt anything we do is.

Normal was never in the cards for either of us. I might as well embrace what I've found for as long as possible before it slips through my grasp. I'll be living on the memories of this for years to come.

I duck my head, pulling myself together before I spin to face him. His hands land on the counter, boxing me in, and I lean back. Another shudder rolls through me when he tips my chin up with his knuckle.

"I'm trusting you to not run, Ember." His gaze is serious.

I could reassure him I'm not going anywhere, but he's been more than a little bossy lately. He scowls when I wrinkle my nose.

"What would be the fun in that?"

"I'm serious. I don't want to have to save your ass when I get back."

Rolling my eyes, I lay a hand on his chest, leaning in close. "I'll do my best to be a perfect little princess and stay where you put me."

He barks out a sharp laugh, then grabs the back of my neck. "See that you do."

His mouth slams onto mine before I can respond. It's quick, hard, and full of something I don't want to name, mostly because it feels like possessiveness. When he pulls back, he grins, then strides from the bathroom, the bedroom door clicking shut shortly after.

I had plenty of plans for when he was gone and all of them included staying in the house. Eating, napping, showering, and doing some more research were all on my list, but now I don't want to do any of it.

I sigh as I make my way into the bedroom. I could clean up the pile of stuff still stacked in the corner of the room. The task requires more energy than I have right now. Even sleeping seems like a chore. I wanted to go with Roman to the hospital, but if Moss is awake, he probably wouldn't be very happy to see me.

I collapse onto the bed, messing up the comforter and tossing several pillows onto the floor. Roman methodically made it this morning, grunting when I asked him why he was fussing with it. I didn't realize he cared so much about making his bed.

After twenty minutes, I've counted seventy-seven swirls above my head, but I might have missed one. Just when I've resigned myself to staring at the ceiling for another twenty minutes, my phone rings and I thank whatever god I can remember at the moment.

I answer, but don't say anything. There are only so many people who have this number, and Roman is the only one I programmed in. It may not be under his actual name, but I'd know if it was him at least.

"It's Nicki," a woman's voice says.

It takes me a minute to place her, but then I smile. "Hello, Nicki. What can I do for you?"

"Your mafia man didn't answer, so I decided to call you." She shushes someone before huffing. "I thought one of you would like to know."

"Know what? Wait, how did you get my number?" I sit up, walking to the window and peeking out the curtains.

"You're not the only one who has skills, honey." She laughs at my snort. "Drake gave it to me."

"Of course he did."

"Listen, there's an old barracks in the Barrens. It's not far from the train station, closer to the river, though. Seems like there's some activity down there. Usually I wouldn't say anything, but with the shit that's gone down recently, I figured I should."

"What kind of activity?" I lean against the wall as my stomach flips.

"One or two guys show up, leave after a little while. Then there's a repeat a couple nights later. I'd say it's a lower gang, but when I went to check it out, no one was there. No sign of anyone using it as a hub. Keeps happening, though. One of my guys has been trying to catch whoever they're meeting, but we've got enough we're dealing with right now. I don't have the extra people to scope it out. Figured Drake could send someone to deal with it."

For some reason, her words send a chill through me. There's no reason to believe it's anything other than random, but a weight sits in my gut. Plus, if Nicki is calling me of all people, it must be a concern for her. We're not exactly besties.

"Okay, I'll let him know."

I wait for her to say something, but after what feels like forever, I pull the phone away to see if she's hung up. It's still tracking the call, numbers ticking by. Biting my lip, I press it to my ear again.

"Don't go alone," she finally murmurs. "I know what you're thinking because I'd do the same, but just don't. Wait for Drake."

"I'll be sure to pass on the message," I say, not committing to anything.

She sighs and I can practically hear her eye roll. The line goes dead, and I slide down the wall. I drop my phone next to me, wrapping my arms around my knees. People meeting in the Barrens shouldn't send a bolt of panic through me. Whatever is going on isn't a drug deal or lower gang. I can feel it in my bones.

Even though I want to bust out of here and go check it out myself, I do the smart thing and grab my phone again to call Roman. He doesn't answer, of course. That would be too fucking easy. I call one more time, but as his voicemail picks up with the automated message, I hang up. Shooting off a quick text to him, I push to my feet.

It's the middle of the day. Nicki said they only meet at night, so it should be fairly safe to scope out whatever is happening. I don't know how thorough the other woman is with these types of things. Maybe I can spot something she missed. I have at least two hours before Roman returns, six before the sun sets. Plenty of time to do a little sleuthing.

A thrill shoots through me as I pull on another shirt and I realize how much I missed this. I've spent my whole adult life chasing leads and moving from city to city. While my time in Synd hasn't exactly been quiet, I miss the exhilaration. And if I can find answers to some of our questions, all the better.

Will Roman kick my ass for leaving? Metaphorically speaking? Probably. Do I care? Abso-fucking-lutely not. Maybe this will be the kick in the nuts he needs to remember who I've become. I'm not the sheltered girl with a sharp tongue I was when we were teenagers. I kept the sass and left the shelter behind. I'm more than he thinks, and what better way for him to understand that than to see what I can do. I fought hard for these skills, gave up my entire future to obtain them, all in the name of finding my best friend. Using them to help Aelia's brother seems like a worthy enough cause.

As I slip into the trees surrounding the Byrns mansion, I hope I'm not making a huge mistake.

Thirty-Five

Roman

"When is he going to wake up?" I ask the doctor gruffly.

TJ's life is being measured with machines. Wires tether him to this world, and I wonder if I'm making the right decisions for him.

The doctor shakes his head, stepping back as he blanches. I shouldn't be the one dealing with this. While TJ defended me—even to Samantha when she didn't want me taking over Synd—we don't know each other. Dealing with medical shit shouldn't be my role.

"Unfortunately, we don't know."

I eye him, crossing my arms and waiting. He hasn't been forthcoming with information on how TJ has been, trying to pull some bullshit about confidentiality. In the mafia, there is no such thing. He knows that, but he's being a dick because I'm not Byrns or one of the Kings. Once Moss was brought in, though, he's starting to understand he doesn't have the authority to keep shit from me.

"What else?"

He clears his throat. "Well, Mr. Moss is in critical condition. We expect him to make a full recovery as long as he doesn't develop an infection. TJ, however, isn't responding to medication."

"Keep me informed of both of their conditions. I'd rather not have to come hunting for answers."

I stride from the room, leaving him pale and trembling. My phone vibrates, but I ignore it for now. The hospital doesn't have the best reception. Nurses fumble out of my way until one steps in front of me, blocking the elevator.

"Mr. Drake, could I have a word?"

I scan her up and down, taking in her scrubs and Crocs. I've never seen her before, but that doesn't mean anything. I don't know people like the others do. Glancing behind me, I sigh. Ember's face flashes through my mind and I grind my teeth. I'm not worried about her taking off anymore, but leaving her alone makes my skin itch.

"What can I help you with?" I ask, turning back to her.

"Not here. It's personal," she whispers as she twists her fingers together.

A pang shoots through me. I swear I'm going soft. Blaming Ember seems like the best option, so that's what I'm going with. That thought doesn't make me balk like it once did.

I may not be able to predict the future, but I'm going to get through our current problems and just see where we land. Making her mine might not be as simple as I'd like it to be. We still haven't dealt with our issues, and fuck knows if we ever will.

The nurse gives me a hopeful look, as if my answer will make or break her. I sigh, gesturing her to lead the way. Giving her five minutes won't put me too far behind schedule. The worst that will happen is I can't help her. No harm, no foul. My phone buzzes again, but still I leave it.

I follow her as she slips around the corner, glancing up and down the hall as she does. Whatever her problem is, she obviously doesn't want someone seeing us together. That's not unusual. People either seek us out, begging us to handle whatever shit they're in, or they avoid us until the last possible second, coming to us out of desperation. I'm sure it's the same for the others when they're here.

I'm starting to regret my offer to run Synd, though. Westmont is a smaller city, barely half the size with half the problems. If I would have known I'd be dealing with petty shit like this, I'd have escaped when I had the chance. I shake my head, recognizing the lies for what they are—a deflection.

The nurse stops in front of a nondescript door, no windows to show what's inside, and I tense. When she glances over her shoulder, she doesn't meet my eye. I almost pull my phone out when it vibrates for the fifth time since I've been here. Instead, I step closer to her, waiting for her to move.

"It'll just take a minute. I'm sorry, Mr. Drake."

She pushes the door open, shuffling inside, and I follow hesitantly. I'm greeted by an empty hospital room. The usual posters reminding people to wash their hands adorn the walls. Random wires jut from the outlets behind the bare bed. Glancing into the bathroom, I find it empty and some of the tension leaves me. Unless someone is hiding in the toilet, I'm fairly confident we're alone.

"I don't have much time, ma'am. I'm late for a meeting," I say, still scanning the space.

My eye catches on the curtain that usually hides the patient from view, but it's gathered against the wall. A choked noise echoes through the empty space and my head snaps toward her. From the corner of my eye, I spot the fabric unfurling and I duck.

A man bursts from his hiding spot, rushing me with something in his hand. Raising his arm over his head, I dodge him, stumbling into a cart. The nurse lets out a small shriek, but I can't concentrate on her. If she comes at me too, I might not be able to fight off both of them.

When he rushes at me again, the man's hood falls back, revealing a shaved head and bulbous nose. It's all I notice before he jabs a needle toward my chest. He clearly doesn't know what he's doing, since my ribs would most likely block the move. At least, I'd hope they would. With the way my luck has been recently, he'd probably get lucky, and I'd end up dying in a barren hospital room.

He snarls, spittle flying from his lips, and I sidestep him as he darts toward me. With the bed behind me, I don't have anywhere else to go as he rounds on me. The last thing I want to do is shoot him, but at least he's in a place that could keep him alive.

Once I overpower him, I'll need to question him. All the others dying before I've had the chance has been wearing on my nerves. His dark eyes bulge, veins straining in his neck.

I wait for his next move, but he just snarls, an inhuman sound emanating from deep within him. He slowly weaves back and forth, like a snake about to strike. When he shifts his weight, I dodge to the side and the injury in my side seizes, taking my breath away. As I struggle to pull air into my lungs, I glance at the nurse who's sobbing in the corner, hand clamped over her mouth.

I shouldn't feel bad for her, but I do. I can't imagine what this man threatened her with. That's the only plausible explanation, unless she merely got in over her head and now reality is crashing down around her. I don't have time to worry about her, though. As long as she stays out of the way.

My attacker rushes me, slamming his shoulder into my stomach, stealing what little breath I have left. A horrid screeching sound fills the room as we crash onto the bed, the force pushing it across the tile.

I latch onto his wrist as he struggles to stab me in the eye with the needle. Usually, I could throw him off, but wetness seeps into my shirt and Ink's words to take it easy filter through the ache.

My shoulder screams in pain as I force his hand further away. I slam my fist into his side, but he doubles his efforts. I'm merely a gnat buzzing around his head instead of a full-grown man pummeling him. The shot of adrenaline from the attack is flagging, leaving me breathless.

The needle drops another inch, hovering over my socket, but I can't look away. My gun is trapped behind my back, another tucked in my ankle holster, to far for me to reach. I should have shot him when I had the chance.

I grunt, punching him in the side of the head, but he barely flinches. My strength drains away and Ember's face floats through my mind. I should have stayed home, tucked in bed with her, worshiping her body, and pretending the outside world didn't exist. Now, she'll have to deal with these assholes on her own. She'll have to endure the pain of another death. She never did accept Aelia's. I wonder what she'll do with mine.

Suddenly, the man's face goes slack, the light in his eyes dying a slow death. I shove his arm away as he collapses on top of me. I roll him off, panting as I stare at the ceiling. Sobs from the nurse filter through the roaring in my ears.

"I'm sorry," she cries over and over before crumpling to the floor, an empty syringe tumbling from her grip.

It takes me a minute to get my shit together, but eventually I sit up, biting back a groan. I wince as I press a hand to my side. It comes away painted in crimson and I mutter a curse. Ink isn't going to be happy having to stitch me up a third time in as many days. He might even refuse.

"Is he dead?" I ask, my voice raspy, and I swallow.

"Yes," she whispers, unable to take her eyes from his prone body.

I stand, swaying slightly before I tower over her, and she cowers. "What did you do to him?"

"Would you understand even if I told you?"

I glance at my attacker, his weapon of choice laying innocently next to his slack hand.

"I don't suppose I would." I crouch down and she flinches. "What'd he say?"

She gasps, tears filling her eyes again. "They have my daughter. I couldn't...I can't..."

She breaks down, burying her face in her hands as her shoulders heave. Sighing, I slip my phone from my pocket. I doubt whoever he's working for even knows she has a daughter. Most of the time, the threat is enough without proof. Any normal person would do whatever they could for their child, even luring a mafia leader into an empty room to be ambushed.

"Rigger, I need some men on the hospital. Send someone"—I eye the woman still losing it—"not scary. They'll need to locate a child. And a cleanup at the hospital. Either float him or hide him in the morgue."

"You want me there?" he asks, his footsteps pounding in the background.

"No. I want you at the house when I get there. I'm on my way."

I hang up, wincing as I stand. When I check my shoulder, I don't find blood at least. Small fucking miracles. The nurse pulls herself together and stumbles to her feet.

"I doubt anyone has your daughter. Did you call anyone after he approached you?" I ask, pressing a hand to my side.

"Yes, but my partner is at work. The nanny didn't answer."

"Usually, they don't even bother to take them. Try to call again, but someone will be by to help you locate her."

"I can rewrap your side," she mumbles, swallowing hard, and I nod.

Sloughing off my suit coat and shirt, I grimace at the stain. I should have kept it bandaged, but it didn't look that bad when I got dressed. I snort, remembering Ember offering to do it for me. Apparently, I should have listened to her. The nurse's hands tremble as she approaches me, but they steady when she starts dressing my wound.

"It's not as bad as it seems. You don't need anything other than some rest and to put new bandages on for a couple days. Is there pain?"

"Aches. I'm fine."

She huffs, rolling her eyes, then fear flashes in them as she peeks at me.

"I'm not going to kill you for being snarky. You did technically help me."

"You mean I saved your life after I put it in danger in the first place?" A small smile plays on her lips as she steps back. "You're all set."

I button up my shirt and shrug on my coat. "Someone will be by to help you find your daughter."

She nods, glancing around the room. Her phone appears before I've made it out the door. Once outside, I check my notifications. Two missed calls and a dozen text messages, most from Nicki, greet me, and my breath hitches. As I slip into the car waiting for me, I read through them. One from an unknown number stands out and I pull it up. Cursing, I yell at the driver to get us home now.

"Nicki, what the fuck is going on?"

"Well, hello to you too, Mr. Drake."

"I don't have time for pleasantries. Did you call Ember and tell her to check something out in the Barrens?"

"First of all, stop yelling. Second, I did call Ember. I did not, however, tell her to check anything out. In fact, I specifically told her to wait for you. If your woman went frolicking off by herself, then that's on her."

"Fuck," I breathe, tapping the driver on the shoulder and directing him toward the Barrens instead.

"You realize she can handle herself, right? She doesn't need you to be her knight in shining armor."

"I'm well aware. What else can you tell me about this place?"

"Nothing. Even if I could, I probably wouldn't, since you're being an asshole," she grumbles, and my hands itch to strangle her.

"Why is it that all the women around here..."

"Be careful how you finish that sentence, Drake. There's quite a few of us who could take care of you without a moment's hesitation."

Despite my frustration, I recognize the threat for exactly what it is. I pull in a deep breath, reining in my chaotic thoughts. I didn't want to leave Ember alone in the first place, but I didn't think she'd bolt off on some random fucking mission the second I left.

"Again, I'm aware," I snap. "Except someone is actively trying to kill her."

"I'm bored of this conversation. I don't have time to educate you on how fucked up your thinking is when it comes to your woman, who might not be your woman much longer if you keep treating her like a damsel who needs saving."

She hangs up before I can respond, which is probably for the best since I have no idea what to say. Tapping my phone against my lips, I watch the buildings fly by. Nicki may be right and I'm a fucking asshole, but I can't just stop worrying about Ember because she's capable of taking care of shit herself. I *know* she can, which is why it scares me so much. She's too blasé about her survival.

By the time we make it to the edge of the Barrens, I've tried to call her a dozen times. It always goes straight to voicemail. I change into jeans in the backseat as the driver pretends he doesn't hear me struggling to get them on. Leaving my suit coat in the car, I wave him off. I may not need to save Ember, but she's certainly going to get an earful about sneaking off on her own.

Thirty-Six

Ember

"Well, this is a fucking bust." I lean against the bricks of a crumbling building.

I haven't seen a single person since I got to the Barrens. Obviously, I didn't expect the streets to be filled, but the silence is slowly suffocating me. I should give up, go home, and pretend I never left. My ridiculous pride won't let me. I can't slink back to Roman with nothing to show for myself. I don't know why I care so much about his approval.

Grinding my teeth, I push from the wall and stomp down the next street. My ignorance of this city hasn't helped. Even after three hours, I still haven't found the building Nicki told me about. She said it was an old barracks, but I have no idea what that means.

I've been searching every warehouse I come across on the northeast side of the Egg. About an hour ago, I figured out I wouldn't know it even if I did stumble across it. I'm still kicking myself for wasting so much time on this wayward mission.

I switched goals to finding anything that might help us figure out who was attempting to kill us. Anders is the most likely candidate, but Roman is convinced he's still in Rima. Roman's inability to listen to reason is one of the things we'll be talking about when I get back. If I'm going to be staying in Synd with him, even for a little while, he's going to have to stop being a stubborn asshole.

My phone buzzes and I dig my nails into my palm before fishing it out of my pocket. Roman's fake name flashes across the screen. My thumb hovers over the reject button, but I can't do it.

"Yes, Drake?" I lean around a corner to check the next street.

"Where are you?" he grumbles, and I rear back.

I expected him to yell and berate me for going out alone. Instead, he sounds defeated. I didn't want to beat him down with my independence. That wasn't the point of this little adventure. I was trying to prove a point, though when I changed from doing shit for me to doing shit for him is a mystery.

"Oh, I'm around."

He sighs and the line crackles. "I know you're in the Barrens, Ember. I need you to tell me exactly where."

"So you can come save me? I'm perfectly fine, Drake. I'll be home when I'm home."

He grunts and I thump my head against the wood of a shack I'm propped up on.

"We'll discuss when you started calling this home later. Right now, I actually need your help."

I straighten, giddiness overcoming me. "Are you telling me the great Roman Drake needs little ole me to save him?"

"Let's not get carried away."

"Certainly sounds like it to me." A grin blooms across my face. "So, where are you?"

"I'm at the old police precinct. It's roughly three blocks from the river by the train station."

I glance around, trying to pinpoint where I am in relation. It's no use, though. I'll have to backtrack to the water and work my way north. Chewing on my lip, I wonder if I should call Nicki for help. She might not even answer, honestly.

"Okay. Are you alone?"

He doesn't sound like he's surrounded by enemies. If anything, he sounds like the words are being violently torn from him. I wipe away my smile, swallowing down a giggle.

"Yes. Don't come in here like a spy expecting to heroically swipe me from the clutches of a villain. You'll only embarrass yourself."

"Well, I'll be there when I'm there, then. Toodles."

"Do not make me ask twice, Ember," he growls.

I hang up before I laugh at him. He's clearly miserable and the last thing he wants to do is ask me for help. I may revel in his suffering, but I'm not vindictive.

It takes me another ten minutes to find my way to the river and start the slog upstream. Several bridges span the water, connecting the city. I finally spot a car crossing one and I hide in a doorway until they pass. I can't imagine growing up in Synd with this area right here. Do the suburban moms clench their butts as they pass through this dark area? Do the elite clutch their pearls, waiting for the big, bad monster to jump out at them?

I shake my head, scolding myself for not paying more attention to my surroundings. This place might not scare me like it does the upper class of society, but I still have a healthy respect for it. Especially after TJ and Roman drilled it into me this wasn't a criminal's playground. Labeling me a criminal felt strange. For once I didn't argue, though.

My feet begin to ache the further I trudge along. Taking the river seemed like a good idea, but now I'm wondering if I should have found the train station first and gone from there. The sun isn't even close to setting or else I'd use the lights as a compass point. When I think I've gone far enough, I skip three blocks down and start the slow process of checking the buildings as I pass.

Stumbling on a chunk of concrete, I curse. When I glance around, contemplating throwing it in rage, my mouth drops open. I'm surprised I didn't notice it as I cavorted around the silent streets for hours. It's decrepit with boards hammered over the front windows. Clearly this is an old police station, though. The harsh architectural corners speak to another place and time.

I hesitate before waltzing through the front door. Slipping the gun I grabbed before I left from my hoodie pocket, I squint into the dark interior. A methodical clanking of metal reverberates through the empty space. My heart hammers in my ears, panic momentarily overriding my common sense. I slowly inhale, then exhale to calm my racing pulse.

Quieting my footfalls, I tiptoe through a door frame, fractured pieces of wood littering the floor. I peek in each room until I come to another entrance. The heavy metal has a small window cut out of it and I stretch to see inside. Cells line the wall, minus the prisoners of years past. The clanking pauses, then resumes.

Easing open the door, I cringe, waiting for the hinges to squeal, but it swings open silently. I peek around the frame, but it's even darker back here. As I contemplate pulling out my phone to light the way, someone clears their throat, and I jerk back.

"Stop playing around and get me out of here, Ember." Roman's annoyed voice floats from the last cell and I sigh.

I grab my phone and bring up the flashlight. Stomping down the hall, I jump when the door slams shut behind me. He growls and I quicken my pace, then slow as I realize what I'm doing. My nerves are shot. Adding an extra skip to my step, I saunter to the last cell, then lean against the wall across from him.

He doesn't look any worse for wear, but I can't imagine how he got himself in this predicament. Glaring at me, he gestures to the lock as if I should know how to open it.

"What exactly am I supposed to be doing?" I ask, tucking my gun away.

His nostrils flare and his eyes fall closed. Probably praying for patience. I wipe the smirk from my mouth as I watch the internal struggle march across his face.

"Get me out of here."

"And how did you get locked up in the first place?"

He bares his teeth, snarling, but I just smile sweetly back at him. He paces away from the bars, then back—a caged beast waiting for the moment he's free to pounce on his prey. Namely me. A shiver runs through me at the thought.

"I thought *you'd* be here since this was the place Nicki was talking about. I thought I saw something back here, but when I stepped inside, I must have brushed against the door, and it slammed shut." He wraps his hands around the bars, knuckles turning white the longer he grips them.

"Did you try opening it?"

"For fuck's sake, Ember. Just get me the fuck out of here," he bellows, voice echoing through the space.

"What'll you give me if I do?" I smirk at his slack-jawed expression.

"You have got to be fucking kidding me. I should have called Rigger," he mumbles, dropping onto the built-in bed and burying his head in his hands.

A pang shoots through me, and I straighten, pushing off the wall. Without a word, I step forward and study the lock. I doubt there are any keys randomly stuffed in some forgotten desk. And while I know how to pick a lock, this isn't a standard one on a house. Maybe he *should* have called Rigger. He'd at least have an idea who to get ahold of. I fiddle with the lock, trying not to make any noise, but with the old metal, it's impossible.

Roman's eyes, almost black in the shadows, burn a hole through me as I fixate on getting the damn door open. When he stands up, though, I step back. Fumbling with my phone, I scroll through the one contact I have, hoping Rigger's number will magically appear.

"Ember," Roman says softly.

"Do you have his number? I'll go outside and call him," I mutter, eyes fixed on the useless device.

I don't even know why I have it. I use my computer for most things, rarely using my phone. There's no one to call, anyway. The only people in my life who would bother are missing or in this room, and I don't even know if Roman actually counts. He's reached out to me a total of one time before I came to Synd, and that was for a favor. I don't know how he knew to ask me, but he did. I told myself I kept the same number all these years in case Aelia called, but it was for him too. No matter how much I tried to smother that little ball of hope within me, it would never fully snuff out.

"Ember," he calls again, more forceful this time.

I can't bring myself to look at him. The screen goes dark, not that it matters. My vision is already swimming, fingers trembling, and the voice inside scolds me for caring. It yells at me to pull myself together. Of course shit wouldn't change between us. Just because we slept together doesn't change the fact that we're constantly at odds. I don't know why this situation is hitting me harder than all the rest, but it is, and I don't know what to do other than get the hell out of here so he doesn't catch me crying.

"Just text me his number. He should know who to call."

I jolt as Roman's fingers wrap around my wrist, tugging me toward the bars separating us. His other hand cups my cheek and his thumb tips my chin until our eyes meet. Biting my tongue, I struggle to drop the mask over my features. I'd rather he didn't know I'm on the brink of a breakdown.

"What do you need?" I ask, voice strained, but at least I'm not crying. Yet.

His eyes dart over my face, searching for something I'm not sure I want him to find. When his brows pull low, I hold my breath. Every muscle in my body tenses as his hand slides under my hair, gripping my neck.

I open my mouth to make some snarky comment, or maybe an excuse to get out of this mess, but he yanks me against the bars, his lips crashing into mine.

It only lasts a few seconds before his kiss eases, coaxing me until his tongue slips inside. I melt the slightest bit, and he growls his approval. Thoughts empty from my head, doubts floating away one by one. They'll attack me later, most likely the next time he spouts some bullshit, but for now I'll bask in the bliss of feeling cherished.

He eases back, resting his forehead against mine, but the cold metal doesn't make it nearly as endearing as it usually is.

"I'm sorry," he whispers, and I jerk back.

I don't make it far with his hand tightening on my neck. I'm so caught off guard I don't have time to school my face. He gives me a soft smile, one I don't think I've ever seen before.

"Getting locked up really changed you, huh?"

Roman's head tips back, a full-blown grin taking over, and I'm caught. En-snared. Bewitched. Maybe I always have been. Maybe I never truly broke free. He's always had a hold over me, but maybe that's not such a bad thing anymore.

Thirty-Seven

Roman

I fucked up, but at least Ember is here to keep me company. She paces in front of my cell, muttering to herself. I swear she's about ready to pull out her gun and shoot the damn lock. Not that I'd blame her. I had the same thought before I called her to save my ass.

"Call Nicki," I yell to Ember when she gets too far away.

It makes my skin itch being here—locked up. I didn't think my time in the Byrns basement had that much of an effect on me, but the longer I spend in here, the more I realize it fucked me up. It wasn't the first time I'd been locked away. My father's favorite form of punishment when I was a child was shoving me in a closet. Once we moved to Westmont, he built a holding cell on the lower level, shoving me down there whenever he deemed me unfit, which was more often than not.

I tried to shield Aelia from his manic behaviors. Once she got older, it was harder to hide our father's tendencies for violence. I can still picture her at ten years old, dark ponytail swinging as she loped down the stairs to sneak me desserts through the small window set in the door. Whenever I scolded her, made her promise to stop, she'd give me a sweet smile, nod. Then she'd show up the next day as if we'd never discussed it.

"I'm not calling Nicki. She probably won't even pick up. You call her," Ember grumbles.

She kicks the bars on the cell next to mine, then jumps around for a while, muttering curses before sliding onto her ass against the opposite wall.

"Get that out of your system?" I lean on my forearms through the bars and lace my fingers together.

"Fuck you."

I can't help the grin from spreading across my face. Then I remember how shitty I was to her, and I sober, glancing away.

"I'm sorry about before."

"That's the third time you've apologized to me. Did you hit your head when you got shot? Maybe this is a side effect of a concussion."

I suck in a deep breath, preparing myself for more groveling. It's not lost on me I told Hawk all those weeks ago that I'd never do such a thing. Once I was shot and she was stabbed, though, I can't seem to get it out of my head that she belongs with me. If groveling is how I convince her, then that's what I'll do. Swallowing my pride won't be easy, but I need to if I stand any chance at keeping her.

"Let's focus on getting me out of here first. Then we can discuss the future."

She rolls her head toward me, narrowing her eyes. "And just what exactly does *that* mean?"

"Em, you realize you've been calling Synd home for the last couple weeks, right?"

Shock spreads across her face, and I grin again. The ache in my chest eases when she pushes to her feet. Pursing her lips, she studies the lock, then pulls out her gun. I back up, holding my hands up, and she rolls her eyes.

"I'm not going to shoot you," she says, giving me a look.

"Didn't think you were, love. But a bullet can ricochet. I'd rather not get an ass full of shrapnel because you got impatient. Why don't you just search for the keys?" It's something I've been pushing her to do for the last hour, but she keeps ignoring me.

"Fine," she growls, fierceness flashing across her face. "I'll go look for the keys, which won't be there because no one would leave them just lying around, even if this is an abandoned police station. And even if someone did leave them behind, they won't be here after all these years. But of course, I'll follow your commands like a good girl and look for the damn keys."

She's panting by the time she's done with her tirade. Her eyes dart to mine and then away again. Tilting my head, I study her until it clicks. I saunter to the bars, wrapping my fingers around the cool metal, and track the blush traveling from her neck to her cheeks. My mouth waters and my cock hardens.

"Be a good girl and find the keys, Ember, and I'll reward you."

She squeezes her legs together, still unable to meet my eye. I know I've won when she scowls, then stomps away. I'd rather not have her out of my sight, but since I'm literally locked up, I don't have a choice. Readjusting myself, I try to ease the ache. When the words "good girl" came out of her mouth, it was like a shot of desire straight to my cock.

"Did you find anything?" I yell.

"Would I still be bumbling around if I did?" she bellows back.

I count the seconds to pass the time until she cries out in triumph.

The giddiness on her face when she comes around the corner has my stomach swooping. A ring of keys dangles from her fingers as she laughs. She gets to work trying them in the lock, jiggling each in turn. When she finds the right one, she squeals, bouncing on the balls of her feet as she slides the door open.

"You're free," she exclaims, grinning.

Instead of stepping out, though, I grab her hips and tug her into the cell with me. She squawks, hands landing on my chest, and I cut off the sound as I cover her mouth with my own. Sliding my hands to her ass, I squeeze, then pick her up. Her legs wind around my waist as I devour her. Stepping forward, the metal rattles when I trap her against the bars. The door slams shut, and she jolts, tearing her mouth from mine. Panting, she stares at the lock, keys still dangling from it.

"Don't worry about it," I say, swooping down to kiss her neck.

"I swear if I get locked in here because you couldn't wait to get your dick wet..." Her threat is lost in a moan as I grind my cock into her, only a few layers of fabric separating me from what I crave.

"Stop talking," I growl.

I push her sweatshirt up, bunching it under her arms, then shoving her bra down to free her tits. Before she can protest, I suck a nipple into my mouth, swirling my tongue over the bud, and it hardens. A whimper falls from her lips and her fingers grip my hair. She tugs, forcing me to the other one. Her head smacks against the metal and she moans.

"How attached are you to these pants?" I ask, snapping the waistband of her leggings.

Her head snaps up, glaring. "Do not fucking rip my pants. I'm not walking around the Barrens without something on my lower half."

I smirk, skimming my hand across her stomach, then between her legs. As I rub her pussy through the fabric, her breath hitches, but the edge in her eyes remains.

"I only need a hole." I say, pressing my thumb against her clit, and she gasps.

"No. Absolutely not. Put me down."

Reluctantly, I let her drop from my grasp. She shoots daggers at me once last time before she pushes me back. My blood heats as she kicks off her shoes, then peels the leggings from her body. Only a thong remains, her tits still on full display.

She reaches for my belt, and I tip my head back. Within seconds, she pulls my cock out, wrapping her hand around my length and squeezing. I groan, fingers gripping the bars above her head as she strokes me.

"Em, you have to stop," I wheeze all while thrusting into her hand.

"Is that so?"

It's the cockiness in her tone that finally makes its way through the haze of pleasure riding me. I freeze, dropping my chin to my chest and panting. She strokes me again, running her thumb over the tip, and I shudder. A few more passes and I'll be coming all over her hand.

Grabbing her wrist, I force her arm above her head, pressing my body into hers. The heat from her pussy envelops my cock and I'm not even inside her yet. Scraping my teeth along the tendons in her neck, I rub my length along her. She whimpers every time I hit her clit.

"Legs around me, love," I grunt.

Digging my fingers into her ass, I lift her, and her heels hit my lower back. I shove her panties to the side and line my cock up with her dripping pussy. I plunge into her in one stroke. She quivers around me, gasping, and I pull out slowly. Surging into her again, she moans. The door clatters with every thrust until it's ringing through the space as I fuck her harder and harder.

"Please," she whines, then bites my neck as she spasms around my cock.

I almost come then, watching her climax roll through her body. Slowing, I drag out her pleasure as long as possible. Her tongue darts out, licking at her bottom lip. Hooded eyes find mine and something settles in my chest—a piece I've been missing for a long time.

"Exquisite," I murmur, then suck her nipple into my mouth.

"Roman," she moans, writhing in my grasp.

"Look at how greedy your pussy is, swallowing my cock."

Her head drops, watching as I leisurely thrust into her. Her pussy clings to me, needy sounds falling from her lips.

"Faster," she gasps.

"Like this?" I barely increase my pace.

She huffs, clenching around me, and I grunt.

"Two can play at that game."

Sliding my hand into her hair, I grip the strands and force her head back. I lick up her throat, nipping at her bottom lip as I slam into her once more.

"This isn't a game, Ember. You're mine. And when you walk out of here, my cum dripping from this pretty pussy, you'll finally understand how serious I am."

Her eyes roll back in her head as I pound into her hard and fast. Her pussy quivers and bliss floods her face, but I don't stop.

Slipping my hand to her throat, I squeeze and her eyes flutter open, desire swimming in the green pools. One orgasm flows into the next, and she sobs, her body going limp in my arms.

"One more," I say between gritted teeth.

She shakes her head, body shuddering. I wrap my arm around her, angling my hips.

She cries out, still moving with me. "I can't!"

"Come around my cock. Now."

My words tip her over the edge. I explode with her as I groan out her name. She clings to me, and I bask in the glow of being joined with her. Her legs fall from my waist. I shuffle back, landing hard on the bench. We're still joined, her straddling me, and I watch as she comes back to her body.

When she leans back, only my hands on her waist keeping her upright, she sighs. I'll stay in her heat as long as possible. Outside this cell are problems and decisions we can't ignore. Inside, it's just us, joined together in ecstasy.

She rolls her hips, forcing a groan from me. When she pushes up, pussy squeezing my tip, I groan. Sinking down, she shudders, forehead landing on my chest.

"Ride me, Ember. Take what you want."

She sits up and starts moving. I swear I almost come again when her hand drops to her clit. As her movements become erratic, I grip her waist and thrust into her. Watching her fuck herself using my cock is the hottest thing I've ever seen. Her pussy flutters around me.

"Eyes on me, love."

Green peeks out from the slits, finding my eyes, and she shudders, her orgasm cresting over her. Collapsing in my arms, I hold her close, lightly skimming my lips across her damp skin. As she tucks her head into my neck, a contented sigh leaves me.

A wave of possessiveness floods over me. Ember belongs to me. I pity anyone who tries to take her. They'll never survive my wrath.

Thirty-Eight

Ember

"You know, it was hot when you said it, but actually walking around with damp thighs is not fun."

Roman barks out a laugh, bringing our linked fingers to his lips and pressing a kiss to the back of my hand. I'm so confused by the turnaround in him. He's still an asshole to everyone else, but there's a softness in his eyes when he looks at me. It's freaking me out. It's also easing the ache I've been carrying for the past ten years, and I don't know what to do with that.

I clear my throat. "We should figure out how we're going to catch whoever is trying to kill you."

"Us. They're trying to kill us, Ember." He tugs me down another abandoned street. "Eventually they'll get annoyed their people keep failing and come after us themselves. They'll mess up and we'll deal with them."

"And then?" I ask, holding my breath.

He pulls me to a stop, raising an eyebrow. I shake my head, trying to yank my hand back, but he stops me.

"Don't do that. What exactly do you want to know, Ember?"

His eyes hold too many questions. They're heavy with emotions I don't want to face right now, especially in the middle of the Barrens.

"I was just wondering when these mysterious mafia men are coming back," I hedge, avoiding his gaze.

He pulls his phone from his pocket, brows pulling low. A single lock of blond hair falls over his forehead. My palm itches to push it back into place, but I curl my fingers into a fist.

"That's not what you were going to say, but we'll have to finish this conversation later."

He pulls me around the corner, his long strides making it hard to keep up. I'm about to tell him to slow down when he stops abruptly and I run into his back. My eyes water and I rub my nose, locking down the cuss words I want to spew at him.

"You really shouldn't be here," Nicki says from the shadows.

She steps into the light, and I breathe a sigh of relief. She's the only sign of life I've seen. Otherwise, it's been skittering rocks and the wind howling through the empty alleys. I was wondering if everyone was exaggerating about people living down here. If I hadn't seen the Egg with my own eyes, I would probably assume they were pulling my leg.

"We ran into a bit of trouble," Roman mumbles, shooting me a look.

I stick my tongue out at him, but he's already turned away. Nicki's eyebrows climb up her forehead, pursing her lips when she spots our joined hands.

"What type of trouble?" she asks, crossing her arms.

"The kind he got himself into," I mutter, and he scowls in my direction.

"Nothing you need to worry about." He clears his throat, rubbing his free hand over his face. "We found the barracks but nothing was there . Are you sure you have the right spot?"

I groan, tipping my head back. Finally yanking my hand from his, I step away. He's glaring at me again, but I'm not going to be lumped in with his asinine comments.

"I swear he just doesn't think before he speaks, Nicki. *I* know you are capable of running shit down here and *Drake* does too, regardless of the bullshit he's spewing."

She shoots me a bemused smile, then turns to Roman and raises an eyebrow.

"I never said she wasn't capable. Stop trying to throw me under the bus," he hisses.

"I'll let it slide this time, but get your shit together, Drake, or you'll find yourself banned again," Nicki says.

Roman rolls his eyes, and Nicki winks at me. Roman told me she doesn't converse with outsiders, namely anyone who doesn't live in the Barrens. She seems pretty friendly to me. Maybe it's just him. I wouldn't put it past him to alienate someone only to find out later he should've been befriending them. Most people think he's condescending, but I'm pretty sure he pushes people away on purpose.

If he never lets anyone in, they can't hurt him. I wonder how much I contributed to that. Most likely more than I'm willing to accept.

"I have a plan, but it will require us to be in the Barrens," Roman says, crossing his arms.

Nicki shakes her head. "I don't control who comes and goes from the Barrens, Drake. I'm in charge of the Egg and that's it."

"We both know that's not true, and it's beside the point. Do you have anyone down here that could help us create a diversion?"

"A diversion." It's a statement, not a question.

Whatever grand plan he's cooked up, he didn't share it with me. He had plenty of time while we were skipping around. I won't call him out in front of Nicki, though. She's busted his balls enough for the both of us.

"Nothing big. I'm not asking you to set the river on fire." He smirks and her nostrils flare the slightest bit.

"Oookay. How about we go—" I hesitate, sucking my cheeks in. "We'll go back to the house, and Roman can give you a call later."

He opens his mouth, probably to spit some more bullshit, but Nicki nods, disappearing into the shadows before he can. He huffs, not bothering to wait for me as he stomps away. I stare off to where Nicki went, wondering if she'd put me up for the night. Probably not. We might have been on the same side when she was berating Roman, but that doesn't make us friends.

Sighing, I start to follow Roman, then stutter to a stop. When I asked him earlier what would happen after we dealt with whoever is after us, I thought he'd brush me off. It's hitting me now that I have nowhere to go.

Sure, I could fuck off to Rima and try to find Aelia, but the longer I search for her, the more I'm convinced I'm headed for heartache. The idea that she's still out there after all this time is a long shot at best. There's no evidence I've found that she's alive. Everything I've found points to Anders being the only survivor. Even if I confront him, there's no way he'll just hand over the answers because I asked nicely. Not that I would be kind about it. Either way, I'm chasing a dream that no longer seems plausible.

"Ember, I swear to fuck all. I don't have time to...Ember?"

I swallow hard, peering at him in the darkness. A tear falls down my cheek, but I don't bother to wipe it away. I didn't even realize I was crying. Slowly, I turn away, stumbling forward until I crash to my knees. Burying my head in my hands, I sob.

I've spent so long with this one goal, the loss of it feels like I'm losing Aelia all over again. When Roman threw me out, refusing to listen to me, I threw all my energy into finding her. I've spent my whole adult life running from the grief of losing her, never fully accepting it—fighting the one person who might understand.

Roman's arms wrap around me, his body covering mine. Bile crawls up my throat, threatening to choke me. My hands land on the gritty street, gravel working its way under my nails and biting into my flesh. As I heave, Roman rubs my back in slow circles with one hand, holding my hair from my face with the other. I can't tell if he's helping or making it worse, but I can't bring myself to shove him away.

Swiping the back of my hand across my mouth, I grimace at the mess. I roll to the side, landing hard on my ass, and I prop my elbows on my knees. I can't look Roman in the eye, afraid he'll notice something in my gaze and read the truth within their depths. He was right all along, and I can't handle admitting that to him.

"Ember." His tone has my head shooting up, despite my resolve to avoid him. "How long?"

My mouth flaps open, not sure how to answer him. He can't know the transformation I've just been through. The harsh lines in his face, the accusation in his eyes, and the tenseness of his muscles makes my skin itch. I feel guilty without knowing what I'm supposed to feel guilty about.

"Don't fucking lie to me. Tell me how long." He sits back on his heels, resting his forearms on his thighs, hands clenched into fists.

"I don't know what you're talking about." Another tear slides down my face.

He scoffs, glancing down an alley before pushing to his feet. When he paces away, I expect him to disappear again, leaving me here alone to pick up the pieces of my shattered resolve. Instead, he rounds back, jabbing a finger in my direction.

"Don't bullshit me. You can't fucking hide the fact you're puking in the middle of the fucking Barrens. How fucking long?"

I huff out a humorless laugh, shaking my head. "I'm not pregnant. And the fact you think I would keep that shit from you is insulting."

I push to my feet, dizziness invading my head, and I sway. Closing my eyes, I breathe deeply through my nose, willing away another bout of nausea. Roman's scent invades my senses, filling me up whether I like it or not. I try to wave him off without opening my eyes, but he grips my wrist, sliding his other arm around my waist.

His fingers tangle with my curls, pressing my face to his chest, and I tremble in his grasp. A war wages within me, each side fighting for dominance—for the right to either pull him closer or push him away. Neither wins as my knees give out and he curses.

Then I'm floating, a weightlessness enveloping me. I tuck my head into his chest and my fingers twist the fabric of his shirt. I'll yell at him later for pissing me off. Right now, I need his strength, even if I steal it silently. Every conversation we've had about Aelia has been disastrous. Another one will likely end the same way. I need him, though. I've fought him for so long, I don't know how to change that.

After ten minutes, I finally have some semblance of control over myself. I'll deal with all the other emotions later. It might be a cop-out, but there are too many problems piling at our door to add one more.

I pull in deep breaths, my pulse returning to normal. There's a new ache resting within my heart, but I doubt that will ever go away. I'll carry the pain of losing my best friend for the rest of my life.

I should tell him to put me down, but I kind of like being carried like a princess. He deserves to have to haul my ass around after the bullshit he pulled. I swallow a snort, remembering his accusations, which were completely baseless. I've been living in his back pocket for the last few weeks.

"Drake," I choke out through the thickness in my throat. "I feel like you've changed."

"I know." His steady footsteps echo through the night.

"Hard time will do that to a person I suppose," I whisper, and he freezes.

My body shakes with the force of trying to keep my laughter inside. He growls, then drops my legs.

I stumble, afraid he's going to dump me fully on the ground, but he catches me around the waist, pressing his chest into my back. His hand wraps around my throat, thumb forcing my chin up. My head swims, even as a shiver rolls through me as his breath ghosts across the shell of my ear.

"You think you're pretty fucking funny, don't you?" He spins me around, trapping my arms between our bodies.

"You're the one who accidentally locked themselves in a jail cell and had to call me to save you," I hiss, struggling against the temporary prison he's caged me in.

All the anger I tried to ignore at my realizations surrounding Aelia wells up, cresting over my senses, and my vision goes dark.

"You're right. For fuck's sake, Ember, you're right." His forehead lands on mine.

"You're an asshole," I breathe, my rage dissipating as quickly as it swamped me.

"I know," he whispers. "I know."

Thirty-Nine

Roman

This entire day has been a shitshow and the sun has barely set in the suburbs. The Barrens seem to darken long before the rest of Synd as if even Ra himself has forgotten those who reside here.

I snort, wondering when I'll stop being obsessed with Ancient Egypt. Glancing at Ember plodding along next to me, I'm transported back to when Aelia and Ember would sneak into my room, stealing the few books on the subject I was able to hide from my father.

"What?" she asks, wariness in her green eyes.

"Nothing," I say gruffly, quickening my pace.

She huffs, grabbing my arm to slow me down again. "Seriously, what?"

"I was just remembering the books you and Aelia used to steal from me."

She pulls me to a stop, wide eyes scanning my face. My heart clenches and I swallow hard. Today has had too many emotions. Too many feelings. I'm fucking over today. She scowls, and I'm once again on solid ground. I know how to deal with her snarky remarks. Her tears are another story.

"First of all, it wasn't stealing. It was borrowing." She crosses her arms, cocking her hip out. "Second, Aelia had nothing to do with it."

She tips her chin up, daring me to call her out. I run my tongue over my teeth, taking the time to process her words.

"Are you telling me you snuck into my room, rifled through my things, found my hiding spots, and stole my books?"

"Borrowed. I *borrowed* your books. And I always put them back. No harm, no foul." She crosses her arms and purses her plump lips.

"Except that's not true," I growl, stepping closer, and she straightens in surprise. "My father found one of them when you left it on my bed. He tore my entire room apart and took everything he deemed unnecessary for a future head of the mafia and made me watch while he burned them. And then he did the same to Aelia."

Her lips part, eyes taking on a faraway look as she peers over my shoulder. She couldn't have known how far Anders would go. He never was a patient man, but I was able to shield my sister for much longer than I thought possible. The only time I didn't...the usual stab of pain shoots through me when I think of Aelia.

"I didn't know."

"Of course you didn't. I made Aelia promise not to tell you."

I turn, continuing toward the bright lights emanating from the train station a couple blocks ahead. When I don't hear her footsteps behind me, I spin around. She's right where I left her, still lost in her own world. Or maybe in the past. I take my time studying her.

A soft summer breeze sends her curly red hair floating around her head, creating a halo. The smattering of freckles across her face seem to glow in the muted light. When I was younger, I wanted to kiss each one of them. It was the fanciful whim of a teenager forced into a role I never wanted to fill, in a future I never wanted to settle for. Now, I can't imagine any other life, but I wonder who we would be were we raised like everyone else.

"But she told me loads of shit you told her not to," she says, brows pulled low over her eyes.

"I shielded her, and she shielded you. I thought that was common knowledge."

She looks so lost, as if I've dismantled her entire world with a single sentence. We've been through enough tonight without adding more shit to the list of trauma we need to unpack.

A shadow looms behind her and I tense. Nicki appears, narrowing her eyes and shooing me away. I grab Ember's hand and haul her toward the station. She yelps, pulling at my grip, but I keep hold of her.

"Stop. Nicki needs us gone," I whisper harshly.

"Nicki?" She whips her head back the way we came, stumbling into me.

I drop her hand, wrapping my arm around her waist instead. For someone with so much training, she sure is clumsy tonight. I wonder how much has to do with her breakdown earlier.

It's just another thing we'll have to deal with later. Everything else is being pushed down the line. I can only hope she'll stick around long enough to hash things out. Now that I've decided she's mine, I'll fight to keep her by my side, no matter where we end up.

I don't imagine I'll be welcome in Synd once the others get back. Even if I wasn't their former enemy, with our current predicament I doubt they'll ask me to stay on. Once again, I'll be left with no purpose, no direction. Except this time, I'll have Ember by my side. Unless she's still set on finding Aelia.

The thought has me tripping over my own feet, practically taking Ember down with me. She grips my side, steadying me. If Ember can't give up on her search for someone who's long dead, our future is over before it's even started.

Shaking my head, I usher her into the car I borrowed from Byrns's garage. It's shitty, barely functioning, but the little sedan blends in. I smirk as I open the passenger door for Ember.

"Why are you grinning?" she grumbles when I slide into the driver's seat.

"This is the same car Byrns used to stalk Lacey."

"You know I have no idea who these people are, right? Like I've looked them up and shit, but I've never met them."

She leans against the window, staring at the trains leaving the station as I pull out of the parking lot. Her fingers flex in her lap, knuckles cracking as she works through whatever is running through her mind. When she pulls her bottom lip between her teeth, I reach over and cover her hands with my own.

"Didn't realize you still did that," I murmur, glancing at her as we pull up to a red light.

She turns, teeth scraping against her lip. "Did what?"

Brushing my thumb across the red mark she's left behind, I stare at her mouth. Her chin quivers under my touch, but I can't pull away. Someone behind us honks, and we jump away from each other. The car jerks forward in my haste, and I bang my knee against the steering column.

After several minutes of silence, she clears her throat. "What exactly am I still doing?"

"Cracking your knuckles, biting your lip. You did that when you were younger, but I haven't seen you do it until now." I shouldn't have said anything, but I can't take the words back.

"Today wasn't exactly peaceful. You still run your fingers through your hair when you're stressed, so you don't really have a leg to stand on, buddy."

I roll my eyes, concentrating on driving. She's the only one who frustrates me enough to muss up my hair. I haven't told her yet that we're moving to the Kings' house tonight. The only reason I set up at the Byrns estate in the first place was because of Moss and TJ. With them out of commission, it feels like the right time to leave. It won't throw off whoever is after us for long, but it might give us a break.

"Don't call me buddy."

"Why not? That's what...you know what? Never mind."

Pulling into the driveway, I circle around the fountain and park. Neither of us moves to get out. If we just sit here, we won't have to deal with anything. It'll be like the rest of the world doesn't exist. Someone would eventually find us, but it might take a while. The silence swirling around us is heavy, filled with unspoken words and unfulfilled promises.

"I'm moving to the Kings' place," I murmur.

Her head thumps against the window. "When?"

"Tonight. There's just a few things left to pick up."

She sighs, fogging up the glass. My muscles tighten and I grip the steering wheel, waiting for her to protest. When she says nothing, I shove the door open and step out. I don't have time to wait for her to decide how much she wants to fight me. I round the hood, intent on forcing her from the car, but she's climbing out before I get there.

I pivot, stomping up the stairs, Ember's soft footsteps gradually following. The house is silent as we make our way through. I sent most of the men away, needing them to clean up the Depot. The fire wasn't as bad as I originally thought, but I've been letting Rigger deal with most of it. He keeps asking me when Byrns is coming back as if I'm in regular communication with them. No one has picked up since I spoke to Ren weeks ago. Hawk's been avoiding my questions about it. Not that he owes me anything.

"Do you have a bag?" Ember asks as I push open the door to the bedroom we've been staying in.

I got used to calling it mine, but this is all temporary. The house, the cars, the position will all disappear in the blink of an eye. I have enough money to go anywhere, but I'm still in limbo. The thought won't leave me, eating away at my resolve to do what I can to rebuild Synd. I don't like not knowing what's going to happen next.

"Most of it has been moved over already. Just your computer and some random things are left." I glance around the bathroom, scanning the space for anything that might have been missed.

"My clothes?" she calls, still standing in the doorway.

"Gone," I reply, stomping to the closet.

I gather up the shorts and tank top in the back of a forgotten drawer, stuffing them into the computer bag I bought her. As far as I know, she hasn't used the machine yet. The last time it was opened was at the store when they installed programs she said she'd never use. Why I bought it if she's not going to even open it is beyond me.

Closing my eyes, I pull in a deep breath, centering myself. It's not Ember's fault we have to move. It's not her fault I've been an asshole. It's not her fault someone is trying to kill her. At least as far as I know.

I grab the bag, making my way back into the room and toss it on the bed. Ember hovers around the entrance, cracking her knuckles again. I shake my head, searching for more things the men missed. I didn't want to relegate them to packing up our shit, but I don't have time for it.

I'm digging through the nightstand when I catch her moving from the corner of my eye. She loops the strap over her arm and drags it off the bed, then steps back carefully. My phone buzzes and I pull it from my pocket. Rigger's text stares back at me. Every time he contacts me, he's delivering bad news. As I'm staring at the screen, another one comes through from Hawk and rage rolls through me. We need a goddamn break, but there's no end in sight.

"Anything else?" Ember asks softly.

"Uh, what?" I glance at her before focusing on my phone again. "No. That's all."

I shoot off a quick reply to Rigger, hoping he's up for dealing with the contractor who's trying to fuck us over. Then I call Hawk, nerves pulled tight as it rings.

I drop onto the bed, head in my hand with the phone pressed to my ear. His voicemail picks up, and I throw the phone onto the nightstand. It clatters across the wood, then drops to the carpet. The screen goes dark, and I rub my hands over my face. The bed dips next to me, Ember's unique scent washing over me.

"Anything I can do?"

"No." I dig my nails into my scalp, hoping the pain will center me.

"Alright. Do you want me to call someone?"

I grit my teeth, part of me wanting to unleash on her all the shit I'm dealing with, all the feelings swamping me, all the decisions I'm being forced to make. The louder half screams, warning me away from exposing myself.

My father may have been a grade-A asshole, but he taught me enough to know that leaning on someone else only exposes me to betrayal. Vulnerability equals weakness, and I'll never make that mistake again. The results always end in death.

"No," I say after a minute of silence.

"I'll leave you to it then," she breathes, annoyance weaving with despair.

I don't bother to stop her when she stands, or when the door clicks shut behind her. I just need a minute to get my shit together. Then I'll chase after her. No matter how much time passes or how many things go wrong, I'll keep chasing her, no matter how wrong I know it is.

Forty

Ember

Everything in me screams to run. The sooner I leave, the less time he'll have to find me. Yet the farther I get from Synd, the more of my heart I'll lose. I doubt Roman would notice the pieces of myself I've left behind.

He didn't even bat an eye when I slipped from his bedroom. He was so lost in his own thoughts, worrying about everyone and everything else except for himself. And me, apparently.

I can't blame him. The men who left Synd in his care didn't care about him. They didn't care if he'd be able to handle it. I'm sure they thought it was a fitting punishment for all his transgressions. And if he didn't make it out alive, all the better.

Bitterness rolls though me and I shake my hands like my emotions are simply raindrops coating my skin. All I need to do is flick the water away and I'll be rid of them.

I push open the kitchen door, taking in the room in the soft glow from outside. I finally convinced Roman to turn off some of the floodlights. He didn't until I showed him how easy it was to sneak onto the property without being detected. Making it look like daylight didn't work, since it only created more shadows. He'd scowled, but the next night they were back to the normal ones lining the house.

I never understood why rich people lit the outside of their houses. My parents did it to show off, of course. "What's the point of having money if no one knows you have it?" my father would say. I guess they all think like that no matter which side of the law they live on.

I open seven cabinets in search of food before I give up, collapsing onto a stool at the massive island. The urge to run overwhelms me again, and I drop my head in my hands, elbows posted on the counter.

"You look like you could use some pie."

I jolt, tipping the stool over as I scramble back, then freeze. An older woman, bemused expression stamped across her face, regards me from across the room. She closes the sliding door she must have silently slipped through without me noticing.

"Who are you?" I ask, reaching for the weapon at my back.

Apparently, I'm not subtle enough since she scolds me with just the rise of an eyebrow and a pointed look at my hand. I drop it back to my side. Guilt and shame flood through me, quickly followed by confusion. I have no idea who this woman is, why she's here, or if she's even supposed to be in the house, yet I am feeling guilty. It doesn't make sense.

"Don't worry, dear. They all feel like that. It's the power of being old," she says, patting her silver hair and then waltzing forward to place a bag on the counter I just vacated.

"Excuse me?"

"All the boys. And their ladies as well. They all have regrets, things they wish they'd done differently."

She grabs items from the sack one at a time. Like Mary Poppins's magic bag, it's never-ending. I wonder if she has some magical food that can heal the hurt inside me—a spoonful of sugar to swallow the bitter reality of my life. I doubt it. Nothing has saved me thus far. The chances of this woman having some cure are far from believable.

"Who are you?" I whisper, wrapping my arms around my waist.

"I'm Marie. I cook for Mason. Have for a long time now. His father hired me when Samantha came along. That man couldn't be bothered to notice the beauty in his midst. Though, that's not surprising in their line of work."

"So, you raised Mason and Samantha?" I ask, not really caring.

I don't know these people. They're like characters in a book, there when I'm reading it, but living in the background of my life. Sometimes I wish I could step into their world—live out their stories alongside them. I doubt they'd appreciate the intrusion, though.

Her laugh isn't tinkling or light like I expected. Instead, it's boisterous and low, bouncing around the room.

"I'm guessing you haven't met them?" she asks, and I shake my head. "Thought so. Those two raised themselves. Or rather, their father tried to corrupt Mason, and the boy did his best to protect his little sister from the same fate. I doubt I had much influence other than what food was in their bellies."

I nod, shuffling forward to right the stool when she turns her back. I don't sit, though, since I'm pretty sure she's going to kick me out as soon as she finds out I'm not supposed to be here.

"It was nice to meet you," I say, stepping back.

She swings around, setting a plate on the counter and points at the stool.

"Sit. Eat."

I rush to obey, almost knocking over the chair again. A fork appears next to the plate and my mouth waters as I stare at a perfect piece of rhubarb pie. Slowly, I take a bite, savoring the tart sweetness and buttery crust. I swallow a moan along with the deliciousness. She sets a bowl of vanilla ice cream and a spoon down as well.

"This is..." I don't have words.

I take another bite and am instantly transported back in time to my grandmother's house. I never saw her anywhere but in the kitchen baking the most delicious desserts. The last time I saw her, she handed me a rhubarb pie, ice cream on the side, just like I liked it. The next day she was gone without an explanation. My mother banned me from going there, but I assume she died. At eight, I didn't understand. My entire life changed in an instant. I holed myself in my room for weeks until my father forced me to go back to school. I met Aelia that day and my life changed again. She's the only reason I survived.

"It's what you need, but the question is why you needed it," Marie says, shooting me a pointed look when I stuff another forkful in my mouth.

I duck my head, scooping up ice cream and finishing off my pie. Maria puts the rest of the food away, grumbling as she tosses several containers out. I didn't realize she was making food for Roman and whoever else comes in here. Roman would either bring me meals or we'd go out. I'm surprised I could even find the kitchen in the first place.

"Another piece, dear?"

I stare at the pie tin, knowing I should refuse. My stomach growls and she smiles, snatching my plate up. Glancing over my shoulder, I wonder where Roman ended up. Is he still frozen on the bed? Did he go into damage control for whatever is happening? Did he even notice I was gone?

"Eat your pie, sweetie. And then tell me why you need it," she demands as she pulls out ingredients.

I have no idea what she's making, but if this pie is any indication, it's going to be amazing.

"You know Drake is going to the Kings' place, right? I don't know how many people are going to be eating your food."

"Well aware. I'm heading over there next, actually. Are you ready to stop hiding?"

I whip my head up, fork halfway to my mouth. "I'm not hiding."

She gives me another look and my face heats. I can't imagine growing up with her staring over the counter, her eyes demanding all your secrets. Although, from what she said, she didn't have much of a hand in their upbringing. Still, it's as if she's staring into my soul.

"Being here isn't easy," I whisper, staring at the half-eaten dessert.

"How do you know Roman?"

"We met in Westmont. His sister, Aelia, is—" My throat closes, cutting off my breath and I cough.

She rounds the island, wrinkled hand rubbing my back, and I drop my chin to my chest. Tears fill my eyes, though whether from choking on nothing or from my almost confessions, I don't know. Marie retreats to her side of the counter, busying her hands in the dough I didn't even notice she was making.

I don't want to finish the sentence, but I have to. "Aelia was my best friend."

"I assume she's gone."

I sniff, swiping my sleeve across my nose. "She died in the attempted coup."

It's the first time I've said it out loud. All the emotions I've been shoving down come boiling out, then tears douse the rage, washing it away, leaving only grief in its wake. My vision darkens and I'm pretty sure I black out. It's the only explanation for why the plate is now languishing on the floor in a million pieces.

Glancing around, I find the stool rocking back and forth. My hands clench at my sides—open, close, open, close. My knuckles crack as I force myself to relax, tipping my head back and sucking in deep breaths.

At least I didn't shoot anything. I swallow hard, then look at Marie, expecting her to be cowering in the corner. I wouldn't blame her.

Instead, she's kneading away, barely paying me any mind. I wonder how many meltdowns she's seen in her years in service to the Byrns mafia. I watch her, tracking her methodical movements. A calmness washes over me as I stare, easing the tension from my shoulders and untying the knot in my stomach. She wipes her hands on a towel hanging from her waist, then grabs a broom and dustpan.

I should offer to clean up the mess, but I can't seem to move. I'm frozen, waiting for the explosion she's sure to have. When she stops next to me, I flinch, squeezing my eyes shut. Her skin is soft, her touch gentle as she cups my cheek and my eyes flutter open.

"No harm done, dear. We all make messes of things sometimes. The important part isn't the mess, it's whether you clean it up."

Silently, I take the broom and get to work. My eyes keep skipping to Marie as she gathers up the dough and plops it in a bowl. Time warps as I attempt to gather every piece, but when I reach down to grab a larger one, Roman's calloused fingers wrap around my wrist.

I don't have time to school my face. My conversation with Marie has rendered the mask of indifference I usually wear useless. Not that I've had much need of it around Roman, anyway. He's capable of melting it away with just one look.

"You'll cut yourself," he murmurs, then takes the broom from my trembling hand. "Good evening, Marie."

"Mr. Drake. Sit," Marie says, using the same commanding tone as she did with me.

He rights the stool, glancing at me before sinking onto it. Another plate appears, this time with several cinnamon rolls. Where she pulled them from, I don't know. I wouldn't be surprised if she conjured them from her magic bag, to be honest.

"You too, dear. You didn't get to finish the last piece."

I slide next to Roman, and we eat in silence while Marie putters around the kitchen. My stomach knots the longer no one speaks. Each second, the silence gets heavier, pressing down on my shoulders until I'm hunched over an empty plate. I don't even remember eating the pie. Sorrow crashes over me at missing out.

Roman's hand sneaks under the counter and squeezes my leg. I don't react, eyes darting to the mess still smeared across the wall. He finishes his food as his thumb draws circles on my leg. My skin heats through my leggings and I don't know how much longer I can ignore it. I clench my thighs together, hoping to ease the desire, but Roman digs his fingers into my flesh.

"Don't leave it too long, you two," Marie calls, and I whip my head up.

The glass door slides shut, and she's gone, leaving us alone. Roman stares at the counter, fingers still latched to my thigh, but I don't think he realizes it. I use his distraction to study him. Dark rings circle his eyes, accentuating the lines framing his face. They weren't there before, at least that I remember. His stubble has morphed into more of a beard, doing nothing to hide his sharp jawline. He looks as exhausted as I feel.

"Well?" His gravelly voice is deeper, tinged with emotions he usually hides.

"Well what?"

"What happened with the plate, Ember?"

I sigh, trying to tug from his grip, but of course he doesn't let me. Pursing my lips, I fold my hands to keep from pushing him off the stool. Lashing out would be easier than answering his questions.

He swings to face me, then turns me as well, tucking my knees between his thighs. Raising an eyebrow, I cross my arms, leaning back as much as possible.

"What happened in the Barrens?" His blue eyes are darker, burning into mine.

I shake my head, biting the inside of my cheek. I've already ripped my heart open enough tonight. First with the realization that I've been lying to myself for years, chasing a phantom that's long since crossed over. And then with Marie's needling gaze and perceptive questions intent on me revealing my soul. Can't he see I'm slowly bleeding out in front of him?

I don't know what he reads on my face, in my eyes, but he nods. Before I know it, he's gathering me against him. Tucking my legs around his waist and guiding my arms around his neck, he stands. I cling to him, burying my head in his neck. I could hide here, pretend my only concerns are how late I get to sleep in, but eventually the real world will intrude.

As we pass one room after another, I turn my head slightly. "Are you going to the Kings now?"

He presses a kiss to my temple without looking. "We'll go tomorrow. Tonight has been enough."

I close my eyes, drifting off before we even make it to his room.

Forty-One

Roman

I peek into the bedroom from the closet for the third time in the last five minutes. Ember is fast asleep, curled into a ball in the middle of the bed. We should have left for the King's place an hour ago, but I didn't have the heart to wake her.

I never did get the answers I needed. Every moment of yesterday plays through my mind, draining me all over again. Whatever happened, I've never seen Ember break down like she did.

"Hawk, I don't have time for subterfuge. Just tell me what the fuck is going on," I grumble.

He's been dancing around the subject the entire time we've been on the phone. He refused to talk to me last night, saying he needed to double check his information.

"I really don't think I should be the one to tell you," he hedges.

"Well, someone better or you're going to have an unexpected visitor."

He sighs, mumbling something to Willow, then sighs again. My nerves wind tighter the longer he makes me wait. It's probably just another thing that's gone to shit I'll have to deal with, but a voice inside screams for me to brace myself.

"I heard from Helms. They're in the thick of it, but Anders went missing. I'll give you one guess where Helms thinks he went."

It confirms everything I've been denying. Of course my father is behind the threats against my life. I doubt he recognizes Ember. Both Aelia and I kept her out of his eyeline as much as we could. He knew her parents, though, so we couldn't hide her completely. I imagine he's targeting Ember merely because of her proximity to me.

Anders idea that a woman makes one weak, especially if one was in love, was fucked up. He always said they were good for continuing a family's line, but not much more. The longer I watched the others and their women, the more I realized he was wrong. Jealousy wormed its way into my heart. I just assumed I'd missed my shot or that love wasn't for me. A painful throb hits my chest as I glance at Ember again, and I rub my fist against the spot.

"I'm not surprised my father decided to come back and finish the job. It's not in his nature to leave things hanging in the balance."

"That's not what you're going to freak out about," Hawk says, then mutters under his breath. I'm pretty sure he's cussing.

"The anticipation is killing me," I say with no inflection.

"I'm sure you won't care, but Mac is on the run. Shane and Sam have disappeared. Mason and Ren are embedded so far into the Guild, no one can get ahold of them. But Helms met someone he thought you might know."

"I don't know anyone. Who did Helms meet?" I shake my head, pacing to the back of the closet. I brace myself, though I doubt anything could prepare me for his next words.

He pauses, sucking in a deep breath. "A woman named Aelia."

My mind short-circuits, instantly rejecting his words. He's still talking, but his voice is muffled. Not that I'm paying attention to him, anyway. There's no way Helms met my sister. She's dead. I've never been more sure of anything in my life, and Helms meeting some random woman with a similar name doesn't change that.

When I come back to reality, he's still blathering on about Helms. I clear my throat, attempting to interrupt him, but he keeps going. I tune him out until he takes a breath.

"So, Helms meets a woman who has a similar name as my dead sister, and you assume it's her? Am I getting that right?"

"Did you not hear anything I just said? She's in with the Guild. She's been here for years. Granted, she apparently doesn't look a thing like you. Helms said she looks like Sam, but Drake, she knows Anders."

My heart skips a beat at his explanations until I dig the heel of my hand into my eye socket, grounding my resolve.

"Hawk, I appreciate this, but there's no way it's the same person. My sister is dead. She has been for ten years. No amount of wishing will bring her back."

"Roman," he says, and I jolt upright at his tone. "Her last name is Drake."

My knees give out, phone tumbling from my fingers. The sound echoes through the empty space. Slamming my forehead against the wooden floors, I press my palms to my ears to drown out the lie. Because that's all it is—an elaborate lie devised by a vindictive asshole who can't just fucking die.

But a voice in the back of my head whispers, *What if it's true?* I can't silence the question, no matter how many times I bash my head against the smooth surface.

I don't know how long I spend on my knees, curled around my despair. When I lift my gaze, I no longer hear Hawk's voice, nor the one in my head. My world rights itself, and I struggle to stand, swaying when I reach my feet. Ember's yawn from the bedroom jolts me fully upright, and I run my hand through my hair. I scoop up my phone, making sure Hawk hung up before I slip it in my pocket.

Stepping into the bedroom, I meet her bleary gaze. Even now, hair a mess around her head and exhaustion weighing heavily on her shoulders, she's enthralling. She glances around as if she's forgotten where she is, then swings her legs over the bed and stands.

As she stretches, arms raised above her head, her shirt rides up, exposing ivory thighs flecked with freckles. I've spent more time than I ever thought I would counting them. If she bent over right now, I'd catch a glimpse of a group of them on her ass in the shape of a flame. It's fitting and incredibly sexy.

She drops her arms, though, tugging at the hem of her shirt. As if I haven't seen her completely naked and writhing underneath me. She glances over her shoulder at me, and I raise an eyebrow at the question in her sparkling green eyes. She huffs, then stomps off to the bathroom, slamming the door behind her.

Reaching down, I adjust myself, squeezing my cock to relieve the tension. It's been too long since I've been inside her, even though it's only been a day. I'd live in her pussy if I could.

Now isn't the time to seduce her. I may not be a good man, but I'd rather not use her body to escape the turmoil within me. I can't erase the image of pressing her against the window as I fuck her from behind, though. It's what I would like to do if we didn't need to leave.

Swiping her pants from the floor, I toss them on the bed as she opens the door again. Her hair is still a mess, but the shirt is gone as well as the tiredness from before. My mouth goes dry as I run my gaze along her curves. She tilts her head, tongue swiping along her bottom lip.

She saunters toward me, swishing her hips in a hypnotic fashion. Like I need another thing to place me under her spell. I can't believe I thought I could fuck her out of my system. The minute she waltzed back into my life, I should have known I'd be lost. That thought doesn't worry me like it once did. If I have to be tied to one woman, I'd choose her every time. Even before she came to Synd, I would've picked her.

Her hand brushes mine as she passes me and my eyes focus on her plump ass, her thong leaving her open to my perusal. The corner of my mouth tips up when I spot a bite mark on her shoulder—a token from our time locked in the jail cell.

When she approaches the large window overlooking the backyard, though, a growl is ripped from me. She doesn't bother to turn when I follow her.

I may have envisioned fucking her right here, but it's early morning. Any of the guards could spot her. I crowd against her back, and she leans into me, resting her head on my chest. Gripping her waist, I dip my head into her neck and sink my teeth into her, hopefully leaving another mark on her skin.

"You're playing a dangerous game, Ember," I murmur into her flesh, then lap at the hurt, and she shudders.

Her arms lift, hands sliding around my neck. She rubs her ass into my cock, my pants and her thong the only things stopped me from sinking into the tight hole. She yelps when I push us forward and her tits meet the cold glass. Ember struggles to untangle herself from the trap I've set.

"Oh no, love. You wanted to be fucked where anyone could see you. And I'll give you exactly what you want."

She doesn't say a word, but stills, panting as I unhook each of her hands and press them against the window above her head.

"Keep them there," I grunt as I drop to my knees.

My resolve has fled. Fucking her right now is a terrible idea. I'll use her body and I won't be gentle. I've checked out, though, separating my emotions from the desire to take what I need from her. My hands tremble and I curl my fingers into my palms, digging my nails into the flesh.

Closing my eyes, I inhale deeply, her scent invading my pores, heating my blood. A whimper escapes her, and I open my eyes before sinking my teeth into her ass, wrapping my hands around her thighs when she tries to get away. Her hands don't move, though.

Releasing her flesh, I press a kiss to the red spot, then trail my fingers over the fabric of her thong. She shudders under my touch, making my cock twitch. Dampness meets me when I reach her center and I swallow a groan. Of course, she's fucking soaked for me. Gripping the fabric, I rip it to the seams, my knuckles sliding through her wetness.

When I stand, I'm careful not to touch her, instead watching as she trembles, head dropped as she pants. I slip my belt from the loops, shoving down my pants and underwear just enough to free my cock. Stroking myself slowly, I run a finger along her spine, and she shivers, a whimper escaping her.

I wrap my fingers around her throat, and her back melts into my chest, trapping my cock against her ass once more. I swallow hard and tip her chin up until I catch her lobe between my teeth. Once I release it, I run my nose along her jaw, watching her tits heave with each breath in the window's reflection.

"Tell me to stop," I whisper, half hoping she doesn't hear me.

It's the only out I can give her. Once I slip into her wet pussy, I'll fuck her with no regard to her own pleasure. She shakes her head and shifts her hips, then squeezes her thighs together, trying to create the friction she so desperately needs. Still holding her throat, my other hand splays against her stomach, halting her efforts.

"I'm not in control, Ember. I'll fuck your pussy, your ass, your mouth. I'll use your body until I'm satisfied, leaving you a quivering mess on the floor. Tell. Me. To. Stop."

Her throat contracts as she swallows, and I think she's going to back down. She'll tell me to stop, and I'll take a cold shower. My hand won't be nearly as satisfying, but at least she'll be safe. Safe from me.

With two words my resolve snaps.

"Use me."

Tipping my head back, I groan. Her tits slap against the window as I force her body forward. I grab her hips until her ass is presented to me, ripe for the taking. A little voice whispers she's not ready for me to take her there, so I kick her legs apart.

Gripping her hair, I turn her head until her cheek presses to the glass and line my cock up with her pussy. I don't bother to check if she's ready. She's already coating my tip, and I'm not even inside her yet.

"Remember, you asked for this," I growl, then slam into her.

Her cry echoes through the room, but I don't stop. I thrust into her, using her body just like I said I would. I'm nothing if not a man of my word. When her pussy flutters around me, I freeze deep inside her. She whines, wiggling her hips, and I pull completely out of her. She sags against the glass. Shoving my pants down more, I kick them off. They'll only get in the way for what I have planned.

"On your knees," I pant, pushing her head down when she doesn't move.

She twists, dropping to her knees and opening her mouth, and I almost explode from the sight. I plant one hand on the window, using the other to hold her head still.

Twisting the curling strands in my fingers, I bury my cock into her waiting mouth. She chokes when I hit the back of her throat, and her nails dig into my thighs, but she doesn't stop me.

I'm entranced by the vision of her lips wrapped around my cock, tears streaming down her face. She coughs, eyes flicking up to mine, and still I continue. She wanted me to use her, and I intend to do just that. When she swallows, I pull away again. I don't want to finish down her throat as amazing as that is. She leans forward, trying to capture the tip again, but I shove her head back and she gasps.

"Good fuck toys do what they're told," I growl. "On your feet, hands against the glass."

She scrambles to obey, and a surge of pride rolls through me. Brushing my fingers along her damp skin, I slap her ass and she whimpers. I step back, admiring the pink hand print I've left behind. I smack her again in the same spot, gritting my teeth when her forehead knocks against the glass, a low moan emanating from her.

"Don't fucking move," I whisper.

Stalking to the bathroom, I grab the bag from the counter that I requested the men leave behind. Upending the contents, I grab the bottle of lube and prowl back to her.

She's right where I left her, pussy dripping. Roughly, I yank her thong off, tossing it over my shoulder. She yelps when I run my fingers along the crease of her ass, trying to get away from the cold liquid. I grip her hip hard. She'll have bruises, but I'm beyond caring at this point.

"I'm going to fuck this plump ass of yours, and you're going to take every inch of me."

I work one finger inside and she whines, breathing out my name. When I add another one, she cries out, her voice a mixture of pleasure and pain. I expect her to fight me when I add a third, but instead she pushes back, body shuddering out her release. I shove my cock inside her pussy, grunting at the force of her clenching around me. Slowly, I move my fingers in and out, opening her as she quivers around me.

Her pussy clings to me as I pull out roughly and she sobs, fingers curling into a fist. I twist my fingers, stretching her. When I remove them, she shudders, and I line up my cock. It takes the rest of my control not to embed myself into her ass.

The last bit of sanity has me adding more lube before I slowly sink into the tight hole.

Ember wheezes as I rock my hips, inching into her further. I'm almost fully seated when she surges backward, taking all of me, and I groan at the feel of her pulsing around me.

"Faster," she breathes, desperate prayers falling from her lips.

The beast inside me takes over, and I grip her hips, laying a hand on her back and pushing her down. Her head slams into the window over and over as I thrust into her. My balls seize and my stomach tightens as I stare at my cock disappearing into her ass. Lust invades my brain, and before I know it, I'm pulling out.

She collapses in a heap on the ground. Green eyes blink up at me, desire lining her blown pupils. Straddling her hips, I stroke my cock hard and fast, tipping my head back as I come all over her tits. Her body bucks as I survey my cum painting her skin. Licking my lips, I squeeze the base one more time before I stand.

Swiping my clothes from the floor, I walk to the bathroom, slamming the door behind me. I should be ashamed of what I did to her. But I can't bring myself to feel anything but immense satisfaction.

Forty-Two

Ember

Almost a week later and Roman is still watching me like I'm about to explode. There's a shadow in his eyes that wasn't there before my meltdown in the Barrens. Or rather, since the morning we left the Byrns estate. It's as if he keeps expecting me to blow up, yelling at him for degrading me. I hope he's not holding his breath. He'll pass out long before I'll acknowledge his supposed wrongs.

We've studiously ignored all the other conversations we should be having. But I am about to lose it on him if he keeps looking at me like I'm a ticking time bomb.

The Kings' house is subdued like a permanent storm cloud has taken up residence overhead. As soon as word spread about the others, the entire place shut down. One guard in particular swooped in, growled questions at Roman, then muttered something about getting back to his charge before practically prowling from the room.

Now I'm posted on a stool in the Kings' kitchen that is an exact replica of the one in the Byrns's house across the city. It was jarring when I kept having déjà vu as I walked the halls until Roman told me the mansions were built by the same people. He went off on a tangent about the history of the city, but I was more interested in how his eyes had lit up, hands gesturing to the various points of the house.

Marie putters around the kitchen, loading the dishwasher while she waits for whatever is cooking in the oven. It smells delicious, of course, but I'm concentrating on the scone in front of me. I'd asked for more rhubarb pie, but Marie shook her head, saying it wasn't what I needed. I shouldn't have doubted her. As soon as the cinnamony sugary goodness hit my tongue, I was lost.

"You're humming, dear," Marie murmurs.

"Sorry." I break off another piece and stuff it into my mouth.

"You shouldn't stop, but I would like to discuss what changed from the last time."

I bite my lip, my mind transporting back to that morning. Roman's way of dealing with the fallout from the disappearance of the others, plus everything else he's in charge of, isn't something I'm going to complain about. When he walked away, I expected to be hurt, but a calmness had rushed over me. I'd finally given him something he needed. I shouldn't be humming randomly. I should be incredibly pissed at him.

"Must be the change in scenery," I mutter.

"So that's what we're going with?" she asks, raising an eyebrow.

"Sure. Not much else to be..." I don't even know how to finish my sentence, not that it matters. Every time I think about the future, or Aelia, or Roman, or really anything other than eating this scone, I get lightheaded.

"Ember. A word." Roman's voice rings out behind me.

I'm sure he thought he was sneaking up on us. Jokes on him, since I knew he was there. I'm sure Marie did too, which is why she didn't push me for more of an answer.

"I'm eating."

"It's a fucking scone, Ember. It's portable."

I hunch over my plate, muttering under my breath, "You're portable."

His heat seeps into my back as he invades my space. I bite my tongue, using the pain to suppress a shiver.

"That doesn't make any sense."

"So? Go away," I mumble, my cheeks burning under his scrutiny.

His hands land on either side of me, trapping my body against the counter. His breath ghosts across the shell of my ear. I should get a fucking medal for how well I'm keeping my body in check. I brace myself for his asshole reply.

Every time it seems like we're on the same page with where we stand, something else comes along and fucks it up. Mostly our own ridiculous issues. Usually, I strike first. If I cut him deep enough, it'll hurt less when he retaliates. At least that's what I say to myself.

"Leaning in closer isn't going away," I snap when the silence becomes too much.

"Well aware, love." His hand snakes around, snatching my half-eaten scone from my plate, then straightens.

"Hey!"

Before I even spin around, he's stuffed the whole thing in his mouth. He grins, blue eyes lighting up with mirth, and my mouth falls open.

Flabbergasted. That's the only way to describe what I'm experiencing right now. I don't think I've ever seen him like this—carefree. Even when we were teenagers, he had too much placed on his shoulders. Protecting Aelia, and by extension me, took a lot of his attention. Who knows what kind of unhinged lessons his father was imparting on him?

His grin fades, shadows eclipsing the joy from seconds ago. I hate it. I hate that he hides himself away behind a mask. I hate that I do the same. I hate that I don't trust my own emotions around him, that I need some form of reassurance he'll never be able to give me.

Peering over his shoulder, I break the awkward connection between us. "Where exactly are we going?"

"Dinner. We leave in five."

He strides out, probably to avoid any more questions. I drop back onto the stool, posting my elbows on the counter, and covering my face. I'm sick of not having a place to land. The ground underneath me is always shifting and the vertigo is getting to me.

"Perhaps you should get ready, dear," Marie says as she pulls the dish from the oven.

"What's wrong with what I'm wearing?" I grumble, glancing down at my t-shirt and long skirt. Granted, I'm dressed like I'm on my way to a music festival, but I think it's cute.

"I assume he's bringing you on a date to some place fancy. They might have a dress code." She says it as if she disapproves of dictating what someone wears, which only endears her to me more.

I snort, leveling her with a look. "The day Roman Drake takes me on a date is the day pigs fly. He probably just doesn't want to risk leaving me here by myself."

"Whatever you say, dear."

"Can I have another scone?"

She shoos me away, pursing her lips like I've asked her to do something scandalous. Clomping toward the front door, I grumble under my breath the entire way. Do I really need another scone? No. Does it piss me off when I'm looking forward to that last bite of deliciousness and someone steals it? Yes. I stabbed a man who kept doing it once. Blew my cover, but that shit is unacceptable. I doubt I'd get away with stabbing Roman. He's unusually hard to get shit past.

"You're late," Roman snaps, but there's little bite behind his words.

"And you stole my scone. You're lucky I showed up at all."

He pulls open the front door, gesturing me through first, and I hesitate. Marie's words keep repeating in my head and I can't get rid of them.

He tilts his head. "Problem?"

"Do I need to change?"

His eyes narrow as he scans me up and down. "What's wrong with what you're wearing?"

"We're going to dinner."

"So? I don't care what you wear, Ember. If you want to change, then be my guest, but you've got about two minutes to do so."

He leans against the open door, crossing his arms as he stares at his watch as if he's timing me.

"I'm fine. Let's just get this over with," I mutter, stomping past him.

His hand grips my arm, and I turn to stare at him. The air stretches, warps, and thins all at once. Tumbling into his eyes, I swear his entire existence marches past, one-by-one, each memory more traumatic than the last. Until all I see is him. I don't want to break the connection.

I didn't need to worry, though, since he glances away first, running his hand through his hair. It flops right back, and I scowl at the perfect fucking strands.

"We're just meeting Hawk and Willow," he murmurs, running his palm down my arm, then tangling our fingers together.

I sigh, letting out all the tension riding me with my breath.

"Then why are we still standing here?" I peek at him from the corner of my eye.

A whole minute passes before he rubs his free hand over his jaw. He needs a trim at the very least. I wonder what he looks like completely shaved. My nose crinkles just imagining it. People would assume I'm robbing the cradle, probably.

"Are you okay?" he whispers.

I rear back, spinning to face him. "Is that what this is about? You think you need to make up for...whatever by taking me out to eat?"

He tightens his grip on my fingers when I try to pull away. "We need to meet with Hawk. I'm not trying to make up for anything."

"Good, because I'm perfectly fucking fine."

"Then why the hell are you avoiding me?" he growls.

His other hand grabs my waist, and I tumble into him. His arms surround me, along with his warmth. A guard shuffles around the fountain, then past the stairs. When he spots us, his head whips forward and he trots away as quick as his stubby legs can carry him.

A giggle escapes me, and I bury my head into Roman's chest, wrapping my arms around his waist. His chin rests on my head as I count each of his heartbeats, wondering how the hell we got into this position.

"I'm not ignoring you," I murmur, rushing on when he starts grumbling. "But I figured out you're right."

"Why do I get the impression I'm not going to be happy about being right for once?"

"Probably because you're not." I sigh, stepping back, and his arms fall to his sides. "You were right about Aelia."

I swallow hard, refusing to look him in the eye. I refuse to feel guilty for the last ten years of my life. Regardless of anything else, I did what I thought was right. I never thought I'd give up, but the fairy tale ending I thought we'd have will never come. It'll be a long while before I feel anything other than heartache over it.

His warm hands cup my cheeks, lifting my head until our eyes meet.

"Not yet," he whispers before pressing his lips to my forehead.

He releases me before I ask what he means. I thought he'd rub it in that I was wrong. It'll come before long—some snide comment when he's pissed, or fake sympathy I know he doesn't feel if he's being particularly generous. Right now, though, he just grabs my hand and tugs me down the stairs.

The drive is silent as he maneuvers his way toward Reaper territory. The Flaming Skillet comes into view, only two bikes parked in the lot. I'm pretty sure one is Hawk's, but the other one is smaller. And pink. I'm grinning before I push from the car.

Willow's face lights up, practically bouncing out of her shoes as I approach.

"What do you think?" she squeals, unable to keep her eyes from the bike for long.

"I think it's very pink. When did you get this?"

"Couple days ago. Hawk got it for me." Her eyes dart to the biker, her entire face melting with love. It's not as disgusting as I used to think.

"I didn't know you knew how to ride a motorcycle." I'm kicking myself before the words are fully out of my mouth. We don't know each other. Crossing paths a couple times doesn't make us friends.

"Oh, I don't. I mean, I've been riding with Hawk, obviously, but he's been teaching me."

"That's great," I say, swallowing around the lump in my throat.

Roman and Hawk start for the diner, and Willow follows while I stare at the pink and chrome gesture of love. I wonder how much I've missed over the past ten years.

Obviously, I never would have come to Synd, never would have met these people, regardless of what I would have done with my life. But I would have met someone. Probably not the love of my life since I'm pretty sure that role has always belonged to Roman whether I like it or not.

A friend, though, would have come along. No one could replace Aelia, but I imagine if she's looking up at me from hell, she's cussing me out for putting my life on hold for her.

"Ember?" Willow's soft voice rolls over me, snapping me from my doldrums.

"Yeah?" I turn to her, hating the pity stamped on her face.

She sighs, waving Hawk on when he glances back. "You know, I never thought I'd find somewhere I belonged. My life was...not easy, but also exceptionally lavish. I'd convinced myself I wasn't worth fighting for because I never fought for myself. I'm still learning, still growing, and very much trying to keep myself from being kidnapped again, but at least I'm doing something, ya know?"

"Sure," I snap. It's almost as if she reached into my brain and extracted all the insecurities plaguing me.

"That's okay. You don't have to admit it. But maybe think about taking a leap into the unknown. And don't give up. Your tenacity is something I admire in you."

She waves, then slips through the doors, yanking Hawk and Roman with her. Tipping my head back, I blink away the tears. I should have asked her if she was okay. The bombs Hawk dropped on Roman were about her friends, including her *best* friend. Yet here I am, wallowing in self-pity. I'm not used to thinking about others.

She's right, I don't want to admit anything out loud, but her words hit me hard. Shoving away the heartache that's been plaguing me for the last week, I ignore the sharp stab of pain behind my eyes. I'll deal with the future when the future comes. Right now, my focus needs to be on exposing Anders. There's no way anyone else is after Roman and me. If I can bring Roman his father's still-beating heart on a silver platter, maybe we'll both finally be at peace.

Forty-Three

Roman

"Do you think they just wanted to chitchat?" Ember asks, tapping her finger against her leg while staring at the dark houses whizzing by.

"Probably. They seem determined to be more than acquaintances, though I can't fathom why," I grumble.

"Missing their friends?" She turns to me, tilting her head.

"Most of the Reapers are still here. Only Helms went to Rima."

"He's the president, right?" Her palm slaps the dash as I take a corner a bit too fast.

I nod, though I don't know if she notices as she's gritting her teeth and clutching the seat.

"I'm not going to flip the damn car, Ember."

"When was the last time you drove yourself? I think you forgot some pointers from driver's ed," she mumbles.

I chuckle, gripping the steering wheel and taking another turn just a little too fast, and she gasps.

"That's assuming I took driver's ed."

My phone buzzes in my pocket and I sigh. The longer I'm in charge, the more I realize why the other mafia leaders had two lines. Byrns gave out my number to everyone he could think of, completely fucking me in the process. If I get another one, only Ember is allowed to call me. And maybe Hawk, but after tonight's interrogation on who I knew in Rima, maybe not.

"Do you want me to get that?" Ember asks.

Normally, I'd hand it over. For all the shit between us, I trust her. Except I'm pretty sure it's Hawk still trying to convince me that Aelia is alive. I don't have it in me to explain to Ember his theories. I'm not convinced she's given up her crusade to find my sister. And after she told me I was right, I didn't have it in me to dash that last bit of hope. This woman is making me go soft. I'm not entirely sure I care anymore.

"It's fine. I'll deal with it later."

"Since you're stuck in a car with me and can't run away..." She bites her lip, and my stomach tightens. "Your father."

The air rushes out of me, relief flooding my body. Keeping shit from her is harder than I thought it would be. Regardless of Hawk's insistence that Helms found Aelia and she's been with the Guild this whole time, I refuse to believe it. Besides, I have no idea what they've done to her, how they've corrupted her. I don't know the inner workings of their organization, so it's possible our father kept her from the worst of it, possibly even brainwashing her. It's the only reason I can think of as to why she wouldn't contact me.

Unless Anders filled her head with lies about me, or hell, told her I was dead. It seems to be his go-to whenever shit goes sideways.

"What about him?" Even though I'm glad she's not asking about Aelia, it doesn't mean I want to discuss my remaining family member.

"I know you're skeptical, but I honestly think he's behind all this." She rushes on when I open my mouth to rebut her. "Obviously, he'd come back to finish the job. You're still alive and who knows what kind of pull he has with the Guild. Maybe he's acting alone."

"If Anders was behind all the attempts on our lives, then why wouldn't he just reveal himself? He hasn't changed much from the last time you saw him, Ember. That man can't handle doing shit unless he's able to gloat about it."

I grip the steering wheel tighter. At this point, we're just cruising around the city. We're supposed to go to Byrns's place to check in, but summer has finally taken hold. It's been a long time since I was able to enjoy...anything.

Until Ember popped back into my life, I hadn't savored life. There wasn't anything to take joy in, anyway. I'd rather not ruin the evening by talking about my father, but Ember seems determined.

"He's lived so long pretending he's dead he probably doesn't know how else to operate. Besides, he always hid behind others. The only reason he came to Synd ten years ago was because he couldn't run the men he'd turned in Synd all the way from Westmont. Who else would go through this much trouble to take you out?"

"Maybe there isn't just one person. Or maybe it's someone after you. They're trying to get me out of the way to take you out. Which is more plausible than my father abandoning the Guild to come after me again." It's not, but I can't imagine Anders caring.

"Maybe the Guild sent Anders to take you out so they can swoop in. Finish the job they started. It has to be a thorn in their side they weren't able to take over here."

Everything she says is logical and well thought out. I wonder how long she's been mulling this over. She's only mentioned Anders being behind the assassination attempts a few times. She drops it at the slightest pushback, never pressing the issue.

I don't care who's behind it. If it is my father, then all the better. I'd like to be the one to take him out. Avenging my sister is my new mission. I figured I'd have to wait until the others came back to put the plan forming in my head into action.

"It doesn't matter either way. Byrns and the Kings are in Rima dealing with the Guild. If Anders is there, I'm sure he'll slip away like he always does. If he's here, then his death will come quicker than I expected, is all."

"You're going to hunt him down, aren't you?" she asks softly, and I glance at her still staring out the window.

"I don't see how—"

An explosion lights up the sky close to the river, and I slam on the brakes. Rumbling echoes through the quiet neighborhood, followed by a dog howling, and a shiver skitters down my spine.

"Drake," Ember says, a warning in her voice.

I don't know if she means to warn us away from the disaster clearly happening a mile from us or if she's urging me toward it. Either way, a second later we're careening down the road. Thank fuck it's past midnight, leaving us the lone vehicle on the road.

"Call Hawk," I bark at her.

Our tires screech as I take another turn, and she gasps. Slamming on the brakes again, we take in the carnage. Smoke obscures most of the rubble, though flames flicker through the shadows.

"It's stone. How does stone burn?" Ember turns wide eyes to mine and I shake my head.

"Stay in the car."

I push open my door, carefully stepping out. Heat billows from the wreckage of a vehicle. I can't even tell what the model is, much less if there's someone inside still. I doubt they survived if they were.

Stepping closer to the railing, I can just make out the lights from the Egg. Other than the fire, it's the only illumination for several blocks on either side.

"Get back, Ember," I growl. Of course, she didn't listen.

Her eyes meet mine and she points toward the river. Jogging over to her, I follow her gaze down. A dark car floats in the water, only its trunk still visible. As I scan the area, the hair on the back of my neck stands up. Grabbing Ember's arm, I tug her back to our vehicle.

"What the hell. What if someone is down there?" she cries out, and I cover her mouth, still glancing around.

"Get in the car, Ember. Now."

I don't know what she hears in my voice, but she obeys without another word. Throwing it into gear, I whip us around, heading back to where we came from. Ember keeps looking back as if she can't pull her eyes away.

"Did you notice the car?" I ask, checking the rearview every few seconds.

"Duh. I'm the one who pointed it out. We should go back."

"It looked exactly like ours."

Her head whips around as if she'll be able to see all the way to the wreckage. Her phone rings and she jolts, tossing it against the dash. It bounces to the carpet, still buzzing. A nervous chuckle leaves her as she picks it up and answers.

"Willow. No, we weren't far. Roman made us leave. There's a car in the river. Another one on the bridge in flames. Half of the stone railing—is it called a railing—whatever. Half of it is gone, I'm assuming where the car went into the river." Ember's eyes find mine while she listens to Willow's response. "Well, Nicki can eat shit if she thinks we had something to do with this."

"Tell her to have Hawk bring some guys to check it out," I say, concentrating on making it back to the Kings' estate.

"You heard?" She pauses. "Apparently not. He thinks the car in the river is the same one we're driving." Another pause. "I don't fucking know."

"Tell him I'll be there after."

She raises her eyebrow, then purses her lips. "I'll deal with it."

Willow's short laugh rings through the small space as I pull onto the Kings' block. It's cut off when Ember hangs up.

"What?" I grunt.

"You think you're leaving me behind to deal with this shit?"

Swinging into the driveway, she braces herself against the door. I almost clip the fountain as I circle it, not that I'd mourn the loss. It's fucking hideous. Throwing open my door, I march to her side, ripping at the handle. I stumble back when it doesn't move, and she wiggles her fingers at me as she smirks. By the time I make it to the driver's side again, she's locked that door, too. And crawled into my seat.

Leaning my hands against the door, I bare my teeth. She taps her arm where a watch would normally sit.

"You're wasting time, Drake. Get in the passenger seat like a good boy, and we can get on our way."

"I'm not fucking playing this game with you, woman," I growl as I contemplate if I could punch the glass. I'd only hurt myself and possibly her. Not worth it.

"Been awhile since this was a game." Her green eyes hold a challenge I desperately want to win.

Glancing over my shoulder at the guard shack, I scoff at the kid behind the glass when he ducks his head. I meet Ember's gaze again.

"I'm driving. Open the door."

"Not a chance, buckaroo. You tried to hide me away in a fucking castle like a princess in distress."

"For your own fucking good," I cry, throwing my hands up.

I feel ridiculous having this argument through a car window. I could just get another vehicle, but then she'd just follow me. She's probably get lost and then I'd have to save her ass regardless. Again, not worth it.

"Well, if it isn't the consequences of your own actions," she sings, then her face drops. "Get in the car or I'm leaving your ass here. You can play Rapunzel and let down your hair for me later."

Knocking my head against the window, an ache forms in my chest. As much as I'd like to leave her here, she won't back down. I don't want my attention divided, but she'll be with me at the very least. Her staying here might be worse. I'd have to tie her to the bed to get her to stay put, and even that's not a guarantee. She probably knows how to get out of shit like that. My cock hardens, imagining her spread-eagle and unable to move. I straighten, adjusting myself as I round the hood.

The door unlocks a second before I reach for the handle and I slide inside. The car jumps forward before I have it closed, and I glare at her while she giggles.

"Hardly the time to be laughing," I growl.

"Hardly the time to get all horny, but here you are." She smirks, almost hitting the curb when she looks at me.

"Keep your damn eyes on the road. Don't make me regret taking you along."

She shakes her head, sighing. "If it makes you feel better to think you're allowing me, then be my guest."

I run my hand through my hair, tipping my head back. If my father is after us, he's expanded to taking out innocent people. Not that he cares. We need to find him before more people die. The plan I have to force him to expose himself isn't a great one, but it's the only one I've got. Hopefully, I can keep it from Ember until after I've executed it. If tonight is any indication, I'm afraid that won't be an option.

"Where exactly am I going?" She taps her finger on the steering wheel to a beat I recognize but can't fully recall.

"Wouldn't have to ask if you'd have let me drive."

"And yet I didn't, so cough up the address."

"Hawk's house. It's in Reaper territory."

"Obviously. Now shut up while I remember how to operate a vehicle."

I grab the dash as she takes a corner too quickly. Gritting my teeth, I clench my ass, hoping my stomach doesn't fall out of the small hole as we make the rest of the journey in silence. As she bumps into the curb in front of Hawk's house, I swing open my door and practically dive from the car.

"You're never allowed to drive again," I snarl at her.

I expect a snappy comeback, but her eyes are fixed over my shoulder.

A strangled cry rings through the air and I whip toward the sound. Alarm floods my system, rooting my feet to the ground. I don't know what happened between their phone call and now, but Willow staggers off the porch steps toward us. Her body buckles and she drops into the fetal position, sobs wracking her body.

Hawk's eyes track her, his mouth parted. He glances at the phone in his hand before his eyes meet mine. Grief and terror war with each other.

Ember snaps out of her trance and rushes to Willow's collapsed form. She curls her body over Willow's, glancing over her shoulder at me. Her wide-eyed gaze screams at me to do something, but I don't know what's going on, much less what to do about it.

"Hawk," I bark and he jolts, his eyes coming into focus. "What happened?"

"Alex," he breathes, glancing at his phone again.

His fingers tremble as he swipes at the screen, then brings it to his ear. Almost immediately he curses, then stabs at the device.

I stalk toward him. "Tell me what's going on, Hawk."

He shakes his head, then glances at Willow still sobbing in Ember's arms.

"Helms…" He coughs, then doubles over to dry heave. I may not have been around long, but I've never seen him look so distraught. When he's done, he stumbles down the stairs.

"What happened to Helms?"

He shakes his head again as if he can erase whatever truth he's been handed. No matter how many times he repeats the move, it won't work. It never works. Once someone is gone, there's no bringing them back. I know that all too well.

"Nothing." He swallows hard. "He thinks Alex is dead."

His declaration hangs in the air between us, heavy with sorrow. Willow's weeping creating the backdrop for their grief. I didn't know Alex well—certainly not well enough to have his death grip me like it is them. Perhaps that's why I'm able to think more clearly.

I grab Hawk's shoulder, steadying him as he tips to the side. "I'm assuming you called Helms and he didn't pick up?"

"It's disconnected. Like he sent the message and immediately destroyed his phone." Hawk runs a hand through his hair. His eyes keep darting to Willow.

"What exactly did the message say?"

He hands the phone over and I scan the text. It's short and riddled with typos. Scrolling up a little, I find the rest of the messages look nothing like the last one.

"Pull yourself together. This doesn't even seem like Helms sent this."

Willow sniffs, bright blue eyes peeking up at me from over Ember's shoulder. Her misery clears just enough for her to nod once.

"Until you get confirmation, there's no reason to assume he's dead."

Hawk shrugs off my hand, and I return his phone. He slips it in his pocket as I tug Ember to her feet. She stumbles and I wrap my arm around her waist. Hawk gathers Willow in his arms and stomps halfway to the porch, then pivots. Tears still stream down her face, but at least some clarity has returned.

"Sorry the night turned to shit. We'll let you know if we hear anything else. I'll call in some guys to deal with the thing at the bridge," Hawk says.

"I'll call you, Ember. We should go out soon. Lots to gossip about," Willow whispers, a small smile playing on her mouth.

Ember scoffs as she slams her head into my collar bone and I wince. Willow giggles, but the muted sound lacks its usual brightness.

Until we have confirmation on Alex's whereabouts, I'm pretty sure she won't be back to her usual self. I don't blame her. I went through all the emotions when Aelia died. Without visual proof, it's hard to deal with the unknown. I'm not convinced Alex is actually dead, but if he is and I've put the idea in their head that he could be alive...they might never forgive me. I wouldn't blame them.

Forty-Four

Ember

"Going somewhere?" Roman murmurs, voice still groggy from sleep.

"Can't a girl pee in peace?" I grumble.

The chilly air spreads goosebumps along my arms, and I shiver. My feet connect with the cold floor, and I yelp, yanking them up and falling into him. His arms circle around me, holding me awkwardly, but I sink into his warm body anyway. I wish I could stay right here, half sitting against him while he makes that rumbling sound of contentment in his chest. I really do have to pee, though.

Untangling myself from his limbs, I sit up, sighing. I dash to the bathroom, not bothering to turn on the lights. My eyes fall closed while I do my business, almost falling asleep again.

Last night was another shitshow, and we didn't get back until the middle of the night. At least the Depot isn't on fire again. The bridge near the Egg is another story. Roman thinks whoever blew it was trying to take us out, but we weren't anywhere near there.

When I mentioned it felt like Anders might be behind all our problems, he dismissed me. I still caught the gleam of concern in his eyes, though. Outwardly, he's still clinging to the idea that I brought these problems to Synd. It's getting a little insulting. Except I can't convince myself that he's wrong. His father seems the more likely choice.

Sure, I blew up an MC's headquarters and dumped most of a high-level gang's stock in a lake, but they didn't suspect me. At least, the president didn't. No way they'd follow me across two states just to retaliate. Synd's issues were happening long before I got here.

"Ember?" Roman's panicked voice rings through the bathroom, bouncing off the tiles and rattling my brain.

I take my time washing my hands, wondering if he'll pull himself from the bed before I get back or just wallow in the covers, waiting for me. Most nights he's been waking in the middle of the night, breath heaving from his lungs. He clings to me, tucking my body close as if I'll disappear if he's not touching me. Clearly, he's having nightmares, but neither of us mentions them. I'm not entirely sure if he knows I'm awake when they jolt him out of his dreams.

Roman's shadowed form fills the doorway, a specter from another dimension. One I'm wanting to seep into, regardless of whether it's a hellscape or not. As long as he's there, I'm sure I'll survive whatever horrors await us. I shake my head, dispelling the ridiculous musings my mind is waxing on about.

"Come back to bed," he mumbles, holding his hand out.

As soon as my fingers intertwine with his, a sharp blaring noise rings out. A flashing light by the door I didn't notice before strobes to a steady beat. Roman spins away, rushing to the door and flinging it open. Two guards hurry past and Roman snags one of them.

"What the hell is going on?" he bellows over the ruckus.

"It's an alarm, sir. Someone shot at a car coming into the driveway." He pulls away, rushing after his compatriot.

"Didn't they tell you about the security system?" I yell as I pull on pants.

I'm reaching for a t-shirt when he grips my wrist and tugs me toward the door. I snag my knife, tucking it into the waistband of my shorts just in case. A tank top isn't exactly what I want to be wearing while dealing with a crisis, but I doubt he'll leave me behind to change.

More guards swarm the front hall, more than I've ever seen here or at the Byrns mansion. Several of them glance our way, dismissing me in the next second. They all shuffle to the side, clearing a path for Roman, and I follow close behind.

"Who was in the car?" Roman asks a tall man who doesn't look like he's smiled a day in his life.

"Couple Reapers."

The man starts to walk away, but Roman grabs his arm, swinging him around. The guard sneers, reaching for his gun. Then, like a switch flipped, he drops his hand and schools his face into some semblance of respect. Resting my hand on the knife at my waist, I wait for him to make a move. Roman might think his borrowed status is enough to protect him—I'm not as trusting.

"Which Reapers?"

"The VP's woman and some other guy. Don't know who it is. I don't keep track of them." The vein in his forehead throbs, ready to explode. "Anything else, *sir?*"

My lip curls, a snarl erupting from my chest, but Roman slides his hand around my waist, then squeezes my hip. The guard glances away. Not before I catch his eye roll, and I tense.

"Go do your fucking job." Roman tracks him as he prowls away.

"You shouldn't have let him get away with that," I say as we hurry down the front stairs.

"Wasn't worth it. The King's men don't know me as well. They'll get it before long."

The car sits idling by the guard shack at the mouth of the driveway. Willow's tear-streaked face glows in the light, and she bounds toward us, skidding to a stop when we reach the fountain. She points to a body lying next to the open passenger door and Roman takes off.

"What happened?" I grunt, eyes fixed on Roman until a crowd swallows him up.

"Hawk was on a run. He wanted me to go along, but I was working with Doc."

"Wait, Doc? I thought Ink was the Reapers' doctor?"

"He is. Doc is the sergeant at arms. It's complicated." She waves away the explanation. "I got a call from Mia that the Flaming Skillet was hit, so we went to help."

"Alone?" I shouldn't be grilling her, much less shouting, but seriously.

"I messaged Hawk," she snarls. "When we got there, though, someone was following us. I tried to lose them, but I'm not a great driver. Doc said to head here. Just as we were pulling in, they started shooting."

"Is Doc hurt?"

I haven't met the man, but he's high enough in the Reapers organization to raise questions. Maybe whoever is after us has expanded their scope to the others as well. Which doesn't rule out Anders, but it does point to me not being the primary target.

"He wasn't shot, but I slammed on the brakes, and he hit his head on the dash. What if I killed him? Hawk is going to be so mad at me."

I chuckle, all the stress and anxiety finally getting to me. Meeting her shocked gaze, I giggle. She gives me a tentative smile, but then turns her eyes to Doc, still lying on the concrete.

"He didn't die. Drake would be running his hands through his hair. Instead, he's yelling at that kid who looks like he's going to piss himself."

She breathes out a sigh, then a bubble of laughter seeps from her. "For the record, I'd be really upset if one of them died. They're my family."

"I get it. Your mind focuses on the least terrifying prospect. In this case, Hawk being upset with you."

I link her arm with mine as we watch Doc sit up and rub his head. Roman crouches next to him, but Doc is still a whole head taller. Roman points back to us and Doc nods, waving to Willow, and she sighs again.

I bite my lip, glancing at her from the corner of my eye. "Listen, this might not exactly be the right time—"

"But can I give you a description of the car?"

"Actually, no. I think I know who's behind all this shit. I'd like to figure out if I'm right, but Roman won't let me out of his sight."

"Probably because he knows exactly what you're planning on doing," she says, raising an eyebrow.

"I don't plan on going and getting myself killed. I just need to confirm some things so we have a clear path on how to deal with him."

"You think it's Anders, don't you?" she whispers, and her fingers dig into my arm.

"It's the most likely scenario," I mutter. Roman narrows his eyes at us. I'm slightly terrified he can read lips.

"What exactly are you wanting me to do? Ask Roman on a date?" She giggles, rubbing her hand over her mouth.

"Maybe Hawk can distract him? They'll leave us together, and I can go off and do my thing. I'll be back before they even know it." I hold my breath, hoping she agrees. It's not the best plan, but it's all I have.

"Why do I feel like a teenager trying to dodge our parents while we smoke pot in the cemetery?"

I turn wide eyes toward her, mouth dropping open. She shakes her head, a bemused smile gracing her lips.

"Just because I was a goody-two-shoes doesn't mean I didn't do shit. Granted, that was before Joseph came into the picture. He was not a tolerant man." She tenses, then adds, "He was my stepfather."

"Was?" Not tolerant in my world meant abusive, usually physically. I'm scared to ask what Hawk did to him.

"Oh, I killed him. Stabbed him in the heart and then slashed his throat. Thought I told you." She grins at me before unlinking our arms and hurrying to Doc's side.

She may have mentioned offing someone, but I probably didn't pay attention. I never would have expected Willow, who can't be much over five feet and sweet as a fucking button, to murder someone. Sure, she took charge of shit down at the Depot, but she definitely isn't one I'd peg to be wary of. I can't tell if that means I'm losing my touch or she's just that good at hiding her dark side. I jolt when Roman steps in front of me, blocking my view of Willow fussing over Doc.

"What's wrong with you?" he asks, barely sparing me a glance before he's typing out a message on his phone.

"Did you know Willow killed her stepfather? Like brutally?"

His head whips up, then a smirk takes over. "Sure did. It was quite gruesome. Honestly, I didn't think she was going to go through with it. When I first saw her, she was a timid little thing. Let everyone walk all over her."

I rear back, blinking rapidly. "First saw her? What?"

His expression darkens and he scowls. "You think I tried to take over Synd without researching every single thread? Helms had a connection to MacKenzie, who was living in Rima. Mac and Willow were friends. Honestly, I'm surprised she and Hawk didn't cross paths long before they did. Though apparently there was a large enough rift after my father came through the first time that a lot of them lost touch."

"My head hurts." Rubbing my temples, I sigh.

"I'll draw you a diagram later." He wraps his arm around my shoulders and guides me back into the house.

"I don't need a murder wall to learn about their lives. Not like I'll ever meet most of them."

He tenses, then shoves me toward the door. "Go back to bed. I'm going to clean shit up here."

I open my mouth, then snap it shut. He's already turned away, striding back to the scene. Of course he'd walk away without saying anything. I probably shouldn't have passive aggressively tried to get him to ask me to stay.

I don't know if *he* even plans on staying in Synd once everyone comes back—if they come back. A chill rolls down my spine at the thought. Roman could be stuck here, taking over for whoever doesn't make it out of Rima, and then what? Accepting that Aelia is really dead is going to take years, but it also means I no longer have a purpose. I don't know where I'd go if Roman doesn't ask me to stay with him.

I shake my head, halting my mind's downward spiral. Nothing happens until I find Anders and kill him once and for all. And I can't do that without Willow's help. I seek her out in the crowd, trying to catch her attention subtly. Willow's gaze bounces between Roman and me, then fixes on me, and she nods. At least something went right tonight. I'm sure Willow will tell Hawk my plan, but as long as they hold off telling Roman, I'll be fine.

# Forty-Five

Roman

I never thought I'd be visiting one of the Reapers to make sure they're okay, but here I am. Three days after Willow almost sent Doc through a windshield, I'm standing on Hawk's front porch a few doors down from Reaper headquarters.

"This place used to be Mac's house. You know, before her dad moved them to Rima. Obviously, she's living with Helms, so I fixed it up. Willow likes living next door to her best friend," Hawk says, making small talk. I fucking despise small talk.

"You realize I don't fucking care, right?"

He chuckles, clapping me on the shoulder before disappearing back into the house. I scrub my itchy palms against my thighs. I didn't exactly want to let Ember out of my sight, but somehow she convinced me to go alone, mentioning Willow might stop by.

It's quiet out here, the faint rumble of bikes the only thing disturbing the silence. Even the noise from the city doesn't interrupt the crickets just coming out for their nightly song.

Hawk drops a beer next to my elbow, then leans on the railing as he surveys the road. He's not the same as when I first got here. Granted, he fucking hated me for kidnapping Willow, so I didn't blame him. I suspect Willow had a lot to do with him letting go of his thirst for revenge. Though every once in a while, he gets a gleam in his eyes. I'm pretty sure he's thinking of all the ways he could kill me. I'm only half convinced he'll never act on them.

"What exactly did you need to talk to me about?" I ask, leaning my forearms on the railing next to him.

"Nothing. Doc is fine. You hear about the break-in at the Byrns house?"

"Attempted break-in. They shot him before he made it across the lawn. He was dead before he hit the ground."

It's like everyone is against me. All I want is one of the hitmen to live long enough to ask who their master is. Confirming that it's my father behind all these half-assed assassins is my number one priority. After making sure Ember isn't caught in the crossfire, of course.

"Guess you'll just have to wait for the next attempt on your life to capture them." He chuckles as if this is a big joke. He's not the one getting shot and stabbed and blown up, though.

"Why did you invite me over if you didn't have something to talk about?"

He hems and haws a little before leveling me with a glare. "I'm still pissed about all that shit from before. But I figured we should clear the air a little. Plus, Willow wants to hang out with Ember. She's worried about the others. She's still struggling with the guilt from how they all treated Lacey. There wasn't exactly a lot of time to make up for all that shit before they took off for Rima."

"Why exactly were you an asshole to Lacey?" I never could work out why they had such a problem with her. If anything, they should have welcomed her with open arms.

"Personally? I thought she was in league with you. It was just a little bit too coincidental that shit went sideways and she revealed herself at the same time."

"And the others?"

I shouldn't care, but out of all these people, I felt Lacey and I were the most alike. She may not have remembered her brother, but she lost loved ones, too. She knew what it was like to be all alone in the world, on the outside looking in. In the month before she left, we had more than a few conversations. She still didn't feel like she belonged, but at least the others were making an effort.

"I mean, Mac had her thing with her brother. The others, I'm not entirely sure. I'm not exactly close to them. We're kind of in a world of our own up here," he says wistfully.

I sigh, slipping my phone from my pocket and texting Ember again. Am I acting like a needy boyfriend? Yes. Do I care? Not entirely. Especially since she isn't answering me.

"Ember told you to get me out of the house, didn't she?" I scowl, leveling him with a glare.

He gives me a sheepish grin. "I think you're smothering her a bit. Willow cussed me out for that shit, too. Having her out of my sight makes my skin itch. Like nothing is right until she's in my arms. You got that?"

"No," I say, but I'm unable to look him in the eye as my palms tingle.

I'm not about to bare my soul to him. He doesn't care about my love life. He's just hoping I don't fucking lose it before Helms gets back. From his point of view, Ember is a distraction. I'm sure if there was anyone else to take over, he'd either take me out or suggest I move my ass along. Probably the former.

"Sure you don't," he huffs, grinning. "You know we're not enemies anymore, right?"

"Not entirely sure what you mean," I mutter, wondering if he's reading my mind. I shake my head, dismissing the idea.

He sighs, pushing back to drop onto the bench. I'd rather not have a heart-to-heart either, but Hawk seems determined to keep me here. At least until Willow gives him the green light to release me. I should just drive to the Kings and make myself scarce in their massive house while they finish their girl's night or whatever they're doing. I'm supposed to be mending fences, though, and I can't do that if I keep everyone at arm's length.

I drop down next to him, cradling the beer in my hand. "I understand we're no longer enemies."

"Were we ever?" He tips the bottle back, scanning the silent street.

"I kidnapped your woman." Probably not the best idea to remind him.

"Did you, though?"

"Of course I fucking did. I stuffed her in my car."

"After asking if she'd feel more comfortable in the backseat."

I glare at him. "I tied her ass up."

"Asking if the bonds were too tight."

"I had a fucking gun to her head!"

"Was it even loaded?" He grins, and I explode from the bench.

My bottle rolls away off the front porch, dropping into the bushes. I wonder if they'll find it years from now, wondering how it got there. I'll be long gone by then, fading from their memories exactly like my family did from Synd's history.

Whether Hawk thinks I kidnapped Willow or not, I shouldn't be fighting him on it. It's not about them seeing me as a threat or because of my ego, though Ember would argue on the last point.

"Why are you fighting being exonerated?" he murmurs, finally taking me seriously.

"Why do you feel the need to let me off the hook?" I spin and lean against the railing, crossing my arms.

"Because I understand why you did it. Just like I understand why Willow never stood up for herself."

"Those aren't even remotely the same things." I tuck my chin to my chest.

"Maybe not, but I still understand. It's something I might have done, had I not found the Reapers."

I raise an eyebrow, and he waves away the questions I'm sure are swimming in my eyes. The revving of an engine followed by a woman hooting interrupts any further conversation we'd have. Not that I want to go down the path he's trying to drag me on. I'd rather just wallow in my own misery, paying for my sins one day at a time. A single headlight pierces the night, and I glance over my shoulder with a sigh.

The garish pink bike rolls to a stop at the curb, and Ember tumbles off. Thank fuck she's wearing a helmet, since I'm pretty sure she smacks her head on the ground before bouncing up. Willow almost tips over as she struggles with the kickstand, and Hawk rushes past me, already scolding her.

"I've got it!" She shoos him away, finally getting it down and swinging her leg over, tumbling into his arms.

I stomp toward Ember, already pissed off. Not only did she take off for half the night, but she stopped answering my texts two hours ago. Then she decided that getting on the back of a fucking bike was a good idea when she's clearly been drinking.

She falls into my arms, and I barely catch her. When I tug the helmet off, I'm snarling. She blinks up at me, hair swirling around her head and a dopey grin on her face.

"You're fucking drunk," I accuse even as I pull her closer.

Mock outrage overtakes her face, and a delicious blush reddens her cheeks even more than they already are. My cock stirs, hardening like it always does when she's around.

"How dare you! I am a fucking lady. And I can hold my liquor, I'll have you know." She giggles, completely contradicting her words.

"What exactly did you give her?" I call to Willow, who has the good grace to grimace.

"We went out for dinner." She toys with the patch on Hawk's jacket, muttering, "And had a margarita."

Ember lifts to her tiptoes, lips brushing my jaw, and I grit my teeth. "I had five."

"For fuck's sake," I grumble.

I swing a squealing Ember into my arms, and stomp toward the car I took from Byrns's garage. Hawk's laughter follows us, and I flip him off, almost dropping Ember when she kicks her legs back and forth.

"Would you knock it the fuck off? You're going to get a concussion."

"You wouldn't drop me." She says it with such conviction I stutter to a stop, gazing down at her. She grins, fingering the button on my shirt.

"Stop trying to undress me."

Somehow, I get the door open and stuff her inside, all while she attempts to get me naked. She's giggling the entire time. I flip Hawk off again before slipping behind the wheel. Ember runs her hands over my chest as I buckle her in, and I almost get out to ask Hawk for a stick. It's the only way I'll be able to beat her off.

It's only twenty minutes tops to the Kings' estate from Reaper territory, and that's with traffic. Ember is determined to use every single one of them to get into my pants. I've pushed her back into her seat at least a dozen times, and we're still ten minutes out. I don't know which event is tonight, but apparently it's just letting out and clogging the streets.

Ember's nails dig into my thigh, and I shudder. I'm not about to take advantage of her, but I can only do so much while trying to deal with traffic. She walks her fingers to the button on my pants, and I yank her wrist away, growling.

"Ember, do not try to..." I grit my teeth as I slam on the brakes, my arm holding her in place.

The light flashes red and a car behind us lays on the horn. I usually don't flash my gun, but the minute I slip it from my holster, the person behind me stops. By the time I slide it into the middle console, Ember has my zipper down and she's tugging at my boxers.

"It's okay. I'll free you," she whispers, and I'm pretty sure she's talking to my cock.

"What the fuck, Em. Seriously, we're not fucking doing this." I push her hand away, then grip the steering wheel as the light turns green.

"Remember when we played truth or dare?" she murmurs, lifting my shirt and pressing her lips against my stomach. My muscles quiver, and I suck in a deep breath.

"No, I don't." I do. I know exactly what she's talking about. She asked me what my secret fantasy was, and I said...

"Road head," she giggles, resting her forehead on my leg.

"I'm not going to let you give me road head while you're fucking tanked."

"You're a stick in the mud. Don't you ever loosen up?" She's still pawing at the elastic of my underwear.

"Fucked you in a club bathroom. And on a balcony at a goddamn gala," I remind her.

Her hand strokes me through the fabric, and my cock twitches. After another minute, though, her fingers drop, brushing my balls, then she stops moving completely. A soft snore floats from her, and I knock my head back against the seat. At least we're almost home. I'll get her inside and hope she doesn't end up puking on me.

When I finally pull into the driveway, my leg is wet. Gently, I push her back into her seat, sighing at the drool stain she's left behind. I don't know how my life got here, but it's not until I'm rounding the hood that it hits me. I'd never do this for anyone else. Shit. I'm in fucking love with her. I'm totally fucked.

Forty-Six

Ember

My mouth feels like a skunk died inside it, and my head has a small hammer pounding away.

"Why won't my ears pop?" I moan, curling into a ball.

"Because they don't need to, love. You're covering your ears." Roman's muffled voice barely registers as his fingers wrap around my wrists and gently pull them away.

"Five margaritas was too many." I swallow a sob. It only makes my stomach roll more, nausea creeping up my throat.

"Probably. Now let's get you back to bed."

His arms slide under my body, and I breathe through my nose as he sets me on my feet. I sway, vertigo hitting me hard. Doubling over, I grip Roman's hip, fingers scrambling to find something to hold on to.

"Do not fucking puke," he growls.

"Too late."

I swear I try to make it in the toilet. It's not my fault he stepped in front of my mouth. And I *do* feel terrible about it. Or at least I will in the morning. Right now, I'm just overwhelmed by the smell. Tears fill my eyes as I peer up at him.

"Sorry," I gasp, dry heaving again.

He sighs, shaking his head. "It's fine."

"Are you mad at me?" My chin quivers, and I swear I'm never fucking drinking again.

I haven't been this trashed since Aelia and I broke into my parent's liquor cabinet. I seem to recall Roman yelling at me for corrupting his sister. He was pissed then.

"I'm not mad."

"I feel like you're mad, but you won't tell me until tomorrow."

He shakes his head again, then turns around. What a ridiculous question. Of course he's fucking mad. Willow probably told Hawk what we did tonight, and Hawk won't keep it from Roman.

I'm surprised he's even helping me right now. Maybe I look so pathetic, and that's why he's waiting until I no longer look like I'm on death's door before hitting me with the lecture.

"Are you going to puke again?" He looms over me.

Squinting up at him, I shake my pounding head. I drop my chin, moaning through the pain. Then I'm dry heaving, not because of the alcohol swimming in my stomach, but because of the smell. Roman picks me up, making my stomach roll again, and I curl into a ball.

"You're going to get it on you," I mutter, cringing away from him.

"It's already on me, Ember. Don't slip."

He sets me gently on my feet, and I cling to him when they skid across the tiles. Opening my eyes, I'm met with steam and a delicious warmth swirling around me. A moan leaves me as I hit the wall, then slide down. Hot water pelts the side of my face, and I turn toward it.

"You're going to fucking drown," he growls, tugging my whole body away, and I whine. "I have to get your clothes off, so stop struggling."

My eyes pop open, and I realize my hands are uselessly flapping at him as if I'm going to fend him off. I lift my arms, letting him peel my shirt over my head. My leggings prove to be harder, and I end up on my back.

"How the hell are these people so fucking rich? I could fit a twin-size bed in here." My voice echoes off the tiles.

"You're just as fucking rich, Ember. I seem to remember your bathroom had an inset tub."

"Co-rec-kia-shun." I enunciate every syllable and wave a finger in his face. "My *parents* are rich. I barely touch my trust."

He snorts, finally getting my pants off. They splat against the floor, and then he starts on his sweatpants. The gray fabric does nothing to hide what he's packing, and I giggle.

"Barely isn't never. Besides, how do you survive? Not like you have a job."

I'm sure he's just spouting bullshit to keep me from passing out, but there's an edge of judgment in his tone. It only makes me want to cuss him out, even though I should keep that shit to myself.

"I actually work, asshole," I mutter.

Roman crouches by my head, elbows resting on his knees. Of course, his dick is right there, hanging out for all the world to see. I scowl at the offending appendage, then lick my lips, though I'm not entirely sure why.

"Ember, I live off my father's fortune and his father's before him. Do you really think I give a flying fuck if you live off your trust?"

I suck my cheeks in, rolling my head to the stare at the ceiling.

"My feet are hot."

He sighs, helping me to stand and keeping an arm around my waist. He's been sighing a lot tonight, and it's starting to annoy me. Gently, he shuffles us toward the water, then tips my head back.

"Please don't waterboard me," I whisper, and he chuckles. "At least you didn't fucking sigh again."

"Tell me what you did tonight," he asks softly as he keeps working on my hair.

I should tell him to stop. The curls are hard enough to deal with as it is without him snarling them up. But his fingers feel nice as they massage my scalp, and with my eyes closed, the room isn't spinning. I can deal with the aftermath of tonight in the morning.

"Willow is nice."

"I agree." He presses a kiss to my throat.

It's quick, probably meant to relax me or something, but all it accomplishes is heating my blood more than it already is. I doubt he'll let me drop to my knees and finish what I'm pretty sure I started in the car. Then again, I'd probably throw up on him. Puking on his legs and puking on his dick are *very* different things.

"I mean, like really nice. I get why you picked her."

He tenses, fingers digging into my hip, and I wiggle to get away from the sharp pain. He brushes his palm over my wet skin, an apology only his flesh can give. Dropping my head to his chest, I wrap my arms around his waist.

"I didn't pick her, Ember. I picked you."

I snort, biting his pec, and he yelps. "I meant to get answers from when you were searching. I get it. Good to know you pick me, though."

The smile he can't see drops from my face and tears fill my eyes. This is why I hate getting drunk. Controlling my emotions isn't something I can do with copious amounts of liquor coursing through my body. Roman may pick me to fuck, to fight next to and with me, for now. But later, when I tell him everything I saw in the Barrens tonight...he won't just be mad. He'll be furious. And then it'll be over.

I may or may not be there to help him confront his father. I certainly won't be here for the aftermath. Because as much as I want to stay, as much as I tell myself I love him, he'll never admit he feels the same. Even with my acceptance of Aelia's death, he doesn't think he has the capacity to love.

I can't fix him. As much as I wish it worked that way, sometimes love just isn't enough.

"Tell me what happened tonight," he says, resting his chin on my head.

"I don't want to."

"Tell me anyway."

He reaches around me, turning off the water, and goosebumps instantly erupt across my arms and back. He drops a kiss on my head, then lets go. Seconds later, he wraps a towel around me, rubbing the fabric along my wet skin. Another towel is wrapped around my head. As soon as I move it'll tumble off, but at least he tried. It's more than he would have done a couple months ago.

The thought pulls me up short, and I stare at his bare feet. Mentally counting back while my head is muddled isn't the easiest, but I could have sworn only a few weeks had passed since I first came here. So much has happened in such a small amount of time. I shouldn't be worried about the future. I shouldn't be worried about anything except tomorrow. Living one day at a time is the way I survive. It wasn't until Roman stepped back into my life that I started wanting more.

I'm consumed in the mindfuck of losing time, it takes me a minute to realize I'm dressed again and Roman is tucking me into bed. I jackknife up and my head sends my eyes spinning. Groaning, I press the heels of my hands to my temples.

"You know this wouldn't happen if you stopped flopping around," he grumbles, tracing light circles on my back.

"It's not my fault the world won't stop spinning."

"I'd argue with you, but I seem to recall you not being able to admit defeat when you've been drinking." He eases me back, then climbs in behind me. "Tell me what happened tonight."

"Why do you keep asking?" I curl my body into his as his arm tucks around my waist, settling under my stomach, thank fuck.

"Because as I was carrying you into the house you kept saying, 'I'll tell him tomorrow.' We both know what will happen tomorrow, though."

"Bold of you to assume I'll even remember this tomorrow," I snap, but there's no bite behind my words.

"You might not. You'll also find an excuse to not tell me tomorrow. Or the next day. Or the next. So, might as well get it the fuck over with."

"With logic like that..." I mumble, tugging the covers up to my chin.

I wait for sleep to get me out of talking to him. Apparently, my mind is in agreement with him. Or maybe it's my heart. Whichever it is, they're a fucking traitor. He wouldn't wake me up just to badger me about a dinner, which I think is what Willow told him. I could lie, but I'm not very good at it. At least in my current state.

"Fine." I scoot away from him and roll on my back. "We went to dinner."

"And after?" His fingers brush my side lightly, sending shivers through me.

"You saw after. It's before..." I bite my lip. "I may have taken Willow somewhere. And we may have done some sleuthing."

His hand pauses, settling under my breast. "Sleuthing."

It's a statement, not a question, and I tense. Peeking at him from the corner of my eye, his gaze is fixed on me, boring into my soul. I bite my cheek, half of me wanting to run away. My morbid curiosity on how he'll react takes over and I stay put.

"It's not like we raided a warehouse or something. Hawk probably isn't going to be very happy, though."

"You went into the Barrens, didn't you? Did you try to get into the Egg? Pick a fight with someone? For the love of all things holy, tell me you didn't go back to the barracks." Exhaustion lines his words, and he snatches his hand away, rolling onto his back.

"We were just checking to see if someone showed up. It's not like we were setting charges or some shit."

He curses, slamming his fists into the mattress, and I flinch. "Did it occur to either of you that maybe that was a fucked-up idea? Perhaps you should have told someone where the hell you were?"

He launches off the bed, pacing back and forth. His hands flex over and over, and I wonder if he's imagining strangling me like in those cartoons. My eyes wouldn't bug out, but I press my lips together to stop myself from laughing at the image forming in my head.

"For fuck's sake. The least you could have done is gone when you were sober," he yells, planting his fists on his hips.

I gape at him, completely speechless. With one sentence, he's sobered me up and pissed me off. I tumble off the other side of the bed, barely getting my feet under me. Not entirely sober it seems, but at least it's enough to keep a coherent thought in my head.

"You think I went to the goddamn Barrens *drunk*? Give me a little bit of fucking credit."

He rears back as if I slapped him. I almost crawl over the bed to do just that. I'm not entirely sure I would make it though, so I settle for glaring at him. It doesn't have the same effect, but it's the best I can do in my current state. My head swims, and I can't figure out if the room is tilting or if that's me.

Closing my eyes, I press my tongue to the roof of my mouth to stop myself from throwing up all over the bed. Sure, there's enough of them in this place to find another, but Roman would probably make me clean the sheets myself and then I'd end up puking again. Tomorrow is going to be a shitshow, I can already feel it.

"I can take care of myself, Roman. So back the fuck off."

I jolt when his hands land on my hips, pulling me into him. Resting my forehead against his bare chest, I breathe him in. I fucking hate this. I just want to know where I stand. I want to stop teetering on the edge of destruction. I want to go back to being secure in my beliefs.

His fingers slide under my hair, gripping my neck, and he leans down. "Just because you can take care of yourself, doesn't mean you have to do it alone."

"Careful," I whisper. "You sound like you're applying for the job."

He chuckles, the rumble echoing through me. "That implies that it's work. Taking care of you is the furthest thing from that, Ember."

"That's not what you said a couple weeks ago," I mutter, butterflies erupting in my gut. At least I hope they're butterflies and not the alcohol insisting on making another appearance.

"Amazing how shit changes when time passes."

He guides me back between the sheets, then pulls me into his chest. As I drift off to sleep, I swear I hear him whispering. It's probably my mind playing tricks on me. There's no way Roman Drake would ever say he loves me.

Forty-Seven

Roman

"What exactly are you wanting from me?" Nicki asks, eyes fixed over my shoulder.

I resist the urge to look. I learned long ago to not take my eyes from the person in front of me. Nicki probably isn't trying to distract me, but I swear she's doing it on purpose. Probably to piss me off.

"Any information about the car bomb the other night. Or the vehicle found in the river."

Focusing on me again, she brushes off her jeans that I swear she painted on, then crosses her arms.

"Nothing new. Obviously, the bomb was rigged. The car in the river is completely submerged now, but it's the same make and model as the one you've been driving. Might be good to switch it up a little."

I roll my eyes, glancing down the alley to the right. A rock skitters in the night, and I search the shadows for Ember's form. I told her to stay put. Not that it's ever worked before. She insists on tagging along. Or going off on her own like she did the other night. Another image of her tied to my bed flashes behind my lids, and I tense.

"We have been. If they were after us, they knew what car we were driving that night and where we were headed. Any idea who that could be?" I swing my gaze back to her.

"No, but that's not exactly my field of expertise. Listen, I know you're not used to this shit, but I'm not your informant. I run the Egg and keep the Barrens in some semblance of order. Nothing more, nothing less." She holds up a hand when I open my mouth. "However, I will tell you it seems like you have a mole. Retrace your steps from that night."

"No one betrayed us," I growl even while nerves shoot through my chest.

She waves away my words. "Listen, I get it. You're in that weird limbo of being in charge but also not. You have people you trust even if you don't like it. Doesn't hurt to reexamine those relationships, as tenuous as they may be."

She turns, the dark swallowing her up. Tipping my head back, I heave out a sigh. I hate solving puzzles. Even when I was trying to take over Synd, I hated dealing with the people. I never knew who I could trust. Constantly looking over my shoulder waiting to be stabbed in the back is a terrible way to live. My father did it for years, becoming paranoid. I don't want to end up like him.

"It wasn't Hawk or Willow," Ember says from behind me.

"Why is it you can never listen?" I don't bother to turn around.

"I do listen. When you're not spouting bullshit." She links her arm with mine, tugging me along. "Are you ready to hear what Willow and I found down here?"

I sigh, steering her down another street as she skips along beside me. Eventually we'll have to talk, but I'm still pissed she went off with only Willow to watch her back. I'm more on edge since I realized how I feel about Ember. It was ridiculous to think I'd ever be able to keep her at arm's length, especially after tasting her. If I lose another person I love, I'll never recover. I'll follow her into the darkness, hoping the devil allows us to be together in the afterlife.

"What did you find?"

"The abandoned jail was set on fire. Nothing really burned other than some of the leftover desks. That big, burly guy, the Irishman, was hanging around." Her nose scrunches then she snaps her fingers. "Mack. That's his name. He said some guys were hanging about. Then a woman came sneaking around. Said she didn't belong. Then boom, fire."

"So, you have no proof to back up your theory that Anders is behind all this," I state matter-of-factly.

"Well, if that's the way you want to look at it, sure. But also—a woman. Any random women who don't fit in down here you can think of?"

I shake my head, mulling over Nicki's words. Willow wouldn't betray us, not that she could have if she was with Ember. I don't know any of the other women who are tied to the Reapers. I don't know enough people in Synd. Hawk might have an idea. Hell, even calling Mason would be better than figuring it out myself. None of those in Rima have been answering either Hawk or me. I'm sure they're dealing with the fallout of Alex's death as well as some of the others disappearing.

"The only place we went was the Flaming Skillet."

Ember freezes, and I jerk to a stop. She stares into the darkness, a calculating look in her eyes.

"What about Mia?" she whispers.

"Who?" I rub the ache in my chest.

"The server at the diner. She's the only one we saw other than Willow. Maybe we should call Hawk to come and ask Mia who she talked to." A shiver rolls through her body, though it's not chilly out.

"Come on."

Grabbing her arm, I rush us to the car parked on the edge of the Barrens. For once, she doesn't complain. We're both silent on the drive to the diner, Ember's fingers flying over the screen as she texts Willow.

"Are they coming?" I ask as I pull into the gravel parking lot.

"Hawk said to grab Mia and bring her to the Kings' place. He'll meet us there." She climbs out of the car. "You think I could convince her to just come with us?"

I step out, meeting Mia's eyes through the front window. Hers widen and she trips back a step, and I slowly shake my head. If she runs, it'll only make shit worse for her. She may be a lousy server, in my opinion, but Hawk seemed to like her. I'm sure her betrayal will hit him hard.

"I doubt it," I answer, prowling toward the diner.

The bell above the door jingles joyfully, at odds with the tension swirling through the air. To her credit, she doesn't run or hide. She waits by a table tucked away in the corner, blocking my view of whoever is seated there. Mia spreads her arms, tipping her chin up in defiance.

"She doesn't have anything to do with this. Leave her alone," she whispers. Her chin quivers, but her eyes are dry.

"We're not in the business of harming innocents, Mia. You should know that. If you come without a fuss, we'll drop her off once we clear this up," I murmur.

She shakes her head, planting her fists on her hips. "I'll go with you but leave her be."

"Not going to happen. Let's go." I wrap my hand around her arm.

She resists at first, then gives in, allowing me to walk her out. I glance behind, making sure Ember deals with the other one. She wraps an arm around the young girl's shoulders. Mascara runs down her cheeks, and she sucks in a shuddering breath. The girl can't be more than eighteen, and I shake my head. Whatever Mia did, I hope she didn't rope a minor into it.

The car ride back is just as quiet as the one to the diner. The younger one sobs silently as Mia rubs her back. Hawk's troubled gaze meets us as we pull into the drive. His jaw ticks as I pull Mia from the backseat, and his eyes follow us as I march her up the stairs.

"Don't put her in the basement," he mutters, and I nod.

I've never been in the Kings' conference room, but it's exactly like the Byrns's, or how it was before it caught on fire. Hawk locks the doors behind us, and the two women shuffle away, huddling on the far side of the table.

"Sit," I command, pointing at the chairs.

Mia drops into one, tugging the girl into the one beside her. She keeps a firm grip on the girl's arm.

Hawk shuffles closer as Ember drops into a chair across from them. I lean against the wall, wondering how she'll play this. Other than Willow, Nicki, and my sister, I don't think I've seen Ember interact with another woman. The girls at school shunned her for the most part, and there haven't been many opportunities for girls' nights since coming to Synd.

"The other one is Mia's brother's girlfriend. Katie's sixteen. No way is she involved in this," Hawk mutters, crossing his arms as he leans next to me.

"Mia, tell me what happened." Ember's soft voice seems to ease Katie since she stops crying.

"I didn't want to," Mia whispers, leaning forward. "He has Kyler. Said if I didn't do what he said, he'd send back parts of him."

"Seems you should have been more concerned with what we'd do to you when we found out," Hawk growls, and Mia flinches.

Ember spins around, raising an eyebrow at him. "Kindly shut the fuck up. Or you can get the hell out. Either one is good with me."

Hawk rolls his eyes, muttering under his breath.

"Drake will, asshole," she sneers, spinning back. Apparently she caught his words.

I straighten, glancing between Hawk and her. I have no idea what she's signing me up for, but I refuse to be put in the middle.

"Have you tried calling him?" Ember asks and Mia huffs.

"Do I look dense? Of course I did. I searched everywhere for him. He's been missing for two weeks."

"And you didn't think to come to us?" Hawk asks, brows pulled low over his eyes.

"And what exactly would you have done? Dropped everything to find him? None of you have loyalty to me," she spits out.

"Maybe not, but since you were supplying information to our enemy, we might have taken an interest," I say, cutting off Hawk.

She scoffs, folding her arms and leaning back. Katie's wide eyes find mine, begging me for something I'm not sure I can deliver. Kyler has been missing for so long, the odds of him being alive are slim. The truth swims in Mia's eyes. It's why she came with us so willingly. She wanted us to know because she's in over her head, but I'm sure her pride and fear overrode all sense.

"Who was it?" I ask.

"If I knew, I would have come to you. He always had his face covered. He's older, though. Had a limp, too."

"Great, so we're looking for an old man with a limp. That's a lot to go on. If your brother is dead, his blood is on your hands, Mia." Hawk slams against the door, attempting to exit. It doesn't budge, and he kicks the wood. I reach up, unlocking it, and he shoves out of the room.

Mia's eyes fill with tears, and she snaps her mouth shut. Her throat bobs as she swallows hard, patting Katie's arm.

Ember spins around again, giving me an expectant look. I nod, finally giving in to her. Anders isn't very subtle, usually. And I assume I'm the one who gave him the limp. There was blood on the floor after I shot into the smoke he disappeared in, like the worst magician ever. I wonder if he feels the ache in his bones every day like I do.

My phone buzzes, and I slip it from my pocket. An unknown number flashes across the screen. I slip from the room as Ember offers them some water. They'll have to stay here while we track my father down. They're not safe anywhere else.

"Drake," I say, answering the phone.

Silence meets my ear. I pull it away, then bring it back. I don't have time for pranks, but I wouldn't put it past Anders to gloat. Another ten seconds lapses in silence and I hang up. I refuse to play his games. My phone vibrates in my hand, the same number flashing, and I crack my neck before pressing accept.

"Don't fuck with me—"

"Roman?"

My fingers go numb, the device tumbling from my hand. A trick. That's what this is. A trick my father set up to fuck with my head. That's the only possible explanation why I'm hearing a voice I haven't heard in ten years. I scramble to pick it up. Even if it is a hoax, at least I get to hear her voice one more time.

"Hello? Are you there?"

I clear my throat, never wanting this to end, even though I know it's a lie.

"Roro, please say something," she whispers, tears in her voice.
I drop to my knees, my vision going dark.
"Aelia?"

Forty-Eight

Ember

"Roman?" I whisper, dropping to my knees next to him.

He doesn't even register my presence. He's locked in some hell, precipitated by whoever is on the other end of the line. I try to slip the phone from his fingers, but he grips it tighter, baring his teeth at me. I stumble back at the raw emotion on his face. It's like he doesn't even know who I am.

"No, don't hang up." Despair laces his tone, and his eyes fill with tears.

The door behind us opens, and I scramble up. Ushering the women past Roman, I glance back at him several times. He hasn't moved, body frozen on his knees.

Apparently, I'm on my own directing them where to sleep. It took some convincing to get Mia to agree. I'll have to make some calls to Katie's mother too, but that's the least of my worries.

Thankfully, Marie is in the kitchen. She fusses over them, putting plates of dessert in front of them. Something cooks on the stove, steam filling the air. I'm shooed away after a minute, and I run through the halls back to Roman.

Skidding around the corner, I slam into the opposite wall. When I catch my breath, I scan the emptiness as if he'll magically appear. Marching toward the conference room, I shove open the door. My heart sinks when I realize it, too, is empty.

Sliding down the wall, I wrap my arms around my knees, burying my head. If only I could disappear as easily as he has. I grit my teeth, forcing the tears away. A gap in the wall catches my eye, and I jump up.

"So, this is how you magically appeared." I open the hidden panel to reveal a staircase. I wonder how many secret passageways they have.

Glancing behind once more, I step into the darkness. I use my phone to light the way, but it doesn't help other than to make sure I don't fall to my death. This tunnel system is a convoluted mess, which I assume is by design.

Every time Roman randomly showed up, this is how he was traveling. He took me through one, but I figured it was a one-off. I huff, wondering if he ever planned on telling me. I can't blame him since this isn't his house. Still, I'm going to be pissed about it.

When I stumble across him, sitting on a landing, I let go of my annoyance. His head hangs low, not even flinching when I drop next to him. We sit like that, him lost in his thoughts and me waiting for him to come back to himself. I want to ask who died. It's the only explanation for his reaction. Catatonic—the exact way he was when Aelia didn't come back. Until I interrupted his downward spiral, and he rose from the ashes of his grief to take his rage out on me.

"You were right," he murmurs. Too many emotions crowd his voice, making it impossible to fully understand where his head is at.

"Right about what?"

"Aelia."

That one name, three syllables, five letters, cut me deeper than anything else. Swallowing around the truth I recently acknowledged, I shake my head.

"No. Aelia is dead." It's the first time I've said it so plainly, and tears fill my eyes.

"I heard her voice. I spoke with her. She's alive. I didn't believe Hawk—"

I rear back, staring at his profile. "What the hell does *that* mean?"

He runs his hand through his hair, clearing his throat. "Nothing. But she's alive. She's with the Guild."

"No, don't shove me off. Did Hawk tell you she was alive? When?"

He blinks, his eyes clearing, and he sees me for the first time since I appeared. He reaches for me, and I stutter away.

As soon as he touches me, I'll cave. He'll explain away his reasons for keeping shit from me. And I'll let him. Every fucking time, I'll let him.

"A while ago," he mumbles. "I didn't believe it."

"You watched me break down. You saw me relive the horror. You *sat there* and said *nothing,*" I hiss. "And all this time, you knew she was alive. Even if there was a sliver of a chance, you should have told me. I thought I *wasted* years of my life chasing the idea that she was alive."

I'm panting, my chest tightening the more I think about it. His tongue darts out, licking his bottom lip as his hands clench over and over. He opens his mouth, then snaps it shut again.

"Fuck you, Roman Drake. Fuck you."

And then I run. As fast as I can, I stumble through the tunnels. A set of stairs looms out of the darkness, and my shins slam into them. I crumple to the floor, sobs wracking my body. Everything hits me at once until only one thought remains.

She didn't call me.

It shouldn't matter. She doesn't know that I'm still here—I'm still looking. There's no way for her to know anything beyond the walls of the Guild. Calling her brother is more important.

Still, jealousy rips through me, choking me with its headiness. My vision blurs, but whether I'm spiraling or crying, I can't tell. It doesn't matter.

Arms wrap around me, heat skates along my skin, bleeding into my pores. Tremors wrack my body as pain pours out of me. Every muscle twists, squeezing my heart until I'm trembling and numb.

I thought losing Aelia was the worst thing I've ever felt. I thought admitting she was dead was excruciating. But this? This is torture.

"No, Em. No. No. No." Roman's voice seeps through the fog, winding through the cracks in the walls my mind has erected around my senses.

It's then that I realize I'm screaming. Over and over. Again and again. *Find her.*

I tense, clamping my lips together to hold in my pain—to bury it deep within my heart where it's always lived. It retreats the slightest bit, refusing to be caged once more.

He grunts when I throw my elbow into his stomach, his arms loosening enough for me to free my own. I kick, hitting his shins as my toes scramble for purchase on the smooth stone. Roman grips me tighter, rolling us to the side. His hand wraps around my throat, cutting off my screams.

As suddenly as the rage hit, it flows away, slithering into the dark to terrorize some other poor soul. My body aches, acid filling my veins to weigh me down.

"I'm not the enemy, Ember," he whispers harshly in my ear. "I'm sorry. I'm fucking sorry."

"I hate you," I sob, tipping my head back, wishing he would tighten his hold, suffocate me if only to put me out of my misery.

"I know."

I push at his limbs, and he drops them. As much as I don't want to leave the safety of his arms, I no longer trust him. It doesn't even matter what else he's hiding. Surely there's more. How could there not be? If he withheld this, the most important thing...

Another sob crawls up my throat, and I cover my mouth to keep it inside. He doesn't deserve to hear my pain. Out of everything I expected to fracture us, Roman not telling me Aelia was alive wasn't even a possibility.

"Don't, Ember. Don't do it." His voice echoes through the darkness.

My phone, the flashlight creating a spotlight on the rough ceiling, lies innocently next to him. It's the only way I'm able to make out the anguish on his face. I swallow the shame and pity that floods my mouth. It burns as it slides down my throat, and my stomach rolls. I push to my feet, my chest heaving while I struggle to gather up the emotions I've scattered upon the stone.

"She's a prisoner. For years, she's been held hostage by those sick fucks, and you want me to what? Leave her? Trust people I don't even know to save her? They don't fucking care about her. They'll save themselves." I glare down at him through swollen eyes. "Fuck you, Drake. You don't deserve her if you leave her to rot a minute longer."

I grab my phone, and his fingers brush my arm. Jerking away, I give him one last loathing look before I force my feet to take measured steps. I have no idea where I'm going, and I'm sure to get lost in this maze, but I don't give a fuck.

Leaving right now isn't possible, anyway. Not only am I in the wrong mental state to fuck off to Rima to save her, but I don't even know how I would accomplish it. If the others haven't been able to do it by now, why would I think I could? Maybe it would be easier for me since I'm only one person.

Taking a turn, another set of stairs appears, light filtering from the open panel at the top. I practically crawl up them, relief flooding through me. I collapse when I reach the conference room, curling into a ball and fighting the misery licking along the edges of my vision.

I don't know how long I lie there, drowning in despair, but eventually I pull myself to my feet. Wandering through the halls, I barely recognize where I'm going until I reach the kitchen.

Mia and Katie have long since disappeared. I don't even care if they slipped out of the house or found a bedroom to crash in.

Dealing with Anders isn't important anymore. Roman can have his revenge, though I wonder if exacting justice upon his father will be as satisfying as it would have been.

I drop onto a stool that looks a little worse for wear. The rest seem perfectly fine, and I wonder what happened to make this one lopsided. A chocolate croissant sits on a plate, a glass dome covering it. I snort, recognizing the cover as the same ones my parents used for their fancy parties—the ones I wasn't invited to. I would sneak down to the kitchen and swipe some of the lobster puffs or truffles.

Gently, I remove the cover, then stare at the pastry. I'm not hungry. In fact, I might ruin chocolate croissants for me forever if I eat it. I have a feeling Marie left it for me, though. After only a few encounters, I trust her to know what I need more than I trust myself.

Picking it up, I nibble on the end. A tear slips down my cheek, dropping onto the counter. I don't bother to wipe it away. I swear I've cried more in the last week than I have in the past ten years.

When Roman threw me out all those years ago, refusing to speak with me, I locked my emotions deep within. I refused to give in until I found her. Since I came to Synd, though, I've been on a rollercoaster I'm still not sure I want to get off of.

Roman slides onto the stool next to me, propping his elbows on the counter and dropping his head in his hands. Ignoring him is the only way I'll be able to keep my shit together, so I take another bite. He pulls another plate toward him, and we eat in silence for several minutes.

I shove the last of the chocolatey goodness in my mouth, planning my escape route when he clears his throat.

"I couldn't do it." He shoves the empty plate away. "If I told you and it wasn't true...I couldn't do it."

"And yet it was true," I say bitterly.

He nods, eyes fixed on the counter. "And then I'd lose you."

"Why would Aelia being alive make you lose me?"

"Because you always loved her more than me. And I don't blame you. I'd pick her over me every fucking day. She's always been the best of us. Neither of us deserve her."

I suck in a quiet breath, closing my eyes. "Loving you would be a long journey to nothingness."

He nods as if I'm confirming everything he already knew. He doesn't realize I'm already there, lost in the void that is loving him—in the understanding that he'll never feel the same. Protective? Yes. Caring for me? Maybe. But never in love. When I started down this path, I knew it would lead here—to nothing. Too much past and no future.

"You can't go to Rima, Ember. I know you don't trust them. Hell, you don't even know them. But I do. I've been watching them for years. They won't leave her behind if they can save her. For criminals, they're actually pretty fucking decent." He says it like he's still pissed about it.

"Probably would have been easier to take them out if you didn't respect them," I murmur.

He sighs, rubbing his temples. "I have to stay here. I can't do anything for Aelia, no matter how much I'd like to. Killing our father is the only way I can atone for never believing you."

"I'm not the one you need to appease, Drake."

He pushes from the stool. "That's where you're wrong. Once Aelia is home, I'll make amends to her. But you? You deserve everything—including a love you'll never accept."

His lips brush my temple and then he's gone.

Forty-Nine

Roman

I haven't seen Ember for twenty-four hours and it's killing me. According to the guards, she hasn't left, but it's not hard to get lost in a mansion like the Kings' place. I don't blame her for avoiding me.

Hearing Aelia's voice again, talking to her, was overwhelming to say the least. I wanted to tell Ember everything she said. It'll have to wait until Ember is ready, but every time I think about it, I die a little inside.

Aelia is as stuck as the rest of us. Stagnant and unable to move forward. At least my sister is doing something good. The need to rush to Rima and rip her from the Guild's grasp threatens to take over several times an hour. Holding back is one of the hardest things I've ever done.

Now I'm left to pace around the halls, pretending I'm not searching for Ember. Instead, I stumble across Mia in the library. Walls of books surround comfy chairs and couches. It appears the room is actually used, with several novels strewn on side tables throughout the massive space.

I find Mia lying face down on one of the couches, and I clear my throat. Her hand brushing the carpet as it hangs off the side flips me the bird, so at least I know she's alive. I settle into the chair across from her and cross my ankle over my knee, folding my hands on my stomach. Hawk has been out searching for Mia's brother, but the vastness of the Barrens doesn't help.

"Enough wallowing. I need information, and you're going to give it to me," I say, and her head turns to the side to glare at me.

She blows her dark hair from her face, but the strands float back and she crinkles her nose. She pushes them back, annoyance stamped across her pursed lips.

"Are you being an asshole because you're fighting with your woman, or are you always like this?"

"We've crossed paths before. What do you think?" I raise an eyebrow, and she scoffs.

"Bona fide asshole. Got it." She flashes me a thumbs up and buries her face again.

"I may be an asshole, but you're a shit server. We both understand we're not going to become best friends and braid each other's hair, but that doesn't mean you're not going to help me."

A clock chimes from somewhere in the room, and I glance around to find it. When I look back, she's narrowing her eyes at me again.

"You don't have hair long enough to braid. And I'm going to shave all mine off, so we'll have to come up with another sleepover tradition to pass the time." She sighs when I don't react. "Fine. What the hell do you want?"

"The man you met—"

"Your father," she sneers.

I nod my head, continuing, "Where did you meet him? In the Barrens?"

"At first it was through a guy. Some lowlife who looked like he was one missed hit away from losing it. He asked me if I could get him Oracle after he threatened to stab me." Most people would have the good sense to be scared, but Mia just rolls her eyes as if this is a normal occurrence. "After I fed him some info that didn't pan out for the old dude, he got pissed and cornered me after work. That's how I knew he had a limp."

"So, you have no idea where he's holed up?"

She sighs, finally sitting up. "Listen, I didn't know what else to do. I wasn't going to follow him to his secret lair. I may be a bitch, but I'm not qualified to pull off some grand rescue."

"And yet you didn't come to the people who *could* accomplish such a feat."

She glances away, jaw set. I don't blame Mia, just like I didn't blame the nurse. My father knows exactly how to manipulate people through threats and fear. Hell, I lived under his thumb long enough I tried to carry out a vendetta against people I didn't give two shits about. I'm the last person to judge Mia for the decisions she's made.

I lean forward, propping my elbows on my knees and letting my hands dangle between my legs. This conversation, while necessary, is exhausting. Especially since I keep getting lightheaded.

"Anders Drake doesn't reveal himself unless he's at the edge of the cliff. You were seen in the Barrens, Mia."

Her head whips back, fear dripping from her eyes. "I didn't have a choice."

"That's neither here nor there. Hawk has people out searching for your brother. Do you have any idea where Anders would go, other than the abandoned police station?"

"He's still there," she whispers.

Slipping her phone from her pocket, she slides it across the coffee table between us. A text thread is pulled up between Mia and Anders. She hasn't answered his last seven messages that get progressively more irate. The last is the worst of all, demanding her presence at the barracks or he'll send her brother's head to her in a box.

Glancing up, I push the phone back, and she cradles it to her chest, silent tears slipping down her face. When her eyes meet mine, I nod. I won't give her false promises.

"If you find Kyler..." A strangled sob cuts off whatever she was going to say.

Pushing to my feet, I tuck my hands in my pockets. "If I do, you owe me a fucking cup of tea."

She chokes out a laugh, swiping away her tears angrily. I leave her to pull herself together. She doesn't want my sympathy, much less my comfort. I'm shit at giving it anyway.

I trip over my feet when I find Ember leaning against a bookcase around the corner. She has a book in her hand, but her eyes aren't moving. She makes a show of holding a finger up and then slips what looks like a receipt between the pages before snapping it shut.

"We need to talk," she says.

Her eyes are blank, face an emotionless mask, and I hate it. I'd rather she scream at me. Hell, I'd rather she threaten to smother me. Anything but this shell of a person standing in front of me.

"Lead the way."

I gesture toward the door, and her breath stutters. Apparently, she's not as detached as she'd like to be. I smile as I follow her out the door and down the hall. I can work with that. She leads us to my bedroom, and my cock twitches. Kicking the door shut, I adjust myself. Apparently, not discreetly enough, as she rolls her eyes when she catches me.

"Can't fucking help it, Ember."

"Well, keep your damn pants on. In fact, go sit there and try to keep your hands to yourself." She points to the chair across the room, and I make my way over.

"Are you going after Anders?" she asks, plopping onto the edge of the bed.

"I don't have a plan yet, seeing as how I just found out where he is."

"I want to go with you." Her fingers pluck at the skin on her knuckles, leaving a redness behind. My palms itch to cover her hands.

"I can't promise you that. If you're staying, I might need you somewhere else," I hedge, glancing at the rumpled sheets behind her.

I didn't even sleep last night, thoughts of Ember consuming me. Though I thought Aelia would dominate my mind, other than my breakdown yesterday, I haven't obsessed over it. The majority of my adult life was spent mourning her, maybe I just haven't accepted her resurrection yet. I thought it would be hard to put my trust in Byrns, Helms, and the Kings to keep her safe, but knowing at least some of them are there to protect her helps. Actually, I wish I could get ahold of Sam. She might not like me much, but she wouldn't blame my sister.

"What do you mean, if I'm staying?" She shifts, not able to meet my eyes. "Thought you were going to stop me from going to Rima."

"You and I both know I can't stop you. But I'd rather you didn't put yourself in harm's way."

She snorts, shaking her head. It might be a ridiculous statement, but if she's in Rima there's no way for me to protect her. Getting into a pissing match with her about whether or not that's my job isn't something I want to start right now.

"I'll help you take down Anders, but then I'm going to Rima."

My heart twists, sending a bolt of pain through my chest. I press my fist against the ache, and she fixes her gaze on me. I drop my hand back to my lap.

"Anything else?" I grunt.

I thought I wanted this conversation. I thought I could handle whatever she threw at me. I could convince her to stay and be here with me. Even if I don't stay in Synd forever, I want her by my side. Wherever I end up, I want her with me.

I can't force her, though. She'll make her own decisions, and if her future doesn't include me, then so be it. I'll have to live with losing her, no matter how hard that will be.

I peek at her from beneath my lashes as she stands, eyes roving around the room, and she wraps her arms around her waist.

"That's it?" she whispers.

"What else is there? You've made your decisions, and I need to make mine."

"So, we're right back where we started. Nothing's changed," she says bitterly.

Lifting my head, I meet her green eyes filled with unshed tears. "Oh, I think a lot has changed."

"Like what?"

Pushing from the chair, I step closer. I tip her chin up with my knuckle, electricity shooting up my arm at the contact. Her tongue darts out and runs along her bottom lip. Brushing my thumb along the same path, I suppress a shudder.

"Everything."

"I don't know what that means."

I chuckle, running my hand through my hair. "Sure you don't."

"Why do you even care what I do?"

I scowl, sliding an arm around her waist and yanking her into me. She gasps and her hands fly to my chest, nails digging in. I hate this timid woman. It's not her. The Ember I know seizes what she wants without giving a damn what anyone else thinks. I hate that I'm the reason she isn't herself. I'm probably not the only reason, but I contributed and that's enough.

"Because you're mine, Ember. You always were."

Swooping down, I cover her mouth with mine, and she gasps. When she melts into me, I know I've won. It's not the same as professing my undying love for her, but she wouldn't believe me if I dropped to my knees and begged her to love me.

Walking her backward, we tumble onto the bed, my body covering hers. She squirms under me, fingers scrambling to unbutton my shirt. Propping myself onto my forearms, I brush my lips along her jaw, her gasps filling my ears. I let her struggle for another minute, relishing the taste of her skin before I stand. Grabbing the edges of the fabric, I rip it the rest of the way, buttons scattering across the floor.

She sits up, nails scraping up my chest as she bites my side. I groan, tipping my head back as she attacks my pants. I've been hard since the library. It's been too long since I've been inside her, but I need to taste her first. She finally frees my cock, licking her lips as it bobs in front of her face.

"Off. Now," I growl, pointing to her shirt as I step out of my pants, tossing them to the side.

She whips the fabric over her head, then unhooks her bra. I bend, sucking a nipple into my mouth, and she moans, fingers digging into my scalp. Swirling the tight bud with my tongue, I ease her onto her back. Whimpers fall from her swollen lips as I switch to her other nipple, giving it the same treatment.

I scrape my teeth over her skin as I grip the waistband of her leggings and peel them off her legs. Dropping to my knees, I bury my nose between her thighs, breathing in her unique scent through the fabric still separating me from her. She jolts, legs clamping around my head when I nip at her clit. She's vibrating, her entire body on edge as I lick her through her lace thong.

"Drake," she groans, grinding her pussy into my face.

"Hmm?" I murmur.

Spreading her thighs, I hook my fingers under the elastic, and she jumps, lifting onto her elbow.

"Do not rip my panties. They're pretty," she snarls, and I grin.

"You're pretty."

"Not the fucking point, Drake. Do not ruin my underwear."

I run my thumb along the fabric, then press her clit, slowly circling the sensitive bud. Her eyes roll back in her head, pussy pulsing.

"Seems I've already done that, love. You've fucking soaked them."

She gasps, head tipping back. "Wash them."

I slip them down her legs, even as the urge to destroy them with my teeth rides me. This isn't about dominating her, fucking her into bliss. No, this is to show her how I feel with my body since the words won't come. Bringing the fabric to my nose, I breathe in deeply, then toss them onto my nightstand.

"What the hell was that?" she pants.

"You smell delicious. I'll buy you a new pair. Hell, I'll buy you a dozen."

Her reply is lost in a moan when I lick her pussy, flicking her clit with my tongue. I groan, bolts of pleasure shooting through me and straight to my cock as the taste of her explodes across my senses. I do it again, just to hear her whimper. Her fingers grip my hair, yanking at the strands as she tries to pull me closer.

Sucking her clit into my mouth, I slip two fingers into her pussy, and she clamps down. Her orgasm takes us both off guard, and I shudder with her.

Gazing at her, I track the flush traveling up her chest as she pulses around my fingers. I'll never get bored watching her come. It's a heady feeling knowing I'm the one who made her feel this way.

"Cock," she gasps.

"Hmm?" I ask, the vibrations of my voice sending bolts of pleasure through her.

"I want your cock. Now."

I chuckle, pulling my fingers from her as she tries to suck me back in. I lap at her core, not wanting to waste a fucking drop. Ember's heels dig into my sides, then she kicks me, and I grunt.

"Did you need something?" I growl into her flesh, then sink my teeth into her inner thigh.

"I will fucking stab you if you don't fuck me right now," she threatens, and I grin.

Nipping my way up her body, I take my time. She writhes under me, muttering threats between moans. Cupping her tits, I push them together and press a kiss to the side of each one.

She growls, rubbing her clit against my stomach, seeking any friction she can. Her hand tries to steal between our bodies, and I grab her wrist. Forcing her arm above her head, I latch onto her nipple, and she shivers. Her other hand grabs my side, then she rakes her nails to my hip. I bite her nipple, and she yelps.

"Don't even think about it or I'll tie you to the bed," I growl.

Her mouth drops open, but desire drips from her gaze. "You wouldn't."

"Try me."

A smirk slowly overtakes her mouth, and I shake my head. I don't have anything to tie her up with, but I'm sure I can find something that will work if she decides to defy me.

She pouts, then grabs the back of my neck, forcing my mouth back to her nipple. As she bucks underneath me, I get back to worshiping her body. I'd die a happy man being suffocated by either her thighs or her tits. They're fucking perfect, filling my hand, nipples hardening under my tongue.

I grip her hip with my free hand, holding her still as needy noises fall from her. Just when I think she's given up trying to touch herself, her fingers slip under my hip. I push off her to stand, and she glares at me. Her eyes drop to my cock, and she bites her lip.

I grab the tie I threw on the floor last night and knot it, creating two loops. It's not perfect, but it'll do until I can find something better.

"Fuck," she breathes, then flips over to scramble across the bed.

I capture her ankle, tugging her back to me. I grab one wrist, slipping the silk over her hand, then secure the other one. She barely struggles, though every time her ass rubs against my cock, I can't help but respond. I pull her to her feet and press her back to my chest. Wrapping a hand around her throat, I guide her arms over my head, the tie keeping her still for me.

"Is your ass missing my cock?" I whisper.

"Yes," she gasps, knees giving out, and I sling my arm across her stomach, gripping her hip.

"What about your pussy? How much does she miss me?"

I dip my fingers between her legs, gathering up the wetness, and she shudders. Pumping one finger in and out of her, I trail it up her stomach, then circle her nipple.

"Do you want a taste, love?"

She nods, opening her mouth, and my cock pulses against her ass. Slipping my finger inside her mouth is almost my undoing. She sucks hard, tongue sliding against my skin, and I sink my teeth into the soft spot by her shoulder. Releasing her flesh, I admire the mark before pulling from her mouth. I slip her arms from over my head and her locked fingers drop to the bed, her ass pushing into my cock.

I lean over her body, whispering into her ear, "Don't move."

It takes everything within me to step away from her. Stalking to the closet, I open drawer after drawer, searching for anything other than my tie to secure her to the bed. I didn't knot them tight, but I don't want to hurt her.

The image in my head of her spread eagle like my own personal feast has me gripping my cock and squeezing. I'm torturing myself as much as I am her.

I'm about to give up when I open the bottom drawer and find lace-lined cuffs, a leash of sorts attached to rings on each of them. I grin, prowling back to the bedroom. Ember is right where I left her, ass in the air, waiting for me to return.

"Good girl," I murmur, then slap her ass hard.

She groans, burying her head into the mattress. The handprint against her pale, freckled skin sends a bolt of possessiveness through me. I drop to my knees and bite the mark while my thumb finds her clit. Ember sinks to her knees, gasping for breath. She's close to coming again, and I pull my hand away.

"You asshole," she cries.

Tugging the silk from her wrists, I massage the flesh before cuffing one and then the other with the bonds I found. She eyes my movements, panting and rubbing her thighs together.

"Crawl onto the bed," I say, my voice rough with desire, and she does, the ties trailing in her wake. "On your back."

She flops around, legs falling open, and I wipe away my grin. Her arms fling over her head, eager to please. I attach them both to the headboard, wondering if the bed frame was purchased for this exact reason. The bedroom was empty when I took it over, but that doesn't mean it wasn't used before.

When she's secure, I trail my fingertips down her skin, working her body into a frenzy again. I avoid her nipples, lingering on the soft undersides of her tits, then her stomach. Her muscles jump under my touch, and I dip my head, kissing my way down her body.

Her hips kick up and I straddle her stomach, my cock standing at attention. She tugs on the restraints, mouth hanging open as if she can catch the tip if only she tries hard enough.

"Do you want to suck my cock?" I grip her chin.

She nods, then licks her lips. "Please?"

"Such manners. If only I had known teasing you was the way to get you to obey."

Her brows pull low as she contemplates my words. I slide up her body and kneel over her face. Using my thumb, I force her mouth open, then guide the tip between her lips. She sucks, trying to pull me deeper, and I groan.

My hand slams against the headboard and it rattles against the wall. It's too much. I thrust forward once, hitting the back of her throat, and she gags. I pull out completely, panting while I get my shit together.

Fucking her mouth would be amazing, as usual, but I need to be deep inside her when I come.

"Wait," she gasps. Clearing her throat, her eyes find mine. "Again."

I shake my head, settling between her legs. "Beg if you want, love, but I'm going to fuck you slowly."

"You can fuck me after."

I chuckle, skimming my hands up her sides, then down to her hips. I grip my cock, rubbing the tip along her pussy, avoiding her clit, and she squirms. Her back arches, heels digging into the sheets, and I thrust into her deep.

Our groans mingle, echoing throughout the room, giving voice to our pleasure. I drop my head to her neck, breathing heavily while I bask in the connection. Her legs wrap around my waist, and I move, plunging into her steadily.

"Faster," she whines.

"Not a fucking chance, Ember. I'm going to savor every fucking second of this."

She gasps when I bury my cock into her, grinding my hips against hers. She whimpers, rolling her hips and I kiss her jaw, then her cheek, and finally her mouth. As I sink into her, my tongue sweeps into her mouth, using my body to worship hers.

"Untie me," she mumbles against my lips, and I pull back, searching her face. "I want to touch you."

"Do you? Or do you just want to play with your clit?" I smirk at her huff.

She clamps around me, and I grunt, dropping my forehead to her chest.

"Fuck me properly and I wouldn't have to," she snaps, but when I glance up at her, still buried deep, a smile plays on her lips.

"Pissing me off isn't going to make me go any faster, love."

Pushing up, I grab her hips, fingers digging into her skin, and I surge into her. The headboard hits the wall with each thrust, and her tits bounce as she closes her eyes and moans my name.

Her legs fall away from me as she spasms around me, shuddering in pleasure. Gritting my teeth, I fuck her through her orgasm, holding myself from filling her up.

Her body trembles, muscles turning to jelly, and I slow. Reaching up, I unhook one arm and then the other, leaving the cuffs on, but she doesn't move.

I cover her body with mine and roll us until she's straddling me, body still tucked against my chest. I run my hands along her skin, kissing the top of her head. I roll my hips, the new angle sending another bolt of pleasure through me.

She pushes up, planting her hands on my chest and my hands drop to her hips. The restraints circle her wrists, though the straps are still attached to the headboard by my head. Ember is a vision, eyes closed, head thrown back while she rides my cock. My fingers drop to her clit, and I circle the bud as she shudders.

Her eyes meet mine and she pushes my hand away, guiding it to her waist. Leaning down, she kisses me gently.

"Fuck me," she says against my lips.

Picking her up, I thrust into her hard and fast. Her fingers bury themselves between her legs, rubbing her clit, and I fix my gaze on her. My stomach tightens and I groan as I watch her touch herself. She sails over the edge, pussy squeezing the fucking life out of me, and I erupt.

She falls onto my chest, and I gather her in my arms as her hips rock back and forth. Her pussy pulses around my cock. I kiss her forehead as her body goes pliant.

After several minutes, I slip from her heat, drawing the covers over both of us. She murmurs, eyes closed even as I tuck her body close to mine. Resting my cheek against her hair, I sigh.

"Fuck, I love you," I whisper, but she's already fast asleep.

Fifty

Ember

Roman is gone. Before I even open my eyes, I know he is. It's not that his side of the bed is cold, or that I heard him slip out. No, it's as if all the life has been sucked from the room, leaving me bereft.

My muscles ache as I stretch, then flop onto my back. Opening my eyes, I stare at the shadowed ceiling. I can't even make out the swirls it's so dark.

Sitting up, I whip the covers back and pad to the window. I fling back the curtains, expecting bright sunlight, but I'm met with darkness. There's not even moonlight scattered behind the clouds. Thunder rolls in the distance, and I shiver. I'm naked, but there's something else making goosebumps run up my body. I spin around, scanning the empty room.

The white piece of paper lying on the nightstand catches my eye. My feet are rooted to the floor, though. I can't make myself move, too afraid of what I'll find. In fact, I already know what it says. Maybe not the exact words, but the voice in my head screams the truth at me.

Roman left without me. He didn't want me to come with when he faced his father, so he snuck away in the dead of night like a fucking coward.

Stomping to the closet, I grab clothes, all black to blend into the night. As I tug on my pants, I curse him under my breath. I should have known he would do anything to leave me behind. Even fucking me to distract me from the conversation we should have been having.

Sure, I was using him too, throwing my newfound resolve to be pissed at him aside. I should have pressed the issue, but then he couldn't have fucked me into oblivion. I groan, my muscles protesting as I pull on my shirt. I can't deny it was hot as hell.

And then he fucking left.

I almost ignore the note altogether. As I grab a gun from the nightstand, though, my eyes keep darting to the neat handwriting. Of course he wrote it instead of texting me. Then I might have woken up. I scoff, but my gaze drifts to it again. I snatch it up, skimming the lines.

My mouth parts and I start over from the beginning. Most of it is as I expected, but the end. The end is what has a tear bleeding into the paper.

If I don't make it back, remember she needs you. You can survive without me, but not her, no matter what's between us. We always knew I was the expendable Drake.

I sink to the bed, brushing my fingers along the lines as if I can reach him through his words. The piece of my soul I thought had long since died wails within me, crying out for someone who's no longer here. Swallowing hard, I fold it, shoving it into my bra, next to my heart.

By the time I'm stomping into the hall, I'm cursing him again. That fucker thinks he can sacrifice himself and tell me in a goddamn letter? Who the hell does that? This isn't a fucking movie. I was right before, he's a coward. And I'm going to tell him exactly what I think of his letter and shove it straight up his ass.

Seething, I storm through the house until I get to Mia's bedroom. I kick the door, not to break it down as I'm pretty sure I'd break my foot if I tried, but merely because I'm that pissed off. I do it again for good measure. Mia's face appears, sleep lines gracing her face.

"Where's Anders?" I snap.

"He's at the barracks, I think," she stammers out, and I pop an eyebrow up. "The old police station in the Barrens."

I nod, turning to dash away, but pivot back. "Do you have a hair tie?"

She nods, disappearing into the darkness, then reappears a minute later with two ponytail holders in her hand. I snatch them up with a muttered thanks and then march away. I don't care what she does with the information. There's no one to tell, anyway. If Anders knows I'm coming, so be it. He probably doesn't even remember me.

Sneaking into the garage is easier than I thought it would be. Keys hang on hooks right by the door and I pick one. They're all fancy as shit except for one beater. It takes longer than I'd like to find the right key for the hunk of junk, since it's sitting on a workbench instead of hanging up, but soon I'm pulling out of the drive, waving to the guard in the shack. He tentatively waves back, a bewildered look stamped on his face.

The streets are empty as I try to remember the way to the bridge closest to the old police station. When I had to find Roman, I was wandering the Barrens and we were staying on the Byrns' side of the river. The Kings' side is still foreign to me, though I'm starting to realize the streets are laid out much the same way as the Byrns' territory. In fact, the west side might be an exact mirror to the east.

When I finally bump over the bridge, lightning flashes across the sky, threatening rain. The last thing I want to do is traipse around in a thunderstorm. Hopefully, I can find Roman, beat Anders to a bloody pulp, dump his body in the river, and be back in bed next to Roman before it starts. That is, after I tell him how spineless he is for leaving a fucking note. Tall order, but a girl can dream.

"Fuck," I mutter as I swing the car into a curb. "This isn't...wait. Fuck yes."

I glance around, making sure no one is in the backseat, even though I know I'm alone. I'm used to talking to myself since I rarely have anyone to chat with, but I still get worried someone is spying on me.

Snorting, I pull the car off to the side and throwing it into park. It takes three tries to get the door to latch shut, and I stick my tongue out at the rust heap.

Thunder rolls overhead, the only sound to pierce the quiet of the Barrens. I check my weapons one last time before dashing through the streets. Nothing moves as I creep around corners and skip past empty buildings. Even the air stands still.

I slide into a shadow, studying a metal shack I'm pretty sure I saw before, and the hair on the back of my neck stands up. Whipping around, I scan the quiet, but nothing jumps out to attack me.

I pull in a deep breath to calm my nerves. It only helps a little. Biting my lip, I contemplate texting Roman, but dismiss the idea almost as soon as it forms.

I step into the light, then jolt back into the cover of darkness when a single gunshot rings out. I scan the area again, straining to hear the next one. Nothing comes, and I slip my gun from the holster, checking the magazine once more. A shiver runs through me as I take off toward where I'm pretty sure the noise came from.

I swing around a corner, skid to a stop, and throw myself behind a dumpster that smells like cat piss and burning metal. Light reflects through the shattered window of the police station, then winks out. I doubt there's a back way into the place, leaving only a frontal attack.

Not knowing how many men Anders has with him freaks me out, but it's not like I'm going to turn around and go home. I slip my phone from my pocket and send a quick message to Willow before approaching the side of the building.

I peek through the bottom corner of the window and crawl over the sill when I don't notice anyone milling about. The inside is quiet, and I wonder if I imagined the light.

Sounds in the Barrens seem to echo, distorting where they're coming from. I could be searching in entirely the wrong spot, leaving Roman vulnerable to Anders's traps. Because of course he'd have traps. Tiptoeing around a half-burned desk, my foot hits the leg. The noise isn't loud, but I duck down, holding my breath.

"Sorry to burst your bubble, Father. I didn't realize you wanted to gloat." Roman's voice rings out.

A low voice rumbles a response, but I can't make out the words. I pass the hallway leading toward the cells, then sneak around the massive front desk, ducking behind it to peek around the corner. The shadowed passageway doesn't seem to have an end.

I swallow hard, checking my gun again. It's a nervous habit from the first time I got into a firefight with someone. Sweaty palms and a gun with no bullets made for an interesting dilemma. Ever since, I end up checking and rechecking, never fully convinced it's loaded.

"Her? Some fuck the Kings foisted off on me. Not that you would understand. I'm sure you don't get laid unless you pay for it now that you're with the Guild."

My skin crawls, thinking about the Guild. Anders running to them when he faked his death isn't surprising, but it is disgusting.

"Too bad your sister didn't have to go through that, hmm?" Anders says. "The Guild found another option for her, though now she's been run through quite thoroughly. It's a shame her mind will be broken by the time she reaches the Auction."

I expect Roman to lose it—explode and beat Anders senseless. But it's crickets. Rage flows through me and I glance at my hands. I'm not sure if my eyeballs are vibrating or my hands are trembling. Either way, I want to pop Anders's head off like a fucking dandelion. My hands tingle and I shake the sensation away.. I have no idea why popping his head off is the only thing I can think of, but there it is, sitting on the edge of my mind.

"Nothing to say? I'm sure you're happy to know she's alive," Anders sneers. "Too bad you won't be able to see her once more, though she's quite embedded in the Guild. Loves her life, in fact. Even if you were able to reach her, she wouldn't want to leave."

Roman's short laugh fills the room as I peek around a door frame. Scanning what was clearly a break room in another life, I find Roman tied to a wooden chair. Anders lounges across a table as if they're having a business meeting. I can't even see a weapon, though only their profiles are visible from my position. For all I know, Anders could have a gun pointed straight at Roman, but I doubt it. I duck back, sliding into a crouch against the wall.

Why isn't he fighting back? A rickety old piece of furniture shouldn't be enough to stop Roman. The fact he was caught in the first place doesn't make any sense. I search the hall, straining to hear anything over the two men in the next room. Anders doesn't even have men, so what the hell happened?

"Are you going to untie me, or have I sufficiently proven myself?" Roman asks.

My eyes fall closed, and I bite my lip. That fucking asshole. His note makes a lot more sense now. Still a damn coward. Which I will thoroughly make him pay for as soon as I get him away from his father. Anders corrupts everything he touches. I won't allow him to steal another person I love. Not again.

"I'm disappointed in you, son. You protected the girl as if she mattered. But I taught you better than that," Anders says, then sighs.

Standing, I peek around the corner again, focusing on the layout of the room. The last thing I want to do is bust into the space and trip over a random chair. Not only would that give them time to react, but it'd be really fucking embarrassing. It doesn't seem like the fire reached this part of the station, though soot covers the floor and ceiling.

"You certainly did, father. What can I say? She was a really good fuck."

My eyes dart to Roman, his ever-present smirk plastered on his face, but it doesn't reach his eyes. My knees buckle and I sag against the wall. Whatever Roman is playing at, he's doing a shit job. Although maybe Anders won't notice. Sure, he hasn't confessed his undying love for me, but I know I'm more than a quick fuck to him.

"I can't deny you that," Anders murmurs, his finger tapping against the table. "You know your mother was the perfect mafia wife. Did exactly as I said—did her duty. Too bad she was only able to provide me with one."

Roman narrows his eyes, then plasters on a blank expression. "One son, you mean."

Anders's laughter has all my muscles tensing. I'm not entirely sure I want to hear what he has to say. I'm only able to make out his profile, but the sharp smile he sends Roman is all edges and hate.

"Of course. Except your sister was not her daughter."

Roman's jaw twitches, the only sign of how affected he is. He nods, waiting for Anders to continue. Roman and Aelia might not look a thing alike, but neither do Anders and Aelia. Everyone just assumed she took after her mother, who supposedly died in childbirth with her.

"Who is her mother, then?"

"So many questions. One would think you're not truly committed to being welcomed back into the fold, Roman."

"If she's not really my sister, then I suppose I don't have any allegiance to her." He says it so nonchalantly, *I* almost believe him.

Anders chuckles, crossing his ankle over his knee and tapping the table once more. He holds up his finger, wrinkles his nose, and then wipes off the blackness on his pants. I can't imagine what he'd be nervous about, but he's not hiding it very well. There's a tremor in his voice as well. Usually, I'd use that to my advantage, but with Roman still tied up, it might just give Anders an itchy trigger finger.

"How unfortunate for you, then. She is my blood. And Byrns blood, though only through marriage."

Roman's entire head twitches, brows pulling low over his eyes. "What the hell does that mean?"

"I'm sure you don't remember much of the fallout we had with the other families. You were quite young. The Kings and the Byrns, bastards the lot of them, decided they deserved more territory than us. Byrns in particular stole something from us, so I took something from him."

"I still don't understand."

An evil smile spreads across Anders's face and he leans forward. "They thought we were less than them, so I fucked his wife. Repeatedly."

He spreads his hands wide as he sits back. "Your sister was the result. Of course, everything fell apart when that bitch went and told Byrns. Shit went south quickly after that."

"That's why we left? Because you fucked his wife?"

"Yes, among other things, I suppose. And now they're gone, with their offspring about to be defeated by the Guild. The question is, are you going to join me or continue turning over a new leaf?" he sneers.

"Synd is ripe for the picking. I'd rather not be relegated to taking orders from someone else."

Anders nods, contemplating Roman's words. I doubt I'm going to hear anything useful, not that I know what I'm supposed to be listening for. I creep back down the hallway, searching the spaces for a distraction to lure Anders out. Hopefully Roman doesn't interfere while I beat Anders to death.

I find a metal pipe, probably from the water system. It's only two feet long and a couple inches wide, but it'll do. I'm glad I picked these pants, as they have extra pockets. Pulling a firecracker from one of them, I grab the lighter next. Willow slipped them to me after she confiscated them from an initiate at the Depot. That's how the fire started, though I never told Roman. I didn't want a sixteen-year-old to be floating down the river for a prank. I'm glad I kept them, though.

I slip out the window again, then light the fuse and duck around the corner, gripping the pipe. What feels like a whole goddamn minute passes and I'm about to check on it when a series of pops shoot through the night. I never understood why people said firecrackers sounded like gunfire, but now I get it. With the racket echoing off the surrounding buildings, I wonder if others will come to investigate.

As silence descends, a shuffle of a shoe rings out, and I hold my breath. Launching around the corner, I swing the pipe as hard and as silently as I can.

I pull up short, trying to stop when I spot Roman's scowling face, but I'm already committed. His hand shoots out, grabbing the metal and wrenching it from my grasp. Panting, I gape at him as Anders appears behind him.

"Well, well, well. What do we have here?" Anders sneers, and I swallow down the bile creeping up my throat.

Roman tosses the pipe to the side and it rolls away, too far for me to reach without one of them catching me first. I tilt my chin up, glaring at Anders. I'll deal with Roman's bullshit later.

"Shoot her, son."

Roman pulls out his gun and black spots swim in my vision. My heart twists and it hits me. I fucked up. And now the man I'm in love with is going to kill me. I am totally fucked.

Fifty-One

Roman

I see the exact second Ember's faith in me dies. It bleeds away along with the color in her face. It winks out of her green eyes, leaving an emptiness behind.

I lock away the pain, convincing myself it's for the greater good. Saving Aelia is the most important thing, even if that means losing Ember. Eventually, she'll understand why I did it, though I might not be around to see the results.

"Move," I mutter, the barrel of my gun twitching to the right.

She shakes her head as her hands curl into fists at her sides. Lifting the gun, I point it at her chest.

"Do it," she hisses.

"Roman, now would be the time. We have other things to attend to."

My father's phone buzzes, and I glance over my shoulder. He's busy texting, probably the Guild.

Ember's fingers grab my wrist. I whip back around as she twists my arm. The gun clatters across the concrete. Letting out a growl, I shove her away and she ducks.

I dive for my weapon, expecting her to grapple for it, though she probably has her own. Instead, she rolls toward the pipe.

Seizing it, she dashes toward Anders, swinging it at his knee. He barely has enough time to yell before the metal connects with his bones and he crumples to the ground. Lifting the gun in the air, I fire off a single shot. She freezes, pipe hanging over her head. She drops it to her side, panting as she stares at Anders.

"Don't do this, Roman. He won't get you what you need."

"And you will?" I sneer, though there's little heat behind my words.

"Maybe not, but he'll betray you long before you find what you're looking for."

Her eyes are still fixed on my father as he clutches his injured leg. He struggles to pull his gun from his back, then points it at her. She kicks it away, snarling at him.

"You're a pathetic excuse for a father. Fuck you, Anders Drake. I hope you rot in hell for what you've done."

Tears glisten in her eyes, and I close mine. I can't let her emotions sway me. I'll never be able to kill her, but Anders will lead me to the Guild. I'll be able to get inside much easier than the others. Then I can save Aelia, like I should have done years ago. I can't let Ember fuck that up.

"Go, Ember," I snap, and her eyes dart to mine.

"No. He deserves to die."

Shaking my head, I prowl toward her when another gunshot rings out, and I jolt. I scan her for blood, but she's whipping her head around. I glance down and find blood seeping into my pants.

The pain hits me, spreading from the wound and radiating up my body. Staggering to the side, I fall into the wall. My gun slips from my numb fingers.

Ember screams, crashing the pipe onto Anders's arm, his barrel still pointed at me. He laughs, then groans as he cradles his useless limb to his chest. Ember throws the metal, then drops to her knees next to me. Her hands rove over my body, probably looking for more injuries. I shove her away, snarling as she lands on her ass, shock spreading across her face.

Anders struggles to stand. His knee gives out once, but he manages, leaning against the brick building. Of course he fucking shot me. Baring his teeth at me, he snarls.

"I knew you were fucking useless, just like your bitch of a sister. At least she paid her dues. You're nothing more than a disgrace to the Drake name."

His words roll over me, none finding their mark. At one time, I would have done anything for his approval. His criticisms would have cut me, shaped me, molded me into his image. I peer at Ember, still frozen where I pushed her. I may no longer care what he thinks of me, but I can't let her kill him.

"I'm sorry, Father," I whisper, and something in Ember's eyes breaks.

Anders scoffs, limping toward his fallen weapon. He'll kill her if she doesn't run. Yet she doesn't. She's too busy pleading with me without words.

Go, I mouth.

Shaking her head, she pushes to her feet, grabbing the pipe as she does. She moves in front of me, standing guard as if she can protect me from his manipulations.

"You've inspired a deep bond in her, Roman. Too bad she was just a good fuck, hmm?"

Another gunshot rings out, followed by my father's cry. I launch to my feet, leg screaming in pain, and I shove Ember behind me. She snorts, dancing next to me instead. Anders lets out a guttural cry, clutching his uninjured leg. At least, I assume it's uninjured since there's no blood.

"What the fuck?" Ember breathes, staring at Anders still writhing back and forth.

"Fuck, his voice is annoying. Every time he opens his mouth, I want to put a bullet in *my* head."

My mouth drops open at the man striding from the darkness. He runs his fingers through his sandy blond hair, grinning. Ember hefts her pipe up, eyes darting between the three of us. I reach over and force it down.

"You're dead," I say. It's honestly the only thing I can think.

Anders lets out a string of curses, each more imaginative than the last, and the man sneers at him.

"Go milk a fucking duck, asshole. You'd already be dead if I didn't think Drake deserved to beat you to death himself."

"But you're fucking dead." I repeat.

Alex's head pops up, shock spreading across his face. He pats himself down, then pinches his arm and yelps.

"Pretty sure I'm alive. Unless I'm a ghost, which would really fucking suck." He grins, then kicks Anders in the side when the man groans. "We're trying to have a fucking conversation."

"Wait, this is Alex?" Ember asks, tilting her head.

"Well, aren't you a delightfully vicious thing?" Alex tilts his head and bites his lip suggestively.

"Stop hitting on my woman, Alex," I growl.

Alex holds his hands up, sliding away from Anders as he smirks. "You know my heart's already spoken for. Speaking of which, I need to get back to Rima now that this asshole is dealt with. You *are* going to actually deal with him, right?"

He glares at me, and my eyes skip to my father. Swallowing hard, I shake my head and Ember swears under her breath.

"Imma shoot him in the head then," Alex says, lifting his gun.

"No," I cry, stumbling toward him.

The smile spreading across my father's face makes my stomach roll. Ember's hand falls on my arm, and I shrug her off.

I don't deserve her sympathy. I don't deserve her love, if she'd even be able to love someone like me. After tonight, I'm sure she'll want me dead, too. The blame will sit squarely with me. I deserve her hate.

"Put the gun down, Alex. Shouldn't you be finding Samantha? Why are you even here?" I snarl, and a shadow creeps into his eyes, muting the green.

"All in good time, Drake. Everything happens in due course," he murmurs.

He steps away from Anders, his gun hanging at his side. I'm sure he thinks I'm going to change my mind, but the pull between keeping him alive and just being done with it is too much. It stretches inside me, making it hard to breathe.

Anders chuckles and it dissolves into a coughing fit. I have no idea how he's still conscious with all the injuries peppering his body.

"These people won't get you anywhere, Roman. Be the man I taught you to be and kill them, or I will. Though perhaps we can sell the girl like I did your sister. She can be your way in."

A gun appears in his hand, though why he hasn't used it before, I can't figure out. When he points it at Ember, my vision goes red. My mind blanks, no longer in control of my body.

When I come back to reality, my fist connects with my father's face. It's not the first time I've hit him, apparently. Ember screams, creating a symphony of sound to the bloody mess I'm making of him.

Alex's hand lands on my shoulder, and my arm swings around as he dances out of the way. I snarl at him, then hit my father again.

"Drake, he's dead."

Blood coats my hands, splattering up my arms. I stumble back, staring at the crimson dripping from my knuckles. I have no idea how long I was beating him, how many times I hit him. Based on the mutilated mess his face is, it must have been a while.

I drop to my knees, despair crashing over me. Not for him—never for him. He deserved every last wound. But he was my only path to Aelia. It's like I've lost her all over again.

"Where's my sister?" I whisper as Alex crouches next to me.

"Last I knew, she was still inside. Dante's got eye on her. He's protecting her. He won't let anything happen to your sister," he murmurs.

"How do you know?"

Alex snorts, and I lift my gaze to his face. "Because he's in love with her. Head over fucking heels. She's stronger than you think, Drake."

I push to my feet, dropping my hands to my sides, and glance around. Ember is nowhere to be found, and I swallow hard. I don't blame her for running. I wouldn't be surprised if she ran all the way to Rima. Straight into the arms of the Guild, thinking she'll be able to slip in undetected.

"I have to go," I mutter, wiping my hands on my pants. It's already begun to dry, flaking off as I attempt to rid myself of the evidence of my father's death.

"Where the hell are you going? I just told you not to go to Rima. We need you here. I can't stay, for obvious reasons. It has to be you, Drake."

"Fuck you, King. This isn't my city. I don't give a flying fuck about Synd. I'm going after Ember."

He laughs, and I snarl at him. He doubles over, hands on his knees as his giggles peal through the air. I curl my hands into fists, resisting the urge to punch him. He points behind me toward the building, then wipes tears away from his eyes.

I spin around, huffing out a sigh of relief. Ember's eyes widen and she frowns, letting out a soft "Oh" as I gather her in my arms.

"Don't fucking do that," I whisper into her hair.

Her arms slide around my waist, mumbling, "I have no idea what you're talking about, but I got your phone."

Closing my eyes, I breathe her in. Under the scent of blood and sweat floats one that's completely her. It eases my muscles, and the adrenaline from the last hour seeps away. Pain radiates from my bruised knuckles and the wound in my leg, and I lean on her for support.

"Let's get you to Ink. Hopefully, he can fix you up."

Alex winces as he tucks his phone in his pocket. "I called in a cleanup. Let's not tell Nicki about this though, hmm? She's still pissed at me for trying to break into the Egg."

Glancing over my shoulder, I cling to Ember. "Why would you break into the Egg?"

"Reasons. Just tell her I skipped town again. But I am going to need one of my cars to get back. Guild isn't going to take down itself." Alex vanishes as quickly as he came. I wonder if he'll bother telling us when he skips town. Probably not.

"Is he always like that?" Ember whispers, and I chuckle. There's no mirth in the sound.

"Let's go dig a bullet out of my leg. Then we need to talk."

She tenses in my arms, but nods. I can't wait for the day shit finally settles and we can just live.

Fifty-Two

Ember

"I sent Mia home," I murmur, closing the door to an office Roman took over.

I hover by the exit, unsure where to go from here. I thought Roman would get stitched up and we'd finally hash shit out, but after almost two weeks, I'm doubting it's going to happen. Granted, he was recovering for at least a week of that. I tried to take care of him, though I'm pretty shit at pampering. I gave up when he yelled at me, giving him the space he clearly wanted.

Now I feel like I'm walking on eggshells in a house that's not mine. I shouldn't even be here, but Willow told me she needed me to stay for a little while. I thought it was to help her, but I'm starting to wonder if it was because she was hoping Roman would come around.

"Hawk found Kyler. He was holed up in some abandoned building in the Barrens. Dehydrated and scared out of his fucking mind, but they think he'll be fine."

"I know," he says, eyes fixed on the papers strewn across the desk.

I sigh, crossing my arms and leaning against the door. Waiting for him to speak these days is like waiting for rain in a drought—annoying and fruitless. Alex left the night Roman killed Anders. Kept saying he'd accomplished what he needed and now he was going to find his woman. When I asked him how he was going to accomplish that, he unlocked a door I never noticed, revealing an entire room full of weapons. He loaded up, making several trips to his car, and then took off into the night. I doubt I'll be seeing him again. I'll be long gone when they get home, if they make it back at all.

"Nicki checked on the police station. Anders's body is gone. Said they floated him?" I didn't understand what she meant, but it wasn't hard to figure it out.

"She texted me."

I tap my fingers against my arm, sucking my cheeks between my teeth. Biting down, I use the pain to stop from screaming at him to look at me. It won't do any good. He's still locked in some battle with himself. Continuing like we are, though, isn't sustainable.

"You blame me." To my credit, my voice doesn't waver.

He sighs, nostrils flaring as he slams his hand on his desk. "What?"

I lock down my emotions, tucking the heartache ripping through me deep within my soul. If I pretend it's not happening, it won't affect me. The mask I've perfected over the years slams down over my features and a calmness sweeps over me.

"Nothing. Anything else?"

His phone buzzes and he snatches it up. He waves his hand absentmindedly while he reads the message, dismissing me. I slip from the room, resisting the urge to slam the door behind me.

I wander the halls aimlessly. Calling up Willow to bitch about Roman would be cathartic, but I'm not going to cause a rift between the only leaders left in Synd. I could leave, go off to some other city, or back to Westmont, or say fuck it and go to Rima anyway.

Admitting to myself I'm waiting for Roman to tell me whether to stay or go is harder than I expected. I'm done waiting. He blames me for killing Anders, for being right about Aelia, for his lack of control. Hell, he probably thinks it's my fault it hasn't rained.

When Roman was ready to chase after me that night, I thought we would figure shit out together. Instead, the further we got from the Barrens, the more he shut down. Why should I stop myself from saving my best friend just because he says so? He doesn't control me. Loping down the stairs to the foyer, I drop onto the last step, staring at the front door.

I jolt when a gong goes off, echoing around the cavernous room. I didn't even realize they had a bell, much less one that sounds like it should be in a fucking cathedral. Pulling open the door, I fight a smile when Willow whips around, blonde hair flowing behind her.

"Hey, want to go for a ride?" Her eyes are bright, but they're lined with concern.

Hawk nods as he pushes past me, and I track him as he stalks up the stairs. As far as I know, they haven't been meeting, but then again, Roman hasn't been coming to bed at night either. They're probably having secret rendezvous at midnight, complete with code words.

"Actually, do you want to help me with something?" I ask, finally making up my mind.

"Uh, sure."

She follows me inside, pivoting when I don't go up the staircase. I've been going a different way each time, telling myself it's for a change of scenery, but really, it's to avoid Roman. Not that it's done any good. Even when we do encounter each other in the halls, he barely notices my presence.

We reach the room I took over a few nights ago. It's down the hall from the one Roman and I had been sharing. Both too close, yet too far. Pushing open the door, I cringe at the mess. Sure, the bed is untouched and pristine, but the rest of the area is a disaster.

"You need me to help you clean your room?" she asks skeptically, and I sigh.

"Actually, I was hoping you could go get some things from the other room while I pick up in here."

I should just tell her I'm packing. Most of the clothes I'm leaving since Roman bought them for me. Dresses and gowns, high heels and flats, and even the makeup—it's all staying. I don't care what he does with it. I'll wire him the cost of everything I take and buy whatever else I need when I get wherever I end up.

"There a reason you can't go yourself?" Willow gathers the laptop I left on the chair, setting it on the bed before sitting.

"I was about to, but then you came, so I figured we could hang out while I deal with all this."

I gather all the towels I've left hanging over various pieces of furniture and toss them in the bathroom. I close the door, unwilling to tackle that nightmare. These people must have housekeepers, but I've never seen them. They're certainly not coming in here. That may be because they have no idea this room is now occupied.

"What's going on, Ember?"

"What do you mean?" I throw clothes on the bed, sorting them into two piles.

"You're short on the phone, strictly business. When I asked you about Roman, you sounded like you were about to burst into tears. Now you want me to, what? Sneak into his bedroom, one I assume you were sharing until recently, and find more of your shit?" She huffs, shaking her head. "Is he kicking you out?"

My head whips up and my stomach turns. "No, he's not. At least he hasn't said he is." I go on to mumble under my breath, "Not that he's said anything to me."

"What was that?"

I sigh, dropping a pair of dirty pants onto the bed. "Nothing. But it's not like I was going to stay here forever, Willow. I know you probably had some grand plan of us becoming temporary best friends until your real ones came back, but I'm not really cut out for that kind of lifestyle."

I spin around, grabbing more clothes. How the hell I ended up with so many is ridiculous. I don't need all this stuff. It's harder to travel that way.

Stalking into the closet, I hide around the corner, closing my eyes. It's not Willow's fault Roman is being a dick. Pushing her away is one thing but hurting her...fuck I'm a bitch. This is why I never had any friends beyond Aelia. I don't deserve them.

"Ember?" Willow's soft voice comes a second before she knocks on the door frame.

"Yeah?" I ask, wiping away tears as I struggle to keep my voice even. I fucking hate crying. Another thing to blame Roman for.

"We're going to pretend you didn't just say all that shit to me. And you're going to go get in the shower."

Her fingers wrap around my arm, tugging me toward the bathroom. I go willingly, mostly because I can't remember the last time I bathed. Maybe that's why Roman has been avoiding me. Snorting, I run my hand over my hair. Definitely greasy. Willow leaves me next to the counter, and I hop up.

She starts the shower, wiping her hand on her pants as she goes digging for clean towels. I doubt she'll find any.

"When was the last time you showered?" She eyes the pile on the floor.

I shrug, watching the steam fog the glass. "Couple days. Maybe more. I was taking a whore's bath most of the time."

She stutters, shaking her head. "A what?"

"A whore's bath. You know—pits, tits, and bits?" I laugh as her mouth drops open. "It's alright. I thought it was called a horse bath until I was in high school, and Aelia corrected me. Roman teased me for weeks."

I sober, biting the inside of my cheek, then hop down. The pity on Willow's face is too much. Everything in this damn house is too much. The sooner I get out, the sooner I can find myself again. I'm not a morose little mouse, waiting for the attention of some man. No matter how much I love him.

That note he left wasn't some grand declaration of his love for me. I shouldn't have stayed as long as I have, waiting for him to open up. The woman I was just a few months ago would have been gone the minute he started ghosting me. Now I'm just pissed at myself for how soft I've become.

I shed my clothes as Willow slips from the room. I don't want to step into the water. Then I'll have to go through the motions of washing my hair, and it just feels like a task I can't complete. I hang up a towel I'm pretty sure is mostly clean inside the shower. Of course they have one that's large enough space to have hooks on the inside of the glass without the fabric getting wet.

"Get in the shower, Ember. You'll feel better when you do," Willow calls from behind the door. I wonder if she's sitting there with her ear pressed to the wood, waiting for me to get in.

Stepping inside, the hot water pelts my skin. At least under the spray, I can't tell that I'm crying. It's the only silver lining. Doing a quick rinse isn't something I can manage, so I start the arduous task of washing my hair. Sometimes I envision shaving it all off, but then I'd find out I have a lopsided head and regret it.

I don't know how long I stand under the water when I'm done, but a knock at the door jolts me back to reality.

"I'll be right out," I call.

The door opens, and I swipe my hand across the glass. Roman meets my gaze through the droplets. He closes the door softly, leaning against it as he crosses his arms.

"Something you need?" I turn my back to him and shut off the water.

I grab a towel, dry off, then wrap it around my body. With my hair hanging in strings around my face I probably look like a drowned rat, but I don't fucking care. I'm not trying to impress him. Not anymore.

"Hawk and Willow left. You want to explain why you tried to get her to steal shit from me?" It's the longest sentence he's strung together in the last two weeks. Of course, it's to accuse me of shit.

"Clearly, I wasn't. Anything else?" I step from the shower.

"You can't go to Rima."

"Never said I was."

Pawing through the pile I left on the floor, I find a towel for my hair and wrap it around my head. I cringe when I spot my clothes scattered across the bathroom.

Crossing my arms and raising an eyebrow, I face him. "Are you going to move? Or is this a hostage situation?"

He steps away, opening the door and sweeping out his hand. I march through as if I'm not practically naked. Even with all he's put me through, my blood still heats when his fingers brush my arm as I pass. A switch for turning off my pussy would be fabulous right about now.

I stomp straight into the closet, slamming the door behind me. It pops open a second later as he follows me. Thankfully, I spent a lot of time in a girl's locker room, afraid of other girls seeing my hoohah. I'm able to get dressed while covering all the important bits.

He watches me, expressionless. The longer he does, the more pissed off I get. By the time I'm done, I'm slamming drawers closed with trembling hands.

"You can't stay here," he murmurs.

I freeze, all the emotions I've been shoving away, refusing to feel, crash into me, and my vision darkens. Blinking away the spots, I try to take steady breaths so I don't pass out. I nod once. Then again.

"You don't belong here," he says as if that explains anything.

I don't respond. I wouldn't, even if I knew what to say. I merely nod again, my head threatening to topple off my neck.

"Say something," he breathes.

"Not much to say. I'll be out by tonight."

"Now, Ember. I'm not waiting around for you to change your mind," he growls.

I spin toward him, marching forward and slamming my palms against his chest. He stumbles back a step, shock on his face. Good. He deserves to feel like the world is tilting beneath him. He deserves to feel an ounce of the pain he's putting me through.

"Go to fucking hell. As if I'd even have the option to change my mind. You'll just continue to ignore me and control every decision, anyway. You can't just throw my ass out as if you didn't—" I suck in a deep breath, stepping back.

"As if I didn't what, Ember?" he snarls, crowding into my space.

Grabbing my wrists, he pushes until my back hits the wall. I gasp when he pushes his hips into me, his cock hard against my stomach.

"I need time to pack," I snap.

"You're moving two fucking doors down. It shouldn't be that difficult."

I flinch, then shake my head. He grinds his hips into me. My pussy begs me to give in, to take whatever he's offering. My mind is smarter, though.

"Let me get this straight. You're demanding that I go back to your room," I say, and he nods. "The room you haven't been sleeping in. For what? A week? Because I'm a good fuck?"

He has the good sense to wince, but then he releases my wrists and steps back. My heart cracks, and I close my eyes, a single tear slipping free. Fucking bastard for breaking my heart.

I never should have come to Synd.

Fifty-Three

Roman

My hand shakes when I reach for Ember. Brushing my thumb across her cheek, I catch the tear she couldn't hide. She shudders, then clenches her jaw. I thought I could deal with everything, and she'd wait. Telling her how I feel could wait.

I'm such a fucking asshole.

Before her, I never would have cared. I would have basked in the knowledge that no one would get close to me. As much as I hate it, I took more from my father's lessons than I should have. He never loved anyone, least of all me. We were all pawns to him. And I turned around and did the same thing to Ember.

I drop to my knees, wrapping my arms around her thighs and pressing my cheek to her stomach. She tenses, but I hold her tighter. She doesn't touch me, yet she doesn't push me away.

"I didn't mean it," I murmur.

"I know," she whispers.

"No, Ember. I meant every fucking word I wrote. My father..."

"Is dead. Anders is dead. And yet you're treating me like I stole away your one chance to save Aelia."

"You're more than a good fuck, Em."

She pushes me back, and I let her go reluctantly. I hang my head, bracing my hands on my thighs. I'll kneel at her feet as long as it takes. She sinks to the floor, cupping my face in her hands. I don't know what she finds as she studies my face, but she sighs.

"Say it," she demands.

"I'm sorry."

She shakes her head, tugging my forehead to rest against hers. "Say what's between us."

Her eyes fall closed, but I can't pull my gaze away from her.

"I love you."

My chest seizes and I hold my breath. Just saying the words out loud sends a thrill through me. It was hard enough to stop myself from putting it in the note. Even then I worried I said too much. Saying it now might not be enough.

She inhales a shuddering breath, then presses her lips to mine. It's not the frenzied kissing we usually have. This is a melding of our souls, an understanding flowing between us through a connection few find and even fewer cherish.

"Say it again," she gasps against my lips.

"I love you," I breathe, covering her mouth again.

I untangle the towel from her head, and it drops to the floor. Gripping the strands, I angle her head to deepen the kiss and she moans. Her tongue darts out, sweeping against mine, and my cock twitches. It takes everything in me to pull away. Her lips chase mine, and I cup her face, stopping her.

"Ember, look at me," I command, and her eyes flutter open. "I'm sorry. I'll spend the rest of my life making it up to you."

"You realize you're usually an asshole, right? I'm used to it."

"Except this time, I made you cry. I hurt you and that shouldn't have happened."

I brush my lips across hers, trying to convey everything I want to say but don't have the words for. I'd do it again, if only to soak her in a little bit longer. How wrong I was thinking this woman would make me weak and vulnerable. I realize how strong she makes me when she stands by my side. Ember gives me something to live for.

"How are you going to make it up to me?" she whispers.

"Whatever you want, it's yours. All I have, all I am, is yours."

Her fingers circle my wrists, and she tugs my hands away from her face. Sitting back, she taps her finger against her lips, contemplating me.

"You're a bastard for everything. You know that, right?"

I nod, swallowing hard. "Pushing you away was an asshole move. I won't do again."

"One chance, Drake. That's all you're getting." Ember narrows her eyes at me. "What are you grinning at?"

"Start moving your stuff back"—she gives me a look—"if you want. Then meet me in my office."

I scramble up, then lean down and kiss her hard before striding out of the closet. My plan might not be perfect, but it's a place to start. Hopefully, Ember feels the same.

"Was the blindfold entirely necessary?" Ember asks, exasperation weaving through her words.

"No, but knowing you can't see makes me hard," I murmur in her ear as I guide her through the trees.

Moonlight filters through the leaves, illuminating the path. Crickets sing through the night, creating a backdrop of music I've seldom experienced. Her head whips to the side, mouth parting when an owl hoots in the distance. I press a kiss to her head, dropping my hand to her lower back and urging her on.

"Where are we going?"

"You'll see. Step here."

She lifts her foot comically high, and I chuckle. I swing her into my arms, and she yelps, clinging to me. Hawk's directions weren't entirely clear, filled with landmarks of rocks that looked like potatoes. Thankfully, I made a few trips before tonight. I step off the path, cradling Ember close. She tucks her head to my chest, then bites me.

"Fuck, Em. Don't do that shit without a warning. I almost dropped you."

She snorts, then sinks her teeth into my chest again. I shudder, tripping on a tree root, and she yelps.

"Don't you dare fucking drop me," she snarls, reaching up to rip the blindfold from her eyes.

I stop, covering her mouth with mine, and she gasps. Sweeping my tongue along hers, I devour her. With my hands busy, it's the only way I can get her to leave the fabric where it is. She'll ruin the surprise and I can't have that. Pulling back, I walk toward the clearing.

I lower her to her feet, keeping hold of her waist to steady her. She presses her back into my chest, and I kiss her neck. Removing the blindfold, I tuck it into my pocket. It'll come in handy later, I'm sure.

"Is that a tree house?" she breathes, stepping from my grasp.

"Hawk said Helms and Mac used to come out here when they were kids. Helms is fixing it up for her as a surprise. So, don't say anything to Willow. Apparently, she's a blabbermouth when it comes to Mac."

As she paces around the clearing, gazing up at the tree house, the moonlight bathes her face. Wonder dances in her eyes, and I sigh in relief.

"Can we go up?" she asks, turning wide eyes to me.

"That's the plan."

My hands tingle and my chest tightens as she climbs the wooden ladder, and I follow. She ducks through the opening before I reach the top. She gasps and I rush up the last few rungs.

"You brought pie," she cries as I crawl into the space.

It's a larger space than I expected when I dropped everything off. Some of the walls still have holes in them, but Hawk said Helms wasn't done with it yet. Ember's eyes are fixed on the small table tucked in the corner with a collection of pie and desserts. Marie demanded I help her grandson find a job for payment, but it's worth Ember's reaction.

"Ember, the pie can wait. Come here."

She glares at me over her shoulder. "Did you just say the pie can wait?"

I laugh, pulling her down on the blanket I laid in the middle of the floor. She keeps glancing at the desserts longingly. When I try to get her on her back, though, she jerks from my hold.

"Are you making me wait to eat pie for sex?" Horror splashes across her face.

I grin, shaking my head. "I'll fuck you while you eat pie if you just lay the fuck down."

She huffs, lowering onto her back with her eyes closed. I settle next to her, lacing her fingers with mine.

"Open your eyes, love."

"Holy shit."

She stares at the large dome skylight Helms had installed before they left for Rima. A million stars scatter across the dark sky, illuminating the world in a way I've never seen before.

"What do you think?" I whisper.

"You remembered?"

"Is that a question? Of course I remember. Now, would you like me to fuck you while you eat pie, or would you like to stargaze some more? Or perhaps you'd like me to fuck you under the stars?"

Fifty-Four

Ember

I don't know this man sitting crisscross on the blanket. He looks like Roman, his mannerisms are the same, but this smiling man can't be him. My Roman is snarky and an asshole. I don't know if I can handle this new version of him. If I snap at him, it'll feel like I'm kicking a puppy.

He shoves another forkful of pie in his mouth, glancing up at the stars. I follow his gaze and shiver at the sight above us. I didn't think he'd remember the random conversation we had when I was fifteen, yet here we are. The lights from the city always drowned out the stars in Westmont. I begged my parents when I was little to take me to the country to see them, but they were too busy pretending they didn't have a child.

"Open," he grunts.

I drop my jaw, and he squirts whipped cream into my mouth. I gag, laughing as it overflows and he pulls me in, licking it from my lips. I swallow it down, grinning at him. Even if he's not acting like he usually does, I can't deny the butterflies in my stomach.

"What happened with Brewer?" I take another bite and savor the sweetness exploding across my tongue.

"Our illustrious fire chief will no longer be a problem."

"So, you floated him?" I'm still not entirely on board with the slang they use in the Barrens, but I'm learning.

"No. You saw the extent of it. He's toeing the line now, though."

I shiver, remembering the altercation between them. Roman was composed until Brewer made the mistake of insulting me. Apparently, Roman doesn't take kindly to someone calling me a whore. I imagine it was the implied insult, since he's called me his good little whore more than once now.

Watching Roman strategically beat the man, bruising his knuckles again in the process, had me jumping him as soon as Brewer dragged his bloody body away. Fucking him in a dirty alley wasn't on the agenda, but I couldn't wait.

Roman leans closer, murmuring in my ear. "Are you imagining my cock deep inside that pretty little pussy as his blood dripped from my knuckles?"

I shudder, eyes falling closed, and I squeeze my legs together. He grips my knees, forcing them apart. His thumb rubs my clit through the thin fabric, and I groan. When he pulls away, a whimper I've never heard myself make comes out of me. Grabbing my plate of half-eaten pie, he sets it off the blanket.

"Don't worry, Em. You can finish it after I've had my dessert."

He guides me onto my back, hooking his fingers into my waistband, and I lift my hips. As he peels the fabric from me, I bite my lip, waiting for the moment he realizes I'm not wearing any underwear.

"Such a dirty little whore, aren't you," he hums, then bites my inner thigh.

Pain mixes with pleasure, and my hips lift of their own accord. His arm snakes across my stomach, holding me still. I squirm underneath him as his breath ghosts across my pussy. After what feels like a lifetime, his tongue darts out, flicking at my clit, and I moan.

Slowly, he works me into a frenzied mess, shuddering and groaning as I grip his hair. Every time I get close to coming, he retreats. No matter how much I tug his face closer, or squeeze his head between my thighs, he resists.

"Open your eyes, love. Let the stars see you fall apart under my mouth."

He swirls around my clit, faster than before. He thrusts two fingers into my pussy, and I clamp down hard. Within seconds I'm sailing over the edge, shuddering out my pleasure with the stars standing witness. Panting, I peer down at him, and we lock eyes. I feel his grin against my skin, and something within me slots into place.

I was never one for grand gestures. They always felt false, like the last gasp of a relationship long since dead. This doesn't feel the same. Every discovery, every kiss, every gesture feels like a promise, one forged in pain and pleasure.

Even when he defended me, he was showing me my worth, proclaiming his love with every bruise. It's fucked up, but it's the only way he knows how. At least, that's what I thought until tonight. Maybe he can do both. Maybe I can have it all.

He licks me one last time, pulling his fingers from me gently, then crawls up and folds his arms over my stomach, resting his chin on his laced fingers. My shirt gathers under my breasts, tickling the undersides, and I shiver.

"Do you need more pie?"

I shake my head, hooking my ankles across his back. "I'd rather you get naked."

"You'll have to untangle your limbs from me, then."

I drop my feet, knees falling open, and he pushes off me. I groan, wrapping my arms around my stomach and rolling to the side. Maybe I shouldn't finish that third piece of pie. It's just so delicious. I sit up and pull my shirt over my head, then grab the whipped cream as he undresses. When he finishes, I hold up the canister and smirk.

"You're not putting that on my dick," he snarls, ripping it from my hands and tossing it out the open window.

"Hey, I was going to eat that!"

"Not from any part of my body you're not. That shit is sticky."

He grabs my waist, pulling me into him, and I rake my nails down his chest. He buries his head in my neck, nibbling and sucking his way to my mouth, sending a flood of heat between my legs.

"Do you want me to feed you pie while you ride my cock?" he whispers, and I grin.

"Great in theory. Terrible in execution. Especially if you don't want to get sticky."

He tips his head back, chest rumbling with laughter. I slide my hands around his neck, and he peers at me. I kiss him and pour all my feelings into it. He retreats, resting his forehead against mine.

"Stay," he growls, and I wrinkle my nose. He shuffles around under the table, producing a pillow.

"I'm not a fucking pillow princess."

He grins, dropping it on top of the blanket. "Maybe not, but I'd rather your knees not hurt later."

He pushes me down, his cock bobbing in front of my face, and I lick the tip. He jerks back, gripping himself at the base and then sliding his fist up. Stepping toward me again, he slips the tip between my lips, and I suck him deeper into my mouth. I hum, and his hands tangle with my hair, holding my head still.

Slowly, he thrusts in again and again. I moan, scraping my teeth along the sensitive skin. He shudders, pulling completely out as he pants. I grip his cock, squeezing, and he grips my hair, tilting my head back.

"Behave."

He grabs my wrist, yanking my hand away, and he tugs me onto my feet. His fingers dig into my ass, hauling me up and my legs circle his waist. I rub against him as best I can, but it's not enough. I need him inside me.

"Roman," I gasp, biting his shoulder as he guides us down, repositioning the pillow.

As he kneels between my legs, I glance at the stars shining overhead.

"Lift your hips, love."

Instantly, I obey, and he slips another pillow under my lower back. Gripping his cock, he rubs it along my pussy, and I jolt every time he hits my clit. I swear he's doing it on purpose, especially with the smug look on his face. Just when I'm about to beg, he slips inside. I groan, hooking my heels behind his thighs and attempt to pull him deeper. Roman's hands dig into my hips, holding me still.

He leans down, lapping at my nipple. Arching my back, I roll my hips, and finally he thrusts, fully seating himself in me. I gasp, grabbing his arms as heat spreads through my veins. He presses a kiss to one bud, then the other, and I shiver.

When he glances up at me, blue eyes burning with desire, my heart skips a beat. I didn't think that was possible. Breath hitching? Okay. Head spinning? Possibly. But legit skipping of heartbeats? No. That's something that only happens in books. Never in real life. Creative license to convey a deeper connection. Yet here I am, having full-on heart palpitations.

"I think I'm having a heart attack," I whisper.

He grinds his hips, somehow pushing even deeper, and my eyes roll to the back of my head.

"That's just you realizing how much you love me," he says, punctuating his words by pulling out and plunging into me again.

"Fuck, I do," I moan.

He freezes and my eyes flutter open. He wraps one hand behind my neck and the other around my waist. Tugging me up, he melds our bodies together.

"Your turn," he says, brushing my hair from my face.

"For what? Because I'm pretty sure I've already come twice. Maybe three times. I can't remember."

He smirks, then surges into me hard and fast.

"Say it," he grunts, never slowing.

"I love you," I gasp as I cling to him.

He shudders, hips stuttering. "Again."

"I love you."

His fingers tangle with my hair, yanking my head back, and his lips run up my throat. A low growl rumbles through his chest as I unravel. Pulsing around his cock, he follows me over the edge, groaning my name as he comes. He lays me down, covering every inch of skin he can reach with his mouth.

Gasping, I roll my hips, and he grunts. I never want this to end. I'd stay like this forever if we could—him buried in my pussy, wringing pleasure from our bodies with only the stars as witness. Nothing outside this bubble exists and I wouldn't have it any other way.

"I could fucking live in your pussy," he mumbles, nuzzling my neck.

"Such a charmer."

"Only for you, love. Only for you."

Fifty-Five

Roman

"Next item on the agenda," I say, staring at the piece of paper I'm holding.

"You realize we don't actually need a list of shit to talk about, right?" Ember says, cuddling closer to my side.

"Hush," I murmur, pressing a kiss to her temple.

She burrows further under the covers, huffing. Her fingers walk across my stomach, making my muscles jump. Latching onto her wrist, I move her palm to my chest. When she tries to tug her hand from under mine, I growl.

"Stop distracting me. I'll fuck you after. Such a needy little thing."

"We already talked about you tossing my ass out ten years ago. We've discussed how you had me tailed all these years, leaving me in *very* precarious situations. Then we got in that small tiff—"

"Where you fucking bit me," I grumble and she smirks.

"That's neither here nor there. We resolved the misunderstanding." She falls quiet, sucking in a deep breath. "And we came up with a plan for helping Aelia, even if neither one of us likes it."

I tip her chin up, kissing her softly. She sighs into my mouth, pulling back. The grief that once lined her green eyes is gone, replaced with uncertainty. We may have come up with a plan, but neither one of us thinks it'll do much good. Giving up trust to people she barely knows, and I only trust as far as I can throw them, isn't easy. It's the only way to not fuck up what they already have in motion.

She clears her throat. "How can there possibly be anything else?"

"Next is telling you what Aelia said when she called."

She bites her lip, and I pull it out with my thumb, brushing the pad against her cheek. Blowing out a breath, she nods.

"I just want to know if she mentioned me. No. I want to know everything. No. Ack, I don't know."

Rolling away from me, she slings an arm over her eyes. I give her a minute, but we can't afford much more than that. As much as I'd like to spend all day in bed with her, we have meetings to attend, deals to broker, and more decisions to make. I've already put it off for three days.

After the tree house, I took her back to the Kings', and fucked her until we both passed out. The next day I ignored every call and text, cussing out several guards who tried to interrupt us. I spent the time worshiping her, making promises I probably can't keep, and then writing my list.

"Is she safe?"

"She's owned by the Guild, so I'm sure you can answer that question yourself. She did say someone is protecting her."

"Dante. Which is who again?" She peeks from under her arm, pursing her lips.

"He's MacKenzie's older brother. A little too old for her in my opinion," I mutter.

She snorts, rolling back and draping herself over me, tucking her leg between mine. Her knee rubs against my cock, which is already halfway to fully hard. Gritting my teeth, I focus on my list again, but the words blur.

"How old is he?"

I shrug, then roll my eyes when she gives me a look. "My age."

"So it's the same age gap as us. Which is only like two years, tops. Which is not an age gap at all."

"Doesn't mean I have to like it. Can we stop talking about my sister while your hand is creeping toward my cock?" I ask, grabbing her wrist again.

"Duly noted. What else is on your list? I can't handle talking about her anymore unless you've changed your mind and we're going to buy a tank." She tries to peek at my paper, but I tuck it away.

"We're not buying a tank to bulldoze through Rima. Even if they couldn't stop us, we'd have to get out eventually and then they'd shoot us."

"We could just go in, tank blazing, and get all the innocents out. Then, boom! Blow up the building." A manic gleam sits in her eyes, and her hips jerk against my leg.

Rolling her onto her back, I rub my cock along her pussy. "Are you wet thinking about blowing shit up, Em?"

She shudders, wrapping her legs around my waist. I grind into her, and she reaches between us. I expect her to go for her clit, but when I lift up, she grabs my cock. When she squeezes, I sit back on my knees and my vision darkens.

"What about your list?" she asks, sliding her fist to the tip and down again.

"Fuck the list," I groan, tipping my head back.

She stops and I glance down, then at her face. "I'll keep going as long as you read your list."

I lunge to the side and snatch up the paper while she giggles. She starts stroking me again as I attempt to read my handwriting.

"Where to live," I grunt, shoving my hips forward.

She guides my cock to her entrance, slipping just the tip in, and I groan. The paper crumples in my fist as I let her take control.

"And where exactly do you think you'll end up?" she asks quietly, and I rock into her as her hand still squeezes the base.

"We. Us. Together," I gasp, gripping her hips and plunge into her until I hit her hand.

Her hand falls away, gliding to her clit, and I plunge into her again. She gasps, arching her back. I surge into her, the list forgotten. We can deal with it later, when we're fully clothed and her body isn't distracting me. I grunt, knowing that will never happen. She could be in a potato sack and still be breathtaking.

"Wait," she pants, nails scratching my stomach.

I freeze, closing my eyes and gritting my teeth. When I'm sure I won't explode, I peer down at her.

"What do you mean us? Are you asking me to move in with you?" She's so serious, I swallow down the chuckle crawling up my throat.

"We already live together, love."

"Temporarily," she says, then bites her lip.

"No." I pull out, plunging into her once more as I glare at her.

"No? You can't just say 'no,' asshole." She shudders as I do it again.

"Looks like I just did. Tell me you're going to defy me and see what happens," I growl.

Her mouth drops open, and I bury my cock into her, fast and hard. She belongs to me, and I belong to her. If I have to fuck that realization into her, then so be it.

I slide my hand to her clit, rubbing hard and fast. Her eyes fall closed as she gives herself over to the pleasure rolling over her in waves. Her pussy spasms around me and I grunt, fucking her through her orgasm. Two more thrusts and I'm emptying inside her, branding her from the inside out.

I cover her body with mine, and her arms wrap around my neck, holding me close.

"Mine," I murmur into her damp skin. "All fucking mine."

"Where to live," she says after several minutes, and I pull from her heat.

She whimpers and I shush her, lying next to her and slipping my fingers between her legs, stroking her pussy.

"Where do you want to live, Ember?"

Slowly, I build her body up again, dipping in and out of her pussy and circling her clit. When she doesn't answer, I cup her and nip at her shoulder.

"Not Westmont," she mutters, and I push two fingers inside her dripping pussy.

"Definitely not Westmont. What was your favorite place you've been?"

She clenches around me as I press my thumb into her clit, curling my fingers inside her. Her orgasm flows over her gently as she purrs under my touch.

"Favorite place, Em," I remind her as she blinks at me sleepily.

"Here. It's the closest thing to home I've ever had. But you don't want to be in Synd."

She cuddles closer when I pull my fingers from her heat, looping my arm over her waist. I pull the covers over our heads, creating our own little fort.

"If you want to stay in Synd, then we'll stay." I kiss her forehead.

"Are you sure? You're not going to get bored and give up on all this?" she asks, a teasing lilt to her tone.

"The stars will fall from the sky, the earth will shatter the very ground beneath us, the rivers will drown all of humanity before you'll see the day that I give up on you."

* * *

Thank you so much for reading Roman and Ember's story!
Ready for the next adventure?
Dive into the spin-off duology Ruins of Rima by pre-ordering Dante's story.
Out August 25, 2023.

If you'd like to hear about the other stories that have been living in my head, sign up for my newsletter (including extra scenes & a novella), visit my website, or follow me on social media visit:
emiliaabraham.com

Special Thanks:

K.B. Barrett Designs-Cover Artist and Formatter

Emily Michel-Editor

Krysten & Hillary-Beta Readers

Crosby Dunbar-PA

Other Works

Also by E. Abraham:

Shadows of Synd:
Under the Shadows: Book 1
Running From Shadows: Book 2
Becoming Shadows: Book 3
Shadows Within Us: Book 4

Ruins of Rima: Spin-off Series
Chasing Darkness (*August 25, 2023*)
Charmed by Darkness (Fall *2023*)

Available on Newsletter:
Holiday Novella

Also by Emilia Abraham:
Stuck at Sundown

Emilia Abraham

After many years of dreaming of becoming a full-time writer, Emilia Abraham took the leap, bringing her words to print. From sweet contemporary romance to spicy why choose and everything in between, she focuses on the happily ever after.

Emilia lives in the Upper Midwest with her husband (who's probably sick of listening to her expound on fictional men) and three kids (who try to steal her post-it notes). When she's not writing, she enjoys reading, playing video games, and consuming copious amounts of energy drinks.

* 9 7 8 1 9 6 1 8 0 2 0 0 1 *